I0596726

JUVE IN THE DOCK

A FANTÔMAS DETECTIVE NOVEL

BY MARCEL ALLAIN

Translated by A. R. Allinson

Bibliographical Note

This Antipodes edition, first published in 2017, is a republication of the work first published by Stanley Paul & Co, London, in 1925. The original translation has been altered to reflect modern spelling and usage.

ISBN 978-0-9966599-4-9

Contents

JUVE IN THE DOCK

1. One and One Make Three!

Discreetly, on tiptoe, with the tread of men who find themselves *de trop*, Juve and Fandor had just quitted Josette de Vautreuil's dwelling. Rescued from the hands of the dread Fantômas, the girl had no further need of their help, nor were they, either of them, the sort of men to wait for thanks.

Out of doors the morning was splendidly fine, the brilliant April sunshine lending a holiday aspect to the day.

"Glorious weather!" muttered Juve. "Fandor, my lad, I'd just love to be off for a run in the country… Pity there's never a chance of it!"

"Why?"

"Why! because the fight's still on! Fantômas is not the man to give us any respite!"

A touch of suppressed bitterness marked Juve's tone. A note of anger quivered in Fandor's reply.

"So much the better!" the young man protested. "Juve, I am all eagerness to join battle afresh. I tell you, when I remember the way he has just escaped us, I feel like going mad with rage!"

As he spoke, Fandor's heel struck one of those iron plates that cover the openings giving access to the sewers. Was it not, alas! by diving down one of these apertures, contrived for the convenience of the sewer men, that Fantômas had once again made good his escape? Where was he now, the scoundrel? Where had he vanished to? Was he still creeping along beneath the Paris streets, or had he already regained the open air? It was barely five minutes since the wretch had disappeared.

But now, as the iron plate rang under Fandor's impatient foot, the journalist gave a sudden start.

"Why, good Lord!" he grunted.

"What's wrong with you?" demanded Juve.

"We're a pair of fools!"

"Eh? what say?… Well, what's to do now!"

Juve in fact might well wonder. His companion's behavior was certainly bewildering. Dropping his friend's arm, entirely regardless of passersby who turned round to stare at the young man, Fandor had fallen on his knees on the pavement and then lain down full length on the ground, gluing his ear to the slot to be found in the middle of these sewer covers for inserting the levers employed in raising them.

"What's taken you?" Juve repeated his inquiry.

"Hush!" ordered the journalist, and vouchsafed but one word more in full and sufficient explanation of his odd behavior—"speaking tube!"

Why yes, Fandor's notion was of the simplest! But it is just these very simple ideas that are often the most ingenious. No doubt, it was an impossibility to pursue Fantômas through the sewers, but could not these same sewers be utilized to spy on his movements? It is a well-known fact that subterranean passages of all kinds constitute excellent conductors of sound. Along their walls spoken words are carried to great distances with great distinctness.

"Fantômas is there!" Fandor reasoned. "He is there with his accomplices. Is he not sure to speak to them?… and are we not bound to try and hear what he says?"

Juve for his part was too keen a police officer not to guess, in one second, the nature of his companion's plan.

"Not bad!" he muttered approvingly, and bending motionless over the young man's shoulder, he breathed an almost soundless question in his ear:

"Hear anything?"

"Yes, someone speaking. Wait a bit… Ah! damnation!" swore the journalist. Along the neighboring Avenue Mozart a streetcar was rattling noisily down the hill, preventing him from catching properly what was being said, perhaps a long way off, in the underground ramifications.

"Well?" whispered Juve breathlessly, when the car had gone by.

"Nothing more now!"—and Fandor got to his feet. He was

very pale, but his eyes were lit with a flame of eagerness and determination.

"Well?" insisted Juve. "Speak out! You heard something?"

"Yes… but only something very vague."

"But still…"

"All I could hear, Juve, was a few words, barely a half-dozen words. The tram passing prevented me catching the whole sentence…"

"And it was Fantômas speaking?"

"Yes, it was He! He said this…" Fandor paused a moment to think, then declared:

"He said this, Juve: 'Now we must separate, all to meet tomorrow at the Admiral's. It's going to be a fine stroke of business…'"

"A fine stroke of business!" Juve repeated the words like an echo. Then a heavy silence reigned between the two friends. Both well knew the full importance of those brief words their grim foe had pronounced.

"A fine stroke of business!" Fantômas had declared. So he was evidently planning some fresh scheme of villainy. Having but just come off victorious, or nearly so, from one battle, he was resolved to carry his grim enterprises to some yet more sinister conclusion.

Juve's fists clenched in a spasm of fury. But now he had declared "The game is up!" but lo! the game was to begin afresh—and already, it seemed, the challenge was thrown down. Fantômas had bidden his accomplices to a rendezvous. Manifestly he was acting on a definite, deliberately thought-out plan.

And to fight the enemy, to win the victory, Juve and Fandor possessed but one vague, inconclusive hint—that "an Admiral" was destined to be the next victim of the Lord of Terror's monstrous machinations.

For a while the two men did not exchange a word. Both were thinking hard, striving to understand something of the new police problem facing them. But surely all conjecture was premature at present. Were they not bound of necessity to wait for further and more detailed information?

Juve was the first to break the silence.

"An Admiral!" he exclaimed, "but there are numbers of Admirals! Do you know how many, Fandor?"

"My word, no!"

"No more do I! Anyway, it's an Admiral now in Paris… Is it an Admiral on the active list or an Admiral on half pay? We don't even know that,"—and the worthy detective, usually so calm, shook his head angrily.

"We know something," he declared, "and it is exactly as if we knew nothing at all. Look you, Fandor, I'd give ten years of my life for one single supplementary detail."

Then, hurrying on, Juve hailed a taxi.

"Rue Tardieu, driver, No. 1."

"We're going home?" Fandor asked him.

"Yes, to dress. In an hour's time we shall be paying a visit at the Ministry of Marine. Possibly they'll be able to tell us if an Admiral is at the moment the possessor of some precious object, some great sum of money—something, I can't tell what, of a sort to tempt Fantômas. What say you? We must make inquiries on the chance,"—and with a discouraged sigh, the police officer observed:

"The public often poke fun at the police, but the public little realize the real difficulties of the work. By God! here's a definite enough case in point. We know an 'Admiral' is to be the object of a felonious attempt by Fantômas, and our object is to prevent Fantômas from succeeding. Now, to do that, we must discover what Admiral is in question… I should very much like to see how the wise men who make fun of us detectives would set about gaining the day under these circumstances!"

Juve proceeded to extract a cigarette from his case, lit up and resumed quietly:

"And we *shall* succeed! We must succeed!"—and said no more.

Passionately devoted to his profession, delighting in the never-ending struggle, policeman against criminal, he might feel distressed by the difficulty of the task at hand, but he was never the man to give way to discouragement.

At his side, Fandor sat absorbed, like his friend, in somber reflections:

"Ah! if only," he told himself, "if only I had thought of listening to what was being said in the sewer five minutes sooner. All I actually caught was the few final words Fantômas addressed to his accomplices before leaving them…"

Twenty minutes later the taxi pulled up at Juve's door.

"Here we are," cried the latter. "What says the dial, eh?"—then he paid off his driver, stepped across the narrow sidewalk and made to enter the doorway, when he was accosted by a man who halted before him, cap in hand.

"Excuse me, sir!… I have been waiting for you. You are Monsieur Juve, I think?"

"I am."

"I have a letter—to be delivered into your own hands."

"Who from, my man?"

"I don't know, sir. It was a gentleman sent me on the errand, Place Pigalle. Seems it's urgent—very urgent."

As he spoke the man was searching his pockets and presently produced a yellow envelope, which he held out to the police officer.

For a moment Juve hesitated, examining the messenger's general appearance. The latter was a man of fifty or so, poorly but decently dressed, and wearing a shiny brass plate on his bosom.

"You are a licensed commissionaire?" he asked him.

"Yes, sir. Monsieur Juve doesn't know me by sight? *I* know Monsieur Juve. I've been living in the district the last twenty years."

"And the individual who sent you, you know him also?"

"No, sir. It was a gentleman in a motorcar. He pulled up when he saw me, called me to him and gave me the letter, saying: 'Whatever you do, look out for Monsieur Juve himself. Don't just deliver the thing at his address. He must get my letter before he goes up to his rooms. Five minutes' delay might spoil everything.'… But if you would look inside the envelope, sir, you'd no doubt see…"

"Who is my correspondent. Why, certainly."

Juve took the letter and opened it. Not a muscle of his face moved as he scanned the short message it contained. But he called Fandor to him: "I'll stand you a drink, my boy… at the *Hermitage*… yes, close by." And added, turning to the messenger: "Thank you, my man. There, there's a trifle for your trouble."

When the fellow was gone, Juve handed the note to his companion, with a curt: "Read that!"

"Who's it from, Juve!"

"Read it, I tell you!"

The missive was of the briefest:

"At a quarter to twelve be at the *Hermitage* café-restaurant. When they summon M. Durand to the telephone, stand by!… A message of grave importance; impossible to give details here; impossible to sign. But for God's sake, come. I dare not phone you at your house; line perhaps tapped."

"And no signature?" asked Fandor in much astonishment. But Juve only shrugged his shoulders.

"You're thinking…?"

"Why, yes!"

"What do you make of that final 'e,' with the broken loop? I know the machine that letter was typed on."

"Whose machine is it, Juve?"

"Havard's… Head of the Criminal Investigation Department, my lad!"

A quarter of an hour later Juve and Fandor were taking their seats under the veranda of the café indicated, without a word spoken. The same doubts filled the minds of both, to the exclusion of everything else. Certainly M. Havard was not a man to have sent a letter of this sort without some serious motive. But what could be the nature of this "message of grave importance," which he had not even dared to address to the police officer's home?

In less than three minutes the two friends were to know. A pageboy appeared, calling out:

"Monsieur Durand!… Monsieur Durand—wanted at the

telephone!"

"Here you are!" cried the detective, and sprang to the instrument.

"You, Fandor, take the other receiver, and listen too. I have no secrets from you,"—and in a ringing voice Juve answered the call:

"Hello! Chief! here I am. It is I, Juve."

But the poor man had to grasp his companion's arm to save himself from falling. A mocking voice had replied:

"Hello!… 'Chief' do you call me, Juve? Oh! you flatter me… Hello! it is I, Fantômas speaking!"—and next moment the voice grew harsh, curt, imperious:

"It is about Fandor, Juve, I'm phoning you. Don't cut me off, Juve! It is Fandor's life is at stake."

Nor was the warning needless. On recognizing the voice, but too familiar, of the Lord of Terror, Juve had in fact been on the point of leaving the instrument. But Fandor's name and the threat that went with it kept him at his post.

"Juve," the voice went on again, "you refuse to believe that I think very highly of you, feel great admiration for your talents… Yet here's a proof of what I say… Juve, I have chosen to give you fair warning. I have chosen to act honorably. Listen to me! I am going to start on a new enterprise—an enterprise that is to be a signal triumph for me… Well, Juve, do not concern yourself with it. Do not attempt to frustrate my plans. Leave off interfering with me!… Yes, give it up, I say, for…"

Fantômas paused for a moment, while Juve ground his teeth in impotent fury.

"For," proceeded Fantômas, "I give you fair warning, if I find you in my road, it is Fandor I shall punish—Fandor I shall kill!… And so, it will be you, yes! you, who will be answerable for his death."

Then came a sharp click. The speaker had hung up his instrument. Communication was cut off.

Ah! this time the scoundrel had struck home. Impervious to all personal fear, Juve could not fail to be terrified by this menace to Fandor's life. With unsteady steps, the police officer stumbled out of the telephone box, only to hear a great guffaw behind him.

"Why, Fandor, what do you mean?"

"Oh! let me have my laugh out, Juve! For my part, I just love these Bluebeard tales of terror."

"But all the same…"

"No, no! say no more, Juve, not a word! Oh, ho! so *I* am to be killed, am I? A fine story, truly! And I'm to take it lying down, am I?… Come, let's be off to breakfast. Jean must be sick and tired of waiting for us."

Fandor was not afraid, not he! And he would not let Juve be alarmed either.

So Juve said no more. He knew his friend's high courage and felt no surprise at sight of the young man's laughing face. He just grasped the journalist's hand and pressed it hard. "You're going to give me your word… that you will be prudent and run no risks… You won't go anywhere without me?"

"Good! very good!… There are new potatoes, and we shall find 'em burnt to a cinder. Hurry up, Juve, hurry up!… By the by, you were finely mistaken, old man, with your 'e' final and your Havard's typewriter!"

"I admit it. Fantômas must know the defect in the keyboard of that machine, so he copied it to give me confidence."

"Very possible! But why did he telephone you at the café here instead of at your own place? In the Rue Tardieu he was still more sure of getting you on the wires, eh?"

"Quite true."

"All the same, Fantômas does nothing at random. You can't suppose, Juve, he did it without a good reason."

"Not a bit of it, Fandor…"

Juve was answering mechanically. He could not get the abominable communication he had just received out of his head. Indeed, was Fandor not talking simply and solely with the object of distracting his companion's thoughts?

The two friends left the café and returned to the police officer's abode.

"Fandor, my boy," Juve spoke at a venture as the pair climbed the stairs, "do you know what you ought to do? You should take a sea voyage. Why not go—go to Australia?"

"Juve, you are not logical. Two minutes ago you wanted me to stick by you, to sit tight under your wing…"

"By going away you'd be playing Fantômas a fine trick…"

"Hold your tongue, do!"—and the young man rang the bell… He was perfectly well aware of the agonies of apprehension his old friend was enduring, but he *could* not for one second accept his counsels of prudence.

The door opened and Jean, the police officer's old servant, appeared.

"Monsieur has got back—and that's a good thing. Those gentlemen must be getting tired of waiting…"

"What gentlemen?" demanded his master.

"Monsieur doesn't know about it?" Jean asked in return. "I thought the gentlemen had an appointment…"

"But, God bless us! who are the gentlemen?"

"I don't know, sir. They didn't give their names. They simply said they'd wait till Monsieur came in."

"Good! I'll go and see them,"—and, winking in an odd way, Juve added:

"Just step into my bedroom, Fandor, will you?"

Throwing off his topcoat and hat, Juve opened the door of his sitting room—and gave a start of surprise. Of the two callers awaiting him, one at any rate was perfectly well known to him. It was the President of the Associated Committee of Insurance Companies against Theft.

As to his other visitor, Juve had never set eyes on him. He was a man of average build and bulk, tall rather than short, with a keen eye and an energetic bearing. Dressed in a closely buttoned blue cloth frock, at once elegant and unobtrusive, he presented the bluff, martial figure of a soldier or sailor.

Without a moment's hesitation, Juve addressed him.

"Admiral, I am pleased to meet you…"

But no sooner had he spoken than he was biting his lips with vexation. His visitor had burst out laughing.

"Admiral?" he protested, "but I'm no Admiral!… I am a busi-

nessman, Monsieur Juve, a dealer in antiquities,"—and little
suspecting how strange his remarks sounded, he concluded:

"Yes, I am a businessman… Alas! if I was an Admiral, I
should not be in such anxiety, such alarm about Fantômas—at
least I imagine so…"

*   *   *   *   *

At this point, to tell truth, Juve indulged in a very ugly
grimace. Albeit he was not vain enough to deem himself infal-
lible, he was nevertheless chagrined at his blunder.

"Worse and worse!" he thought to himself. "Three mistakes
running! First, I thought I recognized M. Havard's typewriter.
Then, I believed it was Havard was going to phone me. Now,
I take an antiquary for an Admiral! Verily I have reason to be
proud of myself!"

But making the best of a bad job, the police officer broke
into a laugh.

"Very good, sir!" he declared, "so you are an antiquary and
you are afraid of Fantômas. That's clear enough so far. Now will
you tell your story."

He pointed to an armchair, and then offering his hand to the
President of the Associated Committee:

"It was you, I presume, sir, who advised this gentleman…"

"Monsieur Thévenot."

"…advised Monsieur Thévenot to apply to me."

"As a matter of fact, it was I, and it was Havard…"

"You have seen the Chief?"

"Not an hour ago. M. Havard sent us on to you, and com-
missioned me to tell you that he gave you full powers to carry
through the matter we are going to lay before you…"

"Well, I'm all attention," observed the detective, whose eyes
had turned for an instant to a piece of drapery that masked one
corner of the room, though no one noticed the fact.

"My dear Juve," the President went on, "it's like this. I can
explain the thing in three words. M. Thévenot has applied to
me with a view to insuring, for a very substantial sum—close
to five million francs—a certain letter, or to be more precise,

a document. The fact is M. Thévenot is afraid this letter may be stolen from him, for the mere perusal of its contents would entail for him the probable loss of an amount equal to what he wishes to insure it for. You follow me?"

"Perfectly. But I should like to have some details…"

"We are here to answer your questions."

"Well then, what exactly is this letter you speak of?"

The President threw a questioning look at M. Thévenot, as though asking his permission to speak out, then continued:

"This letter, my dear Juve, or rather this document, for it *is* a document we have to do with, is strictly speaking a plan—the plan of a place where a treasure is hidden…"

"A treasure? Ho, ho!"

"No need to laugh—I repeat, a treasure, an historical treasure… Anyway, here are the particulars in full…"

The President half closed his eyes, and resumed:

"You are no doubt aware that, when the Empress Eugénie, wife of Napoleon III, left the Tuileries, that is to say on September 4, 1870, she dispatched her jewels to her mother, Madame de Montijo, at Madrid, by a special messenger…"

"And those jewels never reached their destination!… Yes, I know that much."

"Well, sir, they never got there for the very good reason that the messenger who carried them, as it was given out, had really nothing at all in his wallets. The jewels never left Paris. They were buried in some place unknown. It is the plan of this locality that is in M. Thévenot's hands…"

"All quite plain!" Juve agreed. "*But* I don't see what Fantômas…"

"Wait a moment! The plan in question came by pure chance into this gentleman's hands. He discovered it concealed in an old timepiece, behind the dial. Now this precious paper had not been ten minutes in M. Thévenot's possession when he received a message by pneumatic—and here it is…"

As he spoke the President stood up, took a pocketbook from his pocket, and drew a pneumatic dispatch-form from it, which he handed to Juve.

One look sufficed the police officer to master the contents:

"Order to M. Thévenot to take no steps in regard to the plan he has just discovered. Order to the said M. Thévenot to deliver it to me into my own hands. The above injunctions to be obeyed under pain of death. Signed by my proper hand—Fantômas."

"The devil!" was the detective's sole comment. Then after a moment's thought, he questioned:

"When did this message come?"

"Only just now."

"So you hurried off at once to the Department?"

"At once, yes!" declared M. Thévenot. "I was able to get admission to M. Havard through one of my friends, an Inspector…"

"Excellent! and M. Havard sent you on here?"

"No, not exactly. M. Havard thought at first, so I suppose that it was a practical joke… He simply advised me to insure against theft."

"Better and better!" laughed Juve. "Havard has shown he possesses a sense of humor… To proceed—what next?"

"Next, at my earnest request, he allowed me to telephone from his office to the President of the Insurance Committee…"

"And I," the President took up the tale, "I brought M. Thévenot here. I am quite ready to insure this letter, this document—but on one condition."

"And that is?"

"That *you* undertake to protect this paper."

Juve might have been looking to hear these very words. In a moment he was on his feet, rubbing his hands. "So," he cried, "so! Let me tell you this, then!"

Then he went on again, speaking very fast:

"Shall I give you a piece of advice, my dear Monsieur Thévenot? Don't lose a moment! Go to the spot indicated! Get hold of the treasure!… Call up the newspapermen… The jewels once in your hands and the Press publishes the news, your risk is at an end. A find like this will make such a noise the jewels will be unsaleable. No receiver would dare to buy them from Fantômas… What now? You're smiling."

This was true. As he listened to the officer, the antiquary had broken into a smile. "Monsieur Juve," said he, "you tell me exactly what M. Havard told me. Yes! the advice is excellent, *but* I cannot follow it…"

"Because?"

"Because the jewels are in a place where I cannot institute a search without formal permission—and this permission I shall not have before a week is out, or longer!"

"The devil! May I ask…"

"Where the place indicated is. Certainly! It is the Ministry of Marine."

"The Ministry of Marine?… The devil's in it, surely!"—and dropping into an armchair, Juve took his head between his hands, for once nonplussed. He had never looked for *such* a piece of news!

And yet, was it so extraordinary for the Ministry of Marine to be mixed up in the affair? Under his breath Juve muttered:

"The Ministry—the very place all the Admirals are necessarily bound to visit. And I know how Fantômas… Well, upon my word!"—and then, springing up, he marched straight to the curtain hanging at the far end of the room, with the remark:

"This is a serious matter, gentlemen. So I must have someone to help me… I have your permission? Come in, Fandor!"

As he spoke, Juve tore back the curtain. Behind it, the wall showed a wide opening. Standing in this aperture, which communicated with the police officer's bedroom, appeared the journalist.

"Come in," Juve reiterated, and turning to his visitors: "You know Jerome Fandor, gentlemen?" he asked. "Good! and you, Fandor, have heard what has just been said?"

"Without losing one single word."

"And you have a suggestion to make? a plan to propose?"

Never before had the journalist seen Juve so agitated, no doubt of that—and never had he found his friend so much inclined to listen to his advice.

"Juve," the young man began very calmly, "all this seems to me as simple as A B C and absolutely providential. Here we have the bait to catch Fantômas… The gentleman must keep his document. He must go back quietly home. We, you and I, Juve, must hide there. When Fantômas comes this time, by God! we'll arrest him."

Fandor had spoken with breathless eagerness. The gallant journalist's youthful optimism admitted no doubt or hesitation. But suddenly he felt a qualm. Juve had checked his enthusiasm with a look: "Idiot!" he ejaculated. "Madcap!"

Then he asked a question: "You have five million francs to play with?"

"Five millions?"

"Why, yes—to repay the insurance… and suppose we don't arrest Fantômas?"—and folding his arms as he strode up and down his sitting room, Juve proceeded:

"For, after all, we must have a conscience! These gentlemen don't care a hang whether we arrest Fantômas or not. If they appeal to us, it is simply because they wish to safeguard this paper. Therefore, if we fail to do so, if Fantômas beats us, as honest men we shall be bound to pay the five millions. Have you got them, my boy?"

"Not I," laughed Fandor.

"Another thing now," Juve went on again. "It is evident that M. Thévenot, a man of honor, cannot make his search without proper permission from the authorities, but it is equally evident that Fantômas, on his side, will not be troubled by any such scruples. He will go straight to the hiding place. So we must remember that the risk is conditioned in this way: M. Thévenot can do nothing till a week is out, while Fantômas can act at once… Come now, I begin to see daylight in the matter!"

Juve wore the little look of covert irony that always characterized him when he was studying a problem that really interested him. Discussing the thing in so many words, he appeared to be exposing his inmost thoughts, but one never knew if he was really sincere, if the phrases he used did not conceal some trap or trick.

"To proceed," he added, "the whole question is to find out if we can prevent the theft… No, no, this is no everyday affair.

Ordinarily folks send for the police when something untoward has happened. This time I am asked to stop the untoward something from occurring. A very odd, a very exceptional state of affairs!"

Then suddenly the police officer swung round on his heels, to face M. Thévenot.

"You know what Fantômas is?" he asked.

"Why…"

"The most redoubtable brigand that ever lived—and a genius into the bargain, the genius of Evil. He is all-daring, all-powerful, his cunning is limitless. You know that."

"Yes, Monsieur Juve…"

"Then you will understand I must lay down conditions if I am to intervene—and you must agree to them,"—and Juve resumed his seat. He was a trifle pale and the veins in his forehead were swollen. His whole soul was absorbed in a mighty effort of concentrated thought.

"Then again," he began again presently, "I start with the axiom that Fantômas is a man, like you and me. He has a body. He is not an immaterial spirit…"

"Now, now!" broke in Fandor, "you are joking, Juve?"

"Hold your tongue!… But I admit one thing," Juve continued, "that the man is gifted with amazing powers. I know no strongbox capable of defying him, no lock he cannot open, no walls he cannot break through. In one word, I confess there is no place where we can secure your document in safety…"

"Yet…"

"Let me finish, Mister President! Starting from these premises, I say there is but one way to safeguard the document and defy his efforts, and that is to keep it in our own hands…"

"In our own hands!"

"Exactly. What you have under your very eyes cannot be spirited away. The one thing is, to guard the holder from being murdered…"

"But really…"

"Hear me out, Monsieur Thévenot! The point is then to secure the paper on one's own person, for a week, and not to be murdered. That's plain enough, I think… Plain as daylight, eh, Fandor?"

"Now, not to be murdered," Juve concluded, "the best way is not to allow anyone to come near you. Well, I will undertake to guard the document if Monsieur Thévenot agrees to spend a week in my company in a place where no one can possibly get near us from any direction—neither from the right, nor from the left, neither in front nor behind, neither above nor below…"

But the detective might as well have been talking Chinese for anything his audience could understand.

"Neither above, nor below!" M. Thévenot repeated the words. "Where the deuce do you propose to imprison us then, sir?"

"In a summer house."

"A summer house!"

"Yes!—at Robinson."

Fandor had sprung impetuously from the chair where he was sitting, but Juve went on calmly:

"Do you know, Monsieur Thévenot, what Robinson is?"

"I have never been there… I am a Belgian…"

"This is what Robinson is—a hamlet in the Paris suburbs consisting of… of a collection of restaurants. It is a pleasure resort. Young people flock there in crowds every Sunday… Now let me tell you, sir, Robinson has this special peculiarity—there are very big trees there, and in the branches of these same big trees, summer houses, kiosks, if you like, are contrived, where you can breakfast and dine. Each of them forms a special private room. You get there by means of narrow winding stairways encircling the tree trunks, and meals are served by hauling up with ropes and pulleys the baskets in which the waiters pack the dishes."

"And you propose?…"

"I propose this, Mister President—to shut myself up with Monsieur Thévenot in one of these kiosks. We put the document on a table before us—under our eyes. And we stay there a week, till the proper permission comes. Of course, I organize a system of surveillance. Fandor will keep guard halfway up the stairs, the sole means of access from below. In addition, four Inspectors will take post in the trees round, who will keep a watch on the four sides of our eyrie, and look down on its roof. In this way Fantômas will find it impossible to approach, whether from the sides, from above or from below."

Juve had said his say. Taking a cigarette from a box on the table, he was now smoking composedly. Round him his auditors stood lost in thought, while, with eyes fixed on the floor, M. Thévenot pondered the pros and cons.

No doubt the police officer's proposal took one's breath away, but after all, was there not a touch of genius about the scheme? Undoubtedly, in such a kiosk, isolated in midair, on which a rigorous watch was kept from every quarter, no theft would be practicable. Ingenious as Fantômas was, it was surely self-evident he could not possibly circumvent the precautions Juve suggested.

The President of the Associated Companies was the first to break the silence.

"Certainly I was not expecting anything of the kind," he confessed, "but I can see that in this way absolute safety will be secured… Yes, if Monsieur Thévenot agrees to your conditions, Juve, I think nothing untoward can happen."

"And you consent to insure my document for a week?" demanded the antiquary.

"Certainly."

"Well then, I am ready to sign the policy."

"Very good! The thing won't take two minutes,"—and going to the table, the President extracted a form of contract from his pocketbook and proceeded to fill in the blanks, while Fandor drew Juve aside. He was not satisfied with the turn of events, not he!

"Juve," grumbled the young man, "your plan is excellent, *but* we are losing a unique opportunity to capture Fantômas…"

"You think so?"

"God, yes! We had a marvelous fine bait—and we are spoiling it. We knew what Fantômas wanted to steal. We ought…"

"To let him take it?" mocked Juve.

"We ought to leave him the hope of taking it…"

"Really?"

"Why, yes! Look you, it is a question of five millions. Well, I have a mind to open a subscription among readers of *La Capitale*. The funds once got together, you would have no more scruples, and we would lie in wait for Fantômas with the document in our hands…"

"Fandor, you are talking foolishness,"—and Juve, his hand on his comrade's shoulder, breathed low in his ear:

"What, don't you understand then?"

"Understand what, Juve?"

"That that is just what we are going to do—to wait in ambush."

"Oh, Juve! you go too fast. Fantômas this time will never be able to do anything."

"Really?"

"Why, what do you suppose…"

But Fandor did not complete his sentence. Juve's strong hand gripped his shoulder till the fingers almost entered into the flesh.

"I suppose nothing, Fandor," declared his friend. "But I know one thing—that this, this affair is a challenge I am throwing down to Fantômas, and that he will know it is. Yes, I know that much, Fandor, *and* that Fantômas is not the man not to pick up the gauntlet thrown down by me."

"Then you think?…"

"I think nothing," Juve cut him short. "And there is nothing hidden, is there, in all this? You know as much as I do. You know what Juve is going to do. It is open to you to discover what Fantômas will attempt. If you guess it, you are his master, or as good as his master. That's all I have to say. But as for supposing he will make no attempt…" and the police officer shrugged his shoulders. Truly, he felt no doubt in the matter. Well he knew that the man he was tracking down was capable of performing positive miracles. He knew that the word *impossible* was not in his vocabulary. He knew, above all, that his pride as a brigand would not brook his refusing the challenge offered him by his enemy.

For the first time, indeed, the roles were reversed. It was no longer Fantômas who was defending himself against Juve; it was Juve on the defensive against Fantômas. No longer was it the officer of justice attacking the malefactor; it was the malefactor who was to attack the representative of the law. In this deadly encounter Juve was playing his game with all the cool deliberation that was his, all the ingenuity he possessed.

"Shall we be going, gentlemen? Are you ready?" asked the detective.

"Yes," replied M. Thévenot, "the policy is signed."

"Excellent. Let us be off then."

"Immediately?"

"Without a doubt. From this instant war is declared."

"War? Hmm! You use expressions that make one shudder. But in war men are armed… You have…"

"My browning? Certainly. And you, *you* would like a revolver, Monsieur Thévenot?"

"No, I thank you… I am near-sighted… and, and I do not know how to shoot…"

"In that case, I say no more. Fandor, telephone for a motor, will you?"

"Right, Juve. But you're not calling up the Inspectors?"

"Yes, I am. Jean will take a letter to the Criminal Department. I am asking for Henri and Theo, who will bring two comrades with them… Now, gentlemen, shall we start?"

Ten minutes later a car was making its way across the city, carrying M. Thévenot, Juve, and Fandor. The President of Committee had taken his leave, being required elsewhere on business matters.

"I shall go and dine this evening at Robinson," he announced as he shook Juve's hand. "I want to see your fortalice."

No doubt the Insurance magnate found the adventure entertaining. How was he to know that at that moment, for all their cheerful looks, Juve and Fandor, for their part, felt their hearts beating wildly in their bosoms?

A fresh struggle was beginning. Once again Juve and

Fantômas were going to face each other…

Who would win the day, the honest men or the criminal?

*   *   *   *   *

Daring as he was, confident as he had every right to be in his own abilities, yet Juve was not the man to count upon a victory so long as the battle was not even begun. His actions showed as much. Doubtless the police officer had never neglected to take proper precautions; doubtless, under all circumstances it was his custom to multiply necessary safeguards. But this day of all others he showed himself scrupulously careful, meticulously exact in his preparations.

When the car set him down at Robinson, in company with Fandor and M. Thévenot, Juve made straight for a group of young men standing round three motorcycles with sidecars. It was in fact a posse of six Inspectors from the Criminal Department, who had just arrived on their light machines.

"Theo, Henri," Juve hailed them, "come with me. We are going to select our sky parlor,"—and with a wave of the hand he called the other four officers to attention.

"You, gentlemen, meantime are to keep a watchful eye on M. Thévenot here. Nobody is to come near him, not for one second! In any case, I shall not be long gone,"—and as he spoke, the detective moved away a short distance.

A full hour had elapsed when at last he returned to the waiting antiquary, with smiling face and cheerful looks.

"You have found what you were looking for?" asked the tradesman.

"I have."

"It will be easy to keep a watch on?"

"Quite easy. Impossible to circumvent my sentries! You shall see for yourself,"—and at once Juve led M. Thévenot to the foot of a big tree surmounted by a single kiosk and surrounded by four other taller trees. "There stands our home for this week," Juve explained. "We are going to shut ourselves up in that hut aloft there. By my orders, they have carried up two iron bedsteads, so one of us can sleep while the other watches. And now, my dear sir, give me your best attention. Tell me candidly if my precautions strike you as sufficient. This is what I have arranged: there is only one stairway leading to this kiosk; on that stairway Fandor, and then Inspector Henri, will mount guard in turn. No possibility of getting up that way—and into the bargain an absolute safeguard of the underside of the kiosk. You agree with me?"

"By God, yes, of course I do."

"Then, I proceed. In each of those trees, which are taller than our own, I post an Inspector, who will be relieved every two hours. You will see that, from where they stand, my Inspectors will find no difficulty in keeping under observation all four sides and also the roof of our fortress. You have no objection?"

"Good Lord, no!"

"That's all right then. Let us go up. From now on I take it your document will be in perfect safety."

Juve's voice shook a little as he pronounced the words. In perfect safety? But did he not know that nothing could be, anywhere, in perfect safety, so long as Fantômas wanted to get possession of it?

"Well, let us go up," M. Thévenot consented. "But… our meals?"

"We shall hoist them up by means of a rope and a basket."

"My letters?"

"Fandor will send them up by the same road."

"So, we are to enter our prison cell?"

"Our prison cell—you have said the word! Oh! by the way, are you a card player?"

"Yes… why?"

"Do you play checkers? chess? dominoes?"

"I do… But…"

"My dear sir, I have had these games taken up. A week of solitary confinement is a trifle long. We must think of everything," and as a matter of fact Juve was forgetting nothing.

While M. Thévenot, a trifle pale perhaps, was climbing the first steps of the little stairway leading to the kiosk in the treetop, Juve stepped up to Fandor.

"My lad, two words with you—two serious words," he began.

"Out with it, Juve."

"Here are your orders: Happen what may, Fandor—you understand, happen what may, no matter what occurs, remember this, you are to stay where you are, halfway up the stairs, and your eyes fixed on the underside of the kiosk…"

"But, Juve…"

"No 'but' about it, Fandor! You are to stay there, without stirring from the spot. I have also told the Inspectors the same thing. Till I say the word, till I give precise, definite, formal orders, no one is to move…"

"Still, if…"

"Leave 'still' alone!… Now think! Fantômas cannot get to the kiosk because his road is barred every way. Then it is easy to foresee he will try to entice you or one of the Inspectors from his post of observation—and that is just what we must not allow, that is exactly the trick we must anticipate and baffle. Accordingly…"

"I understand, Juve!" Fandor declared, "and I will not stir. Nobody shall stir. But you really think he will try…"

"What!" cried the detective at that moment, "look, there, at the foot of the tree!"

At that spot, someone—who?—with the point of a stick had traced a single word—a word of defiance, a word of mockery, a common slang term of insult—*swab!*

It wanted a Juve to have noticed the thing, but was it not in fact Juve and no other the odious epithet was meant for? Starting back in alarm, Fandor cried excitedly:

"Come then, you don't suppose…"

"I suppose nothing. I read what is written… Now, till we meet again, my boy, and be prudent."

A rapid handshake that surprised the young man by the nervous strength of its grip, and the police officer, taking leave of his companion, in turn followed M. Thévenot up the corkscrew stairway that led to the high-perched kiosk.

The antiquary had paused at the door of the little hut . "I was waiting for you, Juve," he explained.

"Very good! Then I will do the honors. Come along in… you can see the accommodation is of the homeliest?"

And homely indeed the arrangements were. By Juve's orders the place had been swept clear of its usual appointments. The sum total of what remained was five indispensable pieces of furniture—a table, two wooden chairs, two beds. On the floor stood a washbasin for the necessary ablutions. In one corner were the games—cards, checkerboard, chessboard, and dominoes. In another a basket, full of provisions for the evening meal.

"There," cried Juve, "let's settle in!"

Then, stepping to the door, he shot home two massive bolts that had doubtless been fixed there by his instructions.

"Let's see to the lighting arrangements. Is the electricity in working order? Yes!" Juve turned a switch and a globe lit up.

"Excellent! And besides that, here's two pocket lamps… By the way, my men are at their posts? Yes, I can see them… Now, my dear sir, we have only to take one last precaution. We must guard against fire. Here is an iron case. Will you put the document in it yourself?"

"With pleasure," and under the police officer's eyes, two piercing eyes no sleight of hand had ever deceived, the antiquary slipped the precious plan into the metal sheath Juve had brought with him.

"I am to replace the whole thing in my pocket?" he asked.

"No. In that case only you could keep guard of it. Let us put the box here, on the table, in front of us. Now, with your permission, I am going to seal it up,"—and Juve secured the box with a big seal of red wax.

"And now for a bit of relaxation!" he laughed with a cheerfulness that sounded a trifle forced. "I clap my browning in my pocket, and here, within reach of my hand, I lay another. There, that's as it should be!… Shall we read a novel?"

"To speak quite frankly, Monsieur Juve, I'm falling asleep where I stand. Last night I never closed an eye…"

"Well, then, we'll have dinner, M. Thévenot. After that, I promise you you shall get to bed. For my own part, I intend to keep awake every night. I can sleep a bit in the daytime."

Juve seemed absolutely easy in his mind. Was he convinced he had actually taken all possible precautions? Did he deem it proven that Fantômas would feel bound to admit himself checkmated, unable to make any attempt whatever on the position?

It was a question M. Thévenot could not but ask himself. While Juve, on his side, must feel a certain admiration for the antiquary. Certainly no immediate danger was apparent. Still, the very superabundance of the precautions taken was bound to be a trifle alarming.

"This commercial man keeps superbly cool!" thought the police officer. "For sure the Belgians are a cold-blooded race, phlegmatic folk if ever there were such! Not a sign of agitation, not one quiver of the nerves. And yet he knows I fear Fantômas may come at any moment. The fellow's got some pluck!"

But, two seconds after that, Juve broke into a big laugh. No doubt M. Thévenot was courageous enough, but there was an explanation in this instance for his admirable coolness in no way connected with his bravery—the man had fallen fast asleep! Tranquilly, still holding his fork between his fingers, his chin drooping on his chest, he sat slumbering heavily.

"Poor devil!" thought Juve. "That's what comes of finding treasure-trove! Yesterday he can't have dared to sleep a wink. Today he is utterly tired out,"—and the detective was still smiling when suddenly his merriment seemed to be superseded by a sharp pang of alarm.

"How now," Juve muttered, for he himself had just smothered a great yawn.

"A soporific?" he asked himself in a muffled voice, and was on the alert in an instant. Was it, in fact, impossible that some drug might have been mixed with the food and wine sent in from the restaurant? He sprang to his feet, asking himself:

"Am I sleepy? Do I feel 'funny'?" But no! On the contrary, he had never been more "his own man." He had merely yawned because he was hungry.

"Come, come," thought the police officer, "this is no time

for nerves. To suspect everything is just as silly as to suspect nothing! I'm going to finish my dinner in peace and quietness. Then I'm going to smoke a cigarette… Then—but there, suppose I lift that fine fellow on his bed?"

Juve stood up. Then, with a strength no one would have suspected to look at him, he raised M. Thévenot's body in his arms and was carrying him to one of the iron bedsteads when the antiquary woke up with a start and a half uttered cry for help, which Juve promptly suppressed as it rose to the frightened man's lips.

"Hello! It is I, Juve! Don't be afraid. I was going to put you to bed…"

"Put me to bed?…"

"Yes, you were asleep. Good! Don't try to understand, but get off to sleep again,"—and without another word the antiquary did as he was bid. In fact, he had hardly settled down with Juve's help on the bed before he was snoring again.

"Very reassuring!" remarked the detective. "A man drugged with a soporific does not awake so readily. Good! Now to finish my supper. Juve was desperately hungry, and did great execution on the meal the restaurant keeper had provided. Then he washed up, and packed away the remains of his repast in a basket that was furnished with an iron hook at top.

"Tomorrow morning, when it's light, I'll let down all the stuff with a rope… Now for a cigarette, and to make my final round of inspection." No sooner said than done. Slowly and carefully he examined each of the four walls. Everything appeared to be in order, and he went on next to the windows. By his orders a fine network of iron wire had been fixed across each of these.

"If Fantômas *should* come," he muttered to himself, "I defy him to throw my iron box out of window." But presently he shrugged his shoulders, resuming:

"But there, I'm just talking rubbish. Fantômas *cannot* come, that's a fact!"

Stooping to scrutinize the floor, he looked down through a crack in the boarding.

"Fandor below," he assured himself, "Henri to north, Theo

to south, east and west the two other officers! Above and below and on all sides everything is under observation. No, the thing's impossible! Fantômas can do nothing, can try nothing even."

A second cigarette followed the first, and, his nerves calmed and soothed, Juve sat down on the end of the other bed, opposite that occupied by M. Thévenot.

"Anyway," he went on to himself, "Fantômas would never be so imprudent as to attack the first night. No doubt he would wait for the last few days of our watch. Naturally enough, when nothing happens, vigilance relaxes. Hmm, suppose I light up meanwhile. It's so dark I can't see a blessed thing," and getting up, the police officer crossed the floor and, switching on the electric current, rubbed his eyes.

"Ah! but it's a bit dazzling, this light! So much the better, anyway... Now, what time is it?"

His watch marked not quite nine o'clock.

"Let's read a bit. Nothing like it for keeping a man awake—when the book is interesting."

It was peaceful enough indeed this first night of sentry duty. Not a sound was to be heard. By Juve's orders, the whole restaurant had been engaged for the week—the Insurance Company had opened an unlimited credit in his name—and the personnel had been dismissed for the time being. Faintly, a long way off, could be heard the tinkle-tinkle of dance music from the orchestra of a country tavern—the only sound that reached the watcher's ears save, from half hour to half hour, short, sharp whistles from nearer at hand.

"Fandor and the officers signaling to each other to show they are awake," the detective told himself. "Never, I think, have I been so well guarded."

And yet, as time passed and the night grew darker and darker, Juve could not ward off an ever increasing sense of coming disaster. M. Thévenot was still sleeping soundly, while Juve assured himself that a thousand obstacles made an attack from Fantômas a physical impossibility.

Yet at the same moment he was thinking:

"An 'impossibility' he should come!... Yes! But that

does not prove he will not come. Everything is possible to him—everything!"

Then the police officer threw down his novel and got up.

"Bah! I'm as nervous as a young girl! No one can get into this kiosk, that's flat. And in this kiosk there's nobody but Thévenot and myself. Now one man," he concluded, "and another man, that makes two men. Consequently, as the two men who are here—myself and Thevenot—are not Fantômas, I may rest assured that box will *not* disappear," and as he spoke, Juve laid his hand on the metal case containing the precious document. He stroked it lovingly and, lifting it up, examined the seal of red wax he had himself affixed, then restored it to its original position.

"The document is there," murmured the detective, "and I defy Fantômas…"

But the sentence was never finished. The thing was so sudden, so startling, so swift and unexpected that Juve simply had not time to gather what was happening, what could be happening. An appalling crash, a noise of breaking glass… then utter darkness… then a cry, a yell for "help!"

The kiosk was plunged in utter darkness, darkness as black as ink, yet Juve had the impression, the presentiment—his eyes were useless—that a man was there, who rushed to the table and laid hold of the metal case in which lay the precious paper.

The baffling confusion of such moments is nerve-shaking. But instantly Juve bounded forward, straight before him, with a savage oath and a fierce cry of: "Fantômas! Scoundrel!"

His body touched that of an intruder, and for an instant his fingers gripped a coat collar. But a furious, murderous blow of the fist caught him right between the eyes. He staggered and all but fell, stammering out: "Fantômas! Fantômas!"

Only a miracle of willpower kept the police officer on his feet. Groping around, he found his revolver, cocked it and shouted:

"Flat on the floor, Thévenot! I'm going to fire."

The noise of the antiquary tumbling hurriedly out of bed followed. Then in the dark, at random, Juve fired.

Simultaneously loud shouts came from outside:

"Juve, hold on! Are we to come up? Juve, I say! Juve!"

Fandor's voice was breathless, choked by cruel apprehension. Theo, the Inspector's, clear and distinct, as he cried:

"But, good Lord! I saw nothing! Which way did he pass?"

Juve yelled back: "Don't move! He is in here… Fire, if he comes out!"

With the words, he took out his pocket flashlight and pressed the trigger. Why, the whole thing was over in less than a second—Fantômas *could* not have escaped!

The light flashed from the flashlight, dazzlingly bright. But lo! there was nobody in the kiosk—nobody save Juve and M. Thévenot.

"I'm going mad," groaned the detective. Then he gave a quick order: "Don't move, Thévenot! The document is here?"

The box lay on the table. Juve took it, and let fly an oath. The box was empty. The seal was broken and the precious contents gone.

"Juve! Juve! are we to come up?" screamed Fandor. But the police officer did not reply. He was thinking:

"We were here, Thévenot and I. One and one makes two. Never yet has one and one made three. So, it would want a third person, and no third person could have got in. Nor could he have got out again…"

Juve glanced rapidly at the door and windows. The latter were tight shut, the iron trelliswork was intact. On the door the two heavy bolts were still in their sockets.

"Nobody has come in, therefore, and nobody has gone out again. It's self-evident this time!"—and he called out:

"Come up, Fandor. But no one move, except you."

The journalist hurried up the stairs, and next moment was shouting through the door:

"Here I am, Juve. Is he caught? You're not wounded? Open the door, I say."

"Keep quiet, Fandor," ordered Juve, and suddenly snatching his browning from his pocket, he covered the antiquary.

"Strip!" he commanded.

"But… but you must be mad!"

"Strip, I tell you. Not a word!—or else restore the paper! Nobody has come in. Nobody has gone out. You and I were the only two here. I'm not Fantômas. It follows, you are…"

"Juve, Juve! But this is…"

"In two seconds, I shall fire, and kill you, if you don't obey. Off with them! Yes, that's right… Fandor, are you there?"

"Yes, Juve! Yes!"

"I'm going to half open the door. I shall pass out Thévenot's clothes to you. Search them. Unstitch the seams! The document is in them."

"In his clothes?"

"Yes! Because it can't be anywhere else. Otherwise I should see it…"

"Very good, Juve!"

"And if it was not there, Fandor, that would be proof positive of an absurdity—that one and one make three. For in that case there must have been a third person present, when there was nobody at all except Thévenot and myself."

Juve was quite positive. He was sure of this fact. The impossibility of anybody's having come in or gone out was beyond dispute. One by one, he passed out the garments to Fandor, and closed the door, while before him, pale, distraught, discomforted, stood the antiquary, stammering:

"But it's sheer insanity, mere lunacy! What do you mean…"

"Silence!" thundered Juve. "Wait and see…" It did not take long. In a quarter of an hour Fandor was back again.

"Well? You've found?…"

"Nothing, Juve! The document is not hidden there." Juve turned white as paper. Then he mastered his feelings. Browning in hand he stepped up to M. Thévenot.

*   *   *   *   *

Juve was good nature personified. No one who knew him would have said otherwise. But he was also a man of great resolution, perfectly ready to resort to the worst acts of violence, when such acts were rendered necessary by events. For years he had been pursuing the ruffianly Fantômas, and had again and again had proof of the atrocities the wretch was capable of committing. Against such a monster all measures were justifiable. And now he was convinced—and the conclusion was logical—that Thévenot and Fantômas must be one and the same person.

The police officer's brow was black with passionate anger as he advanced a step nearer the trembling antiquary.

"Get up!" he ordered.

"But I am innocent."

"Enough! Hold out your hands!"

"There… Oh! for God's sake!"

"Silence!"

A sharp click sounded. Juve had slipped the handcuffs on the man's wrists. He went on:

"Wrap this blanket round you. There! Now listen carefully—and don't you think I'm joking…"

Then he moved to the door, behind which Fandor still stood.

"Stand by! I am going to open the door. Fantômas-Thévenot is coming out. Take your revolver and cover him. At the slightest movement fire!… In any case don't let him go all the way down, take him only as far as the middle of the stairs." Then, turning to Thévenot, he uttered the one word, "Go!"

Next moment Juve stood alone in the kiosk that had been the scene of these surprising events. No sooner was he by himself than the detective's demeanor showed a change.

"By the Lord Harry!" he growled. "Either I am mad, or the paper is not far away. He hasn't hid it in his clothes. Then he must inevitably have concealed it somewhere else,"—and Juve repeated emphatically, as if anxious to convince himself of the truth of what he said:

"Nobody has come in. Nobody has gone out. It follows either he has stolen the document or I have. I have not; therefore he has! Impossible to discover any other explanation… But now to make a systematic search"—and he started on the most minute and meticulous investigations. As he told himself, was it not self-evident, was it not indisputable, that the precious paper must be in the kiosk, inasmuch as nothing nor anybody could have left it.

First of all, Juve examined the windows. They were still hermetically closed. Next came the turn of the metal trellis. The meshes were intact, and the network was too close for the document to have been pushed through it.

"Now the floor!" But the floor was of oak parquetry, and the joins, if not absolutely perfect, could not have allowed the vanished document to slip out that way.

"Quite conclusive!" muttered Juve. "No doubt of it, the paper *must* be hidden here inside—and I mean to find it."

Nevertheless, an hour afterwards, he had found nothing whatsoever. Nor was this for lack of the most scrupulous and indefatigable search even in the most utterly improbable places. Not an inch of the walls, of the ceiling, of the tables and chairs, of the floor but had been subjected to the minutest scrutiny. Yet the paper remained undiscoverable.

Then, utterly exhausted, Juve sat down, his brows knitted in sheer perplexity. "I'm going mad," he told himself again, and in very truth, his wits seemed to be wandering. Nobody had come in, nobody had gone out, nothing could have been thrown out of the kiosk—and the document had disappeared!

"It's black magic!" groaned the poor man.

Taking his head between his hands, he strove desperately to find an explanation.

"Thévenot is Fantômas—granted! I am ready to allow it. But how did he work it? If I don't find it, I have no proof of his guilt. Well, I can find nothing—nothing whatever."

A momentary smile lit up his set face. The antiquary could not have eaten the paper, swallowed it? Was it not a device often resorted to by evildoers to get rid of a compromising paper? But next moment Juve shrugged his shoulders. This explanation was inadmissible. He had seen the document and knew it was of some bulkiness, consisting as it did of several sheets. He was bound to admit the physical impossibility of anybody's having been able to get into the kiosk or get out of it. He found himself forced to recognize the physical impossibility of M.

Thévenot's having had time to swallow the document in the few brief seconds that had intervened between the going out of the light and the turning on of his flashlight.

"No, that's not it!" the detective admitted. "Then, what *is* it?"

The sound of a loud sneeze made him jump. "Oh, dear! the man's catching cold!… Now for it. Nothing ventured, nothing gained,"—and he left the kiosk.

"Are you there, Fandor?"

"Yes, of course I am."

"And M. Thévenot, where is he?"

"Why, here, standing opposite me, poor devil!"

"Standing there? Come, come, you're not gone mad, are you?"—and Juve tumbled down the stairs four steps at a time.

"It's just abominable treatment!" he cried. "Why, Fandor, you're surely the silliest of asses. *Please* take M. Thévenot near a good fire and let him warm himself. Really, I don't know how to excuse your behavior!"

"But, my dear Juve…"

"Not a word! else you'll put me in a passion. But you, you, Monsieur Thévenot, didn't you understand? And didn't you give Fandor a hint? Oh! I can never forgive him…"

Juve seemed in despair. As for the antiquary, shivering and green with cold, he was manifestly bewildered.

"Understand what?" he asked. "Give Fandor a hint about what? Anyway, you don't suspect me any longer?"

"But I never did suspect you, come."

"Why? What?"

"Suspect you? You? Only a madman could do that. And Fandor, who left the handcuffs on! Come along, do. A glass of grog will warm you up."

Three minutes later M. Thévenot was dressed again, while Juve was explaining:

"My good sir, if I accused you out loud, if I had your clothes searched, if I handcuffed you and told Fandor to cover you with his revolver, it was all to put Fantômas off the scent, who was bound to be somewhere near, within hearing. What I wanted was to induce him to clear out by making him think it was you

I really suspected. Why, it was a feint, and nothing else."

And, without giving the antiquary time to get in a protest against this "feint," without appearing to notice the suspicious glance with which Fandor favored him, Juve continued:

"I said to myself, look you: 'Thus reassured, Fantômas will run for it. We didn't see him come, *but* we shall see him go.' Ah, yes! worse luck, he has diddled us. It's enough to drive a man mad…"

"And the document? my plan?" groaned M. Thévenot.

"Stolen, of course! Spirited away!"

"Abominable! abominable!"

Juve's face took on an expression of profound surprise: "And why, pray? Tell me that!"

"What! You ask why?"

"Of course I do, seeing you only want it in a week's time."

"But I shan't have it in a week's time."

"My dear sir," Juve spoke in a quiet voice of perfect assurance, "that is where we differ—differ entirely. In a week from now you shall have your paper…"

"I shall have my paper!"

"Why, yes! Most certainly you shall. I shall give it back to you…"

"You have recovered it then?"

"Yes, I have… or I shall! Will you be offended if I don't tell you more just at present? And there, you've caught cold too—you're sneezing again. Come, we'll put you in one of my Inspector's sidecars and I'll have you driven home again. You, Fandor, are to take another of their motorbikes and drive me. Theo and Henri will have the third machine. The rest of the Inspectors will return by train,"—and as he gave these directions, Juve seemed so absolutely calm and confident that neither M. Thévenot nor Jerome Fandor found themselves able to pronounce another word. They were dumbfounded by the police officer's consummate coolness.

2. Fandor Disobeys Orders

Juve, however, would have been much mistaken if he thought to baffle so easily the natural curiosity his odd behavior was bound to excite. No sooner, indeed, did Fandor find himself alone with his companion on the great paved highroad that connects Robinson with the capital than the journalist, no longer fearing to embarrass his friend, made up his mind to question him.

"Juve," the young man began, "am I really an ass?"

"If you go making bad blood about it, yes!"

"That's what I shall do, Juve, if you go on telling me you suspected M. Thévenot by way of a ruse and that I didn't understand."

"Then, my dear lad, I won't go on telling you."

"So, you still suspect him?"

"Hmm!… If I suspected him, should I have let him go?"

"Juve, that's no answer."

"Fandor, it's all the answer your question deserves."

"Which means what, Juve?"

"Which means just exactly this, Fandor: you saw the whole thing, not a detail escaped you… So, you know just as much as I do, and there's no need for me to put you wise."

"But, Juve, *I* don't understand."

"Did I ever say *I* understood?"

"How was the document stolen?"

"Do you think I know that?"

"Yes, because you declare you are in a position to restore it in a week's time."

Juve only shrugged, remarking:

"Come, don't let us confuse what is already far from clear. The way the document was taken is one story; the way I shall recover it is another—and these two stories are separate and independent."

"Juve, you're a tiresome beast!"

"You're not very polite."

"Juve, I want to know… Ho, there! Look out! Do you want to kill us?"

Fandor's outcry of alarm was amply justified. As though suddenly struck by a brilliant thought, a veritable revelation from heaven, Juve had thrown up his hands, stood up in his sidecar and then plumped down again.

"The dullard I am," he growled. "Why, it's undoubted! It's self-evident! It's obvious… Oh! the idiot I've been, the born idiot!"

"Juve, have you done gesticulating?" Fandor demanded.

"Gesticulating, yes! But not laughing!"

"May I know what about?"

"No!… Turn to the right…"

"To the right? But that's not the straight road. Where are we going then?"

Juve's voice was a trifle tremulous as he gave the answer:

"Where are we going?… Hmm… Well, to… to see Fantômas."

"Eh, what? You tell me?…"

Fandor had stopped his machine dead, in sheer amazement.

"Speak out, for God's sake! Have done with your mysterious ways! Have you sworn to bring me to perdition?"

"Not at all. Just the opposite!"

"Just the opposite! One wouldn't think so."

"Well, my dear lad, I'm going to tell you. You're listening, eh? Here's a final word—don't you forget it: never worry your head about the thing!"

Juve smothered a laugh, then repeated:

"Don't you worry your head! That's plain enough, eh?"

"Plain? You mean to say…"

"Hush! Not a word! Drive on. You have your revolver?"

"Of course. But…"

"Not a word more, chatterbox. Think! You know as much as I do… Left, here!"

And Fandor said no more. Since he had lived with the police officer, the journalist had enjoyed many opportunities of learning that it was perfectly useless to try to force Juve to explain himself, once he was resolved to hold his tongue.

And then Fandor began to feel really exasperated with himself. It was quite true, after all, he knew perfectly well— just as well as Juve—all the details of the adventure they were engaged in. Ought he not, like him, to fathom the secret the detective had guessed. The motor gathered speed, while Fandor silently turned over in his mind the questions that puzzled him.

"The paper has disappeared… But how?… Juve is sure of recovering it… But in what way?"

Nor had the young man found any plausible solution of these two problems when Juve again signed to him to wheel to the left and turn into a fine avenue of tall trees.

"Go easy, Fandor! No noise," he said softly. Then suddenly the order:

"Halt! Get out here!"

Fandor felt his heart almost stop beating. Was this actually a house of Fantômas'? Could it be that Juve, when he announced that he was paying a visit to the redoubtable Lord of Terror, had been speaking seriously! A thousand questions flashed through the journalist's brain. If Juve knew of a house where Fantômas was to be found, how could he have waited all this time before raiding it. If he knew, for a certainty, that the Arch-Criminal lived in this locality, why was he guilty of such monstrous imprudence as to visit such a spot without having mobilized all the forces of the police?

"Juve told me a lie! Juve was joking!" he thought. "I'm sure of it."

But a cold shudder ran through him as he gazed about him. In this outer suburb of Paris bordering on the enormous cemetery of Clamart are to be found not a few lonely and ill-omened tracts. And how gloomy this avenue with its great trees was! How the wind whistled eerily through the branches! Not another sound to be heard! Not a living being within sight! It was indeed a fit dwelling place for a monster of iniquity such as Fantômas.

The young man moved a step nearer the police officer, who, leaving the sidecar, had gone to a ditch by the side of the road.

"Juve," he began, "tell me…"—but got no further. Juve laid a finger to his lips, enjoining silence.

"H'sh! Listen! We are a hundred yards from…"

"From what, Juve? From where?"

"Hush! hush! Wait!"

Juve stretched himself on the ground and, putting his ear to the earth, seemed to be listening intently. Then, as he got up again:

"Fandor," he whispered, "mind every word I say. This is serious to the last degree… Fantômas is yonder…"

"Yonder?… Where?"

"Within a hundred yards of us!… At home!… in his own house!"—and without giving his companion time for questions that were obviously futile, Juve went on:

"How do I know? Precisely in the same way as I know how the paper has disappeared… Yes! and how I shall recover it… Anyway, in twenty minutes—never worry your head, my boy—you will know everything too!"

Again Juve signed to the other to keep silence, and after listening once more for a second or two:

"He is there," he announced… "This time the day is ours—and how easy a victory! Now, happen what may, swear to remember my orders and to obey in everything… everything whatsoever."

"But, Juve…"

"Yes! who can tell? But listen to me; this is the plan I have decided on. A hundred yards from here we shall come upon a villa—Fantômas'. We are to go in—of course revolver in hand! The door opens on a corridor, at the end of which is a staircase. I shall go upstairs. You are to stay below. Keep a good lookout, whatever you do! Five minutes after I have gone up you will see Fantômas come down. Bar his way. Fire, if he tries to pass. I shall be behind him—and he won't return the way he came, I take my oath to that! You understand?"

"To work!" was the journalist's unhesitating reply. He was strung to a high pitch of excitement. A certain ring in Juve's voice that plainly indicated the grave importance of the game they were playing impressed him deeply. But how mysterious, how strangely mysterious, it all was!

Meantime, without another word, the police officer had started for his goal. He had dropped into the ditch and now, bent double, Fandor behind him, was making his way noiselessly to the gate of a country villa, a house of three stories and presenting a very comfortable appearance.

Juve repeated his previous admonition, but it was purely superfluous—Fandor held himself ready for anything.

Softly Juve opened the gate of the garden, which he crossed. At the far end was a flight of stone steps and at the top a stout door. This door, to Fandor's growing amazement, the detective opened with a key he drew from his pocket.

Again came the detective's whispered warning exhorting to vigilance, and Juve pushed on through the open door into a flagged entrance hall. This he crossed, and the momentary flash of an flashlight, no sooner lighted than extinguished, showed Fandor a carpeted staircase.

"There, stay there!" whispered Juve, "and mind, no quarter!"

Revolver in hand, every nerve on the stretch, the young man took ambush. So extraordinary, so unexpected, was the whole thing it seemed more like a nightmare than a reality, and Fandor pinched himself to try if he was awake or dreaming.

Yes, he was certainly awake, and now he could plainly hear Juve mounting the stairs. One story, a second—was he going up to the third floor then? "Juve is making overmuch noise," he thought to himself.

Then, suddenly, he was near going frantic. Through the silent house a scream of rage had echoed, a cry rather of anger than of pain. And then… absolute silence!

Without one instant's hesitation, as the thought flashed through his brain that it was Juve, his best friend Juve, they were attacking, Fandor dashed wildly to the stairs, revolver in his hand, his own flashlight in the other. Was not his first and foremost duty to go to his comrade's help?

He reached one landing, then another. He was already halfway up to the third floor when he stopped dead… Before him lay something that was surprising, incomprehensible— and only too self-evident at one and the same time.

Truly, this obstacle before which Fandor had come to a dead stop bore a sinister, a dreadful meaning! Impossible, at sight of it, not to realize why Juve had uttered the cry of horror the young man had heard. Impossible too not to shudder at thought of the fate that had overtaken the detective.

This impassable obstacle barring the journalist's advance was, in one word—a hole, a hole of the strangest aspect, dark and manifestly deep, the nature of which admitted of no mistake. While, up to this point, the stairway was like any other stairs, while, up to this height, it was thickly carpeted, here, before his eyes, Fandor beheld a gap where several steps were missing and torn shreds of the carpet, resting on nothing, hanging down into empty space.

What had happened was obvious at a glance. Quite unsuspecting, Juve had reached the fatal spot. Still unsuspecting, he had stepped on the carpet, probably stretched on wires so as to give the appearance of successive steps the same as elsewhere. But beneath his tread the wires had given way. Then inevitably, carried down by the falling carpet that tore under his weight, Juve must have plunged into the void, into the horrid abyss whose existence it had been impossible for him to guess.

In a flash Fandor had mentally reconstituted the tragedy, and all but fainted with horror and distress.

"By God!" he cried, "it was no accident, this extraordinary state of the stairs."

Instantly he realized that the absent treads had been willfully suppressed, and he cried out in impotent fury: "Fantômas! one of Fantômas' traps!"

How could it be otherwise indeed? Had not Juve himself, only a few moments before, assured his companion he was taking him to the dread Arch-Criminal's abode? Was it to be wondered at then if the man the world called The Torturer should have set a snare of this atrocious sort?

Half paralyzed, Fandor fell back, to rest his back against the wall. Fantômas! Yes, it was Fantômas haunted the place where he was, Fantômas, who might at any moment appear, mysterious, unrecognizable as always under the flowing folds of his black hood, clad in his close-fitting suit of black, black gloved and shod in black, the darkling vesture the Lord of Terror ever wore. Was he not, perhaps, even now marking down his victim, ready to spring out next instant and annihilate him?

But presently, by a supreme effort of will, Fandor regained his habitual cool self-control. Yes, no doubt of it, he must confront The Torturer face to face. But what of that? Must not Juve be his first care? Was he not bound to bring succor to his friend?

But where had the police officer fallen to? And was he seriously injured? How came it he did not call for help? Fandor, however, wasted no time in vain conjectures. Heedless of danger, scorning all precautions, he knelt down on the last step overhanging the gaping void and bent over to stare into the abyss—without avail. He even, at the risk of betraying his presence, turned on the light of his flashlight, which he still carried, but its rays were not powerful enough to reach the bottom of this sort of oubliette.

"Ah! but I *will* know, come what may, where Juve is. I am resolved to save him!" the young man swore. By this time he was completely master of himself again. The certainty of danger roused his constitutional bravery. His mind was made up in a moment.

"I am going to call to him… He must know I am here," and he shouted with all the force of his lungs: "Juve! Juve, I say!"

But not a sound was heard in answer, and for some moments Fandor felt the panic fear that comes of absolute, unbroken silence. Not a sound, not a footstep, not even the creaking of a board! Yet Fantômas was there, to a certainty!

But once more Fandor forgot the Lord of Terror. No! it was Juve he thought of. In a faint, no doubt? Incapacitated from answering? Or else, he had not heard, buried in some dungeon so far away that his voice had failed to reach the prisoner.

"I am determined to know the truth," he reiterated—and he fired two shots at random, in the air. But a reverberating echo was the sole result.

This time Fandor was afraid—dreadfully afraid. No, it was not the danger he ran, the danger he must face, the danger of the situation he was in he dreaded; but he was thinking, the sweat beading his temples:

"Dead? Can he be dead?"—and great tears welled in his eyes, the tears strong men feel no shame in shedding, because they come from the heart.

"Juve was dead? He had been killed by the fall?" No! Fandor refused to believe it. There are horrors reason revolts at.

Swiftly, with frantic recklessness, acting as though he deemed himself alone in this strange house, the young man flew down the stairs.

"Down there, where I lay in ambush," he remembered, "there was a door not far off… a door that should open on a stairway leading to the cellars. In the cellars I shall find the oubliette perhaps." He was like a man in a dream, who does things without much knowing how or why.

Reaching the entrance hall, he stopped in amazement. The door he had seen shut was open.

"Why! what!" he stammered, "Fantômas must have come down after all?"

But already he was plunging down the narrow stairs that led, as he had guessed, to the basement regions of the house, and in two minutes reached a circular vaulted chamber. And in this chamber, by the light of his flashlight, he made out a curl of blue-gray smoke! He sniffed the air, and exclaimed:

"Tobacco! It reeks of tobacco… English tobacco!… the sort Juve is fond of!"

A thousand confused thoughts whirled in his brain. Mechanically he moved on, only to stop dead on the far side of a dividing wall. Above his head yawned an opening, going up to a great height. His light directed towards the top of this orifice afforded him a view of the underside of a flight of stairs… some of the steps of which were missing.

"Great heavens!" he gasped, "but this is the place where Juve fell, surely? No, not a doubt of it! But how comes it he is not here now? And I can see no signs of the accident." He bent down, then knelt on the floor, which was of hard earth, and a thick layer of dust had accumulated in it. Yet the dust showed no mark of footsteps, no impress of any sort.

"And yet," the young man spoke out loud, "if Juve fell here, I could not help but find traces of his fall." But there was nothing whatever to be seen.

Then, buried in thought, the journalist left the cellar and made his way back to the ground floor.

By this time he was more puzzled than uneasy. A fleeting smile hovered about his lips.

"Yet another mystery!" he muttered, as he climbed the cellar stairs and regained the entrance hall. "The way the paper was stolen… that makes one; the way Juve expects to find it… that makes two; again the way Juve has vanished… that makes number three."

So saying, Fandor crossed the vestibule, turned the handle of a door and opened it.

"Yes, I must have a look over the house," he thought. "So much the worse if I find myself face to face with Fantômas!" He was almost laughing now. For this third mystery he had a moment before been speaking of, was he already by way of finding a reassuring explanation?

In any case, with a fine recklessness, he did not even take the trouble to extinguish his pocket lamp as he made his way into the room he meant to investigate.

Once inside, he gave an exclamation of surprise, and his visit ended summarily. There was a good and sufficient reason for this; the apartment was absolutely empty, and contained not a single piece of furniture.

The hangings, half torn down from the walls, showed that it had only recently been dismantled.

"Let's look elsewhere," said Fandor, and a second room on the ground floor received a visit.

"In just the same state," muttered the journalist. "Better and better! Now for the first floor."

Thither he proceeded without any undue haste. Only to note his anxious face, in fact, only to observe his look of absorption, it was easy to guess he was thinking his hardest, evidently trying to find ground for accepting the belief that little by little was strengthening in his mind.

"Yes, the first floor," he told himself, opening door after door at random, and without the least precaution, "the first floor is in exactly the same condition as the ground floor. Hmm! it was to be expected..."—adding presently:

"Well, suppose I take my departure."

Putting out the flashlight, the battery of which was getting exhausted, the young man proceeded with the utmost nonchalance to light a cigarette, as he concluded:

"Yes, that's it! Let's be off! Nothing better to do,"—then added under his breath:

"Juve is a scamp, and I shall tell him so!"

This said, he marched out deliberately, banging the door behind him, never thinking of the noise he made.

"A rum sort of house," the journalist grumbled. "A staircase wanting some of its steps, and to make up, carpeted magnificently—and never a scrap of furniture anywhere else!... Ah, well! this will make fine work for M. Havard. I can guess that much... I might even 'hatch out' a fine article to mystify the readers of *La Capitale*... But all the same, what a rascal to be sure, what a confounded rascal!"

Dawn was breaking and even under the great trees of the avenue it was getting light enough to see. Suddenly Fandor stopped dead, looking about him in surprise.

"Oh! ho! and my motorbike and sidecar? Where the devil are they?"

Turning about, he gazed to right and left. Not a trace of the machine anywhere!

The young man's brow darkened.

"I don't half like this," he muttered. "Juve should have known better. He should never have dared..."

But he checked his vexation. Once again he seemed the victim of an agonizing dread. Just now had he not been telling himself that Juve had purposely enticed him to a house he had himself "faked," had he not come to think that, in order to lose him (Fandor), to "drop" him, the detective had deliberately played the game of a voluntary disappearance?

"Just the sort of thing Juve *would* do!" the young man had told himself. "Perhaps he wants to set about a report of his death? Perhaps he wants to put people off the scent and make it believed he is Fantômas' prisoner?..."

But now, noting the disappearance of the police conveyance, he dared not indulge in any such reassuring theory... That Juve, the worthy man, should have gone off alone on a motorcycle, a delicate piece of machinery for a novice to work and one he had never driven before, that was out of the question.

Had somebody else stolen it then? Was that somebody...? Suddenly, startlingly, a new hypothesis flashed across the journalist's brain and froze him with terror. What was there to show that Fantômas had not followed them, Juve and him, while they were on their way to the lonely house? What was there to show that, from motorcar or motorcycle, Fantômas had not at a distance watched their invasion of the villa? And might he not have taken cover, seen Juve come out alone, attacked him, mastered him and carried him off in the sidecar?...

Again Fandor's face was pale as death. If he had felt reassured a moment before it was because, finding no traces of Juve's fall, but on the contrary noticing a smell of his friend's favorite tobacco, he had been convinced that he was guessing right when he supposed Juve to have made off—for the best of motives. But this in no way hindered his having subsequently fallen into a trap!

Suddenly the journalist gave a shrug.

"After all, no!... I'm talking nonsense! If Fantômas followed us, spied on us, he too must have had a vehicle of sorts, a motorcar or a motorcycle, at his disposal. In that case I should come across his mount, if it was he who went off on our machine..."

And lo! next moment Fandor broke into a laugh.

"So then, by Jupiter! I'm not a fool, and didn't Juve tell me—and speaking seriously—that I 'mustn't worry my head about it'? That was meant, I suppose! And I am disobeying orders if I do worry my head,"—and he walked on.

"How far away I am!" he grumbled, "and not a tram to be hoped for this time in the morning… Well, well, let's pad the hoof!… If only I knew where Juve is!"

But to this riddle the excellent young man, cudgel his brains as he might all the way back to Paris and all the while he was tramping wearily across the city to Montmartre and the Rue Tardieu, could find no answer.

He was accordingly very tired and in anything but an amiable mood when at last, fagged out and exhausted, he rang at the door of the police officer's modest flat.

"If only I might learn he is here," the young man told himself. But no sooner had Jean opened the door than that faithful henchman inquired:

"So Monsieur is not with you, Monsieur Fandor?"

"No!… And I doubt if he's coming back so soon."

"Monsieur will come back when he sees fit," returned the old man, unconcerned as always. "I'll leave his coffee on the fire."

"Hmm! if you like… But…"

"Monsieur doesn't think it worth while? Then we might give it to the snorer?"

"The snorer?"

"Yes… can't you hear, sir?"

The journalist listened and satisfied himself he could perfectly well hear somebody snoring in the next room.

"Why, who is it?" he demanded in surprise.

"Someone I don't know, but someone almost as filthy as Monsieur is—no offense meant… A trifle less dust, but a deal more grease!"

"Description's a bit vague," struck in the journalist. "I'll go and see for myself," and he marched into the next room. With a start he recognized the visitor, who was no other than Inspector Theo. Evidently worn out with fatigue, the man was so sound asleep Fandor had to shake him awake.

"Come, bear it like a man!" the young man bantered, "your appeal is refused!"

"Here I am, Chief!" the fellow stuttered. "Good Lord! I've been napping!"—and then, rubbing his eyes. "Hello! why, it's you, Monsieur Fandor. And Monsieur Juve? is he back too?"

"No!… You were expecting him?…"

"Surely. He'd told me to be here bright and early this morning."

"He really told you that?"

"Why, certainly! You seem surprised?"

Fandor was more than surprised. He was struck to the heart. If Juve had arranged to meet Theo, was that not proof positive he had meant to return home? And did it not show conclusively that his disappearance was involuntary? Not wishing, however, to let the policeman into the secret of his fears and anxious to afford himself a chance of thinking things over before making Juve's absence officially known, the young man forced himself to put a good face on the matter.

"Ah! well," he replied, "so be it! But Juve won't be coming back so soon as all that, as far as I know, that is."

"Oh!… He's following up a clue then, eh?… As it happens, I was half thinking *I* had got hold of one too to give him."

"How so?"

Fandor asked the question absent-mindedly. In his present state of mind any ordinary, commonplace talk annoyed him.

"It's like this, Monsieur Fandor," the man went on, a hundred miles from suspecting the other's thoughts, "it's an informer gave the tip to the authorities at the Prefecture. Seems that, tonight, there's to be a grand meeting, a solemn confabulation, something or other of the sort, among the apaches. I thought the Chief would like to be there. It'll be held at a certain tavern…"

"Yes, what tavern?" Fandor asked, more and more absent-mindedly.

But instantly his indifference gave place to amazement, when Theo went on to explain nonchalantly:

"Oh! a shady place, naturally! A drinking den at Javelle. The signboard's lettered 'à l'Ami Ralle.'"

"'A l'Ami Ralle'!" Fandor yelled excitedly, "otherwise 'à l'Admiral'!… And we never twigged it! Oh! bless my heart and soul!"—and before Theo's astonished eyes, he danced a war dance of triumph.

"And old Juve, who was worrying about the Ministry of Marine! And I, who wanted to consult the Navy List! L'Ami Ralle! L'Ami Ralle! Oh! I shall have a word to say to this gentleman, l'Ami Ralle, I shall!"

Then, running to the door of the sitting room, Fandor called: "Jean! Jean!"

"Sir!" came the reply in the old servant's quiet voice. "Two beds, my man, right away, one for the gentleman and one for me. And hey, presto! quick's the word!"

Without giving a thought to old Jean's evident bewilderment, he went up to Theo, and gripping him by the lapel of his coat:

"No, you're not just in a condition, my friend, to grasp the subtleties of the situation. But, anyway, here's a piece of news for you: you and I, tonight, we are going to arrest Fantômas perhaps!… And now to bed with us! I'm dead sleepy too, you must know," and with a push he sent the amazed and dumbfounded Inspector flying into a bedroom next door.

As for him, he darted into Juve's working-room, snatched up a piece of paper and wrote in his best copperplate:

"'*Amiral*,' i.e. '*Ami Ralle*—a drinking shop,'—yes, we must be kind to old Juve," he laughed to himself. "And now to bed!…"—and he was turning the sheet over to dry it on the police officer's blotting pad, when suddenly his eyes filled with tears.

Why, no! Juve was not a "rascal" after all. On the blotter Fandor read a sentence written in blue pencil, a sentence that was at one and the same time a warning, an order, a piece of advice… and almost an admission:

"Never worry your head about it!—Fandor, please note!"

3. In the Hands of Fantômas

Jerome Fandor might well, under present circumstances, have found himself entirely unable to sleep. The recollection of the trying moments he had just lived through was of any-thing but a soothing effect. Juve had disappeared, and try as he might to persuade himself that his friend was in no danger, the journalist could not be really easy in his mind. On the other hand, having resolved to pay a visit to the "Ami Ralle" den, he could not possibly regard the future without some degree of well-founded anxiety.

But the young man had so much of the heedless confidence of his age, and above all, so large a dose of recklessness, such a passion for fighting, that all these excellent reasons proved powerless to combat his fatigue.

"To bed," he exclaimed, "and away for the land of dreams! Napoleon used to sleep for two hours before his greatest battles. I don't see why I should not copy the Emperor's example,"—and fortified by this historic precedent, three minutes afterwards he had shut his eyes and was instantly wrapped in refreshing slumbers.

It was night, or very nearly so, when he opened his eyes. Indeed, it was a sheer impossibility for him to have done other-wise. To go on sleeping was out of the question. Inspector Theo was shaking him with might and main.

"Rouse up, Monsieur Fandor. Just time to dress, and we must be off."

"Righto!" cried the journalist. "A couple of minutes to get ready, and I'm your man."

It was something more than two minutes Jerome Fandor took over his "preparations," but, to make up for it, when he did come on the scene, his appearance won a cry of admiration from Theo. Truly Juve's lessons in the art of makeup had not been wasted! As thoroughly as the Prince of Detectives himself, the young man possessed the cunning art of disguising himself, transforming himself into whatever character he thought fit to assume.

It was now a disreputable street loafer who stood before the Inspector's eyes. Instead of a coat, for his visit to this meeting of apaches that was to be held at the sign of the "Ami Ralle," Fandor had donned a workman's blue slop, foul with the accumulated dirt of ages. Torn, patched and ragged as it was, it was nonetheless a fact that this squalid garment fitted admirably and left the wearer the full and free use of his limbs. On his head he wore a cap without a brim, on his feet an odd pair of military boots that had surely come from some barrack storeroom.

As for his face, this was absolutely unrecognizable. Ordinarily clean-shaven, not wearing even a mustache, Fandor now appeared adorned with a heavy growth on the upper lip and an imposing Newgate collar by way of beard. He had painted in a finely executed black eye of a life-like greenish blue tint, giving him all the appearance of having recently been engaged in some battle royal. Now, a cigarette stuck in one corner of the mouth, his two hands dangling in his side pockets, he demanded:

"A good makeup, eh?"

"First-rate!" agreed Theo, in the tone of a connoisseur. "I should never have known you myself."

The officer's own getup was simple enough. A stonemason's blouse, all splashed with plaster, soldier's gaiters, a cap spotted with cement, composed his accoutrement. He had given himself a pair of heavy false eyebrows that quite altered the look of the eyes, and besides had wound round his head a sort of muffler, a big check handkerchief with ends of dirty cotton-wool sticking out here and there.

"And I?" he asked. "Am I all right?"

"Quite excellent! But that toothache wants some justification. There! there's a walnut, old chap. Swell out your cheek with it, but whatever you do, don't change sides!"

"Ah! Monsieur Fandor, but you're the man for thinking of

details!"—and Theo gave a satisfied laugh.

Surely the public little knows the quiet courage the men who devote their lives to police work must be prepared to show at any moment. Have they a suspicion of the manifold ruses officers of the Criminal Department must employ to gain an entrance into dens of iniquity from which they would never escape alive were they recognized?

"Revolver?" questioned the younger man.

"Why, yes! Yes, and knife!"

"Then we are ready! Away we go."

In the Square d'Anvers, the two men stopped a taxi, ordering the man to drive them to the bridge of Grenelle.

"What ho!" grunted the driver distrustfully. "And the cash? Got any tin?"

"Go on, my beauty!" grinned Fandor, delighted at the distrust the mere look of him aroused. "There, old man, there's twenty shiners on account."

An argument of this sort was not long in convincing the suspicious Jehu.

"They're rum customers," he thought to himself, "but they're in funds, anyway, for the moment."

In the cab Theo and Fandor did not exchange a word. Both were pondering over the hazardous enterprise they were embarked on. A meeting was afoot at the "Ami Ralle,"—no doubt called together by Fantômas… So far, so good! But how to worm their way into the place of assembly? Such resorts are as closely guarded against strangers as the drawing-rooms of the fashionable world.

"Pooh! we shall see," was Fandor's conclusion. "The great thing, after all, is to discover a way of hearing what's said."

Twenty minutes afterwards Fandor and Theo were making a reconnaissance of the locality from a safe distance. It was just a drinking-shop, like another, this tavern of the "Ami Ralle," one of those places one hardly notices, for by daylight they look quite ordinary. It was situated in a narrow alley at Javelle, an alley little frequented, and bordered by wide spaces of waste-land littered with heaps of scrap iron from the factories that abound in that manufacturing district, and occupied with its brown painted facade the ground floor of a small, two-storied house. Before the door a gas lamp with dirty, cracked panes flickered feebly, showing the announcement: "Hotel."

"Ah! this is interesting!" thought Fandor, making a note of the circumstance. He and his companion had climbed the palings of an enclosure nearby. Crouching in the shadow and peeping through the cracks between the planks, they could see without being seen…

"Interesting," the young man continued to himself. "An hotel!… One might ask for a room…"

But just then Theo whispered softly:

"Heavy shutters, eh? and the landlord is bolting them…"

" Why yes, that's true! So everybody must have comet"

"Most likely. Not to attract attention, our friends must have arrived early no doubt. And the landlord's shutting his door, so his customers won't be disturbed…"

In fact, at that moment a fat man, in shirt-sleeves pulled up above the elbow, a corner of his apron tucked into his belt, was busy closing the massive shutters that decorated the front of the house.

"Devil take it!" the journalist swore. "Yet we've just *got* to hear… Ah! good night! what a fool I am!"

"Why?" queried Theo.

"Why, because it's as simple as how d'you do to find out what's going on inside… Don't move, old man. *You* stay where you are, and keep an eye on anyone going in or coming out… *I'm* off on an expedition."

"An expedition?"

"Oh! but it's a fine lark! Say, Theo, in case of alarm, you'll fire a revolver shot to call me, eh?"

"And you do the same, Monsieur Fandor?"

"Agreed, yes! But I'm not going to run any danger, not I! Ah! happy thought; you, Theo, watch the door meantime and try to follow up anybody who may come out… And try to collar him; a hostage can always come in useful."

"But, Monsieur Fandor, I have no warrant. It's not legal."

"Pooh! what's the odds? You'll always be able to say you made a mistake, that you thought you were arresting Fantômas. One can't make omelettes without breaking eggs."

Without another word and never stopping to hear what his companion might have to say, he got up and climbed back into the alleyway.

"Fantômas *ought* to be there," he kept telling himself, "with his accomplices. I must find out what he says, discover his secrets."

With a catlike tread the young man crept towards the brigand's haunt. Verily he had exaggerated when he said he was running no risk. Nothing could well be more perilous than his present enterprise.

On reaching the front of the house, he halted a moment. Then after making sure there was no passerby in sight and no one apparently on the lookout, he gripped a drainpipe in both hands and began to swarm up it.

"Why, he's mad! They must hear him!" thought Theo, as he watched these proceedings.

"What ho!" Fandor was muttering at the same moment. "Once I can reach the roof, I am saved!"

The young fellow was as nimble as an acrobat, as clever as a gymnast, and soon laid hold of the edge of the roofing, and, getting a purchase, hoisted himself onto the sloping zinc.

It was high time! At that very moment a shutter flew open and a beery voice sang out:

"Curse it, man! did you bolt them damned things? I tell you it's no common stunt, this here! Like enough to bring the cops down on us, it is!"

"And *I* tell *you*, old soaker, you've got the jimjams, and its them makes you go seeing things what ain't there!…"

Fandor heard no more. The window was shut to again directly. Satisfied no doubt that nothing was to be feared, the clients of the "Ami Ralle," after a look round outside, recovered their peace of mind.

"Between you and me, my fine fellows!" laughed Fandor. "Now, with a bit of luck, I think I've won the rubber!"

He got to his feet, and as calmly as though he did not stand on the roof of a house where Fantômas' accomplices were gathered, where Fantômas himself was no doubt present, the young man set about sundry odd-looking proceedings. From one chimney to another he went, and after clapping his ear to the chimney-pots, listened for a few seconds, then moved on to another opening.

"For sure, the meeting *must* be going on somewhere," he told himself, "and if the talk is in any room where one of these chimneys comes out, I shall easily hear what they say."

But he heard nothing save a confused, indistinguishable sound—the noise a crowd of people makes, but quite unintelligible.

The journalist was almost in despair when suddenly a cry all but escaped his lips. There, at his feet, an opening gaped in the roof, a broad, square hole, big enough for a man's body to pass, and through this opening came the sound of voices loud and clear!

"By the Lord!" cried Fandor, "I could not wish for better!"— and he dropped to his knees and listened with all his ears.

He had no doubt about the nature and purpose of this sort of extra wide chimney. It was of course an air passage for the ventilation of the hall where the scoundrels he was spying on were to meet. Nor was it difficult to guess that this hall was an underground room contrived in the cellars of the tavern as a safe place of assembly. This air passage had doubtless been made so wide to serve as a secret exit, an emergency exit, in case of a police raid, to facilitate the escape of the clients of the "Ami Ralle."

But there his conjectures ended. Kneeling now and bending over the hole that led down to the black depths of the subterranean regions, Fandor had suddenly heard a voice, distinct, authoritative, imperious: what a thrill ran through him at the sound, what a spasm of rage shook him from head to foot!

"Fantômas! it is Fantômas speaking!" panted the journalist. The words reached him quite plainly and distinctly, so clear he did not lose a syllable. But what was his amazement as he caught their import! Fantômas was there; he could hear him speaking. Yet the man was declaring:

"I shall not be with you tonight… That is impossible… No matter! I have promised payment, and payment shall be made. Each of you will find at his lodging, when he goes back home, the sum he has earned in doing my biddings…"

Then, while Fandor was grinding his teeth in fury, as he recognized Fantômas' voice and the peremptory tones in which he issued his orders, the Lord of Terror went on:

"Now, listen! Important events are preparing. Those who shall serve me loyally will be rewarded magnificently. Here is…"

At this point, from his post of observation, Fandor caught the sound of clapping and a muffled salvo of cheers; these last words of the master had stirred his audience to an enthusiasm that could not be altogether stifled.

Fantômas' voice continued:

"I have gained possession of a document that is worth a fortune. This fortune I shall be master of shortly, and you shall have your share… But you must keep discipline—the strictest discipline!"

A pause, then the grim voice proceeded: "You must, likewise, never let yourselves be caught by gross attempts to work on your credulity. Tomorrow the papers will give out that Juve has disappeared… that he is dead… that I have killed him at a villa in the outskirts. Well, it is false! It is a lie! Never think yourselves rid of him… I do not know where he is. I do not know what he is plotting. But he has *not* fallen by my hand!… So, beware!"

Fandor felt his heart swell with a growing delight. It was really true then! He had not deceived himself? If Juve had disappeared, it was because his disappearance was essential to the success of some ruse? He chuckled: "That rascal of a Juve! 'Not worry my head'! By the Lord!"

Then he listened again… What did *this* mean?

"Beware then of Juve, and of Fandor, more than ever! More than ever, too, feel no surprise if I am some time without your hearing from me… A rumor is going about—it seems His Majesty may be coming to Paris. Perhaps I shall be obliged to go away to welcome him… When I return, I will let you know… Till then…"

But Fandor was no longer listening. All the time Fantômas had been speaking, only by a supreme effort of self-control had he succeeded thus far in restraining himself. Now he found it impossible to master his rage any longer. To know the monstrous villain only a few yards away, to hear his words, to think it was in his power to confront him, to clap a revolver to his head, to master him—and not to make the attempt, was more than the gallant young man could endure.

"I must, I will!" broke suddenly from the journalist. " Nothing venture, nothing have. I will try the hazard!"

No doubt, Fandor was guilty of the most reckless imprudence, but imprudence is, all said and done, but another form of courage. Not another instant did he hesitate. He even forgot the words he had heard just before, in which Fantômas had feigned to make excuse for not coming. Shutting his eyes for a moment, he seemed to behold a nightmare vision—the terrific figure of Fantômas in the horrid panoply of blackness men told of in shuddering whispers. Yes, in that moment of fierce excitement he saw the black, fluttering hood, the black silk tights, the black gloves, the black shoes, that were ever the grim disguise of the Torturer.

"And I am not to hurl myself at his throat, to arrest the scoundrel, to bring him at long last to the scaffold?… But that were sheer cowardice!"

Alas! what the young hero was fain to do was madness rather, utter madness.

Now he lay down flat on the roof, let his legs dangle down the ventilating shaft, and noiselessly explored the darkness with his feet.

"Ah! footholds," he exclaimed, "iron staples let into the stonework! By God! I thought as much."

He cocked his revolver. To the ring on the butt was attached a doubled lanyard, by which he slung the weapon round his neck. Between his teeth he held his unsheathed dagger.

"To work!" he cried. "Down there they must be half a score for sure. I shall never leave the place alive, that I know… Pooh! what matters that, if I can sell my life against Fantômas'… He is all I must trouble about!"

He lowered himself into the black void and began the descent. A perilous enterprise, for the slightest sound might betray him, and if he *were* heard, was he not certain to be killed without even a chance of defending himself? The wretches he meant to face would find it easy work to shoot him down with revolvers in this cramped chimney where he could barely turn.

"A villainous job!" growled the climber. "I wonder if Theo has seen I was going down? No, surely!… Ah! now I've just dislodged a stone…"

He stopped dead, and with beating heart, listened once more. Fantômas was not speaking. Instead, beery, blackguard voices were exchanging low-toned confidences the young man could only half hear.

"To work again!" he encouraged himself. "Nobody's heard the noise I made. A lucky chance…"

He descended another few rungs. At last his foot touched hard earth. Was this the bottom of the ventilating shaft?

But next moment the blood seemed to congeal in Fandor's veins. As he turned about to look and see whereabouts he had come to earth, he had heard a rustle, and a hand, yes, a man's hand, was laid on his lips, stifling the cry of surprise that he was on the point of uttering.

*   *   *   *   *

Doubtless, in the course of his adventurous career, Jerome Fandor had lived through moments no less fraught with tragedy. But never yet had he felt such an agony of surprise and horror as now. He had been convinced he was alone, and was expecting to come out in some back room where nobody could see him. At worst, he thought he only ran the risk of falling plump in the middle of the hall where Fantômas' accomplices were gathered. But this he had not foreseen—this encounter with another man in the narrow shaft he had ventured into, this grim encounter in silence and darkness.

Opening his lips to let fly a startled oath, the young man let the dagger slip from between his teeth. His revolver was still his. Yes, but had he the time to get hold of it?

So swift is thought at times when Death is felt close at your elbow that already Fandor believed he had fathomed the sinister truth. Who could it be, gagging him like this?… Who but Fantômas! For the fraction of a second following his meeting with the unknown aggressor, who was stifling his outcry, he never doubted what was happening, what must be happening. Had he not heard Fantômas speaking? Did he not know how he had announced his absence, informed his accomplices he could not come to join them? Yes, it was all plain enough. Fantômas had hidden in this chimney shaft to be out of his men's sight; it was from there he was addressing them, himself invisible.

No sooner had the thought flashed across Fandor's mind than he summed up in two short words the fate he felt awaited him. "Done for!" the young man groaned in despair. In truth, should ill-luck bring him face to face with Fantômas, there could be no doubt but the brigand would have him at his mercy. Had he not the advantage of position? Did he not know the ground? One shout, one word from his lips, would bring his accomplices to his help. "Done for!" Fandor told himself again, "but we'll make a fight of it!"

And, by sheer instinct, by an overmastering impulse, he bit the hand pressing against his lips, while he tried to seize his adversary by the throat.

But the fight the young man was spoiling for hung fire. Fantômas? *Was* it Fantômas who was there?

No, not a bit of it! A piteous voice articulated: "God Almighty! don't bite! Is that a way to behave? Have you gone stark mad now?"

Fandor thought he was dreaming. That voice, that whining voice, half choked as it was, had surely a shade of mockery, of irony about it? The journalist asked breathlessly:

"Juve, is it you?"

"What!" cried the voice, "is M'sieur Juve coming too? Lordy! we can't *all* of us get in! The thing's impossible!"

Fandor fought hard to keep back a great roar of laughter. Juve? Why, no! It was no more Juve than it was Fantômas he had come upon… It was Bouzille!

Verily that inveterate tramp, that incorrigible vagabond could boast for once of having given Jerome Fandor the surprise of his life! What the devil was he doing there? It was very certain he knew Fantômas, and knew him well, but that only made his being where he was the more astonishing. As a friend of the brigand, why was he not with his other accomplices? Why was he playing the spy in this chimney-shaft?

Fandor whispered:

"Bouzille, quick! tell me, was it Juve sent you here?"

"Juve, M'sieur Fandor! No such a thing! We ain't on speaking terms, us two!"

"Who then?"

"Why, me!"

"You! You came of your own accord? Why? What for?"

"M'sieur Fandor, don't bite me!… But I can't tell you that!"

"But, Bouzille, you *must!*"

"So you think, M'sieur Fandor… But I say no! Well now, I'm going to explain how it be, but it ain't no place for talking, this here! Come away… More by token, I'm devilish hungry!"— and, very calmly, Bouzille made as though to clamber up the steps that Jerome Fandor had just climbed down.

He did not get far. Catching the old fellow by one leg, Fandor brought him to a halt.

"Easy on, Bouzille!" ordered the journalist in the same muffled voice demanded by circumstances. "No good trying to make off, mate! You can't go yet."

"But M'sieur Fandor…"

"Silence! and down with you, quick!"

"How you do go aging a fellow, anyhow!" Growling and grumbling, nevertheless the old vagrant obeyed orders. He came down again, asking:

"To start with, *I* might go questioning *you*, what you be

doing here, seems to me!"

"Well, you're going to see, Bouzille. If I'm here, it's because I'm out to arrest Fantômas."

"Fantômas! Then there's nothing doing, M'sieur Fandor! I can tell you that much, for sure and certain. He ain't there!… Come on, shall we have a glass?"

"Bouzille, you're telling me a lie… I heard Fantômas' voice…"

"Oh! that's all one!"

"What do you mean?"

"Well, M'sieur Fandor, it's a sort of a dodge like. He spouts away into a telephone—a telephone ending in a phone arrangement… only as how it's a business of wireless telegraphy… only there is wires to it. You understand, eh?"

And, strangely enough, he did understand! The fact was, Bouzille was trying to explain that Fantômas was telephoning to his accomplices and that his voice seemed to prove his presence because he used a wireless telephone loudspeaker, fixed up instead of the usual receiver.

"The devil!" exclaimed the journalist. Then he went on:

"In any case, there are his accomplices."

"His accomplices! But they've hooked it, M'sieur Fandor. While you was getting down that there chimney, they've trotted off, them chaps! Just clap your eye there. See, there's never a one left, and the lamp's dowsed,"—and with philosophic phlegm, Bouzille struck up his customary refrain:

"Anyway, that don't hinder you standing me a drink, eh?"

"Righto!" Fandor agreed. In fact, at that very moment, the gallant journalist was thinking to himself that he must by no means throw away the happy opportunity offered by this unexpected encounter with Bouzille. Did not the old scamp's presence in the ventilation shaft afford ample proof that the man was in touch with Fantômas, and was it not highly desirable to win his confidence and so ferret out information that was bound to be worth having?

"Up you go, Bouzille," Fandor ordered. "I'll follow you. Do you know I'm not over fond of dubious tricks… Folks who betray their comrades, for instance!…"

"Oh! M'sieur Fandor! Don't say such things!… I ain't afraid of your telling 'em I was there, I ain't!"

"They don't know then?"

"It's God's truth, M'sieur Fandor, I be so thirsty I can't nohow just get my wits together!"

As he spoke, the old fellow was clambering nimbly enough up the iron footholds and was soon on the roof, where next moment Fandor joined him.

"No offense, M'sieur Fandor," the old fellow then began to question his companion, "but how ever did you get up?"

"By the rainspout, Bouzille."

"I guessed that. But *I've* got a rope. It's more comfortable like. Now I'm in high life, why, I've got to take things easy."

"In high life, eh, Bouzille? You're in high life, are you?"

"Times, yes, as I might say! But mustn't go gassing about the thing here… After you, M'sieur Fandor… best make as little noise as may be, of course."

Fandor was quite ready to take both suggestions. Meanwhile the tramp had uncoiled a knotted rope firmly fastened to a chimney, the end of which reached to the ground behind the house.

"A back door in case of some dirty work in the hall down yonder," he explained. "I've known about it for ages… Lordy! yes, it's meant for getting down by, but I just used it for climbing up… Have a look at it, M'sieur Fandor! No fear of it breaking. It's sound stuff! So let yourself go. There's never a soul in that there big bit of wasteland."

"First-rate! first-rate!"—and two seconds later Fandor was on the ground and in another moment found Bouzille at his side.

"And now we're going?" he asked.

"To the wineshop, of course, so as I can talk… Oh, no! not the 'Ami Ralle.' We might not be over and above welcome there. To a den where they know me…"

To say truth, this establishment where Bouzille boasted he was known was not exactly a palace of luxury. It was a shady-looking wineshop of the sort common enough on the outskirts of the city. All the same the journalist was delighted to find it apparently deserted. Not a customer was to be seen.

"Bouzille, my man, order yourself what you like, and explain yourself."

"For money down, M'sieur Fandor?"

"You shall have five francs for your pains."

"Oh! more than that! I'm done with working for that price these days,"—and rapping on the table, Bouzille shouted to the landlord:

"A tasty saveloy, a gallon of white, three pennies' worth of bread—and no crust, mind you!"

Then, when all was on the table and the old glutton hard at work, Bouzille condescended to inquire:

"So then, M'sieur Fandor, sir, you want to know?…"

"What you were doing in that chimney."

"Well, I was just listening."

"Yes, but what were you listening to?"

"What I could hear, of course!"

"Bouzille, you're making a fool of me!"

"Oh! M'sieur Fandor! How can you say so? You'll just kill me with your cruel speeches! I'd rather have you biting me again, I would so!"

It was hard not to laugh, but Fandor did not relax a muscle. He was in deadly earnest. The confounded old scamp must know many important facts, and he was determined to force him to make a clean breast of it.

Kindness had proved a failure, so the journalist suddenly changed his front.

"Very good!" he said sternly. "I say no more, but the examining magistrate will make you speak, never fear…"

"The beak? But I'm not going before the beak!"

"I say you are!"—and Fandor went on in chilling tones:

"Frequentation of lawbreakers—a crime punishable by law… I've caught you in the act. My duty therefore is to hand you over to the police…"

"To the cops! Hand me over to the police! Me! me, a concierge!"

"A concierge? You're a concierge? Since when?"

"Since this morning, M'sieur Fandor…"

"And at whose house? where?"

"A bite of best camembert, M'sieur Fandor, and I'll tell you."

"So be it! But if you're deceiving me…"

The cheese was promptly set on the table. But mine host was hardly out of the room before Bouzille was objecting:

"When I say I'll tell you… why, you know, I'll be telling you what I do know, of course…"

Then, after bolting an enormous mouthful, Bouzille started off in a drawling voice:

"It was only this morning I got my orders… Three hundred shiners a month wages… Nothing to do but keep the door and store away the boxes that come… Must give out as how it's a shy sort of gentleman what don't see nobody… Must hold my tongue and not blab secrets… It's out at Vanves Malakoff the house is—Rue du Docteur Brauly… I'm never to say 'Majesty,' but plain 'Mister'… Bless you, I know it all by heart. But there, see for yourself! there's the letter…"

At that moment Fandor was so overcome by his excitement that the hand he extended to take the paper Fandor offered him shook violently in spite of his efforts for self-control. "At Vanves Malakoff, Rue du Docteur Brauly,"—but that was the very same address as the villa where he had gone with Juve, the villa where Juve had disappeared! And they were applying to Bouzille to take a post as concierge where silence and discretion was specially required! And there was a "Majesty" in the case—when Fantômas, speaking to his accomplices just now, had actually announced he was going away to meet an arriving "Majesty"!

The journalist felt like losing his senses. His thoughts were boiling in his head, eddying in a wild whirlpool of impossible conjectures and contradictions. Never surely had confusion been worse confounded!

To give himself time to regain his composure, the young man took the letter Bouzille handed him. It was typewritten, and at first the characters seemed to dance before his eyes. He muttered angrily: "Confound it, but I *must* read it!"

"You're saying, M'sieur Fandor?"

But the journalist made no answer. He was running his eyes over the letter the tramp had put in his hand, and soon saw that the latter had not been romancing at all. The document ran as follows:

"What is wanted is a man of discretion, able to keep a secret and clever at not attracting attention. You have been appointed to the post. You will be concierge at the Villa, situated in the Rue du Docteur Brauly, No. 7, at Vanves Malakoff. Your orders are to take up your duties with the least possible delay. You will take in and store away the trunks and boxes that will arrive. You will not appear to know His Majesty. If anyone questions you, you will say the house is occupied by an eccentric. You will never speak the word 'Majesty,' but only 'Monsieur.' Your wages will be three hundred francs a month. The writer counts on you."

"And there's no signature!" Fandor noted with surprise.

"And I don't know who it comes from, neither," added Bouzille. "I knows, of course, every jail in the country, Paris and the provinces, I do, and I've never had aught to do with kings, I haven't!"—and as he spoke, the old chap had a look of sheer bewilderment in his eyes that was a clear guarantee of his sincerity.

"Then, of course again," resumed Bouzille, "since I got the letter, I've talked it over with all the boys—under seal of secrecy, you'll understand—but nobody don't know nothing…"

"And you can't guess what it all means?"

"Oh! guess? I can guess right enough… But guessing's just as often wrong as right, ain't it?"

"No doubt, but what else can we do? So, tell me this: what did you *think*, Bouzille?"

Fandor was now feigning the utmost indifference, and to strengthen this impression he coolly drew a cigarette from his case and lit up. At the moment the old man was gulping down a bumper, but found his voice again presently:

"What I thought, M'sieur Fandor? Why, up to tonight nothing, I didn't suppose nothing… But then I come along to

the meeting place where somebody—if you must have it, where
He was to be…"

"Fantômas' meeting in fact, Bouzille?"

"Well, tonight's meeting, anyhow… there's some names I'm
not too fond of saying. I'm a canny sort, I am, and don't want to
get into no trouble. Well, as I said, I come to the place—by the
chimney, on the quiet like, without showing of myself… and
when he spoke…"

"When he spoke of what, Bouzille?"—and as the journalist
asked the question, he kept his eyes fixed on the vagabond's
lips, watching for the enlightening word to escape amid the old
fellow's verbiage.

And suddenly out it came, this word that gave the clue to
the mystery:

"When Fantômas, just now, spoke of the King of the Fences,
the Prince of Receivers, when he said as how a rumor was
about that he was coming from America, and how he was a
chap as dared buy all the stuff the other receivers were afraid to
touch—why, then…"

But there the vagabond stopped dead.

"Hist!" he checked himself, "when a man drinks, he gets
talking silly! All that stuff's just fairy-tales of course, M'sieur
Fandor, just fairy-tales like they tell the kiddies! You think the
same, don't you now?"

But Fandor at that moment was thinking precisely the opposite. When, an instant before, Bouzille had let him into the
secret how Fantômas had informed his accomplices of the
speedy arrival of the King of the Receivers, he had with difficulty checked a yell of triumph. Had he not, indeed, then and
there conceived a plan, at once simple and sure, to outwit the
Arch-Criminal?

Now, quite another thing filled his thoughts! The way Bouzille, in the very middle of a sentence, had turned the conversation, the clumsy fashion in which the old fellow had tried to
throw his hearer off the scent by declaring his statements were
only meant as pleasantries, was not all this highly significant?

But the journalist suffered no sign of his suspicions to

appear. Still smoking peacefully, he was saying to himself:

"Not a doubt of it! If Bouzille contradicted himself in that childish way, it was because he suddenly got afraid of saying too much… If he took fright, it was because he caught sight of somebody signaling to him to hold his tongue, threatening him if he went on,"—and Fandor was not deceiving himself as to what must have occurred.

"Yes," he proceeded with his soliloquy, "Bouzille saw somebody, that's certain… Now Bouzille sits facing me… Therefore, he can see what's behind my back… It follows it's from behind my back somebody frightened Bouzille and bade him shut his mouth—somebody I should very much like to see!"

He tossed away his cigarette with a careless gesture. Then, springing up in a flash, quick as lightning he swung round.

Then a cry escaped him, a name ejaculated with concentrated fury: "Fantômas! Fantômas!"

Instantly Fandor recognized the fell Genius of Evil. Beyond a row of shabby trees that decorated the front of the wineshop he had clearly distinguished the terrifying figure. In the close-fitting envelope of black silk that molded his slender, sinewy form, the face veiled by his black hood that hid the features no man knew, Fantômas, through the eyeholes of his mask, had darted at his foe that flashing glance none could confront without a shudder.

"Fantômas! Fantômas!" yelled Fandor, regardless of everything save the gallant impulse to come to grips with the malefactor.

Dashing on one side the bewildered tramp, driving back with a blow of his fist the landlord who was barring his way, alarmed to see his customer bolt without paying, Jerome Fandor rushed headlong from the shop to search with straining eyeballs the darkling spaces of the Quai de Javelle.

Twenty yards away Fantômas had halted, and now stood motionless, with folded arms, as though waiting for his adversary to come on.

Without an instant's hesitation, Fandor sprang forward, racing madly for the figure that showed up sharply defined in the circle of light cast by a street lamp, fearless and defiant.

*   *   *   *   *

Fandor's action was prompted by sheer instinct. An irresist-ible impulse left him not a moment for reflection. The Lord of Terror stood there before him. What could he do but dash in pursuit as one pursues a murderer, a noxious criminal that must be caught, imprisoned, rendered incapable of further mischief. Gallantry, and not reason, was the overmastering motive.

It may be he should have asked himself how Fantômas dared challenge him to give chase. It may be, in common prudence he should have remembered he was alone, far from all human help, that it was impossible in this fashion to overpower the Ever-Elusive, whom all the world was tracking down. The fact is, he did not think at all. In a lightning flash of memory he recalled the atrocities committed by the monster. In a swift vision he beheld all the vile incidents of the scoundrel's career of crime. Was he not, truly, the enemy of the human race? Was he not the redoubtable foe, always in flight, whom Juve had sworn to master, even if it cost him his life? And Fandor was surely not the man to show himself less lavish of his blood than the police-officer.

He dashed forward a dozen yards. Still Fantômas never moved. Then he yelled his defiance:

"Between you and me! A fight to the death!"

A scornful, sarcastic laugh was the only answer. And then, still unhurried, Fantômas too set off to run, at a measured pace with long easy strides, merely maintaining the same distance ahead of his pursuer. The journalist neither gained nor lost ground; one simply followed the other without change in the interval between them.

A heartbreaking race! On the riverside quays of Javelle, ev-erywhere bordered by factories, the street lamps are few and far between and afford only a dim and uncertain illumination. Moreover, from the neighboring river a fog was rising, dulling all the little light there was.

In the gloom ahead showed the fantastic form of the Brigand

in his black costume. Not a sound as he ran! His black shoes with their felt soles fell noiselessly on the pavement, while his clinging suit of black and black hood merged in the general darkness and made it more a matter of guesswork than of vision to say if he was really there. It might well have been a phantom that might, from one moment to the next, fade away, disappear, vanish into thin air.

But Fandor kept steadily on, panting as he ran. He muttered: "If only I had my revolver handy!"

The fact was, when leaving the "Ami Ralle," the journalist had been imprudent enough to thrust his revolver into his breeches' pocket. The pocket was buttoned up; so to get hold of the weapon, he must have stopped. If he stopped, it was certain Fantômas would seize the opportunity to disappear, and that must be prevented at any price.

Then suddenly the young man gave a hoarse shout of satisfaction. Baffled no doubt by the darkness, perhaps winded and knowing his enemy at his heels, Fantômas had just turned off sharply to the right and bolted down a narrow lane.

"A blind alley! It's a blind alley!" Fandor told himself. He knew the district perfectly, and was convinced Fantômas would be brought up short by a high palisade of planks. He had the scoundrel at his mercy!

With a last spurt, Fandor dashed down the turning—and then a cry of furious disappointment escaped him. Yes, it was a blind alley certainly, but the fugitive had made no blunder when he turned into it. The pursuer saw him gather himself together for a spring, leap up and claw his way over the obstacle like a cat.

"Well," the dauntless journalist told himself, "where Fantômas has gone, I can go to. The fellow must have been at the last gasp to risk himself like this on unknown ground,"— and he too made his spring and, active as his foe, caught the top of the fence, hauled himself up and threw his leg over.

On the other side he saw a large garden, very untidily kept. In the middle stood a detached house of a dilapidated appearance. Probably it had been a building originally erected as a private residence in days before the Quai de Javelle had become purely industrial. Fandor, however, had other thoughts than these in his head and took no pains to settle precisely where he had got to. For in front of him, a few paces away, Fantômas was now climbing the walls of the erstwhile villa.

"He thinks he'll throw me off the scent," argued Fandor, "but I'm going to give him a surprise."

Very softly he sprang to the ground. Then stooping double and keeping all he could in the shadow, he in his turn made for the house.

"He is climbing up by the front! I'll do the same at this end," he muttered, and set about the second scramble. For a man like the journalist, practiced in all feats of strength and address, the task presented no very great difficulties. A growth of old, matted ivy clothed the walls and gave him foothold and hand-hold. Then slowly and cautiously he peeped over the eaves of the roof before daring to mount it.

He had felt sure all along Fantômas would not guess his presence, and now a silent laugh rose to his lips. At last he had caught the Arch-Villain. Now he could challenge him face to face! Doubtless believing he had thrown off his pursuer, Fantômas, who had likewise reached the roof, was opening a trapdoor, preparatory to lowering himself into the interior of the house.

"So," thought Fandor, "no doubt this is his 'robber's cave.' The building is supposed to be derelict, and he makes it his hiding place."

He lay down flat and creeping noiselessly forward, dragged himself up to the trapdoor which still stood open. By falling on the enemy unexpectedly, had he not every chance of mastering him, forcing him to surrender? He listened hard for a moment, but not a sound reached his ears… Fantômas must have gone on into an adjoining room.

"Nothing ventured, nothing gained," the young man re-peated his usual formula. But this time he took his revolver in hand, after pulling off the safety catch. Then he dropped his legs over the edge of the trap and, holding on by one hand, let himself slip down into the room below. In the twilight he could see but little of the interior. No matter! This much was abundantly clear—the room was empty, quite empty. Fantômas was not there. There was a door in one wall, and by this he had doubtless gone out.

"I'll go after him," Fandor resolved. He could not reach the floor with his feet, by several inches, but there was no difficulty about the drop. The only thing was to fall softly, with as little noise as possible.

"Here goes!" muttered the young man, and let go, alighting on his toes, with bent knees and body lightly poised.

And then a scream of rage, a cry of horror, escaped him, while a peal of demoniac laughter rang out, waking the echoes of the lonely house. The hideousness of the thing! Barely had he touched the floor of the room when the planking seemed to fail beneath his feet, to give way under his weight. With slow but sure movement, silently and steadily, he felt the ground he stood on gradually sinking, like the floor of a lift.

Instantly, in a flash, Fandor realized the peril of his situation. The room was a fake, a gigantic fraud, a trap. It was no mere chance had led him there; far from it, Fantômas had guided him thither purposely, with odious cunning enticing his pursuer to follow him to his doom—and it was he that was laughing derisively, exulting over his enemy's surprise and terror.

But the journalist was already recovering from the shock. The floor had only dropped a yard or two before Fandor was trying to escape his fate. Gathering himself together for the spring, bracing his muscles for an effort on which no doubt his life depended, he took a frantic leap upwards. If he could but reach and grasp the framework of the trapdoor, he might save his life, perhaps? His fingers seized and gripped the edges.

Wielded with savage cruelty, a whip fell across them. The pain was intolerable, and he let go, to fall back miserably on the sinking floor.

But the young man was not beaten yet!

"He is on the roof, no doubt. Well, I will get a hold somewhere else… where he cannot get at me…"

He caught sight of the handle of the door… He managed to grasp it… For a second, he clung to it, and hung suspended. Then the handle suddenly fetched away, and he crashed down again. Once more a sardonic peal sounded, pitched on the highest note of insult.

This time Fandor had hurt himself. The floor, still sinking, increased the distance now separating him from every possible handhold. Yet he sprang to his feet again. The young journalist was one of those men who will never say die, who go on fighting, when the fight is already lost, doomed beforehand to end in defeat.

But what could he do? Plunging him into he knew not what pit of horror, burying him in some gruesome oubliette, the floor was still sinking, sliding now between absolutely smooth walls showing no smallest projection, without anything whatever to make climbing feasible. The tiger trapped in a sandpit with sides that slide and crumble is not more helpless, more incapable of escape.

"A prisoner! I am a prisoner!" groaned Fandor, his voice shaking with anger rather than fear.

Then, with a sudden start, he heard Fantômas' voice, the accursed voice, harsh and peremptory, and now quivering with pride and satisfaction:

"Did I not caution you that you would pay with your life for any new attempt against me?… Did I not telephone to Juve to warn him I would kill you if he attacked me again?… Am I not the master? and my decrees without appeal?… Jerome Fandor, judge fairly—it is Juve, and not I, you must curse…"

But the young man sprang up at this in indignant protest. Curse Juve? What next? Juve was but doing his duty in combating the Arch-Criminal! And urchin-like in his reckless audacity, a very street-Arab in his gay defiance, Fandor uttered a ringing cry that came from the very bottom of his heart: "Juve forever! Good old Juve forever!"

But the cry found no response save from the empty echoes. Had Fantômas gone, left him to his fate? The journalist could only shrug his shoulders, while the floor continued to sink, as though to engulf him in some abyss of unfathomable depth. Calling upon his habitual fund of cheerfulness, his unfailing stock of raillery, he grinned: "At this rate, oh God! I shall soon be getting to the antipodes!"

Next moment he fell silent—something new and unexpected was happening. A sharp click sounded, and the floor stopped in its descent.

"The end of the trip?" muttered Fandor. But he had hardly said it before he found himself biting his lips to restrain a cry of panic.

Slowly, the floor was tilting, swinging over, rising on one side, dropping on the other. He began to slip, to slide. The smooth surface afforded no purchase, gave him nothing to catch hold of and cling to. He slid further and further down into empty space—to come to earth where? Rolling over and over, at first he could frame no guess. He seemed to be on a toboggan run, the slope of which got momentarily steeper and steeper. With a thud he bumped into an obstacle and stopped dead.

Then, as he staggered to his feet, he heard the sharp, clear ring of metal on metal.

"Bravo!" he cried, "the trap is shutting! I am in my death chamber!"

Around him absolute darkness! Not one ray of light could filter into this grim "in pace," this subterranean dungeon. But Fandor was not one to remain inactive. He stood up altogether; his head struck a vaulted roof.

"The devil! The ceiling's not over lofty!"

Feeling round with his fingertips, he followed the run of the walls. They circumscribed a very narrow space. Under the prisoner's pounding fists they gave back the dull, heavy sound of solid stone. On one side only there was what seemed to be a sheet of metal—the door, and this was shut.

"A tomb in very deed!" observed the unhappy journalist, with a dreadful calm. "Ten or fifteen days in it before a man dies of hunger and thirst! A charming prospect!"

His jesting humor did not desert him, for he felt no fear. Ever since, fighting by Juve's side, he first began the campaign against Fantômas he had known the enemy to be capable of any and every atrocity. His mind was made up to sell his very life, if need be, for victory. He was not going now to give way to panic. He told himself with perfect sincerity:

"A happy chance again, Juve's having disappeared. With his genius, he might well have tracked me to this house… like me have penetrated the decoy room, the floor of which will no doubt be back in its proper place by now. Like me, he might have got himself…"

Then with a shrug he sat down again.

"Yes! no doubt of it—hunger or thirst will be the end. They say you suffer most from thirst. Ah! well, one can't choose one's way of death!"

But, suddenly, he sprang up again so impetuously his head struck the vault, as he jerked out:

"Great God! I'm dreaming!"

A sound had reached him—a strange, uncertain sound, a sort of "glug-glug"—he could find no other word to describe it.

"You'd think…" he began. Then, dropping on his knees, he felt the floor—and laughed aloud.

"Hunger, thirst? Not a bit of it! That would be too slow. The quickest methods are the surest. Fantômas, doubtless, don't want me taking up his mousetrap over long. So he is going to drown me."

The prisoner was not mistaken. By some conduit he could not see water was flowing into his dungeon and beginning to flood it. Already it lay some inches deep on the ground. It was rising rapidly, and must quickly fill the narrow space to the top—a matter of an hour, perhaps?

"And no chance of swimming!" growled Fandor, "and no use, if I could. Standing up, I touch the ceiling. I shall drown when the water reaches it—that's all!"

Again he shrugged. One phrase of consternation, of astonishment, would have struck him as an exhibition of cowardice. Fantômas was the Genius of Evil. Was it to be deemed extraordinary that he should have contrived a trap of the sort? Had he not under his orders numerous accomplices, who no doubt had secretly constructed this murderous device in the deserted house.

"One is never satisfied!" he smiled. "Just now I was complaining about having nothing to drink. Now my grievance will be that I have too much liquid!"

The "liquid," as he called it contemptuously, continued to invade his prison. Noiselessly it rose up and up the young man's body. The icy flood encircled his waist in a cold embrace. Then it reached his shoulders, closed round his neck. He thought:

"To make an end, I should only have to kneel down. It would soon be over. Yes, but then suicide is for cowards. A Fandor holds out to the last second."

The water lapped his chin… He began to pant for breath.

"Very natural," he told himself. "The cellar is airtight; the water compresses the air as it rises, which cannot escape. I am breathing an atmosphere under compression."

Next moment, in an instant, with a terrific crash, with an incalculable force of expansion, the miracle happened. Fandor had been right in what he said, but he had not foreseen what was inevitably bound to occur. The explanation was simple. Under the pressure of the air one of the walls of the dungeon had suddenly given way, bursting like a retort under too high a pressure of gas.

Dumbfounded, bewildered, half-dead, all but unconscious, Fandor had the impression of being hurled forward with indescribable violence. His head struck he knew not what. Resistance was hopeless. An agony of pain overwhelmed him. He shut his eyes, ceased to struggle and fainted away.

When, twenty minutes later, the young man came to himself, his amazement passed all measure.

"Where the devil am I?" he cried.

Memory had come back, clear and precise. He recalled the explosion, perfectly well. But what had been the result of it? Where was he now? The light was dim, but he could make out, flowing beneath a vault of stone, a stream of foul water, bordered on one side by a narrow footway. Tossed up like a piece of wreckage by the current, he lay half on, half off, this pathway.

"A sewer!" he exclaimed. "I am in a sewer!"

"After all," he reflected, "it's simple enough. There were bound to be sewers passing near my death chamber. The explosion must have burst in one of these, and the rush of water carried me into it—there you are!"

Making a prodigious effort to master the weakness that oppressed him, he got to his feet, and it was then, as he stood staggering, striving to collect his wits, that he seemed to hear, did actually hear perhaps, a voice saying:

"He must be drowned, surely?… Anyway, my trap is destroyed. No matter! I will see to that when I get back from Bordeaux."

At the sound Fandor started violently, shaken by a new spasm of horror. He had recognized the voice!

He stammered: "Fantômas! Fantômas!"—and still weak and exhausted, lost consciousness for the second time and fell a lifeless bulk, struck down, overwhelmed by the sheer terror of the dread name he had uttered!

4. Fandor's Recklessness

Three days afterwards, in anything but a good temper, Fandor was leaving the office of the Compagnie Générale Transatlantique at Bordeaux.

"Why! yes, my fine fellow, you're only doing your duty, I grant you that, in sending me to cool my heels outside," the young man was grumbling… "But you forget one thing—that I'm not fond of cooling my heels out of doors, not at all fond!"

And, to tell the truth, he had to all appearance very good reason to say so, for the weather was atrocious, one of those equinoctial gales when the wind drives blinding squalls of rain before it and the angry heavens seem bent on annihilating the earth for good and all. Without paying much heed to the fury of the elements, however, the journalist went on his way, following the line of the quays at which the big ships tie up when they come up the river. He was still growling to himself:

"The good man is polite, a master of words, an expert in the art of taking cover behind the regulations. Oh! I can't blame him for that! It is really not his fault if he refused me every single thing I asked him!… Only he doesn't know me!"

Fandor's hands were buried deep in the pockets of his topcoat. He removed one of them to shake an angry fist expressive of the boiling rage within his bosom.

"He does not know me!" he repeated. "He does not know the Journalists' Association either!… Forbid my going on board, indeed! Refuse me information! I shall be on board in the course of the day, and I shall gather my own information, my man! Ah, ha! we shall see about that!"

In truth the journalist had reason to be annoyed, albeit he had no genuine cause for complaint.

Three days earlier he had escaped from the sewer where he had recovered consciousness the same evening without any great harm done. He had walked on at random till he caught sight of what the underground workmen call a manhole. He had then pushed open the iron plate closing the aperture, an easy thing to do from the inside, and as chance would have it, coming up in a deserted lane at Grenelle, had found no difficulty in making off unnoticed.

"Rue Tardieu," he ordered the driver of the taxi he hailed presently. Arrived there, he found Jean as unconcerned as ever.

"Monsieur has not met the master?" he inquired, without seeming to observe the deplorable state the visitor was in, so used was he to the most surprising accidents.

"Alas, no! But Juve is not the point. Juve will return when he sees fit, Jean. Now pack me a portmanteau. I'm off on a journey."

The young fellow's preparations did not take long. The same evening an express was carrying him to Bordeaux. On arriving there next day, he instantly set about his enquiries.

"I know Fantômas is to come here," he told himself. "I know this is the place where steamers coming from America arrive. I know that a King of the Receivers is expected… By the Lord! it strikes me forcibly all this means something!"

This, in fact, was the plan Jerome Fandor had decided on. He would join this King of the Receivers, keep a watch on him, follow him like his shadow and wait for the moment when Fantômas would inevitably put himself in communication with the new arrival.

"Fantômas has stolen this paper, which is very difficult to dispose of," he calculated. "Why should he not apply to this same king of the receivers of stolen goods? It is a logical conclusion, seems to me a perfectly natural inference."

But the quest was at a standstill. King or no, the American "fence" was certainly not traveling under his own name, advertising his trade and profession.

"Majesties are always incognito!" grumbled the journalist, turning from one steamship office to another all the length of the interminable Quai Bacalan. A pleasant job, truly! And then, I don't belong to the police; I have no authority to demand official information."

For all that, thanks to his knowingness as a newspaperman, he gathered certain official pieces of news. They were expecting the arrival in the roads, within the next forty-eight hours, of the transatlantic mail boat *Niagara Falls*. On this vessel, a suite, the suite de luxe, had been reserved for a personage whose name was a secret.

And Fandor had given a sudden start the instant he had succeeded in extracting this bit of news from an employee of the Compagnie Transatlantique.

"Ho! ho!" he thought, "this means something too! Whoever travels with so much mystery he actually forbids his name appearing on the passenger list?"

Ten minutes later, he was in the Manager's office of the famous Company, from which he was now coming out.

It was this same Manager he had designated in his own mind "my fine fellow," the man he was mentally cursing by all his gods. True, he had been treated with perfect courtesy, *but* he had obtained no further information whatsoever.

"The Company's secret, my dear sir!" he had protested. "The traveler wishes to remain anonymous. I have no authority to commit an indiscretion…"

"Or to permit me to go aboard the tug that will go out to meet the ship?"

"The police regulations forbid it."

"But…"

"Apply to the police!"

Fandor had said no more. He had left the place in a flame of anger. Now he was thinking:

"There is a mysterious passenger on board the *Niagara Falls*… a 'swagger' passenger, for he occupies the suite de luxe… a remarkable passenger, for he comes by the Bordeaux line instead of Le Havre, a much pleasanter way… So… so, I mean to see this traveler, I mean to know who he is!"

Under the ever worsening downpour, the young man swung round on his heels so impetuously he bumped into two passersby who were following him.

"Sorry!" he apologized.

"No harm done!" replied one of the men. Fandor went on his way. A taxi was prowling near, empty. He hailed it.

"Tell me, the pilots' headquarters?"

"It's not at Bordeaux, sir. It's at Le Verdon…"

"Far?"

"Not over near. Monsieur wants to go there?"

"Yes, and post haste, my lad! Top gear! And don't spare the 'pepper'!"

Fate had been kind. He had come upon a first-rate chauffeur. The vehicle was off at once, and soon reached the little harbor by the riverside known as Le Verdon, from which the pilot boats put out to meet incoming steamers and con them into port.

"There, sir!" the driver pointed, "that's the pilot office yonder."

"Excellent!"

Bending to the hurricane that was still blowing hard, the journalist had taken a step or two in the direction indicated when he pulled up sharply.

"What! people abroad, here? In this awful weather!" A car had driven up and was stopping a short way off. Two passengers were getting out, whom he scarcely noticed, full as he was of his own concerns. He was just about to knock at the door of the office when a sailor, muffled up in his oilskins and wearing a sou'wester, approached him.

"You're wanting?…"

"To see a master pilot."

"I am a pilot, sir!"

"Very good! Then we can have a talk. I am a journalist."

"I'm listening."

"They're expecting the *Niagara Falls* in, aren't they?"

"Yes! she should be riding outside by now, or she'll be there soon. The weather's thick; they've not semaphored her yet…"

"All the better. We shall have time…"

"To do what, sir?"

"Mister Pilot, why, to go aboard,"—and without giving the

other time to reply, Fandor went on:

"For go aboard I must. Of course I shall pay what's right and proper... I'm on *La Capitale*. The paper's wealthy. Name your price, and let's be off."

Fandor at this moment never doubted of the success of his enterprise. Doubtless he was aware that the great liners dispense as a rule with the actual services of the licensed pilots, while paying the established fees. But he also knew that a pilot could quite well launch a boat, take him out to sea and, as the phrase goes, "put" him aboard the *Niagara Falls*.

"After that, I'll clear up things," he thought to himself. "If the King of the Receivers is on board, I shall find him... unmask him... keep him in view..."

"Oh! so you belong to *La Capitale!* It's my paper... Yes, for sure, ordinary times it could be done all right, what you wish... But today..."

"Today?"

"Today, my dear sir, if you were Jerome Fandor in person, you'd never persuade me to take you out to sea!"

"Because?" Jerome Fandor asked impetuously, without a word to say that he was actually the famous journalist in question, but almost boiling with rage and impatience at the difficulties raised by the seaman.

"Because," replied the man with quiet determination, "because I value my life and my men's lives. The weather is terrific."

"Good! You're not afraid, of course?"

At the word "afraid," the old sea dog seemed to flinch.

"Afraid? No, young sir! I am not afraid! But some things are impossible... On the open sea, in my boat, I should laugh at the storm, by God! But, here it's the river. To get out, to cross the bar, can't be done! We should be holed on the rocks and sink. My boat draws too much water..."

"But the liner?"

"The liner will not try to come in. She'll lie to in the offing, or if the weather gets worse, put out to sea again. You see..."

The young man was grinding his teeth. Oh! these material obstacles, against which the most resolute can make no headway.

"But I *must* get aboard!" he reflected. Then, laying a hand on the sailor's arm:

"Pilot, everything's not a question of money... This is a matter of the last importance... Can you take me?..."

"No, sir! And nobody could. The bar is too dangerous. There's only a small boat could find water enough, spite of the troughs 'twixt the breakers..."

"Well then, in a small boat?"

"There are none!... And, besides, the backwash would capsize the craft."

"That's your last word..."

"My last word... I know the sea."

Fandor's eyes fell in bitter discouragement.

"Very good I and thank you... If there's a lull..."

"The glass is falling."

Fandor said not another word. He went back to his conveyance. But this time he gave a little start of surprise. The two men were half hidden behind an old boat drawn up on shore and had their eyes fixed upon him!

"What!" exclaimed the journalist, "one would think..."

He moved a step forward in their direction, whereupon the two men half turned aside, seeking to avoid him...

"What ho!" growled the young man suspiciously. His keen eye had looked them up and down and made a discovery.

"The two fellows I knocked against on the Bordeaux quay... By God! So they were following me?"—and the journalist grew white with anger. Their appearance was certainly against them, these two loafers. They looked both poor and disreputable.

"So, it would seem Fantômas is having me shadowed! Am I being followed, I wonder, by a couple of scoundrels who have been sent to meet 'the King'?"

He thought things over rapidly. Clearly this same King of the Receivers must be a person of high importance in the underground world of thieves and swindlers. Was it not, indeed, a well-known fact that the great criminals of all countries are in constant communication? Was it not probable that the coming of this American crook, this King of the Fences, had been duly arranged and organized? What wonder then if his own arrival at Bordeaux had been noted? What unlikely in the supposition that Fantômas had been informed of his doings and had taken due precautions to checkmate his efforts. Not a doubt but the Arch-Criminal had his own nefarious, villainous police force to baffle the activity of the genuine defenders of the law and honest folk.

"I must find out!" thought Fandor. "I must make certain of the fact. If I am really being shadowed, it means I have guessed right—this King of the Receivers is on board the *Niagara Falls*… Clumsy fellows too!" he weighed them up. "They don't know how to work it. They give themselves away with grotesque simplicity. I am going to get rid of them quietly, after which, I'll see…"

Bending head down to fight against the fierce squalls, the journalist went back to where his driver was sheltering behind a house.

"Listen here," he said, "we are going back to Bordeaux. But I ought to give you fair warning. I am a journalist and I'm making an investigation. It's quite possible therefore that at any moment I may be prevented from coming back to where I'd told you to wait for me. Look, here's a hundred francs on account, that way you'll not risk losing what I owe you…"

"Very good, sir!"

The man seemed surprised, and looked at his fare inquisitively.

"Come, drive on now!" ordered the latter. "Back to Bordeaux. No need to go fast—half speed!"

Back in the cab, which set off citywards, Fandor thought:

"The driver doesn't trust me. Those two gentlemen escorting me must have said a word to him, told him some cock and bull story!… Hmm! Maybe I'll have to get on the job quick…"

Slightly raising the blind covering the little window in the back of his conveyance, Fandor scrutinized the road behind.

"Why! of course," he observed, "the other taxi is following.

That's plain to see! Oh! but Fantômas' policemen are a poor lot!"—and the reporter chuckled. For all the annoyance he felt at his failure to induce the pilot to put to sea, he was delighted by this full confirmation of his conjectures. Did not the two wretches by their very presence prove him to have been perfectly right in his conjecture that the King of the Receivers was actually on board the *Niagara Falls?*

"The scent is hot!" he told himself. "Fantômas cannot be far off. Yes, I shall unmask the ruffian in the end, never fear."

But suddenly a new idea struck him. It was a winding road they were on and in very bad repair. He muttered:

"With all these jolts and jars, the shock will never be noticed. With a wind like this blowing about his ears my driver won't hear a thing. Bravo! it's a fine opportunity!"

Opening the door softly, he slipped out onto the step, shut the door to again behind him and sprang to the ground.

"That's the ticket!" he laughed boyishly, and in two strides was across the road and hiding behind a bush beside the track, a turn in which had prevented those in the other taxi from seeing anything of the maneuver. In fact, he had not been lying concealed three minutes before the pursuing vehicle drove past him and went unsuspectingly on its way.

"Pleasant journey!" the young man called after it. "And now, let's think!"

The word seemed the forerunner of some important decision. But what decision could he take? What mortal power can contend against the fury of the elements?

"Wait till the sea goes down? Yes, what else can I do? But who can tell if, between then and now, Fantômas will not, by wireless and code, warn His Majesty to beware of me? Oh! curse the storm!"

At that moment the loud rattle of a motor engine running free with the clutch out cut short the journalist's reflections.

"What!" he exclaimed, and ran to the edge of the roadway. There, under the river bank a magnificently appointed motorboat was moored. A mechanic was busy on board examining some part of the machinery. Hands in pocket, Fandor remarked:

"My word! a fine craft that!"—then, raising his voice:

"It's a private boat, eh?"

"No," the mechanic shouted back. "She belongs to the engineer of the Lighthouse Board."

"Going to put off, eh?"

"Yes, and go to sea… you're talking now. Only she's thirsty, she is! Twenty gallons of gasoline, that's nothing to her. There, she's just full up. I've put over twenty tins in the old girl!"

"Bah! it's Government pays," laughed Fandor. "And you, you're a Navy man?"

"Not I! I'm a fitter… I take 'em out for a trial run, that's all."

"That's the game!" cried the journalist, and leapt lightly on board.

"Hey! What's taken you now?" demanded the man.

"Oh! nothing. But there, take that, will you?"—and he pulled a banknote from his pocket.

"You're not mad, likely?" queried the man in overalls with a startled look.

"Yes, I am, pretty near," Fandor declared. "Listen here… I'm a journalist. I *must* get put aboard the *Niagara Falls*… out in the roadstead. Five notes same as this one if you'll do it—under pretext of a trial run… Are you on?"

"But I can't!"

"Six notes, then!"

"But it's dog's weather."

"Seven?"

"But I tell you the sea's terrific."

"Say ten notes… all in a lump!… Bargain good?"

"Oh, you're the devil of a fellow!… And if we go to the bottom?"

"We won't!… Now then! Ten notes I'm telling you! You're never going to make me think you're a funk?"

"Not I… Only…"

"Thanks, mate! That's the style!… I've won!… Set your old roundabout going. Just now, first I set eyes on you, I said to myself: 'Yonder's my man!' Now, you'll take the helm! Capital!

I'll take on the engine. Don't you worry! I know the job. Oh! by the by, it won't be ten flimsies, it'll be fifteen—and they'll put your likeness in *La Capitale*. Push off! Right away for the herring pond!"

The young fellow spoke with such an air of authority that the mechanic was abashed.

"All the same…!" he protested feebly.

Finally he got the engine going.

"If we capsize…" he was beginning again.

"Go on! if we do upset, why! we'll just sight a whale, get astride his back… and so ride back to port!"

"You're a good plucked one, anyhow!"—and away for the open sea, where the waves ran mountains high and the white spume was flying all around the frail craft.

Would she live it out?

*   *   *   *   *

At first, rash as it was, the venture seemed at any rate possible. It was blowing hard, no doubt, in the estuary of the river, but still the waves were not actually breaking. It was simply a heavy groundswell that tossed the boat up and down like a plaything but did no harm.

"First-rate!" remarked Fandor in his usual joking way. "The little lady has got legs! She goes fine!"

"Yes," retorted the mechanic. "But presently…"

"Pooh! sufficient for the day, eh?"—and slyly, like an expert engineer, he pushed the accelerator a bit further over, speeding up the engine and driving the boat faster than ever to meet the breakers chafing and foaming on the bar…

"We'll get there, never fear!" declared the journalist. "One always does get there!…"

The roar of a gun cut him short.

"Whoa!" he cried. "What's up now?"

"The semaphore station, of course," snapped the mechanic. "Is it for us?"

"Seems like it… The alarm gun… Look out for the signals."

"No use! I cannot read them!"

"They're warning us it's impossible to put to sea."

"They are mistaken then, those folks!"

"Hmm… You'll be able to see for yourself what it's like the other side of the point."

And so he could. In another minute the young man could appreciate the madness of his enterprise. Once round the last cape intercepting the gale blowing in from the open ocean, the sea showed white with spindrift flying before the wind like great snowflakes. A sight at once terrible and superb, this fury of the raging elements! Under a low, leaden sky across which the clouds were driving before the storm at giddy speed, the waves were breaking with a sullen roar in furious cataracts of foam, a very avalanche of water that rose and fell with titanic fury.

The rain lashed their faces. So fierce was the hurricane they were forced to turn their backs to it to breathe!

Fandor swore a big oath, but not for one instant did the thought occur to him to turn back. Moreover, it was fine to see how the mechanic at his side was infected with the like enthusiasm.

"Dirty weather, by God!" his voice rose above the gale. "But we've sworn to make good—and make good we will!"

Next instant began a wild, mad struggle for the light craft. Lifted like a feather by the enormous waves, she seemed to drop into a bottomless abyss as she pitched down into the trough. But unceasing, untiring, the good engine, heart of steel that beat on rhythmically, imperturbably, drove her steadily forward.

The sailor stood clutching the wheel, arms braced, legs wide apart, his whole body stiff and taut, face to the blast. Fandor, seated on the floor boards, one hand clutching a projection of the woodwork, the other on the oil feed and carburetor, nursed the engine. For one instant let him lose his head, show one second's clumsiness, and, in this hurricane, the engine would "heat" for certain and come to a stop. Then, drifting helplessly to leeward, the boat would inevitably go ashore, or, no longer answering her helm, would be capsized by some swirling eddy.

"Damned dirty weather!" growled the sailor.

"True for you!" agreed the journalist.

"If ever we get through, we'll be lucky!"

"We will… D'you see the *Niagara Falls?*"

"Can't see anything!"

Fandor raised himself a bit to look. It was true enough. In this hurricane, these furious squalls, all this hurly-burly of the elements, nothing *could* be seen—nothing but the raging waters, nothing but the clouds that raced past, torn and tattered by the gale.

"She must be in the outer roads… lying off and on," observed the sailor, and both fell silent.

A fine thing the battle of the human will against the blind forces of Nature! The boat seemed to fly over the waves. At times she would disappear, buried under clotted masses of foam, while the whole hull groaned, as if weary of the struggle and ready to break up.

Still on they went. From time to time Fandor would rise to his knees and then with a swift glance scan the near horizon.

"Good Lord!" he growled, "a transatlantic liner's big enough surely, not a thing that can hide itself!"

Then in sudden triumph:

"There! there!…" he cried.

Running back and forth all the width of the roadstead, rolling tack for tack, tossed about like a straw herself, the great ship could be made out in the offing. Not that she was in any danger. So long as her engines held good and she had sea-room enough, she could scorn the fury of the storm. Yet how fragile a thing the giant of the seas looked and how small in this welter of the elements.

"Straight ahead!" from the sailor. Then stooping and bending over towards his companion, he bawled in his ear:

"But how to get aboard?"

"They'll throw me a line…"

"And you'll be dashed to bits against the side!"

"Not I! Don't you worry!… Only, you, about getting back?"

"Oh! getting back?… A wind behind… no danger at all!"

"Sure?"

"Quite sure! I shall only have to let her rip… So *you,* you needn't worry about me, neither!"

"My word! you're a trump!" said the journalist admiringly. "See, there's my pocketbook; the notes are inside…"

"Bah! no hurry for that… We shall see each other again… Marius Capoulin, that's how I'm called."

"And I Jerome Fandor."

"Jerome Fandor! God bless my soul!"

"Hist, man! port your helm!"—and no more was said.

To exchange these few broken sentences, they had had to yell, watching for a momentary lull. And already, under the steersman's hand, the boat was describing a wide circle, making a circuit round the liner, so as to come up under her lee, and thus be sheltered by her massive hull.

"Mustn't waste one second!" urged the sailor. "Look! they've seen us… God! but they think we're going to be lost, in desperate danger!"

It was quite true. From up on the bridge, the officer of the watch had made out the boat. Unable to credit such a piece of reckless daring, he had guessed it was some craft surprised by the storm and come to beg for help. Yet what help could be given in such weather? The officer growled:

"Idiots! freshwater sailors! Let 'em run before the wind for the river mouth. They'll get out of the mess that way—safely enough even… But to try for here, they'll be capsized twenty times over!"

Then, as the boat came nearer, he bawled his orders through the speaking-trumpet:

"Engine room, slow down… Helm, hard aport… a brace of ratlines to save the men!"

He could do no more, only haul aboard from their frail craft the two men that formed her crew. That done, the boat would go to her doom wherever the wind might take her. The whole maneuver was executed with such frantic rapidity the very actors themselves in the drama hardly knew what was happening. From the foremast a boom was rigged to starboard, swinging out over the water at each roll of the ship. From this boom a rope hung, lashed home to a winch. The two castaways must grip hold, and then, between two rolls, they would hoist them aboard.

"Ready?" asked the Captain, who had hurried onto the bridge. "Let go!"

With a creak and grind the winch revolved...

Alee of the great liner, partly sheltered from the hurricane by the enormous hull, the boat seemed a child's plaything the waves must surely break to bits.

"Stand by!" roared the Captain through his speaking-trumpet, and then stood silent, watching his orders carried out, while the hands looked on in shuddering suspense. A second too soon or too late, a clumsy shift of the helm, and the boat would crash into the side and be smashed to pieces.

The ropes ran out... dropped lightly on the boat's deck... a man gripped hold.

"Haul in!" thundered the speaking-trumpet, and the winch revolved again.

Three seconds more, and Fandor was scrambling on to the bridge.

"Your mate?" queried the Captain.

"Going back ashore."

"Oh, ho! so you weren't castaways, after all!"

"Not a bit of it!... We were making for you on purpose."

"For me? for my ship? But..."

"Let me introduce myself, sir!—Jerome Fandor, reporter at *La Capitale*... entrusted with an investigation."

"God Almighty!" swore the sailor, dropping his heavy hand on Fandor's shoulder, who flinched a little under the force of the impact.

"Come on to the roundhouse, to my cabin!... A journalist! You're a journalist!..."

He took a step forward, drawing the young man after him. But Fandor clung on to the rail of the bridge.

"My mate? the mechanic who brought me out?"

He scanned the horizon, trembling with agonized suspense.

The boat had vanished. Next moment, however, he was reassured. Clapping his binoculars to his eyes, the officer of the watch sang out against the wind: "Back in the river mouth, safe and sound! Wind astern, he made good weather! But for coming…"

"Now, sir, if you please!" Fandor broke in, turning to the Captain. "I want to speak to you…"

In a few minutes Fandor was ushered into the Captain's cabin. No doubt the *Niagara Falls* too was dancing to the tune of the tossing sea, but the huge steamship did not indulge in the wild leaps and bounds of the frail craft the journalist had just left.

"Good!" he remarked with a smile, "but you're comfortable enough here. You'll give me ten minutes, sir!"

"Speak away. But I ought by rights to clap you in irons for your rashness. Anyway, what is it?"

"Your deluxe deck cabins are engaged, sir?"

But hardly had the young man uttered the words before he saw the Captain give a start and bite his lips.

"Oh, ho!" he exclaimed… then: "Why, yes, that's so."

"Engaged by whom?"

"I don't know."

"You won't tell me, you mean."

"No! I really don't know! But what's that to do with you?"

"I wish to interview its occupant,-discreetly…"

"Indeed?"

"Yes! About a serious matter. Will you send him in my card!"

At this crisis Jerome Fandor was resolved to act on his favorite maxim: Nothing ventured, nothing gained! He had thrown all hesitation to the winds. He reasoned thus:

"If this passenger is the King of the Receivers, I am convinced Fantômas will try to join him in order to offer him the precious paper stolen from M. Thévenot. Therefore, all I have to do, and do it I must, is to keep my eye on the 'King'; in other words, this same passenger, so as to get on Fantômas' track again, get in touch with the scoundrel in spite of all tricks and, who knows, master him."

From that to a firm determination to interview the man was but a step.

"Still, my coming aboard the steamer," Fandor further reflected, "cannot fail to have been observed. Doubtless, in this atrocious weather, the passengers are none of them on deck and have seen nothing of my arrival. But the hands, the stewards, the whole crew is in the know. No hope, therefore, of the King of the Receivers not hearing the news in five minutes from now. So, why not play the open game, cards on the table?"

And this he proposed to do, to make himself known to His Royal Highness and inform him that his identity was an open secret!

"I don't belong to the police," he would tell him; "nor is it you I have to deal with. I shall not denounce you; I shall not give you away. But my intention is not to leave you, not for one second!… It is Fantômas I am fighting, because he is an atrocious criminal, the enemy of the human race. And I know he is to meet you… I do not ask you to give him up to me. But I hereby inform you that I am going to keep a watch for him by remaining at your side…"

Thus, surely, the King of the Receivers would be forced to bow to the young man's will, only too happy not to be denounced by him to the Criminal Department.

Meantime, as he faced the journalist, the Captain of the *Niagara Falls* had turned curiously pale and was evidently making violent efforts to master his embarrassment. Presently he went:

"Very good, sir. So be it!… I'm going to do what's needful to secure you an interview. Will you give me your card and wait here a few minutes?"

Left to himself, Fandor lit a cigarette.

"So there we are!" he chuckled to himself. "As easy as winking too! Now, when I do meet His Majesty, the scene may likely be a trifle… a trifle violent!"

He was still laughing when the cabin door unclosed, and framed in the opening, Fandor beheld the Captain followed by four sturdy hands. Instantly, instinctively, he divined that something out of the common, something sinister, was afoot.

"Well?" he demanded. But the Captain vouchsafed no reply. Turning to his men, he beckoned them to advance, and two seamen took post on either side of the astonished journalist. Then at last the Commander of the *Niagara Falls* spoke:

"Sir, I have to regret the decision I have been forced to adopt. But I have received orders by wireless, which I cannot possibly disobey…"

"That means?" queried Fandor.

"It means I must put you under arrest!"

"Put me under arrest! Put me under arrest!"

"And have you clapped in irons!"

"But this is sheer insanity! Why, pray?"

"I have orders to arrest all who come aboard my ship asking to speak with the passenger you named to me!"

"But, good Lord, man! these orders don't apply to me."

"Oh! yes, they do!"

"But, I am Jerome Fandor."

"No!"

"What do you mean, no?"

"You are not the journalist Fandor… You are Fantômas!"

"Eh, what? What do you say?"

"You are Fantômas, for Fantômas it is who wishes to meet my passenger."

"By God! but I never looked for this!" cursed the young man, for the moment more bewildered than alarmed. The mistake was so monstrous he thought it might yet be cleared up.

Suddenly a new thought flashed across him.

"Juve is on board?" he asked. In fact, he had instantly guessed what must be the true state of the case. Juve, more prompt than himself, must have chartered a boat and anticipated him in putting out to intercept the steamer. Yes, Juve must have followed out the same line of reasoning as himself and, like him, determined to set a trap for Fantômas alongside this dubious Royalty… Who, but Juve, indeed, could have given the order he had been told of?

The Captain's answer was decisive: "No! Juve is not on

board…"

"The message came from him, anyway?"

"I cannot tell you that!"

"But you don't still mean to arrest me?"

"It is my duty to."

"But still…"

"I warn you not to resist! My orders are in case of violence, to blow your brains out…"

"That all?"

"Submit, Fantômas!"

"I am not Fantômas! I am Fandor!… and if I submit, it is because I can claim no right to show fight against honest men like you… Come, do with me as you will… But promise me one thing. Juve is certain to come aboard the moment you reach port; well, swear to confront me with him… without an instant's delay!"

"Very good! I promise."

His heart swelling with frantic rage—and truly he had reason enough to be angry—Fandor allowed himself to be led away by the sailors, who closed round him and held his arms fast, obviously determined to give their prisoner no chance of escape.

"To have come so far only to get myself clapped in jail like a criminal!" thought Fandor disconsolately. "The clumsy fool I am!"

Then suddenly he broke involuntarily into a laugh: "Ah! and the two chaps who dogged my steps in their taxi?… the shady couple I took for emissaries of Fantômas? Of course they were officers from the Department? men sent by Juve?"

Yes, now he could reconstruct the whole adventure of which he had been unsuspectingly the mystified hero. They had refused him all information at the Company's offices, because Juve had given instructions to that effect! He had been followed, because Juve had made up his mind to have anybody shadowed who manifested an interest in the mysterious passenger!

"And my arrest," he cried, "well, that puts the lid on!"

Meantime they were haling him off along a series of cramped

passageways, and down to the lower holds. Then he was shoved into a dark cockpit where two ponderous chains were clamped to the walls, ending in iron rings secured by padlocks.

"Hold still, fellow!" one of the seamen ordered. "We're to clap you in irons, Fantômas!"

Still unresisting, Fandor let them fix the fetters on his ankles; still without a word he watched his jailers depart. But his heart was boiling with impotent fury, boiling with ever increasing passion.

Left to himself, the young man suddenly burst out:

"And when I remember the King of the Receivers is in the ship… that he will hear, very likely, of my capture… Ah, no! not that! Juve himself, for all his calm composure, could never endure it! I must and will see this self-styled Royalty! I must, cost what it may!"—and Fandor gave vent to a laugh that was a threat, and then took off his collar!…

For sure, he meant to have recourse to one of those bold devices, the very audaciousness of which had often served him so well. But what could he do, what artful maneuver could he attempt, a prisoner in irons?

*　*　*　*　*

Truly Fandor's boast that he would succeed in this enterprise he had undertaken, but which had just been so disastrously frustrated by his arrest, seemed nothing better than a piece of empty bravado. The irons, always carried aboard ship in case of mutiny, though hardly ever used nowadays, are strongly made contrivances, not to be broken easily.

His action too in snatching at his collar and ripping it from his neck, appeared a mere exhibition of childish peevishness. Thus to vent his disappointment on his collar could only mean that the young fellow had completely lost his power of self-control. Nothing of the kind, however! As a fact, Fandor was perfectly calm and collected, guilty neither of babyish petulance nor of idle boasting. But to make up, he *was* guilty of another and more heinous fault, the consequences of which might be incalculable. Poor Fandor, his besetting sin was recklessness!

His unoffending collar in his hand, meantime, the journalist listened for a moment to what was going on about him.

"What's happening," he laughed presently, "is that nothing's happening! And that's just the very best thing I could wish for. However careful I am, it's bound to make a bit of noise… But what matter? The storm's kicking up row enough itself!"

He laughed again, and ripped up the collar, muttering between his teeth as he did so:

"The Captain is no expert evidently at locking up jailbirds, dangerous fellows like me, escaped convicts such as I! In a prison they'd have searched me, at the hulks they'd have collared everything I had about me. Here, nothing of the sort! Well, I'm going to show gross ingratitude… Curse it! a brand new collar too! Ah, well, what must be, must. Indeed, when I took the precaution, I said goodbye by anticipation to my six francs I paid for it!"

Fandor grinned all to himself as with an expert finger he searched the lining of the unfortunate collar he had just massacred.

"Here's the thing!" he chuckled. "Guaranteed finest metal! best make! With it you could cut the steel hawsers of an ironclad, if need be!"

From its cunning hiding place Fandor had extracted a short, slender saw blade, the kind of saw used for cutting metal. Certainly a locksmith would have wondered to see this lilliputian tool. But a convict, a real convict, would have felt no surprise. It was, in fact, one of those extraordinary treasures usually found among prisoners' "swag," articles these latter take such pains to hide from the warders. Manufactured as a rule by ex-workmen fallen into criminal ways, these minute saws represent in the eyes of men condemned to penal servitude the sole and only real chance of escape. Nothing can withstand the finely forged, beautifully tempered steel of which they are made. In the hands of a resolute man such a tool spells the certain assurance of being free whenever he chooses.

"It'll try my patience a bit!" Fandor told himself. "But what a happy thought of mine the other day to hide the thing away in my collar!"—and as he spoke, the young man was already hard at work. He had said truly when he opined that it would call for infinite patience to saw through with a tool of the sort the solid chains that held him prisoner, but Fandor had no lack of this desirable quality.

"Besides," he reflected, "I have loads of time; the storm won't have blown itself out before tomorrow morning. It will be time enough if I'm loose by midnight or thereabouts... Crouching on the ground, his body bent over his fetters, he proceeded to pick out a link that looked not quite so substantial as the rest; then, with a rapid to and fro movement, never stopping but to give the saw time to cool off, he fell to work.

"A tiresome job!" he muttered after an hour's work, "but freedom at the end of it! Never say die's the word!"

Not that there was any prospect of such a catastrophe, nor did the journalist fear anything of the sort. On the contrary the result of his patient and persevering efforts was eminently gratifying. After hours and hours of stubborn application the hard metal of the prisoner's fetters was successfully cut through.

"There!" he cried as he got up from the floor, "it's just fine to stretch one's legs!"

He kicked off the irons! He was free! But next moment he turned pale and stifled a fierce oath of chagrin. In the exultation of his newly won liberty, he had paid no attention to a sound of approaching footsteps. Already the door of his dungeon was opening. What to do? To let himself be seen at liberty meant being instantly put back in irons and, no doubt, kept under watch and ward by a sentinel. He cast a swift look around, but could see no means of hiding.

Then, suddenly, a bright idea occurred to him. Dropping to the floor, he cowered down, squatting on his feet and pulling the end of the broken chains under him. Then, closing his eyes, he began to groan dismally:

"Oh! how ill I feel! how ill I feel!"

"Your rations!" said a surly voice.

The door was open now, and, blinking his eyes, Fandor made out a seaman standing in the opening. He groaned louder than ever:

"How ill I am! I am very ill! I'm dying! oh! stop the ship rolling!…"

A gruff laugh was the only answer he got.

"Oh, oh! seasick, are you?" grinned the sailor. "Right-oh! folk don't die of it!… and I shouldn't care, nor nobody wouldn't, if you did croak, Fantômas!"

Then he asked:

"And the rations? Shall I take 'em away again?" The prisoner took care not to answer, and two minutes after, he found himself alone again. The seaman, delighted with the unexpected windfall, had evidently appropriated the rejected food for his own supper.

"The brute!" Fandor apostrophized the fellow, "and I'm just dying of hunger—not to put it more coarsely! However, to business!"—and treading cautiously, he stepped up to the door of his prison and glued his ear to it.

"Nobody! not a sound!"—and he opened the door. It was not fastened, for the sea laws ordain, for fear of shipwreck, which is always possible, that men in irons are never to be locked in.

"Better and better," the journalist expressed his satisfaction, as he examined his surroundings. I am at the far end of a deserted passageway, which must take me somewhere in the ship. Reckless of consequences, for to meet anyone might prove disastrous, he made his way along the sort of corridor in which he found himself. Right at the end was a closed door.

"I only wish I knew what's behind it!" grumbled the journalist. "But there, luck's on my side. I don't hear anything,"—and he opened softly, to find an iron stair, as steep as a ladder, leading to the decks above his head.

"Well, let's up!" decided the young man. "But where am I going to come out? It wasn't this way they took me down to prison."

He mounted slowly. The storm seemed to have abated somewhat, but the ship was still rolling and pitching in a way that forced him to cling on to the rail. In a few seconds, however, he had reached yet another door barring the road.

"Too many closed doors hereabouts!" growled Fandor. "I shall be catching a headache directly. Anyway, I can't well go back, having got so far"—and he pushed open the door without more hesitation. Fate, always capricious, seemed to have turned in his favor. This time he found himself in a wide space in which were ranged rows and rows of pallets.

"The 'tween-decks, eh?" Fandor asked himself, "emigrants' sleeping quarters, likely!"

Then, with a quick cry of delight: "Something better than that, by God! For sure, I've the devil's own luck on my side."

He was certainly in luck's way this time. The place he had reached was nothing more nor less than the cabin-stewards' sleeping quarters, as was proved by a heap of aprons, dusters, and brooms lying higgledy-piggledy in one corner.

A man would have to be a "Silly Billy" indeed not to know what use to put this bit of good fortune to!

In two minutes his whole appearance was altered. Dressed out in a long apron, a dishcloth under the left arm, a duster in the right hand, Fandor was, to all appearance, transformed into one of the ship's menials.

"Deceive anybody at a little distance!" he assured himself, "and that's all that's needful. I've not the least wish to let 'em see me close. Now to be off!"—and he hurried away. An iron ladder, or to be more precise, a very steep iron stair, led to the upper regions. He climbed halfway up the steps. Then, as he looked about him, a smile rose to his lips.

"The promenade deck!" he chuckled. "By God! I'm coming out on the promenade deck. I couldn't ask for better!"

He was wrong, however. This back stairway, for the use of the men only, did not open on to the promenade deck, reserved for passengers, but on to the afterdeck. In any case the mistake was of no consequence, for there was another stairway leading from this part of the vessel to the upper deck. He was up this in two seconds, with all the more satisfaction inasmuch as the state of things on the afterdeck was dreadful. Everywhere the sea came roaring and foaming in over the bulwarks in torrents.

"Let's get on," Fandor told himself. "The way's open to the

suite de luxe,"—for with his characteristic obstinacy of purpose the young man had entirely refused to abandon his project of paying a visit to the traveler he suspected of being the so-called "King of the Receivers." He made straight for the poop.

"The special staterooms are always that way," he remarked. "Besides, I noted on the plan of the steamer I saw at the Bordeaux office the number of the one I'm concerned with—No. 220. So, if I come upon a door numbered 220, I shall know I've got to the right place... Ha! there it is!"

There was nobody on deck, a circumstance amply accounted for by the state of the weather, while the officers were no doubt gathered on the bridge in view of possible collisions—a danger always to be dreaded in the crowded waters outside a great harbor.

"Yes, there it is, not a doubt of it!" Fandor repeated... "Well, now for it!"

What he proposed to do was sheer madness. To rap at the door of the stateroom and appear before its unknown occupant was simply to risk having an alarm raised in less than no time. Nevertheless, knock he did.

"He calls himself a King," he said to himself. "Well, I shall address him as 'Your Majesty' on entering. No matter what the man's effrontery, he is bound to be dumbfounded, struck all of a heap, and that's all I ask to give me time to convince him he has everything to gain by holding his tongue,"—and, a smile dawning on his face:

"A funny job all the same!" he went on with his soliloquy... "Here's a crook, a criminal, who has only got to sing out 'Stop thief!' to have me jailed... of the two of us, he's the one whose story they would believe, you may be sure of that!"

After knocking, Fandor stood stock still, listening... Not a sound! not a movement within!

"The fellow's asleep—the sweet sleep of innocence! Ah, well! I'm going to wake him,"—and this time he battered with his fists on the door. Still not a sign of anybody waking up inside.

"Come, this is a bit too thick! Even aboard steamships the cabins, even the special staterooms, are not such vast apartments!"

A couple of vigorous kicks shook the panels. It was labor thrown away!

"Damn it! is the man dead?" Fandor cursed. "No, that can't be! Anyway, I'm going in, unless the door's fastened."

It was. A solid lock resisted all the journalist's efforts.

"And to think," he muttered, "that any moment I may be heard and interrupted!… What's to be done?… I know! I'll just try one of my little sleight of hand tricks,"—and after a rapid search, he extracted from his waistcoat pocket a long instrument looking something like a corkscrew.

"There!" he said, as he inserted in the keyhole this picklock contrivance… Two minutes fumbling among the wards, and— pray, have the kindness to walk in! With a dexterity many a burglar might have envied, the journalist had forced the lock, and the door was open.

"Nobody awake yet? Very well! In I go, and pull the door shut behind me," and he suited the deed to the word.

"Now, where the devil is the electric switch? Oh, here it is! Now, let's light up the show!"—and in an instant the cabin was brilliantly illuminated. Jerome Fandor had sprung back, meantime, and set his back against the door, ready for anything.

But now his quick eyes, searching the place, looking for the bed, looking for the man he expected to see in it, rounded under the shock of an astounding discovery. The cabin—not a soul was in it—was the strangest, the most surprising sight. The bed stood bare, without bed-furniture of any sort, no sheets, no blankets, were to be seen; pillows and bolster were innocent of pillowcases. The dressing table and washstand were in the same condition—no little bottles, no brushes, no soap, no towels! To make up, on floor, chairs, tables, lay a thick layer of dust, while the whole room had that airless, shut-up smell there is no mistaking.

"Why!… Why, the place isn't occupied!" exclaimed the astonished man; and yet there before his eyes, ranged along the bulkheads, were three enormous trunks, solid, substantial trunks, a trifle worn by much traveling.

"Still," he further remarked, "the suite has certainly been engaged. There's the luggage to prove it."

The fact is he was utterly at sea as to what it could possibly mean. The Captain's behavior, what he had said about persons "who should come aboard asking to communicate with the passenger occupying the special suite," all showed that the latter *was* really and truly occupied.

"The thing's past understanding!" muttered Fandor in a voice that trembled slightly… But perhaps the answer to the riddle's to be found in the next cabin?"

This was a bathroom, and he found it in the same derelict condition. Then he visited the remaining stateroom, which completed the special suite de luxe of the *Niagara Falls*. The furniture was shrouded in dust sheets.

"Nobody! nobody at all!" exclaimed Fandor in a sort of fury. "But why?"

He went back to the trunks and stooped to examine the biggest of the three.

"There, I'm not making a mistake after all. The label shows that much!"

It was a fact. The trunk bore a label inscribed "Special staterooms, *Niagara Falls,* No. 220."

"No! I'm making no mistake. I am actually in His Majesty's cabin, *but* His Majesty's not there! Why? oh, why?"

The bewildered journalist sat down, and holding both hands to his head, strove to unravel the seemingly incomprehensible mystery… Suddenly he started up.

"I've got it, by God!… There's an explanation for everything. Why, of course, my man missed the boat and his luggage went off without him." Yes, it seemed very plausible. Moreover, simple as the explanation was, the theme admitted of sundry highly interesting variations. Had the King of the Receivers missed the steamer by mere misadventure or very much on purpose? King as he called himself, the man was only a receiver of stolen goods, a lawbreaker, after all. Why not suppose that, at the moment of sailing, he had had a panic, had dreaded being recognized?

"It's that, or it's something else; I don't care which!" Fandor suddenly declared, summing up the situation. "But what am I to fix up now?"

For a long time he sat silent, thinking. At last the young journalist's speaking countenance was lit up by a crooked smile:

"Why, certainly," he soliloquized, "it's the best thing to do. To begin with, there's no positive proof he's not hidden away somewhere on board. Then, it's quite likely Fantômas is not aware of His Majesty's absence, if he is not there. In fact, I run no great risk, unless it be of letting in the light on a whole host of mysteries."

So, without more ado, the journalist set to work with amazing activity. Once more utilizing his "nightingale," he forced the padlock securing one of the big traveling trunks and threw it open. It was a sort of large basket covered with mole-skin. Coats, trousers, underlinen, were piled up inside…

"Quite a regal outfit!" laughed Fandor. "Ah, well! Necessity knows no law. Since I'm a cabin steward, I'll do my job as such and pack all this gear away." But, truth to tell, the merry-hearted young fellow had a very odd idea of tidying things away! He took out the contents of the trunk by armfuls, rolled them up so as to occupy the least possible space, and shoved them pell-mell into a chest of drawers.

"The key in my pocket, they won't find the stuff just so easily!" grinned the amateur steward. "Anyway, there's the old trunk empty… I'm keeping back, though, just a few articles of underwear; it'll make softer lying… Now, have I forgotten anything?"

Again he cast a searching look round the cabin. But, once the chest of drawers was re-closed, there was nothing to betray his having been there save the wide open, empty trunk.

"Now we'll shut off the light and unbolt the door," concluded Fandor… "Ah, yes, there's the padlock of the trunk too. It's broken, true, but that'll never be noticed. If I close it shut, it'll look just the same as if it were locked. There we are!… Now to entrain in our padded railway car!"

After unfastening the cabin door and turning off the light,

he groped his way to the empty trunk, and got into it. A shake brought down the lid into place, while working with his pick-lock through the chinks in the basketwork he managed to re-close the padlock, to all appearance as securely as before.

"That's that!" he told himself, calm as ever inside his strange prison. "I shall soon see who will make it his business to take over His Majesty's luggage at the far end… And I'd wager it'll be Fantômas!… Anyway, there's no hurry about it. I shall find that out all in good time, perhaps. There's another point a deal more urgent—when they come to unload on the wharf, shall I be head up or head down? Down would be decidedly unpleasant!"

He stifled a laugh, then gave a yawn.

"I'm dead sleepy!"—and five minutes after, just as if he had not been embarked on the maddest, the most perilous, of adventures, the journalist lay sound asleep at the bottom of his trunk!

5. The Pleasures of Traveling

The journalist was tired out, as he had every reason to be, after the many adventures of which he had been alternately hero and victim. The trunk, moreover, in which he was now confined, was stiflingly hot, while the want of air made his situation still more oppressive. These circumstances were quite sufficient to account for the heavy sleep that weighed down his senses and left him indifferent as to all future eventualities till the moment when a loud, coarse voice roused him from his lethargy.

"That there trunk," the man was saying, "is a bit of heavy stuff, it is!… We can dump it in the net, and swing it out on to the wharf! It won't break, never you fear!"

Instantly Fandor tried to shift his position, but that was impossible, and next moment he recalled vividly and exactly the peculiar situation in which he found himself, and pulling a wry face:

"So," he thought to himself, "we are in port, and they're unloading cargo. What the devil are they going to do with me?"

But he was left no more time for reflection. Heaved up with a mighty effort, the trunk was deposited on the back of a dock porter, and Fandor to his alarm and consternation, heard the man saying:

"You'd think somethin' was moving inside! Sure, it's badly trimmed. Well, if it do shift, I'll just pitch the whole thing over. Not such a fool as to strain my back, I ain't!"

"And the brute would do it too!" thought Fandor.

"Hmm! I've no mind, neither, to have my bones broken by the fellow!"—and he balanced himself all he could in his narrow prison, trimming the load as far as possible.

"Damnation!" he swore next minute, as the trunk was pitched down anyhow on the ship's deck, and he felt the blood rushing to his head. As he had feared, the trunk now stood upside-down.

"And no chance of shifting!" he told himself. "I couldn't help making a noise! Oh God! the fright they'd get if someone opened my package,"—and distressing as his situation was, he all but broke into a mad fit of laughter.

Alas! he was grave enough next instant. Suddenly a new thought had flashed across his brain. "And the custom house?" he ejaculated. When he crept into his hiding place, he had completely forgotten one thing. Did not the Customs, as a rule, require every piece of luggage to be opened? Was it some wretched tidewaiter would have the surprise of his life on dis-covering him!

"Good Lord! what a nincompoop I am!" groaned the young man in consternation. "Fancy never to have thought of that!… No, no doubt about it. I'm going to be caught out, like a naughty schoolboy in a scrape!"—and one by one, all the sound reasons that made his detection almost a certainty passed through his mind.

Was it not obvious that the occupant of the special state-rooms was kept under observation? Did not his own arrest, the way he had been shadowed at Bordeaux, prove the same?

"So," Fandor summed up the situation, "there's no doubt whatever about it. On finding the passenger is not on board, they'll seize his luggage and search it. The only hope left me is that it may be Juve who does the job."

And the young man pulled a face of acute annoyance even more expressive than before. No doubt, if he found Juve again, safe and sound, his feelings would be those of sincere pleasure and satisfaction, but then, Juve would certainly not spare him some cutting gibes at his madcap adventure!

"Well, anyhow," he told himself finally, "I've always got an answer ready—the clever way his agents followed me about at Bordeaux!"

But something new was happening, and with a muffled groan, he felt the trunk being moved again. This time he found himself right side up again, but he was swinging to and fro in a fashion there was no mistaking.

"The net of the crane discharging the baggage," he told himself. "I only hope it's a good strong one!… Good! here I am on the wharf!" A short and swift journey through the air at the end of the arm of the crane had in fact landed Fandor on terra firma. The trunk was hauled bumping across the cobblestones of the wharf and shoved into a corner.

"Now for it!" thought the prisoner. "In two minutes the custom house officers…"

He broke off in a fury, cursing under his breath: "Fool! idiot! clumsy lout!"

But what stirred his wrath was more of a comedy than a tragedy. At best, inside his confined prison, it was with difficulty he could breathe thanks to the feeble current of air that reached him by way of a chink in the lid. Now, in pure innocence, someone had sat down on the said lid! The chink blocked, Fandor's supply of air was cut off, or all but cut off.

"Come, come! none of that!" he growled. "If that good man—or good woman—don't shift, it will be my duty to take my tiepin and, jabbing it through the crack, teach him trunk lids can prick shrewdly." However, there was no need to interfere. Of his own accord the offending individual got up, hailing:

"Customs! Hi! this way!"—knocking on the lid of the trunk as he shouted.

"Quick work!" thought the journalist, hearing and understanding perfectly well. "In three minutes I shall be caught, like a rat in a trap!"

Then he gave a great start of surprise.

"You're crazy, man!" a voice was replying. "Diplomatic baggage. Read the label… That trunk's not to be searched. Clear it right away, along with the two others…"

"*Diplomatic* baggage?" Fandor asked himself. "Well, it beats me! What does it mean, anyway? I can't have slipped into the shoes of a real Royal Highness by any chance?"

After thinking a while, he resumed:

"But the thing's past understanding every way you look at it!… *Diplomatic* baggage? But diplomats' luggage isn't exempt at the Customs—only ambassadors' dispatch cases are… Ah! but, that's the devil of a bump!…"

It was, in fact, the devil of a shock for the traveler in the trunk, which had just been lifted again and pitched onto a truck with the charming gentleness dock laborers always show on such occasions.

"They're going to break my bones, that's certain!" groaned the unhappy young man. "No, never again will I hide in a package that isn't marked: 'Glass with care!' That's the least I can do by way of precaution."

Between the wharf-side, however, and the Bordeaux goods station, whither to all appearance the truck was bound, Fandor had little to complain of. He was put right side up this time, and if his position was uncomfortable, it was at any rate bearable. At the goods yard, alas! it was far otherwise. Bumped about, tossed onto a luggage transporter, then shoved into a railway van, trunk and traveler had a rough time of it.

"What a journey!" growled Fandor. "What an infernal journey! By heavens! I think I was a cursed fool ever to undertake it!"

But he was grumbling merely for the sake of grumbling. Never had Jerome Fandor regretted even for one second any enterprise that might serve his ends in a police investigation.

"The great thing, after all, is to get there!" he reflected, "the all-important point is to reach a place where I can learn interesting and illuminating facts!"

Hardening his heart against ill fortune, he settled down as best he might to get to sleep when the train conveying him presently got underway.

"Who sleeps, dines!" the journalist comforted himself with the proverb. "But that doesn't hinder my being damned hungry—hungry and thirsty into the bargain!"

…When, many long hours later, Fandor reached the Paris terminus, he had still other grievances to complain of. His hunger and thirst were in no way alleviated, but these sufferings were aggravated by intolerable cramps. Constrained as he was in the most uncomfortable of postures, unable to move a muscle, humped together in one unvarying attitude, Fandor felt a deadly numbness creeping through every limb.

"If I had to stand up," he thought, "I couldn't do it. A pretty state of things!—when I consider that perhaps in a few hours' time I am going to find myself face to face with Fantômas or else with the King of the Receivers."

But, once again, his reflections were cut short. The doors of the van were opened, porters laid hold of the trunks and pitched them out on the platform.

"And the Octroi?" the young man asked himself. "Will it be as accommodating as the Customs?"

Once more he was reassured. A porter was singing out in a big voice:

"Ah! diplomatic baggage! We've got our orders… Best put 'em on one side… Seems there's several of them trunks… They're to be loaded up on a truck right away. It's waiting now."

"So much the better! I'm in a hurry to get done. Successful or not, my job must finish. I'm played out!"

Making heroic efforts to shake off the torpor that was creeping over him and above all not to groan at each fresh jolt that threw him against the walls of his prison, he gathered that he was being lifted and set down on a motor wagon.

"Air!" he told himself, "I must have more air to breathe… Else I'm going to faint—and that would be a pretty job!"

At the imminent risk of dislocating his arm, the journalist managed to extract a knife from his coat pocket and cut sundry holes in the walls of his trunk. He was overjoyed at the result.

"To breathe is good!" he chuckled, "but to see is better still! I can breathe fairly well, and I can see, more or less. Hurrah!"

No sooner had he obtained this gratifying result than the wagon started away.

"Off we go!" cried the young man, with his wonted light-heartedness. "Now, I wonder where they're taking this *diplomatic* baggage to."

The fact is he was intensely interested to know this. Ever since he had heard the trunk he was hidden in spoken of as "diplomatic," he had been vainly cudgeling his brains to comprehend what justification there could be for the title. And, little by little, Fandor had come to a conclusion that had at least the merit of being not unlikely. *Diplomatic?* no, the King of the Receivers' luggage could not really and truly come under any such category! But was it impossible that they had arbitrarily given it that description for the very purpose of avoiding awkward questions at the Customs and the Octroi?"

"In that case," Fandor told himself, "it must no doubt have been the police who acted in this way… Unless I'm greatly mistaken, Juve, just like me, was watching for the arrival of the 'King.' That individual was not on board the *Niagara Falls?*… Very good! But his baggage was. Juve must have made the necessary arrangements for this same suspicious luggage to be conveyed to Paris absolutely intact, and to that end it must have been labeled 'diplomatic.'"

Certainly Fandor's explanation possessed at any rate the merit of ingenuity… But, alas! the truck carrying Fandor and his fortunes had not proceeded more than a few yards from the railway station before the journalist was compelled, willy nilly, to abandon his hypothesis. The truck was not going at all in the direction of the Prefecture of Police, to which, in the regular course of events, baggage destined for the Criminal Department would have been conveyed.

"Wherever are they taking me?" Fandor sighed wearily. "Where the devil are they going to lift my lid? And who is going to lift it?"

At one moment he was in the depths of despair, at another he was persuading himself that all was for the best. He argued:

"If I fall into the hands of the police, I have nothing to fear—but neither do I discover anything… and they'll take me for a fool. If, on the contrary, this luggage reaches either of the two, whether the King of the Receivers, arrived, I suppose, by another route, or Fantômas himself, well, I shall make some extremely interesting discoveries… But I run every risk in the world of losing my precious life over the job!"

The disabling cramps that had benumbed his limbs deprived the young man of any hope of making a fight for it. But was there any actual danger of his falling into the brigand's hands? As the truck rumbled across Paris towards some unknown destination, Fandor asked himself the question a hundred times over. Logically he felt bound to admit there was nothing to negative this supposition. He knew that Fantômas had gone to Bordeaux. Was it inconceivable that the Master of Crime should have been successful, in the absence of the King of the Receivers, in getting "His Majesty's" luggage delivered to himself? Many a time had the scoundrel carried through far more complicated enterprises.

But now, clapping his eyes to one of the holes he had contrived in the trunk, Fandor gave a sudden start of amazement and let fly an oath:

"God Almighty! Why..."

His heart stood still, and he panted for breath before he could complete his sentence:

"Why! it's the Sceaux road we're on, the road by Fontenay-aux-Roses!... Then..."

His brain reeled. If the truck was making for Sceaux, was it not natural to suppose that the baggage was to be delivered at the villa where Juve had so mysteriously disappeared?... And was it not at this same villa that Bouzille must have taken the post of concierge for the express purpose of being at the orders of the King of the Receivers?

Fandor was prepared for all adventures, but not for this! He had heard Fantômas himself declare he had had nothing to do with the disappearance of the police officer and that he did not know where he was. Fantômas therefore did not know the house, did not live there at any rate... Who, then, was its occupant? Must he admit that it was actually the King of the Receivers? But then he had gone through every part of the accursed house and found it empty from basement to garret.

A poignant sense of anxiety came over Juve's friend and comrade, as the thought suddenly occurred to him:

"Suppose I have made a terrible mistake, after all! Suppose the 'King' has been in France since long ago! Suppose it was *he*, he who had made the attack on Juve, who had carried him off prisoner!…" If he was Juve's assailant, many circumstances that seemed incomprehensible became clear enough. To begin with, Fantômas might have been quite sincere in his declaration of ignorance as to the police officer's whereabouts. Then, did not this supposition of the American criminal's being already in France supply a sufficient explanation of his failure to find the man aboard the *Niagara Falls?*

A horrid sense of dread chilled Fandor's heart. So far he had not felt any great anxiety about his friend, deeming Juve's absence to be due to a ruse. But the police officer had no reason to fear the King of the Receivers at the time he took Fandor with him to the house at Sceaux. When he told the young man "not to worry his head," he had certainly only been anticipating the possibility of attack on the part of Fantômas.

"Juve! Juve! my poor old Juve!" groaned Fandor, oblivious of his own danger, thinking only of his lifelong friend, his comrade in so many battles, so many dangers. Unnerved, unstrung, he fell back and resigned himself to his fate. Nothing mattered now. His energy was for the moment exhausted, as will happen at times to the strongest natures. For long minutes he lay inanimate, almost unconscious.

Suddenly he roused himself, trembling with excitement. A voice was saying:

"Yes, this is the place, wagoner!… And I'm the chap as is concierge here—and a rum billet it is!… Just heave me down them packages!… I'll take 'em upstairs… Then, we'll go see, you and I, if the pub nearby's got any stuff fit to drink, eh, mate?"

"Bouzille, by the Lord Harry!" Fandor muttered hoarsely from the bottom of his box. No, there could be no doubt this time. The goods were actually being delivered at the house where the old tramp had stated he was to be employed as concierge; and the house was the house of the King of the Receivers.

"Juve?… where is Juve?" groaned Fandor. Then he made a supreme effort to recover his composure. Juve, no doubt, had fallen in the grim duel he was fighting with the enemies of mankind. Well, was he to bewail his friend, or avenge him?— and the gallant journalist cried without an instant's hesitation:

"To avenge him!"

Then he quieted his quivering nerves and forced himself to continue his watch. Cramp, fatigue, were forgotten. Assured that soon, very soon, he would find himself face to face with the King of the Receivers, Juve's murderer, he was ready instantly, prepared and ready for the fray.

Guarding against the slightest movement that might betray his presence, his eyes glued to the hole he had pierced in his prison wall, Fandor watched from his hiding place the comings and goings of the wagoner and Bouzille. Looking very proud of his post as concierge, the old tramp was opening the front door wide. Then going back to the gate he laid hold of the big trunk.

"Give a hand, mate, to hoist it up?" he begged, "and I'll soon have it indoors."

Three minutes later the trunk was set down in a half-empty room, while behind the concierge the wagoner was bringing in another big basket.

"There!" he panted. "A lumpy one, that… Well, there's two more. Each take one, and then for a liquor up!"

Two more packages were brought into the room, after which, the wagoner and Bouzille, now sworn friends, marched off together, leaving Fandor gasping with surprise and bewilderment.

"*Four* trunks!" he grunted. "There are four trunks!… But there were only three before—only three on board the *Niagara Falls!*"

Still he hesitated. Was he quite sure? Had he made a mistake? Had his eyes deceived him?

"Anyway, I *should* like to know…" he was beginning, when he stopped, his tongue cleaving to the roof of his mouth, trembling in every limb… He had heard a noise—a rustling of straw, a creaking of wickerwork, and the sound came from close beside him!

His eye at the hole giving him a view of anything happening near him, Fandor now beheld an astounding sight—a sight at which his heart stood still in his bosom.

Slowly, softly, cautiously, the lid of one basket, the lid of the fourth trunk in fact, was opening, pushed up from the inside!

There could be no mistake as to what caused the movement.

"There is someone inside!" panted the astonished journalist hoarsely. "There's somebody hid in that trunk, same as I am in mine!… Why didn't I think of that when I found the cabin on the steamer empty?"

But there was no time for further reflection. Events trod so fast on each other's heels Fandor could hardly follow them, without in the least understanding their import.

The lid continued to open. Who was raising it? Placed as he was, Fandor could not see, but he could guess. Who was there? The King of the Receivers, of course!

And then—was he going mad?… What kept the man so long in coming out of his uncomfortable quarters? Suddenly, the journalist saw two hands, followed by two arms, stretched out of the half-open basket, and calmly unfolding a newspaper— for all the world as if the owner of those hands had no other thought but to read something or other for his amusement!

6. Juve's Temper Is Ruffled

Still there *are* circumstances in which the most phlegmatic characters, heroes the most hardened to the direst surprises, lose their heads a little. At that moment Fandor had never a notion what to think or what to believe. Who, in this house of mystery, could thus be calmly reading the paper? Who, under these tragic conditions could be amusing himself by skimming through the news of the day? He muttered:

"It's the King of the Receivers, anyway, who is there..."

Such was the first thought that occurred to the young man, and, in fact, it was the outcome of an entirely logical chain of reasoning. The house, as Fandor knew, was intended for "His Majesty's" occupation. On the other hand, this same "Majesty," the King of the Receivers, had been found missing from the *Niagara Falls,* where he should naturally have been. What conclusion was possible but that it was he who was in the other trunk, having, in all likelihood, chosen this mode of conveyance in order to balk possible inquiries on the part of the police?

"Yes!" Fandor told himself "all this is clear enough... But what I cannot understand is why he doesn't come out of his box. What is he waiting for? He has reached the end of his journey."

This question the journalist was asking himself was so natural, so inevitable a one, that Fandor abandoned any attempt to find another solution.

"If I understood this much, I should surely understand, or at any rate guess, other things."

Then he had a happy thought. "But," he cried, "what a fool I am! If I were to read what the fellow is reading, I should discover what he is after—in all probability, anyhow."

From the place where his trunk stood, Fandor could not see

the unconcerned reader. But to scan the newspaper, which he held at arm's length in front of him, that would be easy enough. He strained his eyes first of all to make out the headlines, and immediately one of these drew his attention:

Tragedy on board the "Niagara Falls" during a storm, he made out, printed in heavy type.

"It must be my disappearance that's referred to?" he guessed at once. "No doubt they asked themselves what had become of me when they found my empty irons,"—and little by little he managed to spell out the paragraph. It was not an easy job at the distance, but by dint of perseverance he succeeded at last. The article ran as follows:

> A tragic incident marked the last crossing of the steam packet *Niagara Falls* of the Transatlantic Line. During the terrible storm which forced the ship to lay-to outside the mouth of the Gironde, a passenger, whose name the Company refuses to divulge, but who occupied the special suite *de luxe* No. 220, disappeared.
>
> By a startling coincidence the Captain, a few moments before, had put in irons an individual who had been picked up from a boat and whom there are strong reasons for suspecting to be… Fantômas.
>
> The brigand in question having effected his escape and not having been recaptured, we may well ask ourselves the alarming question if it was not this notorious, this redoubtable criminal who murdered and threw overboard the unhappy traveler who has disappeared.
>
> The police are investigating this double mystery, but wisely preserve absolute secrecy regarding the first results of their inquiries.
>
> We shall keep our readers duly informed; but at present we limit ourselves to putting this question to the authorities: shall we never be delivered from Fantômas? Is the nightmare of his villainies never to have an end?

"So then," thought Fandor. "It is I, at present, who am supposed to have murdered the King of the Receivers. What will Fantômas think of that I should like to know! It comes to this, I am making him the culprit of a crime he has not committed."

But his reflections were interrupted at this point by the sound of a laugh. A laugh? No, he could not be mistaken! The mysterious occupant of the trunk beside him was laughing— was laughing heartily!

Fandor was seized with a sudden access of mad anger. What was Fantômas thinking? But did not this merriment supply the answer to that question? He shut his eyes for a second, thinking:

"Why, it is he! it can be no other! There is a trunk too many—his! And why is he there? Because he is asking himself what has become of the King of the Receivers… It is because he is waiting to know… Because he does not believe in the tragedy reported by the newspaper…"

Jerome Fandor's mind was made up. Cost what it might, was it not his duty to elucidate the mystery? Whichever it was, Fantômas or the "King," the man hiding in that trunk was an enemy!

"I mean to find out!"—and, moving slowly and cautiously, he drew his revolver from his pocket and pulled off the safety catch.

There was a faint click… Had the other heard it? But, doubtless, the young man's mysterious neighbor had not thought of listening, being fully persuaded he was entirely alone. He did not stir…"

"On we go!" Fandor encouraged himself, and with infinite daring, supplemented by practiced skill of hand, turning round a little in his prison and using his picklock, he unhitched the padlock that—to all appearance—secured the lid.

"This time," he thought, "the fellow must have heard… But what matter? If he's going to bolt, I shall be out in a jiffy and after him!"

But even now the man seemed to have heard nothing! He was still reading, calmly folding and unfolding his paper, hardly moving at all.

"Well, if the chap's deaf, so much the better!" muttered the journalist, and very softly, very cautiously went on with what he was doing—a mad, impossible enterprise surely. He was trying, in fact, to get out of his trunk without attracting the attention of the man he meant to attack unawares.

"I shall clap my revolver under his nose!" he was saying to himself. "Buried in his basket as he is, I defy him so much as to try to defend himself."

He had certainly good reasons for anticipating victory, if once he could come face to face with his foe… but could he? It took the reporter ten whole minutes to raise the lid of his trunk without any noise. At last it was done. Then, getting to his feet, mastering by a final effort the cramps that made the slightest of his movements an agony, he began to lift a leg over the edge of his box, ready to step down on to the floor.

And it was at this very moment, just as his foot was all but touching the ground, that the unknown spoke.

"Fandor," the voice said, "put down your revolver, I say! You have a mania for playing with firearms. An accident soon happens. You ought to know that!"

Such was Jerome Fandor's amazement and delight that for a moment he stood dumbfounded, without an answer to the mocking words. Then with a hoarse cry of joy:

"Juve!… it's you, Juve! My dear, good Juve! it's you!"

"Why, of course!"

"But yet…"

"Who did you suppose it was?"

"But, but I don't know!… Fantômas! The King of the Receivers!"

"Really? Well, you made a mistake…"

"But why…"

"You're not going to start out on a hundred and one questions?"

"Oh! yes, I am!… Why not have spoken? You knew I was there?"

"No doubt."

"Well!… In that case?"

The lid of Juve's basket flew wide open, and the police officer's face appeared, frowning angrily.

"Can't you answer?" thundered Fandor.

"Look here!… I didn't speak to you because I'm in a bad

temper!"

"In a bad temper?"

"Furious, if you like that better!… Furious with you!"

"With me?"

"Yes! You are the last word in madcap fools. You play havoc with all my plans… You cover the police with ridicule. At Bordeaux…"

"Oh! the two policemen? So it was you set them on my track?"

"On *your* track? Not I! I didn't know you were at Bordeaux. They were to shadow anyone who got into communication with the King of the Receivers…"

"Oh! so you knew…"

"Fandor, you'll be the death of me!… Yes, I knew… I knew then, and I know now, a heap more things than you. Besides, I can see no mystery in any of these occurrences. It only takes two seconds of thought to understand what's happening and what's going to happen. But of course *you* never think! And so you cause me the most vexatious difficulties. So there! Now, you can go away, if you feel aggrieved."

Juve must indeed have been angry with his friend to treat him so ill. But the fact is the latter did not feel in the least aggrieved. He too knew something, and that was that Juve loved him as a son. If his old friend said cutting things to him, he was bound to admit, all in the dark as he was as to the why and wherefore, that Juve had good reason for speaking so. The young man assumed a contrite air, that was far from being natural to him, and asked:

"Juve, if you're down on me like this, it means I've been acting foolishly."

"You may well say that!"

"I should like to know how, please!"

"You have only to think of what you're doing now."

"But I'm doing nothing! nothing wrong!"

"Yes, you are, by being here."

"Very good. Then I'd best go away?… Now I begin to understand."

"Oh, ho! you begin to understand! You really do?"

"Yes! You disappeared on purpose, eh?"

"Why, yes!…"

"To keep me away from you? To save me from drawing down Fantômas' vengeance on my head?"

"Perhaps! And then? You're for asking more questions?"

"Certainly I am! Juve, you knew the King of the Receivers was coming here?"

"Upon my word, no!"

"Oh!… So that wasn't what you suddenly discovered that time in the sidecar when you very near upset us?"

"No, it was not that, Fandor…"

"Then what was it?"

"The way in which the document was stolen."

"What! you know…"

"Why, yes! And you ought to know too."

"Juve, you bewilder me!"

"A reason the more you ought to *think,* to go back home to the Rue Tardieu and think."

"Oh, well! I'm agreeable. I'll leave it at that… But another question: You know how the document was stolen; do you know how to recover it?"

"Certainly! In the same fashion."

"In the same fashion?"

"Yes! I shall make it reappear in the same way it disappeared."

"It's not possible!"

"I say it is! You'll see."

"When?"

"That depends on someone else, not on me."

"On the King of the Receivers?"

"And on you, Fandor!"

The reply left the journalist speechless. He perfectly well understood that Juve did not choose to enlighten him. But he hoped to force him to some indiscretion, lead him on to let slip some hasty word that should give him a hint of the truth.

"Juve," he began again, "it is the King of the Receivers you are expecting here!"

"If you know it is, why do you ask?"

"You can guess what has become of him?"

"I do not guess. I know, without the possibility of mistake."

"Do you also know when he is coming?"

"He is not coming."

"But if you are waiting for him?"

"It was you told me I was waiting for him."

Fandor was beginning another protest at this raillery, which he thought had gone on long enough, when suddenly, with a peremptory gesture that brooked no reply, Juve silenced him:

"Hush! not a word!… Listen…"

The sound of a drawling voice was heard:

"So you've come to take 'em back again!… That's a rummy go!… Why, they've only just brought 'em… Ain't five minutes gone since the wagoner went away. But if them's your orders…"

"Bouzille!" ejaculated Fandor. "It's Bouzille!"

"And they've come to fetch the trunks!" added Juve.

"But, but…"

"Oh! hold your tongue, chatterbox!… And be off… or else copy me!"—and with the words the police officer slipped back into his basket, and ensconced himself comfortably inside. The lid fell back on top of him, and re-closed with a sharp click.

"The devil!" growled Fandor at the same moment. "Must start on my travels again! The thing's getting beyond a joke… And Juve, who was waiting for something!…"

On the staircase outside, meantime, Bouzille's footsteps could be heard, accompanied by other heavier steps. From one minute to the next the old tramp, now concierge to the King of the Receivers, might come in.

"Not a moment to lose!" said Fandor. "Let's get back in our box. Juve can say all the silly things he chooses to me, but I'm not going to leave him. What he does, I shall do!"

More nimbly than ever, Fandor opened his trunk, slipped inside—not without pulling a wry face.

"Ah! but the padlock?" he reminded himself.

But Bouzille, followed by a railway employee, was already entering the room.

"There you are!" he informed the man. "Them's the four trunks, yonder... I'll give you a hand to get 'em downstairs. Then, if so be you like to stand me a glass..."

Then the old man gave a start of surprise.

"Look there! Look at that one, why, the padlock's broke! When they was unloading, no doubt!... Oh! it'll still hold. I'll fix it up... And I've got a bit of old rope downstairs, and I'll cord up that there trunk..."

A few minutes more and the trunk, duly corded, was loaded on a truck, where, as Fandor noted with satisfaction, it lay close by Juve's.

"All right!" he thought. "Soon as Bouzille and the driver have gone, I'll give my mentor a hint,"—but he was not to get much satisfaction out of that.

"Juve," the journalist was hailing his companion a second or two later. "I'm in a damned unpleasant fix. They've corded up my trunk."

"Well?" asked the police officer in a muffled voice.

"Well, I shouldn't be able to get out, if I wanted to."

"What of that?"

"What of that! But you shouldn't say that! You may want my help."

"Not I!"

"But I say yes. Come, Juve, don't be nasty! You can open your basket; so open it and put out an arm and cut the rope half through, so that I can break it if I try."

"I won't. That's flat!"

"But really..."

"My good lad, I told you not to worry your head! I tell you so again. I repeat the advice in view of future events: don't you worry yourself. Don't do it, whatever happens!... And now, hold your tongue; here's our men back..."

"Bouzille!"

"Yes, and the railway man... Hush!"

It was high time. The driver was bidding Bouzille goodbye and climbing onto the driver's seat, he sang out:

"So long, mate! I'm off now, straight-oh! for Batignolles...

Then a bit o' dinner…"—and the clutch was jammed in, and the truck jolted off.

"Alas!" thought Fandor, "I could do with a bit of dinner too!… I'm like enough to lose the habit of eating, if I go on much longer traveling about the country in boxes!"

The young man's usual good humor was quite restored now. True, he had not the faintest notion what was the meaning of these adventures in which he was mixed up, but he felt sure that Juve, for his part, was following a definite clue, marching towards a sure and certain objective. Was not that enough? Was it not his sole aim and object to be his friend's faithful comrade? Had he another wish in the world save to be always on the spot whenever Juve might have need of an aide-de-camp?

Arrived at the Batignolles goods yard, however, a disappointment awaited him. As luck would have it, the trunks were unloaded at a spot where employees were constantly passing to and fro. Moreover, night was falling, and it was getting impossible to see where the basket that held the police officer had been put.

"Come, let's be off to sleep!" thought Fandor, "that's the best thing I can do. I'm sure to wake up when they come to shift my trunk." He shut his eyes, and was fast asleep in a moment. What better, indeed, could he do than renew his vigor in view of the adventures that, in all probability, were still before him?

Loud voices roused the young man from his slumbers. What was happening? Who was it that seemed so angry—angry or amazed? Fandor listened with all his ears.

"Empty, you're asking?" someone was saying. "Well, what of it? It's just a basket 'returned empty'. That's all there is to it!"

"Go on!" retorted another voice, "and the weight on the ticket? Eighty kilos, it's marked…"

"Then it must have been robbed on the road?"

"Very like!"

Fandor's face paled… This empty basket… This basket that should have weighed eighty kilos, suppose it was Juve's basket. He wanted to look out and see, and half turned in his trunk.

Alas! he had not done moving before a yell of terror rang

out.

"God have mercy on us! Something's moving inside! Yes, inside this 'un, the one I was leaning against. Quick! quick! go fetch a constable!"

"Caught!" muttered Fandor under his breath… "Well, well!… But Juve?… Juve?"—and once more his heart sickened in an anguish of alarm and suspense.

*   *   *   *   *

Anything but pleased at being involved in a serious matter that might demand the concoction of a detailed report—a job he hated—the police officer they had summoned soon arrived on the scene, accompanied by a deputy stationmaster who had also been informed of what was happening. The former, a fat man with a red face, had his opinion cut and dried from the first.

"In railway yards," he declared, "whenever trunks are in question, it's always the same old story—it's a woman cut up in little bits you find inside!"—and the officer was deeply morti-fied at the laugh with which a porter greeted his remarks.

"How now?" he asked the man, "that strikes you as funny, does it?"

"For sure!" declared the other stoutly. "For a woman cut up in bits, it wriggled about fine, whatever's inside there!"—and he pointed to Fandor's trunk.

"Open!" commanded the representative of the law. "Must see first, before saying anything!"

Yet, when the trunk was opened, when Fandor popped up from it like a jack-in-the-box, the policeman evidently found himself no less disinclined to say much, for all he vouchsafed was a startled oath. Then, recovering himself, he demanded:

"Now, whatever were you after inside there?"

In sheer amaze, meantime, the railway employees had all fallen back, so that, had Fandor been an evildoer, he had a fine opportunity to take to his heels. But he was thinking of some-thing very different. No sooner was he free of his novel prison than he had darted to the basket where he expected Juve must be. He lifted it with trembling hands, and it was in a tone of horror he too cried the one word: "Empty!"

"Empty! what of that!" queried the policeman. "What had you put in it, eh?"

"Juve, my poor friend Juve!" groaned Fandor.

But truly nothing the young man said could well heighten the stupefaction of his auditors.

"Juve? You say the famous Juve was in that basket?" asked the policeman, turning an apoplectic red.

"Yes!… Certainly he was!"

"Then you had killed him, villain!"

Fandor's only reply was a shrug. What they said to him, what the constable thought of him, what the railway men, who were staring at him with mingled amazement and terror, might believe, he cared not a jot. What had become of Juve, that was all that mattered.

With his own eyes he had seen the detective re-enter the basket. A few minutes after, when Bouzille and the driver were going off to drink at the wineshop, he had spoken to Fandor… Therefore, he had obviously been in the said basket—and he was not there now!"

"When did he disappear?" the journalist asked himself. "How? Why?"

Dreadful presentiments tortured him. Black thoughts filled his mind. This time he could not help but conjecture some atrocious crime. He sprang to the empty basket.

"Open it!" he cried in a voice that rattled in his throat.

"But no one has the keys…"

"Well, use a hatchet!"

"But, but we've no right to! Must know first who it belongs to…"

"To the King of the Receivers… But…" Fandor broke off. His last words had blanched the gallant constable's face.

"Oh, Lord! oh, Lord! it's the devil of a business this!"

Then suddenly the man screamed:

"But, God A'mighty! you're a madman!"

Fandor's quick eye had seen hanging on the wall a whole

battery of implements for use in case of fire, of which a hatchet was the chief ornament. Seizing this, instantly, with one blow, before anyone could stop him, Fandor split the lid of the basket.

"Hi! you, my man!" yelled the constable. "I'm going to…"

But again the representative of law and order was cut short. Fandor, who had knelt down beside the open trunk and was examining the interior, gave a cry of: "Blood!"

Then, next instant, he corrected himself:

"Good Lord! it's all my eye!"—and he burst out laughing.

But at the moment a shudder ran through all the onlookers. The inside of the basket was, in fact, splashed with blood… How could the young villain have the effrontery to declare it was "all my eye"? How could he laugh?

"Wretch!" cried the constable.

"Oh! the artful fellow!" retorted Fandor, who seemed in the clouds.

"Blood!" pursued the constable. "Proof positive of a crime!"

"Poor rabbit! poor duck! poor hen!" Fandor chuckled under his breath. Then he deliberately turned his head, and by fixing his eyes on the object that had just before arrested his attention, he drew the looks of all in the same direction, thus nullifying the effect of Juve's ruse. This time for sure, the police officer would have had cause to accuse him of making "blunder after blunder"!

Then he broke into another peal of laughter. His anxiety was relieved, not a trace of it left! And there was an excellent reason for this. There, a couple of steps from the blood-stained basket, full in view, lying at the foot of a pillar supporting the roof of the shed where they were gathered, the journalist had remarked a bottle, a red bottle, a blood-red bottle. The trick was obvious. Firmly resolved to debar Fandor from any share in the perilous enterprise he was engaged in, Juve had determined once again to break the clue, to disappear and foster a belief in his death.

The police officer as a matter of fact was gone from his basket. Only, wishing to make his disappearance dramatic and at the same time to mitigate his friend's anxiety, he had left behind him in the trunk these bloodstains—bloodstains an explanation of which he afforded the young man by leaving where he must see it the bottle he had used for holding a supply of blood, rabbit's blood, duck's blood, or hen's!

Juve, indeed, had not been particular as to details; but he had felt no doubt whatever that Fandor would set about an investigation on the spot to elucidate the mystery of his disappearance, but on finding the bottle, as he was confident he must do, the young man would see through his friend's trick and would say no more. At the same time, who save the journalist would ever suspect such an odd contrivance?

But Fandor was not destined to have much time to weigh what had occurred. A heavy hand fell on his shoulder.

"Come along! To the station house!"

"What! You mean to arrest me?"

"By God! Yes, my fine fellow!"

"So be it then! I'll go quietly,"—and, as a fact, he did not offer the smallest resistance, and was soon brought before the Commissary of Police. There he gave his name, satisfied the magistrate of his identity, and, thanks to the scare produced in that worthy's mind by this information, was at once conveyed to the Criminal Department and admitted to M. Havard's private office.

"In five minutes I shall be free," thought Fandor, on reaching the police headquarters. "But what the devil am I to try then? Where and how to find Juve? Yet I do not choose he shall join issue with Fantômas, and I not there."

Suddenly the young man gave a start.

"Ah! but Juve has good reason to call me a fool! It's as simple as 'how d'ye do?' I've got a happy thought."

But he had no time to elaborate this happy thought that had occurred to him. They were taking him to see M. Havard. It was with a smile on his face Fandor entered the Chief's room. Not that any great cordiality, if the truth were known, as a rule marked the relations between the generalissimo of the police and the reporter! In fact, Fandor nursed a grudge against M. Havard in consequence of sundry acts of injustice he had committed out of professional jealousy to Juve's detriment. On his side again M. Havard cherished some feelings of resentment against the journalist who had not invariably deemed everything admirable in the activities of the Department. Still, the two men respected each other.

"Good day, Monsieur Havard," Fandor said with outstretched hand. "I am a prisoner, but I have come to ask you to release me… You know what has been happening… And you understand?"

The Chief reached for a voluminous bundle of documents.

"Certainly!" declared M. Havard. "Certainly I know what has been happening… You purloined a trunk on board the *Niagara Falls*… Then, concealed in the said trunk, you traveled, without a ticket, from Bordeaux to Paris… To end up, you were going to repeat the same swindle, if chance…"

"Oh, come!" the young man tried to interrupt the flow of the great man's eloquence.

"Let me finish!… If chance had not brought about your discovery, again hidden in a trunk… and two steps from a bloodstained basket…"

"But…"

"Silence, and listen to me! You understand of course I do not accuse you of the crime…"

"That's a good thing!"

"But I am bound to examine into the other charges brought against you…"

"You are speaking seriously, Monsieur Havard?"

"Do I look as if I were joking?"

"And yet you know quite well the motive of… of the misdemeanors you are blaming me for?"

"On the contrary, I know nothing about it."

"Come now!… Well, Juve…"

"Poor Juve?" sighed M. Havard.

"Poor?… Why poor?"

"Does not everything point to his death? Indeed, I am surprised to see you so cheerful."

"Oh! You… you are surprised?"

"Since the theft of M. Thévenot's document Juve has disappeared, don't you know that? Surely you should be desperately anxious—if you are really Juve's friend."

"Eh, what?… You say?…"

Fandor had grown pale with anger. The notion that the sincerity of his affection for Juve should be called in question was like to make him lose all patience, but a moment's thought decided him to say nothing. Juve vouchsafed no sign of life. Juve had arranged impressive stage effects by leaving those bloodstains on the basket he left behind him. Juve had most certainly not acted without a purpose… Was he to spoil his plans by replying to M. Havard's silly accusations?

"Blunder upon blunder!" thought Fandor. "Juve told me I was making blunder upon blunder!… I must hold my tongue!"—and he said not another word.

M. Havard resumed:

"In any case, it is high time for all this business to be elucidated. Public opinion is more than ever disturbed. This last theft of Fantômas' proves, or would seem to prove, that acts of imprudence have been committed. An end must be put to these fantastic tricks you are constantly indulging in—with what purpose I cannot say… You have been guilty of delinquencies. You have been mixed up in the Fantômas affair. Very well! An Examining Magistrate shall be instructed and you will explain your conduct to him…"

"So, you arrest me?"

"Certainly I do."

"Monsieur Havard, will you allow me to tell you what I think of you?"

"Come, take care! No insults, please!"

"Monsieur Havard, I have a sincere admiration for you!… You are a genius! Failing to arrest Fantômas, you imprison Fandor!… For certain, your name will go down to posterity!"

"Enough! enough!"

M. Havard rang his bell and, pointing to the young man, ordered the two Inspectors of the Department who appeared in answer to his summons:

"Take him to the Depot. Here is the warrant."

"Very good, sir!… Solitary confinement?"

"Obviously."

"Pardon me," put in Fandor, "but I am entitled to see an advocate."

"You have one?"

"The official counsel of *La Capitale,* Maître Nervas."

"He shall be informed."

"Monsieur Havard, my respects!"—and guarded by the two officers, Fandor left M. Havard's office a prisoner.

Now, if the journalist submitted with a good grace that was plain to see to the stupid arrest he was the victim of, but which all the while could not but fill him with boiling rage, it was equally apparent that M. Havard, on his side, harsh and unjust as he had shown himself, was not really very seriously angry. Scarcely, indeed, was the journalist out of the room before the Chief of Police got up, walked to the door of his office, and opening it, asked:

"Well? Did you hear? Are you satisfied? Come in, do!"

And it was—Juve, who came in! Juve, laughing quietly to himself.

"Excellent! excellent!" he declared. "Poor old Fandor! And to think he never said a word, not to spoil my plans… I could see that was it! And to think it is I who am having him arrested!"

"False-hearted friend!" laughed M. Havard.

"You may say so, Chief! Indeed, I'm asking myself if he will ever forgive me… Fact is, I will not have Fantômas killing the lad. He is almost a son to me, is Fandor… Now I know him safe—in prison!"

"Of course. But…"

"Allow me, Chief, before proceeding to other matters, to give you one piece of advice. You know Fandor is no ordinary fellow? Lock the door of his cell tight, whatever you do. He is quite up to escaping…"

"Good! good! Never fear. It's not he troubles me!"

"It is Fantômas!…"

"Yes! You have some hopes, Juve?"

"Great hopes, Chief. This time, if my instructions are properly carried out, it will be Victory. Mind you, since the theft, I have done good work. I shall recover the stolen papers… and I shall arrest Fantômas…"

"Thanks to the King of the Receivers?"

"Yes! Fandor too has guessed it. It's a sure thing, Fantômas will want to sell him the document…"

"Granted! But where is he, this King of the Receivers?"

"I know that, Chief."

"Just as you know the way the document was stolen?"

"Oh! as for that… It is so easy to understand that…"

"That?"

"That I shall employ the same method to recover it."

"But when?"

"That is the one thing I don't know, Chief. But it depends on you."

"On me?"

"On the orders you give,"—and with a smile, as he lighted a cigarette, Juve announced, counting on his fingers:

"Firstly—have the marks I left in the basket taken… and communicate them to the Press… Then spread the report that I am dead, dead and done for…"

"It shall be done, Juve."

"So that a subscription will be got up to erect a statue to my memory. When the donations roll in, the public will be convinced…"

"Very good! And then?"

"Then, secondly, organize the raid. There are seven individuals marked with green. They must be captured, all the seven…"

"Why?"

"Hmm!… Let's proceed… It's essential, but I would rather not let you into the secret… Thirdly—give your officers formal orders not to arrest the King of the Receivers…"

"But, but…"

"Understand me clearly, sir! The King of the Receivers is an infamous scoundrel… his name is enough to show that… But it is through him I propose to catch Fantômas… If they collar him, there's no more to be done! You will arrest him later on—after…"

"I would rather at once."

"Possibly! But that would be a blunder. It's to avoid that, to a large extent, that I am having poor Fandor jailed… Besides, there's nothing to prove your men will be in a position to arrest him, is there?"

"That's true. His description?"

"Easy enough to recognize. Short, bearded, wearing, I think, a white curled wig… But he may change all that… And a hump…"

"Hump behind or in front?"

"That I don't know, sir! You ask too much… He is said to have a hump. He certainly has an American accent. I can't tell you any more. It's a fine thing I've got hold of that much information."

"Quite right, Juve. You gained it…?"

"By artfully questioning sundry international thieves at the Depot. That was my yesterday's job…"

"I congratulate you."

"So now I'll bid you good day."

"Right, Juve!… Oh! by the by, you'll be at the round-up tonight?"

"Certainly, unless I am detained elsewhere. You will be there, Chief?"

"I think so…"

"Then I'll look out for you, in case of need… But there's only one thing of prime importance—to arrest the gentry marked with green, search them and take possession of anything interesting they may have upon them."

"That is to say?…"

But Juve was getting to his feet, casting a startled look at the clock.

"By the Lord! Eleven o'clock already! Goodbye, sir! I talk too much, forgetting I have a heap of things to do!"

Juve exchanged a cordial handshake with the Head of the Criminal Department and took his departure—but only to reappear next moment. The door he had just closed behind him reopened and he popped in his head.

"And, of course, sir, you keep Fandor's cell door double locked? That's all-important."

By a quaint coincidence, at that same moment, Fandor, in the prison cell to which he had been conducted, was soliloquizing under his breath:

"So I am a prisoner! Very good! It's an accident like another. The main point is not to let the thing go on forever. Well, it should be about eleven o'clock now? Barring accidents, I shall be free say at three o'clock this afternoon. That's all that's needful. I have nothing to do before four…"—and, strange to say, the young man seemed sure of his fact! He appeared to entertain no doubt whatever that he could be at liberty at the hour he fixed.

7. "I'll Give You Something to Cry For"

It was just half-past two of the afternoon when Fandor reached the culminating point of his fury. At first, it is true, he had taken his arrest with a smiling face and even a jesting tongue, and this because he knew very well it could have no serious consequences for him. Then, little by little, he had come to adopt a harsher view of M. Havard's attitude, for he was hardly likely to suspect the truth, that M. Havard in sending him to prison had done so to please his good friend Juve.

"The idiot!" he was growling to himself. "To arrest me, me of all people! And why? Why! because I took a journey without a ticket, shut up in a box! Ho, ho! so that is the notion the police have of the way of doing things—they don't catch Fantômas, but think it quite in order to leave the whole world at the mercy of a hideous criminal, while they ruthlessly imprison a harmless journalist doing his duty as a reporter!"

He went yet further in the bitterness of his heart:

"But no, it is not the journalist they abominate in me—it is the friend of Juve. Well, I mean to teach him there are some practical jokes that cost their contrivers dear!" Fandor was quite wrong, but he had no suspicion of the fact. This and that combined to lead him to the same resolve. No sooner was the young man inside the four walls of his cell than he was instantly planning how to get out of it again. But the task he proposed to undertake was no easy one. Say what you will, to escape from a prison is never easy, while to escape from the Central Depot is more difficult than from any other jail. A place of detention of a special sort, a place where prisoners awaiting trial are lodged in close proximity to the Examining Magistrates, the Depot is installed in the basement of the Palais de Justice itself, and both its situation and its internal arrangements and organization contribute to the peculiar strictness of the surveillance practiced. No doubt prisoners do often escape from the Palais de Justice, but these escapes reported by the newspapers invariably take place in the corridors when they are being conducted to the magistrates' rooms for interrogation. From the Depot proper no one has ever escaped save by the complicity of some traitor within the building itself.

"Very good!" the journalist admitted the fact. "But I, Jerome Fandor, I mean to get out. There, my mind is made up!"—and the prisoner began to pace up and down the narrow cell in which he was confined.

As a mere place of detention for birds of passage, the Central Depot is organized on peculiar lines. The prisoners' cells are not like those in other prisons. To begin with, some of them are quite large, and several prisoners occupy them in common. Others, on the contrary, are very tiny, more like cages than anything else—miniature dungeons in fact, having at one end a grating reaching from floor to ceiling and giving on a small courtyard where a warder is constantly on guard. It was to one of these latter that Fandor had been taken. Now, to tear down the grating, cross the courtyard, escape the warder's eye, then traverse the open halls and corridors of the prison, and finally get past the porter at the gate, all this was so manifestly impracticable as to make the journalist appear to have acted like a fool when he resolved on escaping! A man, short of being a fool or a madman, does not resolve to attempt the impossible.

…At five minutes to three, nevertheless, Fandor was beginning to exhibit signs of extreme impatience when the jailer's steps were heard approaching his cell.

"At last!" muttered the young man, while the jailer, halting before the grating, demanded:

"Jerome Fandor? Are you Jerome Fandor?"—a shade of respect noticeable in his tone. Indeed, the fellow must assuredly have been greatly surprised to see the famous journalist in such a place.

"Yes! that's my name," Fandor replied, without giving a thought to the impression produced on the warder.

"Then follow me!" ordered the man.

"To the 'parlor'? It's my counsel, is it?"

"Yes!"

Fandor said no more, but his eyes had begun to sparkle.

"Good for you!" observed the warder. "You don't waste no time! Run in this, morning—and here's your counsel at your orders already!"

But Fandor was in no mood for talk. "Let's get on," he suggested, and the warder led off with a curt, "This way!"

They had to cross the courtyard and penetrate still deeper into the very heart of the prison.

"Capital!" Fandor muttered to himself as he glanced about him on the way. "Solid walls and sentinels everywhere. Just what I wanted!"

Meantime the jailer was opening a door secured by massive bolts, and invited his prisoner to go in.

"Maître Nervas is at the lodge. He'll be here directly." Fandor, without troubling to reply, began a cursory examination of the room where he was going to meet his defending counsel. This was of the simplest—nothing more nor less than a cell like the other, only closed in all round, provided with three articles of furniture and three only—a table and two chairs.

"Not over and above luxurious!" thought the journalist. "But never mind. By the by, a looking glass would have been a convenience, naturally. But there, it's not indispensable."

The key turning in the lock made him jump. Outside the door the warder was speaking as he drew the bolts, evidently giving explanations:

"Yes, Maître, it's always managed this way… I'm going to lock you in with your client, so as you'll be free to talk. Then, when you want to come out, you'll ring! Yes, there's a bell. Then I shall come for you… and they'll take Jerome Fandor back to his dungeon… There, you can go in, Maître!"

The door was thrown open, and a barrister in gown and toque approached the journalist, only to be greeted by a cry of surprise from his client:

"But… but you are not Maître Nervas!"

In fact, Jerome Fandor had long known, indeed had long

ago become the friend of the leader of the Paris bar, famous for his daring advocacy, his biting wit—and his generous heart. But lo! this was not the great advocate—a man of sixty or thereabouts, but quite a youthful junior, a callow, almost beardless stripling, and evidently in a great state of nervous trepidation.

"Maître Nervas' secretary!" he announced himself. "I am his secretary…"

"Very good! And Maître Nervas has asked you?…"

"Oh, no! I have come on my own authority… Maître Nervas is out of town… Yes, for a couple of days… In two days he will be delighted to put himself at your disposal, but I thought you would no doubt be glad to have a talk with me… Oh! Monsieur Jerome Fandor, I don't know yet what you are accused of, but I have such an admiration for you…"

Fandor burst out laughing.

"Hmm!" he returned, suddenly interrupting, "you are very kind, my dear sir… But will your admiration outlast our interview?"

"I feel sure it will," declared the young lawyer. "But what is the charge against you?"

"Traveling without a ticket in a trunk?… Robbing the said trunk! But that's not the question…"

"Not the question! Why…"

"Wait a minute. Tell me something in confidence first. Will you be so good as to inform me how your father brought you up?"

At these words the budding barrister looked so utterly amazed that Fandor went on to add:

"It is a most important point… Was he severe?… just?… patient?"

"Why, why… he was… he was like most other fathers, I suppose."

"Well then, that's all right! My dear sir, please recall the days of your childhood a bit… When you were naughty, when you sulked or cried without rhyme or reason, what used your father to say to you?… I repeat it is a highly important point!"

For the moment the young lawyer was near asking himself

if he were not dreaming a bad dream. What could such questions mean? He had spoken nothing but the truth when he proclaimed his admiration for Jerome Fandor, in fact he might really be said to be a worshipper at the shrine of his genius. But all the same he could not help the question—was not his hero poking fun at him?

"Well?" insisted the journalist.

"Sir," the youthful advocate stammered, "I must own, since you press the question, that my father was a little hot-tempered… In such cases, when I was peevish without reasonable cause, my father used to bestow a cuff on me, accompanying the blow with an emphatic warning: 'There, my lad,' he would say, 'I'll give you something to cry for.' Only…"

"Excellent! excellent! Well, my dear sir, let me tell you your father was doing nothing new. All fathers—and some mothers—do the like under similar circumstances. And that is the very thought that inspires me! I reason by analogy! M. Havard has had me arrested for nothing. I want to teach him to be just. So, I mean to get myself arrested for something!…"

"But, really…"

"Wait a moment. I have, as a matter of fact, committed no misdemeanor. To teach M. Havard to arrest people for something, I am going to commit a crime!"

"You're joking?"

"A crime, perhaps a crime of violence. And you are to be the victim…"

"Oh! Come now…"

"Hush! Not a word… You are to be the happy victim…"

"The happy victim!"

"Undoubtedly. Your portrait will be in all the papers. *La Capitale* will send to interview you… In short, you will 'awake to find yourself famous'!"

"But, Monsieur Fandor, I don't see… I don't…"

"Of course you don't! No, you don't understand. Well, you are going to understand. After all, it's as simple as A B C…"

Fandor appeared to be vastly amused. He could read as in an open book the thoughts that terrified his young companion.

"For sure," he reflected, "Maître Nervas' secretary is asking himself if I am mad. So much the better! A pennyworth of fear will help the lad to make up his mind… With his employer I should have had to use force, and that would have been risky. With him things will go like clockwork."

The journalist drew a handkerchief from his pocket. "Follow me carefully," he said. "You see this handkerchief?"

"Certainly I do…"

"It is clean. It is small. Suppose it soaked in chloroform, impregnated with a drug."

"But why? Why?"

"I am going to explain… Suppose this… suppose I catch you by both wrists like this with one hand, and with the other pinch your nose…"

"Help! help!" screamed the young lawyer in panic terror.

"Hold your noise, do!" Fandor cut in, releasing his victim. "You don't suppose, among all these suppositions, that I'm going to murder you?"

"No, but…"

"You are still alarmed?… That's a pity, for, great heavens! I don't wish you any harm… But to continue… keeping my distance, d'you see, to reassure you… Well then, I pinch your nose with one hand, holding you meanwhile with the other. Now, what happens?"

Utterly dumbfounded, the young lawyer could only stammer:

"Why, why!… I suffocate?"

"Go along! Not a bit of it! You open your mouth to breath…"

"Oh, yes!… so I do."

"Then, quick as a conjuring trick, I pop this handkerchief into your mouth… Once again, what happens?"

"By God!… Why, you kill me!"

"Hmm! You are far too prone to look on the dark side of things!… No, I don't kill you… I put you to sleep, the chloroform sends you to sleep…"

"Monsieur Fandor, let's stop this nonsense!"

"Not for one moment!… Ah! don't ring! I'm watching you!…

Well, now you're asleep. So then I appropriate your gown and toque, and take out of your pocket the pass that permitted you to come here… You gather my meaning?"

"I gather you are joking."

"Never, my dear sir! I never joke! Once dressed out as an advocate, I make off—naturally… Meantime the warders discover you, and note the outrage you have been subjected to… And I do assure you, you shall have your interview all right!…"

"Or else I shall be struck off the rolls. There's no chloroform on your handkerchief, so they will suppose I have lent myself to this farce… and… and it is infamous what you ask me to do."

"A mistake, sir! I do not ask, I order!"

"Oh! come now. Why…"

Fandor's eyes blazed suddenly.

"Young man!" he articulated in a stern voice, "you claimed to know me. If you spoke the truth, you must be aware that I am not a man to be diverted from any purpose I have resolved on… I am anxious to persuade you, but *if* you force me to use violence…"

"Oh! you would never dare…"

"But I *should* dare, I most certainly should! Now, try to understand what I say. My dear sir, if I propose to escape, this does not mean I wish to fly from the law. I have no crime weighing on my conscience. No, it is only that I intend to rebel against an arbitrary act on the part of M. Havard… It is also because I consider I am bound to follow out the campaign undertaken against… against… but there, why not tell you the truth?… against Fantômas."

"Fantômas!" stammered the young advocate.

"Yes! Fantômas has stolen a document. Juve and I have sworn to get it back from him, and what is more, to put it out of the scoundrel's power to do any further harm. This said, you can realize I have something better to do than stick here in prison. Come, allow me… Why, what's wrong with you?" Fandor broke off abruptly to ask the question, then he burst out laughing.

"Oh, Lord!" he exclaimed next moment. "Poor lad! Truly I

am a brute, but I'm a brute that's rather pleased than otherwise."

This last speech admitted of a simple explanation. Panic stricken—after all, his agitation was not unnatural—on hearing Fandor mention the dread name of the Lord of Terror, the trembling secretary of Maître Nervas had fainted right away.

"Upon my word!" Fandor concluded gravely, "I don't know if I should really have ventured to use force. But, things being as they are, I should be a precious fool not to take advantage of the opportunity, without hesitation or compunction. So now, 'on with the play!'"—and bending down over the secretary, who had sunk helpless on a bench at the far end of the room, Fandor removed his gown, then his toque, and dressed up in them. After that, well pleased with his new outfit, which rendered him quite unrecognizable, he turned his attention to his victim who was to take his place in the eyes of the jailers.

"I relieve him of his collar," he muttered. "They've taken my best. I remove his necktie—prisoners are forbidden to wear neckties… Ah! I shall have to slip my coat on him, I suppose. By God! it's more complicated than I thought. But I'll manage it,"—and manage it Fandor did, effecting with an adroitness to match his daring the exchange of his own clothes with those he ruthlessly stripped off his victim.

"His pocketbook? Well, I'll leave him that… His boots! Ah! they're like my own, the warders will never know the difference. There, that's just capital. Now for his attaché case… Where's the pass, I wonder. Ah! better and better! Here it is… Nothing to do now but prop him up against the wall, sitting head in hands on his bench… The light's pretty dim, thank goodness! And I'll hide him all I can from the warder who comes for me… There now, let's ring!"

Once again Fandor was attempting a mad scheme, a forlorn hope, one of those pieces of recklessness that may have the very worst consequences if they fail. Was he going to be caught this time? or was he destined to escape?

He pulled the bell with a perfectly steady hand. When, in answer to the signal, a warder—it was not the same one— opened the door, all he could see was just the back of an advocate bending over a despairing prisoner and plying him with encouraging and consolatory phrases.

"Come, keep up your courage!" he was saying. "All this won't be half as bad as you fear… Look the situation calmly in the face… You'll find it will all come right in the end."

The advocate looked round at the warder with a smile. "Now, my man, I'm ready,"—and he went on ahead, while the jailer was shutting the door again and telling the prisoner: "I'll be back in two twos…"

By that time Fandor was striding rapidly down the corridor. Looking very dignified in his gown and toque, he kept a pace in front of the warder, so preventing the latter from seeing his face.

"Right or left?" he asked.

"Right, sir! The stairs right facing you… You're not going out, I reckon, as you're still gowned? Going back into the Courts?"

"Obliged to!"

"Then, sir, will you, please, give up your pass."

"Here it is, my man! here it is!"

Two seconds more, and standing alone on the stairs that lead from the Depot to the upper parts of the Palais de Justice, the journalist uttered a deep sigh of relief.

"Free, I am free! The great thing now is to get myself a coat, or an overcoat. Ah, well, I shall find that in the Press Room,"—and walking slowly across the vast Salle des Pas Perdus, he reached the Galerie Marchande and made his way into the quarter reserved for press reporters attending the Courts.

His entrance caused an instant sensation. The special reporter of *La Capitale* hurried up to him.

"What! Why, I must be dreaming! Is it you—you in counsel's rig?"

"Hush!" replied Fandor. "Don't attract attention! Old man, I'm going to offer you a 'scoop.'"

"A 'scoop,' eh! Well, what is it?"

"I'm giving you the chance of a rattling good article if you'll lend me your overcoat… Agreeable?"

"Why, sure! But what's the game?"

"Wait a bit!… Here you are—I write a couple of lines, and you show them to M. Havard… No need of more explanations… You understand, I'm sure!"

Fandor was laughing as he spoke. The reporter bowed.

"Away we go!" he cried. "Here's my topcoat…"

"And here's my letter. Take it right away!"

"Agreed!"

Fandor stripped off his gown, slipped into his colleague's overcoat, put up the collar, and made off.

"Must hurry up!" he muttered. "All this has made me late. Well, well! if I don't find him today, I shall see him tomorrow."

Then he burst out laughing, as he hailed a cab.

"Havard's face! Oh, Lordy! Havard's face, when he gets my note!"

The note was short and sweet. Fandor had written: "With my best respects, I beg to offer you a bit of good advice—to see to the speedy release of Maître Nervas' secretary, with whom I have exchanged personalities. With no ill will, but with no wish to see you again too soon!…"

And he had actually signed his name at the end.

8. Kingly Generosity

Unjust as he sometimes was towards Juve, whose celebrity, and even the exceptional talents the great detective possessed, he regarded with some jealousy, M. Havard was not really an ill-natured man. But to make up, he *was* very punctilious and extremely touchy. On receiving the journalist's little missive and hearing of Fandor's escape, M. Havard fell into such a frenzy of rage that for a moment he seemed on the verge of an apoplectic stroke.

"A pretty state of things indeed!" he sighed mournfully. "Oh! but Juve had a happy thought when he asked me to arrest Fandor under the first pretext that turned up, in order to shelter his young friend from all danger!… Arrest Fandor! An easy job that was!"—and the distracted Chief began striding up and down, as he resumed:

"So here I am now with a ridiculous affair on my hands! All the papers, *La Capitale* at their head, are going to make a mock of me!"

The thing seemed likely enough. In fact, hardly a minute later, the Chief's anticipation was amply confirmed, when he saw his office invaded by Maître Nervas' secretary, who had been speedily recognized and released and now wore the triumphant smile of a young man suddenly elevated to the rank and dignity of the Man of the Hour.

"It's abominable! it's idiotic! it's absurd!" the Head of the Criminal Department was still muttering savagely two hours later. "Why, tomorrow, I may expect to serve as 'Aunt Sally' for every confounded newspaper fellow short of a joke… Juve shall pay me for this!"—and he banged his fist down savagely on the top of his unoffending desk. Then he went on more mildly:

"And yet, no! I must not quarrel with Juve. He is the only creature who can get me out of the trouble, by giving me a police triumph that will shut the critics' mouths. Ah! if only he could really and truly succeed in recovering the document or in unmasking Fantômas!"

M. Havard punctuated his sentence with a sigh that spoke eloquently of his feelings. Did he indeed expect Juve to succeed? or did he not rather fear but once again Fantômas would be the one to win the grim struggle?

"Well, we shall see tonight what the roundup will yield," the Chief concluded. "If it is successful, I shall at once send a communiqué to the press."

The words were hardly out of his mouth when there came a knock at his door.

"Come in!"—and an usher appeared on the threshold.

"Is Monsieur at liberty? It's someone come from Monsieur Juve."

"From Monsieur Juve? Why! what d'you mean?"

The Chief turned pale with astonishment. Juve, so all the world supposed, had disappeared. Juve was dead in the eyes of all men! He alone, or practically alone, believed, or rather knew, that the famous detective was alive and well, and hard on Fantômas' heels—and now somebody was come to the office from him! M. Havard passed his hand across his brow with the lost look of a man who feels his wits deserting him. What to do? what reply to make Y what decision to come to? A thought flashed across his mind:

"Could it be a trap? Could it be someone Fantômas had sent to find out exactly what I think about Juve's disappearance?"

Anything in fact was possible once the dread name of the Arch-Criminal was involved in the business.

But now the usher was repeating:

"It's someone from M. Juve… or about a letter from M. Juve. I didn't quite understand perhaps, sir!"

"Idiot! Tell him to come in."

M. Havard had reached that state of nervousness in which even the most self-composed characters lose their heads. Meantime, the usher had returned after a momentary absence, and throwing open the door, announced:

"Monsieur Thévenot!"

Once more M. Havard found himself starting involuntarily… What had the unfortunate antiquary come to tell him? Doubtless he was proposing to make complaint of the meager results so far obtained by the police in their investigations. "A nice time to come, truly!" muttered the exasperated Chief, biting his lips with rage. What answer could he give the man? Was not he too entitled to turn the police into derision? He had warned the Department beforehand that Fantômas meant to rob him. Thereupon the Department, to prevent the robbery, had sent him to Juve in person, the most able of its detectives.

And the theft *had* taken place! And not a soul had understood how it had been committed! And Juve, to crown all, had put about the report of his disappearance or death!

"He is going too far, is Juve," it suddenly occurred to M. Havard. "He never thinks of the ridiculous part he makes me play. Whatever am I going to say to my worthy visitor?"

Still M. Havard was too much a man of the world to suffer his feelings to be guessed. The Head of the Criminal Department is never a man that needs instruction in the art of dissimulation. Very politely he greeted the caller:

"What! is it you, dear Monsieur Thévenot? Alas! I have no news to give you yet… But investigations are proceeding…"

He broke off short in his sentence. M. Thévenot had burst out laughing.

"News!" he cried. "But it is I am bringing you news."

"Come now!"

"Certainly I am! And I'm crazy with delight."

"You have recovered the document," panted M. Havard.

"Not yet! No! But, tomorrow…"

"Tomorrow? Tomorrow what?"

"Well, tomorrow we shall recover it."

"Impossible! What makes you think so?"

"Juve does!"

"Juve?"

"Yes, Juve!"

And while the Chief was asking himself what attitude it behooved him to adopt, M. Thévenot continued:

"Juve never really disappeared, never really died! The prince of detectives! A genius!"

"I quite agree with you. He *is* a genius... But I don't understand. You have seen Juve?"

"He has written to me... Yes, here is the pneumatic I have had—not an hour ago."

"Let me see it!" said M. Havard, trembling with excitement. In an instant he had recovered his good humor, his smiling optimism. If Juve was really confident of recovering the stolen paper, what did he care for the Press's caustic comments on the arrest of Maître Nervas' secretary? A mere communiqué of a dozen lines announcing the successful issue of the affair of the stolen document would convert the critics into admirers of the Department's acumen.

"Show me your letter!" M. Havard repeated.

"Here it is..."

As he took the paper the antiquary handed him, M. Havard, from sheer force of habit, practiced one of those professional tricks that never fail to surprise people not accustomed to police methods. Instead of at once reading the missive, the contents of which piqued his curiosity so highly, he turned the letter this way and that between his fingers and carefully examined the writing through a magnifying glass.

"It really comes from Juve, surely?" stammered M. Thévenot, who had turned pale during this lengthy scrutiny.

"Yes, it's from him all right," declared M. Havard. "His hand is too familiar for me to make a mistake,"—and now, without more delay, he read over the letter to himself half aloud. It ran thus:

"I know where the stolen document is hidden. You can recover it without running any danger, for step by step I am tracking down the culprit, who, being the only one who knows the hiding place, will not be so foolish as to go there to surprise you, having me at his heels. You must go therefore to the little house at the top of Montmartre adjoining the tavern of the Green Rabbit. Go down into the cellars, which are in ruins.

Search under a great heap of debris and open… what you will find there. The word is *Genius*. Then inform M. Havard. He will send a communiqué to the Press. I will get to work at once, to attempt an arrest I cannot venture on before, for fear of spoiling everything, and because events I am expecting will make it easier later on. In any case all this is to be done tomorrow towards late afternoon—not before and not after.—JUVE."

"Extraordinary, eh?" observed M. Thévenot as M. Havard finished reading.

"Upsetting, very!" the latter confessed.

And indeed it was! Once more he felt himself to be the sport of the most baffling perplexities. What did it all mean? How came Juve to have written to M. Thévenot instead of communicating with his Chief? And what a strange place to choose for hiding the paper! To leave so precious a document in the cellars of a ruined house open to the first comer, was such a proceeding really worthy of Fantômas? And then, how understand Juve's being cognizant of so many important particulars and never breathing a word at the time of his last visit to police headquarters? But for all the disturbed looks of the antiquary, M. Havard never flinched. Above all things, he must not let his real feelings appear. All he said was:

"Juve is a police officer among a thousand!"

As a matter of fact he was thinking to himself:

"All this is too surprising for anything… If the letter concealed a trap, this is just the way it would run."

Then, correcting himself: "But no!" he added. "If this message were really a ruse, it would be written more artfully, would read more convincingly! When a trick is intended, a man sets about the job more cunningly than this."

Only half surmising the other's doubts, M. Thévenot declared:

"Naturally, I had hardly got the letter before I started off to see you… To begin with, I wanted to be quite certain it really came from Juve. But you have no doubt as to that? "

"Oh! not the least in the world!" M. Havard affirmed stoutly, that being really the very point he was debating with himself.

"Besides, I wanted to ask your advice. I am told I must wait till tomorrow. But I tell you I can hardly hold myself. Don't you think we might act today?"

"Oh, no! not that!"

"Still…"

"No, no! If Juve says tomorrow, we must obey his orders to the letter."

"But… suppose he was mistaken?"

The Chief made the mental correction:

"If we were mistaken? If we were being misled?"

But aloud, he declared emphatically:

"Juve never makes mistakes!"—adding as an afterthought:

"Besides, between now and tomorrow many things may occur to change the aspect of events. Look here, this very evening I may see Juve…"

"You have arranged a meeting with him?" M. Thévenot interrupted with a start of surprise. "You knew where he was, of course?"

"Not a bit of it! I have never set eyes on him since his disappearance…"

"Yet you say that tonight…"

"I may see him. Yes! Because it seems to me to be beyond a doubt he will write to me too; and because, as a matter of fact, he may likely put in an appearance here…"

"Not if he is tracking down the culprit step by step."

"Ah! yes, that's true… But, anyhow, we must wait. About that there can be no doubt,"—and among all the falsehoods the Chief of the Police was unblushingly piling up one on top of the other—was it not his official duty?—this last statement at any rate was the truth, that it surely behooved them to await developments. For had not Juve given it clearly to be understood that he would be present at the roundup he had wished to have organized?

"If he comes, I shall see him in a few hours' time," M. Havard told himself. "Then I shall know what to think of this letter. Till then, I must do nothing; it is the wisest course to take,"—and he proceeded to curb his listener's impatience by dint of a string of consoling phrases and appeals to his sense of logic:

"Come now, Monsieur Thévenot, would you wish, by an ill-advised precipitancy, to compromise a foregone conclusion, a certainty of eventual success? Juve is not the man to speak at random. He writes you: 'Do this tomorrow!' There it is, tomorrow you must do it! 'Not before! not after!' Those are his very words. You cannot but follow his instructions. Four and twenty hours to wait, what! the deuce, that's not long."

"You are quite right. Only..."

"Only?..."

"Only I have another thing to tell you... to confess to you..."

"Speak out, M. Thévenot!"

"Well, this is it... I'm not a bigger coward than other folk. But all the same... in one word... do you think it is wise for me to visit this house all alone, to go down into this ruined cellar, to...?"

M. Havard, in the course of his career, had come across many "brave" men of M. Thévenot's kidney. Without a moment's hesitation he cut in:

"On the contrary, sir, it would be the height of imprudence. It would be a piece, well, almost of madness. Never think I will let you commit such a folly. I will go with you... Or I will go alone, if you prefer it."

"Oh! with you, I shall feel no alarm..."

"Good! then be here tomorrow at four o'clock."

"At four, very good... You don't think it strange for Juve to have actually wanted to send me there by myself?"

"Pooh!... yes, *and* no!... It is possible, you know, Juve may not have wished to associate me with this glory of discovering the paper?... He is a trifle vain."

In saying this, M. Havard was quite gratuitously crediting Juve with a fault that was altogether foreign to his character. He was confusing the detective with himself. Without disputing this innuendo, however, the antiquary held out his hand to the Chief of Police, saying:

"Men are... what they are! Perfection is not of this world. For my part, if I recover my paper, I shall be so grateful to Juve

I would not for the world..."

"Allow yourself to blame him, even for his defects? You are quite right!"

The visitor took his departure for good, while M. Havard, left alone in his room, again manifested evident signs of agitation:

"This beats everything!" he growled. "There are many strange things I might have looked for, but never such a surprise as this! *Is* the letter from Juve?... Or from someone else? From whom in that case? From Fantômas? No, no! Fantômas would surely have deemed it simpler and more adroit to avoid recourse to such a ruse as this."

The Chief might have long continued these dubitations, without ever coming to a definite conclusion, had not his eye suddenly fallen on a table clock standing at one corner of his writing desk.

"Six o'clock!" he exclaimed with a start. "Good Heavens! and I ordered my men to be here at five. They must be tired of waiting. Well, no matter! A man cannot be in two places at once."

His nerves still quivering, he rang his bell.

"Hervé," he ordered the clerk who had hurried in, "tell the Inspectors waiting outside to come in."

"Very good, sir!"

In a very few minutes the Chief's office was invaded by half a score detectives representing the principal agents of the Central Brigade, and thereupon in the tone of a superior officer issuing his orders to his lieutenants, M. Havard began:

"Gentlemen, I have called you together in order to give you the precise instructions necessary for the carrying out of an important roundup you are to execute tonight. I ask for your best attention..."

He made a pause, then proceeded:

"This roundup is to further the investigations instituted by Juve in connection with Fantômas... I need not say more on that head..."

Another pause emphasized the gravity of the situation, and needless to say not one officer present failed to listen with all

his ears when M. Havard resumed: "The scene of the oper-
ations you are to carry out is the goods station and carriage
depot of Vaugirard Point du Jour. The particulars I have been
at the pains to collect and tabulate authorize me to state that
every night the railway coaches parked in this yard serve as
refuges for numbers of vagabonds. Many are harmless; others
are nothing more nor less than dangerous criminals. You will
therefore take care to be armed and ready to defend yourselves… You understand me?"

The approving nods with which the Inspectors greeted this
speech sufficiently reassured their Chief on this point.

"Now for your more particular instructions," he continued.
"You will surround the trains standing there as rapidly as possible. Every individual found in them will be arrested. I would
point out, however, two important details: you will arrest, first
of all, there is every probability, seven vagabonds whose hands
are stained a green color. These seven will be immediately
handcuffed… and searched. Every article found on them will
be handed over to me. I shall be found, during the roundup,
near the signal box… Is this quite understood?"

Another series of affirmative nods showed the Chief that his
meaning was clear and his orders would be obeyed.

"A second most important point," he went on. "Among these
vagrants you are to rouse out there is reason to believe will be
found an individual wearing a white wig, speaking with an
American or English accent, a short man, and humpbacked?
You hear what I say, a humpback? A humpback is easy to
recognize. So I must have no mistakes on this point… This
humpback you must carefully avoid interfering with. Under no
circumstances must he be arrested. Nor yet must you act in
such a way as to give him the impression that you are purposely
leaving him at liberty. The man is being shadowed. You are not
to rouse his suspicions and break the clue. He must be allowed
to escape, but thinking all the while he is being pursued…
Those are the orders!"

M. Havard seemed to be thinking, hesitating to issue a
further order, but finally spoke out:

"A third important point," he announced. "I am not sure, but I think Juve will be on the ground. He has his instructions. You will therefore leave him to do as he pleases, without appearing to recognize him, for it is possible he may be disguised, made up to look like a vagrant himself. At the same time, if it can be done without attracting attention, you will let him know I am at the signal box and that I have urgent and serious reasons for wishing to see him… That is all. You can go. Take proper measures for everything to be carried through in the best possible way. Give your orders accordingly to the constables under your command. You may dismiss, gentlemen!"

One by one the Inspectors took their departure. When the last of them had left the room, M. Havard heaved another sigh.

"How I wish I were four and twenty hours older," he said wistfully. "What will be the result of all this? I seem to be fighting in the dark! With his everlasting discretion, Juve is very wearing to the nerves. I wonder, is he leading me to a prodigious success, or to a lamentable failure?"

…But there the Chief of the Criminal Department was asking himself a question he was compelled by the force of circumstances to leave unanswered!

* * * * *

"Halloa, my bully boys! So every night, I calculate, you doss here on the quiet, eh? in the cars?"

"That's so, Your Majesty!"

"Really now… and you never have a knock-up with the police?"

"Oh, never!… There's no rumpus never made here… We turn in peaceful-like and snores our fill… Yes, the cops just leaves us alone."

"Really… just leave you alone, do they? Curious! very curious!… And you guys, you all know each other, I reckon?… Hi! you there! confound you! The champagne's for the whole crew, I tell you. So pass it along lively, my lad!"

Shouts of laughter and loud applause greeted this speech. Surely never since first the lines of carriages standing in the

Vaugirard sidings had been invaded by a whole tribe of homeless vagabonds, had the place witnessed such a scene of jollity and merrymaking.

About six o'clock that evening, just as each man was climbing into one or another compartment, preparatory to stretching himself on the Company's cushions for a sound night's rest, there had appeared, trotting into their midst, a quaint-looking little old man, with a smooth, round face, long white hair and a hump—such a hump as surely Dame Nature never designed! Dressed decently, but unpretentiously, the unknown—for indeed no one there had ever set eyes on the man before—had clapped his hands and in a queer, squeaky voice and a strong American accent had started haranguing the company:

"Halloa there, mates! Anybody give a hand with the champagne? It's my treat, my beauties!… But it's devilish heavy too… So, I reckon the heftiest of you had best help get the stuff unloaded—to drink to my good health, lads, afterwards."

Seeing it was a question of drinking, and more than that, drinking champagne, the old fellow's audience was quick enough to understand, while the sensation produced by the unlooked-for invitation was prodigious. Nor was it long before the crowd hustling round the little hunchback was more fully informed as to details. Among these homeless wretches, these night prowlers, there happened to be an Interpreter, a former employee of a Tourist Agency, and he lost no time in questioning the newcomer in English: "What might you be wanting, sir?"—and in five minutes the whole crew knew all about the matter. The hunchback was no other than the "King of the Receivers" of whom the whole Paris underworld had been talking for days past.

Reaching Paris by motorcar, and so avoiding inconvenient inquiries on the part of the police, he began by announcing his wish to spend the night in the railway cars like the rest. He made a further announcement, a more notable one still, to the effect that, desirous of celebrating his arrival, he had had a handcart loaded up with bottles of champagne wheeled to the top of the embankment overlooking the railway yard, suggesting at the same time that the wine was there for no other purpose but to be drunk.

At this the general surprise had been succeeded by admiration and gratitude—and before long by intoxication. In fact to unload the bottles in question had taken hardly more time than had been needed to drain them dry. Indeed there were not a few of the drinkers who had had no dinner, nor yet breakfast; so the poor devils had very quickly succumbed to the effects of the liquor.

"Wonderful chaps these Americans!" was the conviction a large proportion of the hunchback's guests gave voice to, while others expressed their astonishment:

"If he's so rich, why don't he put up at an hotel?"

Then all fell silent to listen. An inexhaustible talker, truly, this King of the Receivers—and a stout drinker. All the while he was doing ample honor to his own good wine, passing from group to group, always laughing and chattering in his queer voice:

"So much for those dead men; there'll be more of the same tomorrow!" he promised, pointing to the empty bottles that strewed the ground. "Plenty others! Every night, if you like. I pay! I'm a King, and I pay royally. My business is gigantic, worldwide!"

Then he danced a jig, before starting afresh:

"The police? Oh! they never catch me—never, I calculate! Slip through the net, I do, every time!"

Presently, under the genial influence of the champagne, the most agreeable confidence began to reign even among those who just at first had received the hunchback with frowning looks. After all, this King of the Receivers, was he not famous as a great criminal, one of the brotherhood of lawbreakers who are past masters in wickedness and whose names enjoy something almost like veneration?

"Seems as how every mortal thing you offer him, he'll buy," men were whispering to each other in dark corners, gathered in unsteady, staggering groups. "Stolen bonds nobody else would look at, *he* takes 'em. Jewels you could never 'dip,' *he* mops 'em up… Why, no! not without his percent, of course! But rather than lose everything, a cove must hand over a bit,"—and before long the hunchback was surrounded by a mob of ill-looking scoundrels, squeezing and shoving, watching his face, seeking for a chance to speak to him apart.

The truth is, the unhappy beings who live by thieving are well aware that the word danger involved in their dismal trade does not reside in the thievery itself. To rob is comparatively easy—but to profit by the robbery, to sell the stolen property, to "dip" the piece of jewelry, the bond of which the police have a description, the banknote the number of which is known, there's where the risk comes in! And they know it too, the receivers, the "fences," who habitually exploit the light-fingered crew's fears. They offer so little, so very little, when the "stuff" is difficult to handle.

"But that chap's the King of 'em, so they say… Show him what you choose, he'll bid you a price. Yes, and he's from America into the bargain. He knows a trick or two! Once a thing's gone through his hands, seems he can sell it back to the bloke as owned it before you pinched it! The beggar won't know his own, he won't!"

…However, by half-past eleven no more drinking was going on in the railway yard and no one was left to warrant the peculiar dexterity of the King of the Receivers. For this there were excellent reasons—the bottles were all empty and the habitués of the place were dead drunk.

But, by themselves in a first-class carriage, a half score individuals were still talking, surrounding the King of the Receivers. Oh! *these* were not drunk, nor even merry! Grim-faced ruffians, with the downcast eye of the habitual criminal, men always ready for deeds of blood! In fact, among all these poor wretches who spent their nights in these improvised shelters, these men, who had scarcely tasted the gratuitous champagne, represented Crime at bay. Doubtless they could all, or almost all, have afforded themselves the luxury of a room in a lodging-house. But the police keep an eye on such places; the proprietors are often secretly in the pay of the officers of justice.

Wherefore they prefer chance quarters for the night, whence escape is easy, if they have to fly to escape jail or the scaffold.

All now, in low voices, each man distrustful of his neighbor, were for drawing the King of the Receivers on one side to make him offers such as these:

"See here, Your Majesty, I have some good stuff, diamonds… Is that in your line?"

"Your Majesty, a gold watch or so, would you care to buy now and again?"

"Now, silver plate, heavy metal, would that suit you, eh?"

Meanwhile, the "King," notebook in hand, was nodding an approving and benevolent head.

"Capital! capital! dear boys! Of course, I say yes. But I'd have to see the stuff first, please!"—and he proceeded to jot down with a nimble pencil the various rendezvous suggested and agreed to in divers shady haunts of which they gave him the addresses.

A King indeed this American "fence." Merely by the way he listened to the offers made him, they could see he was both wary and open-hearted, managing matters frankly and freely, looking after his own interests of course, but quite realizing a man of business must be reasonable. No, it was not in the French "fences" to behave so honestly and act so quickly, with such a scorn of consequences, such a fine contempt for the police. Enthusiasm grew by leaps and bounds.

Then suddenly, in an instant, came the catastrophe, the hideous catastrophe that was only too common. A shrill whistle sounded; hurried footsteps indicated an encircling movement. On all sides acetylene torches flared up.

"A police raid! a roundup!" howled the terror-stricken crowd. In the "King's" compartment a wild panic broke out.

"Caught, by God!" the fellows swore savagely, their faces contorted with rage, "we're surrounded, hemmed in, done for!"

"And the King," grinned one of the ruffians, who had turned pale as death, "it's all up with him, like the rest of us… In five minutes his goose is cooked!"

"Really! Why! no, I don't think so!… But one can never be

sure. Here, take the things—a little present for each of you! Not worth while keeping 'em, if the French policemen are to clap their hands on my collar!"

One and all stood rooted to the spot in amazement… An extraordinary fellow, this King of the Fences! The danger was instant, imminent—yet the man's coolness remained entirely undisturbed. He was explaining:

"All the lot won't be taken, *I* calculate. So, for those who aren't, I've got something good… See here! I open my strongbox."

A laugh—and the most utterly unexpected movement rounded off the sentence. The old fellow was actually opening his hump!—which was a fake, and served him for a strongbox. And no less strange the article he drew from this hiding place, to wit a bottle full of green paint, sticky green paint.

"Stand back, you!" he ordered, "and then pick up your presents; and then go!"

This time no interpreter was needed to expound His Majesty's intentions! With a swift, decisive gesture the King of the Receivers dashed to the carriage floor the bottle he had taken from his hump. It broke into a thousand fragments, showing mixed with the paint it had contained a treasure of incalculable price. Higgledy-piggledy, in the mess, could be seen diamonds, rubies, emeralds.

But why, why, a bottle of paint as casket for these fabulously costly jewels? Only the King of the Receivers could have answered the question… and Juve too, perhaps. But it was no time for elaborate explanations. Juve was not there, and, to make up, the constables were coming nearer and nearer.

These, formed up in four straight lines, had started from the four sides of the railway yard, and were now all moving on the center, the crowd of vagabonds, caught in this human dragnet, flying in confusion before them.

"Quick, my lads!" growled the King of the Receivers, "quick, each take one, I tell you—and I wish you luck!"

With an activity hardly to have been expected of a man of his age, the American had slipped outside while his companions were still tumbling over one another on the floor, each eager to outdo his neighbor in picking up out of the splash of paint the jewels the "King" was leaving behind with the evident intention of not being found with them in his possession.

A criminal, for sure, of high gifts and much experience, a man trained never to lose his head even in the most disastrous circumstances. Very little perturbed, it seemed, by the loss of his treasure, he was no sooner outside the carriage than he began to scrutinize with a wary eye the tumultuous scene enacting on every side.

The lines of police were on the point of coming together. One of them, moving alongside the train, was visiting each separate compartment and turning out the occupants. And now the constables were stooping, searching underneath the carriages for anybody trying to hide there.

"Always the way!" muttered the King of the Receivers to himself, "both sides, inside and underneath—but never on top!"

Then, deliberately, but active as ever—was he really as old a man as he looked?—he sprang onto a buffer, grasped the tube of the pneumatic brake and so hoisted himself onto the roof of a luggage van, where he lay flat on his stomach, motionless and unseen by the police officers.

"No!" he repeated, "never on top! They never look on top!"

Ten minutes afterwards, in fact, the constables were past his hiding place, and he was free to scramble down to the ground and under cover of the darkness worm his way out of the trap.

"A dangerous villain!" M. Havard was saying to himself at almost the same moment in the signal box where he had installed his temporary headquarters, as Inspector Theo hurried up to report the first results of the raid.

"A great success, sir!" announced that vigilant officer. "A hundred and eighty captured!… The seven fellows stained with paint are being searched at this moment…"

"And the King of the Receivers?"

"No, *he's* not among the prisoners—never been seen even!… But he was there, all the same, not a doubt of that… The seven green paint chaps declare with one voice their jewels were given them by him…"

"Their jewels? What do you mean?"

"What! sir, you don't know? And I who supposed this roundup was for no other purpose except to recover these stones and pearls…"

"But what stones? What pearls? Do, please, explain."

"Fact is, sir, I know scarcely any more about… on each of the villains they found pearls, diamonds and… but look there, sir, what Henri is bringing you."

M. Havard stared in bewilderment. The fact is he was entirely ignorant of the reason why Juve had asked him to secure the special arrest of seven individuals "stained with paint" in the roundup he wished carried out. Not once, however, had the great man made the smallest allusion to precious stones or pearls. "So another mystery was on foot?" he asked himself, as more and more nonplussed, he looked at Inspector Henri, who having finished searching his prisoners, was bringing the jewels he had found on them to his Chief. Mechanically almost he asked:

"And Juve? Has anyone seen him? Has he been given my message?"

"Nobody has seen him yet, sir!"

"So much the worse! And those fellows marked with paint, do you know them, Theo? Are they a good catch?"

"Oh! a very good one, sir! They are all dangerous characters. Most of them are wanted at this moment for crimes of violence or robberies… In any case…"

"In any case what? Say what you've got to say."

"Well, sir, it's an extraordinary thing, but they are the only really dangerous prisoners captured in the roundup. The rest are poor harmless devils, vagrants. But it looks as if all the fellows with green paint on their fingers are a fine haul."

"Oh!" said M. Havard, and did not venture to add another word. He was by no means so naive as not to guess this was no result of mere chance. On the contrary, he clearly understood that Juve had foreseen eventualities and that if he had advised the arrest of the seven delinquents in question, it was for the very reason that he was well aware the capture of these seven was of importance. Only, having guessed this much, M. Havard was puzzled to the last degree with the absorbing question how Juve had come by his information. Was it, he pondered, because the detective had kept so close a watch on the King of the Receivers that he knew perfectly well in what company he would be found?

"Strange! mighty strange!" the Chief thought to himself. "So it seems the message to M. Thévenot was correct in every particular. Was Juve actually tracking down the delinquent step by step? Could the King of the Receivers be the delinquent in question? But no, surely not!… Was it not rather Fantômas?"

The Head of the Criminal Department shook his head in mingled mortification and bewilderment. With that confounded Juve a man always felt as if he were fighting in the dark, the victim of willful mystification—and then, when he did condescend to explain what was happening, you had to confess it was all perfectly simple and a moment's thought would have enabled you to guess the solution of the most involved problems…"

"Tut, tut! Damn it all!" M. Havard ended aloud, a very angry man surely to give way to such an explosion of temper. "Give me the jewels!"

"Here they are, sir!"

"Thank you. How many are there?"

"Seven, sir! Each of the scoundrels had one."

"Good! very good!… But… but… I'm not going crazy, am? I'm not dreaming? It's not a nightmare?"—and M. Havard began turning over and over in his hand the precious stones the Inspector had just handed him.

"What is it now, sir?" asked Theo respectfully.

"What is it? what is it?" cried the Chief. "Why, it's this— something that beats everything… These stones are shams! Those pearls are imitations—and poor ones at that!"

"But, sir, it isn't possible!"

"Really? Well, look…"—and M. Havard, with a disdainful gesture, pitched down on the asphalt floor of the signal box one of the pearls found in the possession of the rascally recipients of the "King's" generosity. Then he raised his foot quickly and stamped on the pearl.

"There!" he cried, removing his foot.

The pearl was smashed into a thousand pieces. The test was decisive. A real pearl does not break; a sham one is shivered to bits with the greatest ease.

"Upon my soul!" exclaimed Theo, "it's the first time ever I've seen such a thing—thieves carrying 'bogus' stuff on them… Hmm! it's enough to drive one daft!"

"You're quite right!" approved M. Havard succinctly. "Fact is, *I'm* going crazy too, I think. Good night to you!"—and pulling up the collar of his greatcoat with an angry jerk, the Chief, visibly put out, took his departure.

…He little suspected that he would have been still more surprised had he chanced to be present at a brief scene occurring but a short way off at Javel, at the tavern of the "Ami Ralle"!

*　　*　　*　　*　　*

As the roundup proceeded, ruthlessly sweeping in all the poor wretches who every night came to seek shelter in the railway carriages at the Vaugirard yard, the King of the Receivers had never for a moment lost his cool self-possession. Calm, as every good Yankee boasts to be in face of danger, he had found a way to outwit the police and leave the yard without so much as being seen. Once safe outside, this Royalty of a new sort gave vent to a little laugh of amusement, then whistling between his teeth an American marching song, slipped away in the darkness, as unconcerned as if he had not just escaped arrest, under circumstances obviously threatening serious consequences.

A man of resource, this King of the Fences! a fellow with more than one card up his sleeve to play! Nor was this the first time he had been in Paris, for he lost not a moment in picking up his bearings, like one perfectly well aware of where he is and where he is going. Making a shortcut, he reached the riverside and followed the quays as far as Javel, which he reached not half an hour after his escape from M. Havard's men. Once there, he made straight for the "Ami Ralle," the same shady tavern where Fandor had spent such an eventful time.

"Best respects to the company!" he greeted the half dozen customers he found inside, a broad smile lighting up his round face. "More by token, I warn you not to go Vaugirard way. I tell you straight, the cops are there."

Then he gave his order: "A quencher, landlord! I've got a damned thirst on me!"—and subsiding in a corner without seeming to take any notice of the attention he roused, he sat down quietly to his drink…

At the time five or six customers were seated at the table playing an interminable game of cards, while apart by himself, lost in thought, a tall, thin man, with flaming eyes, seemed to be waiting. He never looked at the newcomer, nor did the latter look at him.

After some time, more customers burst in, red with running and quaking with fear. The fact is, no matter how well a police raid is organized, there are always some of the criminals who slip through the net. These were of the number, and they began forthwith to tell their story.

"We'd been drinking champagne… yes, champagne!… The King of the Receivers—oh! a toff, you bet your life!—treated us… What ho! and the cops are upon us!… Of course, there's a stampede—naught else to be done! The scores o' chaps them police gentry mopped up!… But look, that's not the rummiest go… Before he hooked it, the King, he'd shared out a whole treasure of pearls and stones among the boys—so's not to be nabbed with the stuff on him… Well, seems as how the pearls are all 'bogus,' and the stones ditto!"

The tale created a prodigious sensation. In his corner the man with the eyes of fire started violently, and pulled down his soft hat over his brow so as to hide his eager glances.

"Anybody as can twig the game has only got to speak!" the narrator concluded. "I say we did ought to tell Fantômas. If the King is a traitor playing us false, he mustn't be let carry on his tricks no further."

But a fresh surprise now stirred the company to still more breathless amazement.

At that moment, red with fury, stammering with passion, his round face distorted with a look of hate, the King of the Receivers had left his corner and leapt into the middle of the room.

"And *I* say, by your leave, I say it's a pack of lies! I swear the stones and the pearls were good, and I defy any man to prove the contrary. If policeman Havard says those jewels were sham, *I* tell you they were real! Look you here, here's more of them. By your leave, are *they* true or false?"

He held out the diamonds. They were taken and passed from hand to hand. No, no possibility of doubt! *they* were genuine and represented a small fortune.

"And I tell you straight the others were the same... But I won't be accused like this! I won't be called a traitor, I won't! And I laugh at Fantômas!"

Quite honestly, meantime—there is "honor among thieves," for they know the smallest trickery would be punished by death—the diamonds were restored to their owner.

"Yes!" the old man was now bawling, "yes, I laugh at Fantômas... I'm ready to meet him face to face... I'll write to him, too, if I so choose."

A chorus of guffaws broke out.

"Write to him? Write where? What! d'you suppose we have his address?"

"But *I* have it, anyway!"

"Bah! Let's have a look at it!"

But the King of the Receivers shrugged his shoulders.

"If Fantômas, by your leave, don't tell you where he lives, why, neither will I, that's flat... Fantômas is a great genius and I am a king—and we're not going to get in one another's road, I calculate. So there!"

Very swiftly the moods of this strange man succeeded one another. A moment before he seemed boiling with rage—now he was smiling again.

"Really and truly now," he asseverated, "I'm going to write to him, and I shall see him tomorrow. There, I've said it and I mean it. Now I reckon I want paper, a stamp, ink."

They looked at him in amazement. Was he actually going to write to Fantômas? Did he really know the way to get a letter into the hands of the Lord of Terror?

But, entirely unconcerned, he sat down at a table and in a big American hand wrote two or three short sentences, signed the letter, and then directed an envelope. Was he acting a part? or was it all genuine? The others would have given a good deal to know. But, without paying the smallest heed to their inquisitive looks, the old man sealed up his envelope and slipped it into his coat pocket. Then:

"Listen to me!" he said gravely. "I say this, by your leave, to all of you—tomorrow morning I shall send my letter, by special delivery—'pneumatic,' you call it, I reckon. And tomorrow afternoon, I'm going to see Fantômas. And tomorrow night, I'm coming back with him here to drink champagne—and I invite you all… And now, I'm going to sleep. One can sleep here?"

A nod answered his question in the affirmative. Certainly you could sleep in the place; all you had to do was to lie down on one of the benches. But surely, was he not guilty of the rashest imprudence, this King of Receivers, who carried, and the others knew it, genuine diamonds on his person, who gave out he had put Fantômas' address on the envelope that lay there in his pocket, in calmly going off to sleep in this sinister tavern of the "Ami Ralle"? He lay down there and then and shut his eyes, but sleep apparently refused to come. Three times he got up again, then presently his face relaxed, his breathing grew regular, he was asleep—and no one seemed to be paying any more attention to him.

Suddenly a shiver, a general shudder of horror, ran through the night prowlers and vagabond wretches assembled in the tavern room. From the deep shadow, where the man with the blazing eyes had been sitting, a strange, appalling figure had appeared. All knew it instantly, asking themselves in panic terror when it had glided in and from where. It was a tall man, of slim and supple build… A man? Nay! a shape of horror familiar to all as the embodiment of terror and the theme of blood-curdling legend!

Shod in black—shoes with triple soles of felt, gloved in black, it wore floating over the face, hiding the features, a sort of mask or hood, pierced with two holes through which gleamed the hard, cruel eyes. The whole body was straitly molded in the silk of close-fitting black tights.

Hushed voices, quivering with anguished dread, muttered in trembling tones:

"Fantômas! It is Fantômas!"

The grim Lord of Terror lifted his hand, and all fell silent. Only the panting of quick-drawn breaths was heard. He took another step forward. In his hand was a long stick, one end armed with a wad of cotton-wool that looked damp.

Then the wretches gathered at the "Ami Ralle" saw Fantômas slowly raise his arm and apply the wad of cotton-wool to the sleeping man's nostrils.

"Is he killing him?" quavered a voice. Then the grim silence fell again.

Asleep as he was, the King of the Receivers seemed to make an effort to avert his face, but he cannot have had time. His breath, quickened at first, slowed down. A livid pallor over-spread his features.

"Fast asleep!" announced Fantômas. "It's what I wanted,"—and he gave a short, scornful laugh. Putting down his stick, he stepped up to the American, who lay insensible, evidently over-come by some powerful soporific.

"The letter?" Fantômas spoke again. "Now for this letter he professes to send me!"—and with the words, he searched the pocket in which the King of the Receivers had secreted his missive.

"Yes, that's it!" exclaimed the brigand, examining the address. "A remarkable man truly! How comes he to know?"

Deliberately, with the cool composure of a master who knows himself equally admired and feared, he crossed the room to the big urn in which the coffee, ever ready day and night, was boiling.

"Must make sure what it is he wants with me," he observed,

and taking the letter between two fingers, he held it to the steam
issuing from the open percolator, till the envelope came open.

"Yes, it's just what I thought!" he said, when he had read the
brief message, and refolding the paper, he slipped it back in its
envelope and closed the latter. Not one of his movements was
lost on those about him, who one and all seemed spellbound
by his presence. Quietly stepping back to the sleeper's side, he
returned to his pocket the letter the contents of which he had
surreptitiously mastered. Then turning about, he waved his
hand for silence and spoke:

"Now, all of you, you are to go. This man is under my pro-
tection and I shall see to him tonight… Here are my orders for
tomorrow: you will all meet at Robinson, about two o'clock.
You will come two at a time, discreetly, without attracting attention. You will proceed to the restaurant of the 'Red Chestnut.'… Yes, the place where I stole the antiquary, M. Thévenot's,
document… You will drink in moderation. Anyone getting
tipsy I shall punish…"

Fantômas paused, as if to give more weight to his words.
But this was needless. All present were members of his gang,
and were his accomplices, and all knew what ruthless severi-
ty he showed when he meant to punish his subordinates. He
resumed:

"You will be there, and I shall join you. Perhaps I shall want
your help. In any case, while waiting for me, you will notice
all the loiterers you may see. If you guess the police are among
them, if you recognize any officers of the law, you will take care
not to smoke. If, on the other hand, you have noticed nothing
suspicious, you will light cigarette after cigarette. A simple
enough signal, eh?… You understand me?"

At this moment—a note of tragic irony!—the criminal,
issuing his orders to his accomplices, vividly recalled M.
Havard giving his instructions to his police officers.

"Very well!" he concluded, "I see you understand. Now as
always, the man who serves me well will be well rewarded. Now
you can go. I wish to be alone here."

He was promptly obeyed; while the King of the Receivers

was tossing feebly on his bench, struggling no doubt against the effects of the soporific he had inhaled, the tavern emptied rapidly. The only two left in the room were the sleeping man and, motionless in a corner, Fantômas, who had resumed his previous aspect, that of a vagrant, with blazing eyes.

The night passed peacefully, marked by no incident of any kind. Once or twice the sleeper turned on his bench like a man seeking a more comfortable posture, but Fantômas sat rigorously still, never moving a muscle.

At last it was dawn; at last heavy footsteps sounded on the pavement, footsteps of workmen and laborers making for the neighboring factories at the summons of sirens and hooters calling them to their daily toil. Soon the landlord of the "Ami Ralle" appeared yawning and proceeded to take down his shutters with the nerveless movements of a man still more than half asleep. Then Fantômas took his departure, without a word. Three minutes more and a group of mechanics, little suspecting the sinister nature of the tavern they had lighted on, came in to drink their "morning" of white wine. It was the awakening of Paris and her working population.

The King of the Receivers sat up on his bench with a cheerful: "Well, here we are!" Then, with parted fingers to serve as a comb he arranged his long white locks. Then, after swallowing a cup of black coffee boiling hot, he too left the place. Deliberately, like a man remembering an important duty, he made for a neighboring post office and slipped the envelope Fantômas had unfastened into the "pneumatic" box. As he went he never looked round or took any of the precautions men adopt who wish to keep concealed. He appeared absolutely unperturbed. Yet, had he no recollection of what had occurred the night before? Had he no suspicion, even the vaguest, of having been put to sleep by means of a drug?

Some way behind a man followed on his track, but presently remarked to himself:

"If he was afraid, he would turn round from time to time; if he thought anything was amiss, he could not be so entirely unconcerned. No, no! I am getting over-suspicious!"—and the man stopped dead, wheeled about, retraced his steps and dis-appeared in the direction of Grenelle.

The man was Fantômas! Now, at that same moment the King of the Receivers was sauntering at a leisurely pace along the quays, admiring apparently the splendor of the first beams of the rising sun reflected by the rippling surface of the river. Yes! he seemed perfectly calm, this American stranger! Yet a very tempest was raging within him, a whirlwind of thought.

"Ah, well!" he was thinking, "why should I hesitate? Yes, the first thing to do is to return the diamonds to the jeweler who lent me them… I don't care to expose them to any further risks."

He gave a short laugh, then resumed his self-communing:

"Poor fellow! What retrospective terror he would experience if I let him know how his diamonds passed through the hands of some of Fantômas' most formidable accomplices!… if I con-fessed how I slept in the most abominable of thieves' kitchens, with his gems in my pocket all the time!"

His Majesty broke into another laugh, then proceeded with his soliloquy:

"But there, I do wrong to mock at other men's fears. I have not shown so much bravery myself so far… When I gathered they meant to drug me asleep, when I guessed Fantômas was holding a soporific under my nose, I admit my courage failed me, and I asked myself if I should ever awake."

Surrendering himself to the sentiments these reflections roused in him, the King of the Receivers gave a shrug, criticiz-ing his own behavior apparently:

"To be afraid, well, that's no disgrace, after all. What *is* dis-graceful is to lose one's head and spoil the whole thing!… And that I did not do! Yes! I can fairly say that much of myself. When I knew I was inhaling a drug, I told myself, 'if you are recognized, friend Juve, you're a dead man,' and yet I never moved!…"

Juve?… The American then was Juve?…

The King of the Receivers, for it was indeed Juve who since the day before had worn the personality of that Monarch, continued his self-examination:

"True, I passed a bad quarter of an hour—but that's all! Besides, I had no choice of means. Cost what it might, I was bound to win their confidence. I was bound, by my way of acting, to make it believed I was actually the King of the Receivers… To have thrown myself at Fantômas' throat, one man against many, in the midst of his henchmen, would have been simply silly. I should have got myself killed, and nothing gained. He would have escaped, without my even succeeding in getting Thévenot's redoubtable paper out of his hands… No, no! I did well to try the ruse. I have not lost my night. Havard will be pleased—later on!…"

Surely at such a moment Juve might well have been puffed up with inordinate pride. The night he had spent in that thieves' den, the "Ami Ralle," within two yards of Fantômas, his mortal enemy, letting himself be put to sleep, losing consciousness, knowing well the risk he ran, was it not an exploit worthy of all admiration, one of those acts of courage that take away one's breath with amazement at their intrepid daring.

Instead, he was asking himself simply:

"And the trick of the sham pearls? Well, anyhow, there's seven fine blackguards I've got arrested without striking a blow. It was a sure thing, indeed, that, by posing as the King of the Fences, I should collect round me all the gentry who had a something on their conscience. Yes, that was inevitable… But will Havard have gathered what the game was, I wonder. The imitation pearls in particular must have puzzled him… But, hang it! I couldn't well go throwing about real jewels. I was not sure enough about arresting my men for that. It was quite enough to have real gems in my pocket…"—and the worthy man chuckled. A hero of unparalleled modesty, what caught his imagination was the amusing side of his exploits.

"And Fandor?" he exclaimed suddenly. "How he must be cursing down at the Depot! Fact is, he would never have left me a free hand, if he had been at liberty."

Fully convinced that his young friend was still in custody, Juve went on:

"Yes, he would be wanting to dog me again this afternoon…"

But at the thought suggested by the words, the police officer grew serious again.

"Ah!" he muttered in a hard voice, "this afternoon, yes, what will be happening this afternoon? Will Fantômas come as agreed upon? Shall I succeed in wresting Thévenot's document from him? In a word, shall I be able to arrest the monstrous villain?… What has he been doing, arranging, preparing while I lay asleep, unconscious, under the influence of his dope?"

For a moment the detective was lost in thought. Then he spoke his final word, expressive of his firm resolve to do and dare, to face every risk: "Ah, well! we shall see! we shall see!"— and confident he was no longer being followed, in haste to arrive at the grim crisis that still lay before him, he redoubled his pace.

9. The Last Word

The smoke of many cigarettes floated up to the cloudless summer sky. The order given by their dreaded master to the wretches who were Fantômas' familiar spirits, his vile accomplices, had been faithfully obeyed. Ever since one o'clock of the afternoon, by tram, by train, two by two, or three by three, the scoundrels whose task was to secure that Arch-Criminal's safety had been arriving at Robinson. Passing through the picturesque little domain, one after the other they entered the restaurant of the "Red Chestnut," and sat down to drink, like any other peaceable citizens, come out to enjoy the air and naturally entirely unacquainted with one another.

Yet all were there for one and the same purpose. Fantômas had instructed his men to spy out the land, make sure no body of police was massed there, that no detective, so far as could be seen, was there in ambush. It was agreed that in the case of any suspicious interloper being present, no one must smoke, but on the other hand cigarette was to succeed cigarette without intermission between each watcher's lips. Now, having found the latter to be the state of things, all the frequenters of the "Ami Ralle" gathered at the suburban resort were puffing smokes, each harder than the other.

But were they all quite so much at ease as appeared? As a matter of fact, the different groups had for the last few minutes been exchanging furtive looks of anxiety. Two o'clock had struck, and no Fantômas had appeared. The master, as a rule—and they all knew it—was punctual to the instant. How came it then that this time he was not at the "Red Chestnut" at the appointed hour? Knowing nothing of their commander's designs—he never admitted his subordinates into the secret of his plans—Fantômas' emissaries were tortured by a gnawing suspense that increased from minute to minute.

"Mighty queer!" growled one of them. "There's something not just straight going on!… He should be here by now!"—and the sentiment was echoed by all his fellows.

Under its artfully contrived aspect of rusticity externally, the "Red Chestnut" is quite a luxuriously appointed resort. From time to time sumptuous motorcars drove up to the door, while fashionable women, prettily dressed children and young men in sporting kit were sipping tea within.

"Say, old man, I don't feel comfortable-like among all them toffs," one of the most forbidding-looking of Fantômas' henchmen confided to his neighbor. "Sure, the master must have been 'dingo' to send us here!"

But his remark got no answer. The comrade addressed, starting up in sudden amazement, had held up his hand enjoining silence. In the courtyard a superb car, a thirty horsepower of a good make, had stopped. From it, yellow gaitered, immaculate gloves on his hands, elegantly dressed, evidently by a good tailor, his hat under his arm allowing the wind to play with his white locks, a man had alighted—a man at whom the ill-omened band stared dazed with astonishment.

"No doubt of it!" they cried. "It is he! it is the King of the Fences! it's the queer customer of last night."

But great as was the general astonishment to see the metamorphosis, the radical transformation of the individual who yesterday looked like a poor ragamuffin and today showed as the most elegant of gentlemen, this astonishment would surely have changed to deep alarm, to panic terror, if, by any chance, they could have guessed that this King of the Receivers was in very truth no other than Juve.

Meantime the great police officer was playing his part with supreme art and supreme nonchalance. Well he knew he was there to meet Fantômas; he knew that a few seconds at most separated him from the moment of the most dreadful, the most desperate encounter. And yet, calm and collected, he was issuing orders to his chauffeur, as phlegmatic as ever. Was he not bound, indeed, to wear an aspect of perfect confidence? Was he not bound, up to the very last moment, to embody in the eyes of Fantômas the personality of this King of the Receivers, who was to earn him—he had no doubt about the matter—the most brilliant of all his victories? He was thinking:

"The trap is ready. Fantômas will tumble into it… I will have it so—and so it must be! A little coolness, and the man is mine!"

With one glance of his quick eye, meantime, Juve had already scanned the assembled company.

"Yes, all the men of the 'Ami Ralle' are here," he said to himself. "So be it! it is a sign he is suspicious. Well, what matter? I hold him in my hand!"

With a curt nod he dismissed his chauffeur, who could not know who he was and little suspected he was in the midst of a grim tragedy. Then he took three steps forward.

"Ought I to show that I recognize the wretches?" he now asked himself. "But no! it would be unwise. Time enough presently,"—and he advanced another three steps with the air of a customer looking for a table to suit him.

Suddenly he began to smile.

"Ah! my dear sir!" he cried.

A dozen yards away he had caught sight of the antiquary, M. Thévenot, and walked straight to where he sat.

"I am late?" he asked politely.

The antiquary rose. Seeing Juve was to meet Fantômas, surely this man Thévenot once again fell under suspicion of being Fantômas? If it had not been so, he would never have accosted him. But the police officer was smiling amiably, while Thévenot for his part appeared greatly astonished.

"I am making no mistake?" he stammered. "You are really…"

"Precisely! The King of the Receivers! Yes, I am he!" declared Juve, "and very glad I am to find you… We can talk here, I reckon?"

"No!" replied Thévenot, "don't let us stay here… I received your letter, sir… and I know who

you are… and I must tell you you are making a mistake…"

"Really? How so?"

"I am not the person you suppose!" asseverated M. Thévenot. "You take me for… for… for Fantômas…"

"You are Fantômas!" said Juve.

"No, no!… God, no! Juve thought so too. But Juve has recognized his mistake… and I have come to meet you here…"

"Exactly so, my dear sir," interrupted the other, still playing his part with consummate art," that's so, I calculate, exactly as you said, we had best go where we can talk in private. You take me?"

"Certainly!… Come with me. Have no fear—I have not notified the police…"

"Oh! I know that," declared Juve. "I am with you, sir. Lead the way,"—and he followed M. Thévenot, his blood positively boiling in his veins. He was sure, convinced the man was really and truly Fantômas. True, the fellow denied it. But then, he was well capable of piling lie on lie with shameless effrontery. To unmask the villain would not be difficult, now.

"This way!" the antiquary invited his companion. "In the kiosk we can talk comfortably."

"True for you!" chimed in Juve. "I am quite of the same way of thinking."

It was the same airy kiosk where the incomprehensible theft had been committed. Juve made as though he had no smallest suspicion of the fact. Truly, the moment was one calling for all his talent as an actor!

No sooner inside the narrow cabin, halfway up a great tree, than M. Thévenot sat down and proceeded:

"I received your 'pneumatic' this morning, sir. You wrote to me in set terms that being the 'King of the Receivers' you desired to enter into communication with me for the purchase of the stolen document… From this, I repeat, I guessed you imagined I was Fantômas… Well, the thing's monstrous! I confess, at first, I thought of informing the police… Then, I chose rather to come and meet you… I am not Fantômas!"

"You are!" Juve said coldly. "I know you are."

"But it is not true! What makes you think so?"

"You ask that? Well, I understand how you stole the paper…"

"Come, come! I swear."

"No need! I am going to tell you how."

Juve could feel his heart thumping in his breast, but no trace of hesitation troubled him. With his marvelous insight he read the thoughts of the other like an open book. M. Thévenot was indeed Fantômas. But before making any definite move, before offering to the man he supposed to be a receiver of stolen goods, the document he no doubt carried on his person, he wished to be certain he was not falling into a trap.

He wanted proofs. Well, he must be convinced by proofs that he was unmasked and that to deny would avail him nothing.

"Yes, I am going to tell you exactly how," Juve repeated. "See here, you were alone, Juve and you, in the kiosk, and nobody could come near, either from above or below, either from right or left, or from any direction whatever. That was so, was it not?"

"Why, yes!… But…"

"Wait a moment!… Then came the theft. And nobody had come in or gone out. That is correct too, I calculate."

"I deny it."

"Very good! And Juve was not the thief. It follows, I reckon, seeing it was not Juve, and there was only he and you, it must have been you!"

"But what could I have done with the document?"

"Oh! quite simple, again," Juve declared. "See here, you took the paper, and in the struggle with Juve, you slipped it into his own pocket. Then it was quite OK for you! They might search your clothes; of course there was nothing to be found there! They might search the kiosk; again of course there was nothing to be found… And then Juve, baffled, came out and apologized to you. Oh! Juve had no notion he had the paper in his pocket, and that it was he himself was given the job by you to convey it out of the kiosk. Come, you can see for yourself I guessed right, eh? You hid it in Juve's pocket and retrieved it again from his pocket, after he went out."

The antiquary shrugged his shoulders, then made further protest:

"With what object, I ask you, should I have done that? If what you allege is true, it would follow I was robbing myself. After all, we must be logical; this paper you accuse me of having put in Juve's pocket, for him to carry it out of the kiosk and for me to steal it back again from him afterwards, this paper belonged to me."

"Perfectly true!"

"Then where did *my* interest come in?"

"Oh! I'm not quite a fool!… And the insurance, my dear man?"—and the self-styled King of the Receivers threw himself back in his chair to have his laugh out, then he observed:

"I say again—the paper was valueless. The whole thing was a very cunning swindle devised by you. You were to insure the document for a heavy sum… then you were to steal it… and then you were to be paid the insurance money. But I offer you an alternative scheme. To get payment of the insurance is a risky job. Therefore I say: I will buy the paper from you, and *I* will claim instead of you. Now, what's your price?"

Juve remained absolutely self-composed, imitating with rare success the American accent and queer voice of the foreigner he was supposed to be.

M. Thévenot, however, sat unmoved. He was thinking things out. Suddenly, he shifted his position, laid his right hand on the table that divided him from Juve and seemed absorbed in the contemplation of the wristwatch he wore.

"There is the paper," he said.

With his left hand he had searched his clothes and from a secret pocket had drawn forth the document.

Juve broke into renewed laughter. For once he really needed a few seconds' respite to mask his agitation and recover his self-control.

So he had not been mistaken? So this man Thévenot, whom no one had dreamed of suspecting, was really the dread Fantômas, the author of the audacious theft? So he, Juve, had guessed exactly how this vile criminal of genius had contrived to carry out a robbery that all men deemed impossible, inconceivable?

And then—thought travels fast—he reflected.

"He is surrendering, confessing! Then he is convinced I am really the King of the Receivers… I have nothing else to do but arrest him! "But at the same moment he was deciding to clap the handcuffs on the Arch-Criminal, Juve felt an agonizing doubt growing on him. Fantômas had called together his accomplices to defend him. Juve, on his side, rather than risk giving the delinquent warning of his danger, had not brought one single colleague with him. Not a policeman was within hail! Not a soul would come to his help when the decisive hour struck.

He bent over to look out. Through the window he could see children playing under the trees, harmless promenaders conversing cheerfully together. To what peril he was going to expose these innocent beings if a fearful battle ensued, if Fantômas' colleagues tried to wrest his prisoner from his grasp!

Then he rebuked his own hesitation. Was it not his bounden duty to act with the utmost ruthlessness? And he made up his mind:

"I slip the handcuffs on him, first… Then I hold him at the muzzle of my revolver. At the smallest suspicious movement I blow out his brains. Afterwards, no doubt, his accomplices will kill me to avenge their leader. But I need only not defend myself, and it will soon be over!… Then all will take to their heels. The children and the rest will barely have time to realize what is happening…"

He got to his feet. He had completely recovered his quiet self-command. In five seconds the thing would be done. The great matter was to take up a good position to clap the handcuffs on the criminal, the Arch-Criminal, without his having time to defend himself, to suspect anything even…

He took a step forward. But he must say something, must distract the man's attention, prevent him from taking the alarm. Still playing his role as King of the Receivers, the detective exclaimed:

"Come now! By this time, I calculate you must know I have guessed right that you are Fantômas?"

"I do!… Your Majesty has made no mistake." The brigand said this in the calmest of voices, his eyes still riveted to the dial of his watch.

"The moment is come!" thought Juve. His handcuffs lay open in his pocket. He took them in his right hand, he was ready for instant action.

Fantômas' eyes turned to look fixedly into his.

"But I know another thing!" announced the Lord of Terror.

"What is that?"

The fierce eyes that seemed to bore into his very pupils shook Juve's composure. He must wait till they were averted. To act at that moment would have been impossible…

"Oh, ho!" sneered Fantômas, "so you can't guess what else I know? Your Majesty would like a laugh?"

"Why, no! I am waiting for you to explain…"

"Well, this is it…"

The blazing eyes blazed more fiercely still.

"This is it… I know this too, that… that you are Juve."

A terrible moment, a moment of tragic disappointment!

With one bound Fantômas was on his feet. With one bound Juve stood before him, barring his way to the door. Each man, officer of the law and lawbreaker, leveled his revolver…

Juve was the first to speak:

"Fantômas, hands up!" he roared. "One movement, one cry, and I fire! Quick, hands up, I say!"

"Juve," scoffed Fantômas, "by God! yes, it is Juve, the great Juve who stands before me! How could I ever have let myself be so imposed upon? But, Juve, it is your own perspicacity has been your undoing! You alone could have guessed…"

"Surrender, Fantômas!" thundered the police officer. "And throw down your weapon. Take care, am I to fire?"

He had his finger on the trigger as he spoke, and Fantômas dropped his revolver.

"Is it the hour of my defeat then?" he asked, and *looked at his watch.*

Juve came close to seize the malefactor, the steel of the handcuffs glittering in his hands…

"Yes! it is the hour!" announced Fantômas—"to the second!"

And punctual to the second, a hideous, an insane, an inconceivable catastrophe befell, overwhelming in its sudden horror, its appalling swiftness…

Juve was within a few inches of the villain. Suddenly the man took a leap in the air. No! he was not trying to escape from the kiosk! That would have been a physical impossibility. His leap was to the ceiling of the building; it was the beams supporting the roof he gripped, and hung there suspended.

"Fantô…" stammered Juve, but the word was cut short, choked in his throat as he uttered it.

A terrific crash shook the frail edifice. A rushing wind whistled past in a sudden, fierce tornado. With an appalling noise of rending timbers the whole fabric, walls and floor collapsed in ruin. It seemed to have been torn bodily from the tree it was built on, or rather the tree itself had been uprooted.

Juve was pitched headlong into space, crashing down amid a tangled mass of debris that plunged to the ground beneath to the accompaniment of the terrified screams of the panic-stricken crowd in and about the restaurant. The unhappy man was fully conscious as he fell, his eyes dilated with fury. Was he going to be killed? Was he going to be crushed and maimed on striking the earth along with the fragments of the ruined kiosk? What matter if he were? In the swift flash of a dying man's last thoughts he found time to realize what had happened: by clinging to the ceiling of the hut, the only part of the building that had withstood the shock, Fantômas had saved himself from the fall his enemy Juve had suffered. Fantômas was safe! Fantômas was going to escape!

Had he not, in very deed, taking his spring at the precise second he had waited for, in some sort proved his hideous genius? Undoubtedly it was he who had organized the collapse of the kiosk at a preordained moment, prepared the catastrophe that saved him so opportunely from the hands of the law…

But how had he contrived the disaster? What cataclysm, obedient to his orders, could have thus worked his will? As he rolled on the ground in pain, injured perhaps, certainly bruised and bleeding, Juve growled out the words:

"A cannon shot!… It was a cannon shot!"

*　*　*　*　*

Less than ten minutes after the collapse of the kiosk Juve opened his eyes. Rescuers had hurried to the spot and raised the fainting man from the ground. But no swoon was likely to last long with Juve. He was one of those eager souls whose ardor is such they despise bodily pain and scorn physical hurts.

He found himself lying on a bed, half undressed and surrounded by four persons who were bending over him with anxious faces. On a chair lay his white wig, on the floor his sham mustache. The false chin he had stuck on to round off his face and render it unrecognizable dangled half unglued from his real chin.

"Oh!" he exclaimed, with an evident effort to force his memory to recall recent events, then quickly added:

"One of you gentlemen is no doubt a doctor?"

"Yes, I am!" said one of the strangers bending over the police officer. "But you mustn't talk, you must rest…"

For all answer, Juve sprang up to a sitting posture on the bed.

"Have I any bones broken?" he asked. "Please tell me!"

"Nothing serious," replied the practitioner. "A rib broken, I think, a bad sprain of the right wrist… perhaps internal contusions. A fortnight's rest will put you on your legs again…"

"Really?… But might I ask for my boots back?"

"Your boots? Whatever for?"

"Why, for… Ah! I see them over there,"—and before the others could say a word, Juve was off the bed, and picking up his boots which lay in a corner, began to put them on.

"It's simply madness!" protested the doctor.

"It is a matter of police, doctor!" retorted Juve sternly. "Do you suppose I can sit still and do nothing for a fortnight?"—and springing up, stretching his arms, trying joints and muscles, he declared:

"Never fear, I feel quite fit… Good! now for more important matters!… Of course Fantômas is far away by this time?"

"Fantomas!"

"Why, yes! you don't know? nobody knows yet? Well, it's simple enough. I am the police officer Juve, as the papers in my pocketbook have already told you. As for the individual who was in the kiosk with me, it was the antiquary Thévenot—and Fantômas to boot!… So there you are!"—and Juve broke into a laugh; but noting the look of utter bewilderment that appeared on the faces of his auditors, he proceeded:

"Naturally you are asking yourself if I have lost my wits. Well, the landlord of the restaurant here knows me. It was on his premises a theft was committed, the theft in the kiosk everybody has been talking about… He will guarantee what I am telling you, gentlemen."

At that moment someone came forward whom Juve had not as yet seen. It was no other than the landlord of the "Red Chestnut" he had just referred to.

"Monsieur Juve!" he began, "I did not recognize you just now…"

"That was because I was 'made up,' my dear sir. You want the story in two words? You recollect the theft committed at your place? Well, I was positive the thief could be nobody else but Thévenot, and that, consequently, Thévenot was Fantômas. Unfortunately I possessed no proof… How was I to unmask the fellow?"

"Yes, how?" repeated mine host mechanically. "An idea struck me," Juve continued, "a happy thought. I invented, from head to heel, a personage who had never existed, who was a pure creature of my imagination—the King of the Receivers… First-rate! As King of the Receivers, I was dead certain, sooner or later, to tear the veil off Fantômas…"

In the little room to which Juve had been carried you could have heard a pin drop. Through the reports in the Press all present were acquainted with the general course of the events of which Juve was explaining the hidden springs.

"So there you have me resolved to create this character of the King of the Receivers," resumed the detective, "but it was necessary to get him believed in, to accredit the new ambassador, so to speak, to assure the underworld of crime of the bona fides of the unknown stranger. I set to work at once. I engage an old vagrant, Bouzille, the most garrulous of men, as concierge, quite confident that through his chatter everybody would hear of His Majesty's arrival... And I was not disappointed!"

Juve gave another laugh and went on:

"Then a word on the phone to the Officer of the Transatlantic Line, a message by wireless in code to the Captain of the *Niagara Falls,* and it was clear His Majesty would arrive by that boat. Oh, ho! and I had a success I never looked for; I took in even my best friend Fandor! I created a suppositious King of the Receivers. Fandor, on his side, is determined to find this same King—who never existed. I'm not done laughing yet at the poor lad! After throwing off the track the two officers of the Department detailed to Bordeaux with orders to shadow anybody who should busy himself about the imaginary steamship-passenger, he hid himself in one of the trunks I had taken care to have put in the stateroom of the boat by way of making things more complicated... All the same, Fandor was logical enough. He argued: 'If we go the same way as the trunks, the King of the Receivers is bound inevitably to come one day to claim them!' But for me, who counted on Fantômas looking after his luggage, that did not suit my book. Accordingly, I broke off the clue, forcing Fandor to lose touch of the redoubtable monarch!"

Again Juve laughed at the recollection.

"So far, so good! but what to do next! Things were hanging fire. So, by God! I said to myself, 'nothing ventured, nothing gained,' and myself disguised as the King of the Receivers, I organized a big police raid, a roundup, the only object of which was to bring me acquainted with Fantômas' accomplices. The thing was a success. I was able to arrange a meeting with Fantômas here... and... and the rest you know!"

At the last words Juve's voice lost its cheerful note. No doubt he could congratulate himself on the extraordinary astuteness he had displayed in laying for the Lord of Terror a trap into which he had momentarily fallen, but he was bitterly ashamed to have missed the final and decisive victory.

"Alas!" he declared mournfully, "everything has to be begun afresh... Fantômas no doubt had his suspicions... and now, of course, he cannot any longer masquerade as Thévenot, nor can he ever claim the insurance money for the stolen document… No! but he has escaped, he is at liberty. His cannot-shot saved him!"

"His cannon-shot?" questioned the doctor breathlessly.

"Why, yes!" declared the police officer. "Oh! so that puzzles you, eh? Well, that is the last point that needs explaining. Why did the kiosk collapse? Because a shell or a cannonball cut clean through the stem of the tree that supported it. By God! in some villa of the neighborhood Fantômas must have planted a fieldpiece with which at their leisure they took a deliberate aim at the confounded tree. After that, what more simple? At a moment fixed beforehand, or on some signal noted doubtless through a telescope, his accomplices opened fire. He escaped by clinging to the roof, which did not collapse like the rest of the kiosk, this being carried on timbers nailed to neighboring trees. I, on the contrary, was hurled to the ground. After that, it was mere child's play for the villain to make his escape in the general confusion."

In these few, rapid words he had explained the amazing adventure that had just reached its climax. Now, ready, dressed, without a sign even of still remembering the risks he had run, he concluded:

"Happily there are no victims besides myself—and that is the main point. As to Fantômas, I shall yet find track of him! But one result is gained—he is no longer, he can no longer be Thévenot."

Then the detective gave a sudden start.

"Oh! but I am crazy; it's that fall has dazed me. I'm forgetting things that should be done at once… His car? the car he drove up in as Thévenot?"

"Gone, Monsieur Juve!"

"Mine then? Quick! my chauffeur?"

"Your chauffeur, Monsieur Juve," said the doctor, "is making repairs; all his four tires and his spares have been punctured!"

"By the Lord!" swore Juve, "Fantômas, anyway, has forgotten nothing… But you are on the telephone?"

The police officer was taken to the instrument. He was evidently in great pain, and was limping badly.

"Hello!" he called in a voice that was quite steady, for all the martyrdom he was enduring," Hello! put me through to the Criminal Department, please, in Paris."

The receiver dropped from his hands. The telephone operator was saying:

"Impossible, sir!... All communication with Paris is cut off... The cables have been divided by sections along the roads... Robinson is left isolated—neither telephone nor telegraph working."

10. Revenge Is Sweet

Juve was right. Fantômas, that scoundrel of genius, was not one to forget anything… While the unfortunate police officer was taking a fall that should by all logical deduction have cost him his life, the brigand, seizing the opportunity of the panic created by the startling accident, had made all haste to escape. Climbing down from the tree to which he had clung, he mingled with the crowd, then hurried to the garage where a swift car, engine already started, was waiting for him.

"Drive on!" he ordered. "And quick's the word,"—and not three minutes after the cannon shot Fantômas was making at top speed for Paris.

For a time he said nothing. He was rather pale and was biting his lips like a man in a rage. He was thinking:

"I have escaped, it is true. *But* Juve has unmasked me!… Who is the victor, he or I? No matter, let us say a drawn game… Now for my revenge… I shall win this time!"

Turning to the chauffeur, who, crouching over his wheel, was driving at a giddy speed:

"Slow up!" he ordered. "About Juve's car?"

"Disabled, Chief! Can't start—tires burst, magneto put out of gear…"

"And the other cars in the garage?"

"Disabled too—petrol watered!"

"Capital!… The telephone and telegraph wires?"

"All cut, Master!"

"Better and better!… and the gun crew?"

"Gone, for sure, by car. Your orders have been scrupulously observed."

"Everyone shall be rewarded… Pull up now."

"Alongside that car there?"

"Yes, it is waiting for me. Juve is a man of resource. I've been thinking he might find a way to give a description of the auto at the Paris barrier. It's best for me to change cars."

A second later Fantômas was off again. His new car, however, was going at quite a moderate speed. To begin with, Fantômas was anxious not to attract attention, and in the second place the Lord of Terror did not wish the jolting of the car to interfere too much with what he was doing. From beneath the seat the brigand had extracted a makeup box, in all respects like those used by actors and actresses. In fact, was he not a comedian himself, an actor all day and every day on the stage? Did he not, by himself, fill a hundred different parts? As he went on with his clever makeup, Fantômas was muttering:

"Mustn't put on too much red! Let's make ourselves a bit pale. I want M. Havard to think I'm feeling a trifle frightened… Ah, ha! there he is! The game's beginning, the game that is to give me my revenge!"

At the same moment, in fact, M. Havard was beginning to get a trifle impatient, when at last he saw a motorcar pull up in the Square d'Anvers and the antiquary step out of it…

"I am late?" Fantômas asked.

"Barely five minutes."

"Nothing new?"

"Nothing whatever."

"Then… we're to go—you know where?"

"Seems to me that's what we're bound to do."

"Monsieur Havard, I shouldn't like to drag you into a risky business…"

"Never fear for me! It's my trade… Besides, I've taken my precautions…"—and the Head of the Criminal Bureau linked his arm in that of the man who was still in his eyes, as he had always been, "the antiquary Thévenot."

M. Havard was a man of courage. He had not failed to observe his companion's pallor, but he himself was quite undisturbed. Since the night before, indeed, ever since reading the startling "pneumatic" bearing Juve's signature and summoning M. Thévenot to Montmartre, he had felt many doubts. Without a word of news of the police officer, not yet knowing what precise purpose the roundup under his direction had served, convinced, as he could not but be, that the King of the Receivers did actually and veritably exist, M. Havard's most clearly defined impression was that he was struggling in the midst of incomprehensible dangers and his unassisted reason could afford him no sure clue to the situation. For the rest he could only call up his personal intrepidity, which was of a very high quality.

"Perhaps Juve's letter is not from him at all," he was thinking, "but there is nothing to prove it. In any case the fact that a trap is possibly to be feared gives me no right to ignore an indication that may be of great value… And then, what a triumph if I should actually succeed in coming face to face with Fantômas and arresting the villain!"

Such, to tell the exact truth, was the secret motive that influenced the Head of the Police… He did not positively believe a trap was laid for him; he only suspected it. But this suspicion, far from inducing him to draw back, was actually a further incitement to be up and doing. If Fantômas had had the effrontery to send the letter signed *Juve* himself, well, he would only have to fight him with his own weapons, to catch him in the trap he thought to catch others in.

Alas! what decision would poor M. Havard have taken if he could have guessed that the Fantômas whose mere name, despite his bravery, made him shudder, was no other than his present companion, this M. Thévenot he was at that moment talking to as a friend and whose pale face and scared look he was making quiet fun of in his inmost thoughts?

At the Chief's last words, however, the supposed antiquary had given a start.

"Oh!" he asked, "you have taken precautions?"

"Of course!"

"You are taking police officers with you?"

"Oh, no! that would not have been wise…"

"Why so?"

"The officers, my dear sir, might perhaps have attracted attention. If the letter inviting you to Montmartre conceals a ruse, it is advisable, whatever we do, not to seem to suspect anything."

"Granted! But then, I don't see…"

"What precautions I can have taken? Why, these! Last night and this morning, I've sent, on the quiet, my best sleuth-hounds to surround the house named. They have orders to keep concealed, but to blockade the premises, so to speak. You understand? They are posted all round the building. They are all ready to come to the rescue in force, if need be…"

"Capital! But how are you going to call them up?"

"In the simplest way in the world. I have my pockets stuffed with those toy bombs schoolboys are so fond of letting off. At the smallest indication of danger, I throw these down, and hearing the bang, my men rush up."

"Upon my word! You make me feel quite safe," declared Thévenot. But the words bore a double meaning. It was not the antiquary whose mind was relieved by what M. Havard said… It was Fantômas!

While speaking, the two men had taken their seats in the Montmartre funicular and alighted at the top of the hill, just below the basilica of the Sacré Coeur.

"This way," M. Havard gave the word. "I know the road. I can see in my mind's eye the very house you've been directed to… There, look, I can see it from here."

Yes, there it was. In a narrow lane sloping steeply down the declivity, one of the last of the Montmartre alleyways, one of the few remaining corners still preserving the picturesque aspect of that old-world quarter, M. Havard pointed to a building fallen largely to ruin.

"We are going to walk past the place first," he went on. "We must make sure there's nothing in the neighborhood to suggest danger."

But, as a matter of fact, everything seemed quite peaceable. The lane was deserted. At the far end some children were playing. Further away, two workingwomen were talking together.

"Upon my word," said M. Havard, turning back again, "I'm

beginning to think my plans were needless. Your letter must really have been from Juve. Let us go in,"—and they crept into the dilapidated house…

Ah! what would have been the Chief's terror if only he could have guessed the delight his companion felt at that moment!

"He is mine," Fantômas was saying to himself. "It's between us two, Juve! The game is started—the game that will give me my revenge!"

But in a voice that shook with pretended alarm:

"Monsieur Havard," stammered the bogus antiquary, "you're going too fast! Before going down into the cellars, ought we not first to search the house?"

"Pooh! what's the good? If there was anything plotting against us, you may be sure we shouldn't find it out in five minutes. Let's make haste, rather!"

Then, stooping down, he discovered in the floor a wooden trapdoor half rotted away, which he raised:

"The stairs to the cellars!" he announced. "I'll go down first… Oh! no false shame, you know. If your pulse is beating a bit too fast, stay where you are! I will go alone."

"No, no! I'm not such a coward as all that."

Fantômas was playing his part with cruel perfection. With a devilish satisfaction he watched the Chief of the Criminal Bureau marching so innocently into the ambush laid for him. He asked:

"You have your 'petards' ready to hand?"

"Why, yes! Of course I have… Look here, would you like my revolver?"

"No, no! keep it…"

At the bottom of the steep stairway the two men reached the floor of the cellar, and simultaneously both uttered the same exclamation:

"A strongbox!"

Yes, there in that tumbledown cellar, half buried under masses of fallen plaster, a gigantic strongbox could be seen.

"By the Lord! I begin to think Juve has made no mistake!" cried M. Havard, throwing the light of his electric torch on the big safe. Stepping a pace or two nearer, he added:

"The word to open the lock is 'Genius.' Let's see if this detail too is correct,"—and slowly and methodically the Chief formed the required combination of letters. As he spelled out on the dial the final "s," the door of the safe flew open.

"So, ho!"… he began, but got no further!

Quicker than lightning, Thévenot, or rather Fantômas, caught him by the shoulders and pushed him into the strong-box—and in an instant the door slammed to on the wretched man with a crash, succeeded only by a faint, dull, stifled cry.

"So there!" cried the Lord of Terror. "Oh, ho! he can let off all his 'petards'; only the slightest, barely perceptible sound will penetrate those steel walls."

Then a ferocious laugh, and with a sort of hoarse wild-beast roar:

"Revenge!" he yelled. "Yes! the game is up, and my revenge begins!… A fine hostage, Juve, I've taken this time!"

And, with a grin of satisfied hate, he drew his handkerchief from his pocket and brushed off the flakes of plaster that had soiled his coat sleeves, as profoundly unconcerned as though he had not that moment committed a hideous, a murderous crime!

*　　*　　*　　*　　*

"Now what am I going to do next, I wonder… To tell the unvarnished truth, to be quite candid with myself, I am bound to admit that, properly speaking, I am in the position of an escaped convict and that I deserve a round dozen years of hard labor!"

Fandor had just made his escape from the Depot by an un-paralleled piece of audacity and was still within twenty yards of the Palais de Justice when he put this grossly exaggerated view of the situation before himself. Yes, he had certainly broken bounds, but did he actually run any risk whatever of such a sentence? The misdemeanors M. Havard had laid to his charge were not in reality very serious, and this fact materially diminished the importance to be attached to his escape, which, anyway, had been accompanied by no act of violence or other grave offense. The journalist was too reasonable a man not to see this, and presently he added philosophically:

"All the same I don't believe the Court will be sitting for many a day yet that would condemn me for such trifles. But," he went on, "that is no reason why I should let myself be recaptured. Indeed, I have committed worse than a crime; I have made a mock of an official, and that official M. Havard! It would not be good for my health to come under his jurisdiction again!"

Even as he spoke, the young man broke into a laugh that had no touch of malice about it.

"Poor old Havard, I must have brought him very near a grave attack of apoplexy. Juve will have to make it his business to patch up a peace between us."

But hardly had Fandor said the words before his mood changed and his face lost all its cheerfulness. The mere utterance of the name Juve reminded him instantly of the grim possibilities of the inquiries he was engaged on.

"Where is Juve?" he muttered. "There is no doubt the beggar, the good friend I should say, wants to keep me out of his road, is afraid of my getting into trouble… But that is only a reason the more for my finding him and forcing him to accept my help."

Absorbed in such reflections, the journalist was wending his way along the sunlit quays in the direction of the Trocadero. Presently he began talking to himself again:

"Besides, it's close on seven o'clock… Hmm! it's over late for paying visits. Or else it's too early. Suppose I wait till dark night before I try to find Bouzille."

In fact, ever since the moment of his arrest, Fandor had been resolved to ask Bouzille for the information he was so badly in need of. For was not Bouzille, in Fandor's eyes at any rate, the concierge to the King of the Receivers, an individual the journalist was a hundred miles from imagining to be impersonated by Juve…

"That's the way!" the young man concluded, "I'm going to sleep for an hour or two; then, towards midnight, I'll go and knock Bouzille up. Either I shall be wasting my time, or I shall force him to speak out..."

The decision the journalist had come to was logical enough. True, a rearrest could involve no very serious consequences for him, but it was equally certain that a second sojourn in jail would put back all his investigations—and this was a contingency he dreaded above all things. So, was it not the wisest course, in order to avoid falling into the hands of the police, to postpone his visit to Bouzille till late at night.

"For, after all," Fandor agreed, "there is nothing to tell me that the house where this queer sort of concierge is to be found is not watched. Too many things have happened at Sceaux for the attention of the police not to be thoroughly aroused..."

Alas! the most artfully devised precautions are often the very ones Fate chooses to thwart by the simplest circumstances. Fandor's plan was excellent. It had one fault only—it took no account of the fatigue under which the journalist labored. Since the time he left Bordeaux, in fact, Fandor had gone through so many adventures that he was literally exhausted. It was only his nervous energy kept him going. But the moment he gave way to sleep the nerves would inevitably exact the penalty Nature imposes on every excess.

"Sleep! Yes, but where?" the young man asked himself. "At home? As well throw myself straight into the arms of the police! At Juve's? That would be every bit as bad! Well, upon my word! Necessity knows no law. I'll just sleep here, and have done with it!"

At the moment he was passing under the Pont des Arts, and at this late hour not a soul was to be seen in the neighborhood.

"A man can sleep sound under bridges," he remarked to himself, and deliberately climbed up into the iron framework of struts and girders, settled down as comfortably as possible and shut his eyes, thinking to himself:

"In a couple of hours, I'll start away for Sceaux..."

In a couple of hours!... When the sleeper opened his eyes, when he got his wits together again and was fully awake, he gave a gasp of consternation.

"Why, what! What time is it then?" It was broad daylight, and a hot sun was beating down. It was late in the afternoon!

"Good Lord! what time can it be?" Fandor said for the second time—and in the peace and quietness of the place, like a mocking answer to the question, a clock began to strike. Aghast, the journalist counted the strokes: "Three... four... five! It's five o'clock!"

He leapt to his feet. "Five o'clock? Five o'clock in the evening? But I've been sleeping, then, like a dormouse, like a log, like a Judge on the bench! Five o'clock in the evening! Yes, but the evening of what day? By the Lord! it was yesterday I turned in. I've been sleeping near on twenty-four hours! I can never forgive myself!..."

Certainly the gallant fellow had good excuses to make, but he never so much as thought of them. The sentinel who succumbs to fatigue in face of the enemy, does he not deserve to be court-martialed?

"I have been asleep!" the young man reiterated, "and meantime, God only knows what may have happened!... What has Juve been doing? What has Fantômas attempted? Oh! curse it! curse it all!"

He was down at the foot of the bridge in less than no time. Four steps at a time he climbed the little stairway leading from the strand to the quay properly so called. A newspaper woman stood there, and he bought a *Capitale*. Three minutes later his rage had reached a climax of fury.

"For the first time in my life, I have mulled things," he reproached himself. "The article here is idiotic. *I* ought to have reported these events. I am disgraced... And then... oh! good God! good God!"

For some minutes Jerome Fandor stood silent and abashed, so upset was he by what he read. The paper he was skimming was, in fact, an evening edition. Concisely but clearly the events that had occurred at Robinson while Fandor slept were reported in it. Finally, after glancing through almost the whole sheet, the young man swore savagely.

"Juve! So the King of the Receivers was Juve all the time!

And he very nearly got himself killed! And I was not there! And Fantômas has slipped through his fingers! I deserve to be the laughing stock of all my colleagues. I was asleep all that time. I was positively asleep!"

He took up the paper again to scan the very latest news—and started violently. A headline, in block letters, announced: "Fate of our Collaborator, Jerome Fandor."

"This is the last straw," groaned the journalist, and he read:

"If, as we have seen, a certain number of facts have been explained by Juve the celebrated police officer, other incidents still remain shrouded in mystery. Thus, at *La Capitale*, we are greatly disturbed about our gallant collaborator, Jerome Fandor. Contrary to his habits as an able and sagacious journalist, our valued and astute reporter appears, as a matter of fact, not to have known anything of the tragic incidents at Robinson, nor even to have given them a thought. We have had nothing from him, not even a word on the telephone, or a telegraphic message. This silence is surprising, and, we repeat, disturbing. We are unwilling to record here sundry fantastic rumors to the effect that Jerome Fandor had been arrested by the police and taken to the Depot, but had subsequently escaped...

"We are the more unwilling to do this inasmuch as, on the one hand, we can vouch for Jerome Fandor as a man of impeccable honor, and as, on the other hand, we have been unable at the Criminal Department to obtain any information in the absence of M. Havard, who, having left his office three hours and a half before, had not yet returned at five o'clock, to the intense surprise of his staff.

"In any case, we sincerely hope that nothing untoward has happened to Jerome Fandor. We can only conjecture that weighty reasons make this silence of his obligatory, and that perhaps, by his talent and daring, he too, as Juve has already done, is going to make sensational discoveries that will throw a new and startling light on the tragic episodes primarily connected with the dread name of the Ever-Illusive Fantômas."

Fandor threw down the paper angrily.

"So there they go with their cock and bull stories, expecting

me to provide them with sensational discoveries forsooth. It's
flogging a dead horse, that's what it is! How could I do anything
of the sort, I should like to know. I was asleep!"

The young man was in the vilest of tempers. Furious with
himself at having succumbed to fatigue, he was still more in-
censed against Juve, who, by creating the personality of the
King of the Receivers, had made an utter fool of him.

"I say it was Juve's bounden duty to have taken me into his
confidence," he grumbled. Then with a shrug he added more
tolerantly:

"After all, I know very well that, if Juve did let me go wandering off on a false scent, it was because he was bent on keeping
me out of the fray… No, I cannot be angry with him."

Fandor's rages were never of long duration, and five minutes
after he was his cheerful, confident self again. He was now
telling himself:

"In any case, this is plain enough—to rehabilitate myself, I
must bring off some striking success. Well, here goes for the
great triumph! Juve has let Fantômas get away. It's my turn now
to try my luck!"

Ten minutes afterwards Fandor was jumping into a taxi and
driving off to the Sceaux terminus. An hour more and he was
approaching the famous villa which he had visited twice before,
first with Juve, on the day the police officer had disappeared,
the second time with Juve again, but packed away in the trunk
of the imaginary King of the Receivers.

"The house don't bring me luck, that's certain!" he grumbled. "But I must find Bouzille. He was concierge here; perhaps
he's here still?"

Cautiously, for it behoved him to beware both of the police
and of Fantômas, the reporter scrutinized the place from a
distance.

"Peaceable enough to look at!" he remarked aloud, still absorbed in his own reflections. "Nobody to be seen. The shutters
are up, besides. Can I have had the ill luck to arrive too late,
after Bouzille has gone?"

Suddenly he gave a start.

"Why, no!" he corrected himself. "One of the chimneys is smoking." They're cooking inside… but who, I wonder."

Fandor was not the man to hesitate about the best way to find out. In a moment he had leapt over a wall and dropped into the garden; then, walking on tiptoe and avoiding any noise that might have revealed his presence, he crept up to a window that stood open on the ground floor. Peeping in, Fandor had to bite his lips to stifle a cry of astonishment. In the room before his eyes stood a man, and the man was Bouzille. And the tramp was occupied in the most unexpected fashion. Wearing a white cap and, tied round his neck, a long apron, in which he got his feet entangled every now and then, Bouzille was stooping over a saucepan and stirring its contents with all the solemnity of a "cordon bleu"!

"Who the devil is employing him as a cook?" the journalist asked himself. But he had barely had time to make the query before Bouzille turned round, and, catching sight of him, lost hold of the saucepan in his panic, upsetting the sauce he was concocting on the floor.

"M'sieur Fandor," the old scamp stammered. "Good Lord! And I wha ain't so much as got time for a drink, I ain't!… Why, here's the fourth time I've gone and spoiled my white sauce, and that's put me back above a bit. Come in, M'sieur Fandor. How goes it, sir, with you?"

For all answer the journalist clambered through the window and marched straight up to the tramp. Oh! he knew his man! At the first glance, beneath the pretended good humor of the old man, he had divined his embarrassment and trouble.

"M'sieur Fandor," Bouzille started afresh, "what is it brings your honor to see me again? What! you don't know? I'm not concierge no more. It was Juve engaged me o' course. It's in the paper, it is! But there, you've long ago known what the game was, I'll warrant you."

"Bouzille, I'm not talking about that."

"About what, then?"

"Who are you cooking that stuff for?"

"M'sieur Fandor, that's a secret."

"Is it for Juve?"

"Oh! M'sieur Fandor, I don't so much as know where he is!"

"For Fantômas?"

"M'sieur Fandor, you've got a reason for coming to see me?"

"Answer my question, instead of trying to put me off. *Is* it for Fantômas?"

"Never, M'sieur Fandor, no how! I wouldn't do such a thing! A scoundrel like that there!… And then, my cooking wouldn't be good enough!"

"Who for, then?"

"That's a secret, I keep telling you…"

But, while speaking, Fandor was scrutinizing every nook and corner of the room, and his astonishment waxed greater than ever. On the floor in a recess stood an open basket, of the size and shape of a portmanteau, already half full of appetizing viands. Was Bouzille going to carry his cookery to some dining table in town? Jerome Fandor pointed his finger threateningly at the old tramp:

"Oh, ho!" he said, "so you have secrets?… That's why, no doubt, I'm directed to take you to the Criminal Department."

"To the Criminal Department? But I'm an honest man, I am!"

"You can tell M. Havard that."

"But I don't want to see him."

"May be. Only he's expecting you… Come, off we go!"

"M'sieur Fandor, it's not God's truth what you're telling me?"

"It's just every bit as true as what you are telling me, that this cooking you're doing is not for Juve—or for Fantômas!"—and taking advantage of the trepidation he read in the old man's face, Fandor went on:

"Once, twice, three times, will you answer? No? Very well, I'll keep you prisoner." A sharp click, and the journalist had turned the key in the lock; simultaneously he had sprung to the window, so that Bouzille was veritably a prisoner.

"So then!" Fandor said sternly. "You'll be let out when you've made up your mind to speak…"

"But I can't say anything."

"Why not?"

"Because I've sworn on my life to hold my tongue! M'sieur Fandor, you wouldn't surely wish to get me into trouble, bad trouble?"

"You admit then, my man, you've seen Fantômas? That it was he gave you your orders?"

"M'sieur Fandor, but that depends…"

"No, it doesn't. Now no prevarications. Is it for him you're preparing these victuals?"

"For him and not for him, M'sieur Fandor! How can I tell? Come, must be a bit reasonable. Lookee, they never tells me nothing… and *I've* a-got to go explaining everything! One day it's M'sieur Juve hires me for concierge. Did he ever tell me it was he was the King of the Receivers. Not he, not a bit of it! Well then, Fantômas, he orders me to cook meals. D'you think he tells me who for?"

"Where do you take your cookery to, Bouzille?"

"Oh! M'sieur Fandor, no! mum's the word! If I told you that, it'd be all U.P. with me right away. Anyhow, *you* won't kill me… while he…"

"Very well! Please yourself! But I've given you fair warning— you're my prisoner, and you won't leave the place till you have answered my questions…"

"But it's assault and battery and brute force you're using agin' me?"

"Speak out, and you are free…"

"Not to say, M'sieur Fandor, as how it's a work of charity like I'm doing, a-carrying of this here grub… If you go stopping me, who knows it mayn't mean a man's death?… death by starvation?…"

Suddenly a wild surmise darted through Fandor's mind… For certain, it was Fantômas had instructed Bouzille to prepare these meals and carry them… But who could he be supplying with food by the old tramp's hands, if not a prisoner? And who could this prisoner be, if not Juve?"

"Bouzille," cried the young journalist in a ringing voice, "I give you my oath if you don't answer, I'll…"

But the threat was never completed, sheer surprise had taken away the speaker's breath…

Bouzille, the ineffable Bouzille, was beating the air wildly with his arms, and next moment had sunk, a lifeless mass, to the floor.

11. The Calamities of Bouzille

Assuredly Fandor was no weakling, or a man more easily upset than another. He had gone through so many hair-breadth adventures, found himself involved in so many mysteries, incomprehensible or tragic, so often confronted the direst perils with a smile, that as a rule, whatever happened, he preserved his coolness. For all that, when Bouzille dropped fainting at his feet, the young man was so utterly dumbfounded he rather lost his head!

"Impossible!" was his first incredulous exclamation. Then he told himself: "But, great God! I can't have frightened him to such a degree as to give the chap a fit?"

He bent over the old vagrant, felt his heart, and added:

"And yet he has fainted—fainted right away, fainted like a young girl or a silly woman… Who is to be trusted then, I should like to know!"

Quickly recovering his calm and not overanxious, now he gathered it was merely an ordinary fainting fit not likely to have any serious consequences, he once more stooped over the old fellow, loosened his collar and began to fan him.

"Silly old fool!" he growled. "To turn up his toes like a fine lady with the vapors! Upon my word! I'll just swill a jugful of cold water over his head…"—and he took a step towards a sink there was in the kitchen and looked about for a water jug. But a new thought brought the young man to a halt.

"Ah! Juve was right perhaps. 'Blunder on top of blunder,' he said, speaking of me and my doings… Suppose I think a bit before waking Bouzille up."

The old vagabond was not a man he disliked—quite the contrary. Doubtless he knew him to be capable of many blameworthy acts; doubtless he was aware that the old man had rather elastic notions about honesty… But all the same he was not altogether a bad man. Chance, which often does more to mold human destinies than men's own free will, had led Bouzille into the Paris underworld of crime. There he had come acquainted with Fantômas, and by persuasion or by force, often by the latter, had been induced sometimes to be his accomplice. But he had also, and many times, helped the police! And he very certainly professed a respectful and trustful admiration for Juve and Fandor.

"No!" reflected Fandor, speaking his thoughts out loud. "No, the man's no scoundrel… And he knows very well I'm not the sort to play him a dirty trick… But then, why… why did he faint?" and he stared down at the old tramp, still lying unconscious on the floor, with a puzzled look.

"Odd!" he muttered, "and most extraordinary! I ask him who his dishes are meant for—and the question sends him off in a dead faint! It must be a very tremendous secret?"

Then, next moment, he struck his forehead like a man who is smitten with a new and startling idea.

"Ah! but it's not anything I said or any question I asked him could have upset him to such a degree… It's something he saw, something he caught sight of behind me…"

The window was open. Was it not possible, in fact, that behind the journalist's back, in the garden of the villa, somebody had come up to this window and from there had made a sign to Bouzille, a threat? Fandor felt himself turn pale. Who could, by a single gesture, perhaps merely by showing his face, have so terrified the old man? The journalist answered his own question:

"Fantômas! it was Fantômas!"—and the dread name chilled him to the marrow of his bones. Again Fandor stood buried in his thoughts. "But," he pondered, still speaking his thoughts aloud, "if it was Fantômas Bouzille saw behind my back, without my suspecting his presence, why did he not kill me? Yet Fantômas has sworn my death—and what an opportunity for him to strike me down!"

His conclusions appeared to Fandor perfectly logical, yet at the same time self-contradictory. Fantômas had evidently been there; yet he had not murdered him. Why? The whole problem raised by Bouzille's fainting fit was involved in the words.

"Very good!" said Fandor, "there's one person can settle the question—and that is Bouzille. He must confess, I must make him confess, the reason why he fainted." He returned to the sink again, filled a jug with water, and returned to the tramp.

"Cold water, there's nothing like it for calming the nerves!" he grinned.

But once again the journalist stopped in the act of poising the water jug, preparatory to pitching the contents in Bouzille's face.

"But, on second thoughts, no!" Fandor reflected. "Blunder on top of blunder! To wake him up now would only be another piece of foolishness. Must search him first. What's to prevent my finding some hint bearing on the prisoner he has to feed with his cookery?"

He put down the water jug, and softly and cautiously set about searching the old tramp's pockets. Alas! this was neither a rapid nor an easy operation. In Bouzille's pockets was a miscellaneous collection, including a little bit of everything. There was a broken packet of tobacco strewing its contents over a tattered bag containing three worthless prizes won at some fair. There were rusty penknives, between whose jagged blades were caught torn and dirty papers, mostly notices of forthcoming race meetings!

"They're not pockets," sighed Fandor. "They're ragbags, scavengers' ragbags!"

Suddenly he gave a start. His hands had lighted on a clean sheet of paper. Now a clean sheet of paper was obviously one that had not long been in the old vagrant's possession. Did it contain some all-important revelation? With a shaking hand Fandor unfolded it, his heart thumping hard in his breast in a very agony of suspense.

It was a strange document, this paper chance had thrown into his hands. It showed, to begin with, traced in pencil, a kind of drawing or plan, evidently meant to represent a group of streets and houses. One of these houses was distinguished by a mark in blue pencil. Below were a few lines typewritten, which the journalist read at a glance:

"If Bouzille does not wish to die, if Bouzille wishes to win forgiveness for his dealings with Fandor and Juve, he will convey to the place indicated a copious dinner. Bouzille will find in the cellar the chest that holds the diner. It is provided with a trapdoor. Through this aperture he will pass in the needful provender. This done, he will go, without exchanging a word with the diner, and will forget all about his errand. Treachery or indiscretion will be punished with death. Strict obedience will be magnificently rewarded." Signature there was none at the end of this extraordinary effusion.

No sooner had Fandor read the lines than he seemed to have gone suddenly mad.

"Damnation!" he swore savagely. "And here am I wasting my time. Bouzille refused to enlighten me. But something told me all the while that cooking was for a prisoner… for a prisoner of Fantômas… for Juve without a doubt, for poor old Juve!"

He set to work at once, acting with incredible rapidity. Without a trace of pity left for the old fellow, who still lay unconscious, the young man tore down the cords of the curtains in an adjacent room. With these he tied Bouzille's hands and arms and legs. His handkerchief served to gag his prisoner. Then, picking him up like a parcel, he hauled him to a cupboard and pitched him in.

"There!" he growled, panting with anger. "I don't want to take him with me, and I do want to be able to find him, if need be… A jug of water to revive him this time—and then I'm off."

Under Fandor's shower-bath Bouzille opened his eyes, as expected, but by that time the door of the cupboard was shut upon him, and a turn of the key made all secure. Fandor sprang through the window, climbed the garden wall and so away through the darkness.

"Not a moment to lose!" he thought as he made for the high road. "It was Fantômas who scared Bouzille so… Bouzille dared not speak because he knew he was there… And if Fantômas did not kill me, it was because, fearing the old fellow had already blabbed, he thought best to get ahead of me, to hurry straight to his prisoner… Oh! Juve, Juve! shall I ever get to you in time?"

Very terrible the agony of a man who knows a foul deed is being done, and who is far away, alone, utterly unable to bring instant help to the victim. The night was calm and quiet and this out-of-the-way bit of suburb entirely deserted—not a soul to be seen or heard save from time to time, on the high road, more than a hundred yards away, the swift passage of motor-cars making the best of their way back to Paris.

"Oh! I shall get there! I mean to and I shall!" panted Fandor, hardly knowing what he was saying.

Soon he reached the high road. Suddenly he heaved a sigh of relief; before him, a few steps away, a car was halted. The engine was still running; only the driver, the only occupant of the car, had got down to relight his lamps, which had gone out.

"Now for it!" muttered Fandor. "It's Juve's life I'm defending!"—and he dashed up to the vehicle. With one bound he was on the driving-seat and had the accelerator pressed hard under his foot. Next instant, the engine well started, he threw in the reversing gear, and the car plunged to the rear, leaving its startled owner watching his vehicle backing away from him.

"Help! help!" he yelled, but already it was too late. Fandor had changed speeds, slipped by the first, scamped the second, and going ahead again on the third, had made a rapid swerve and grazing past the stranger whose property he was stealing, was off and away full blast on the fourth, before the bewildered driver quite knew what catastrophe had befallen him!

"Shout away, my good man!" the reporter was saying to himself meanwhile. "Tomorrow you'll have your car back… and I shouldn't wonder but *La Capitale* will offer you a new one to indemnify you… Yes, that's the least they can do!"

He did not vouchsafe another thought to the robbery he had committed. Convinced he was going to Juve's rescue, Fandor was nothing now but one concentrated embodiment of speed! Fast and furious, steering with an incomparable mastery, he reached Paris. Like a bombshell, under the very eyes of the

startled officials of the octroi, who stood expecting his declaration of petrol, he scorched through the barrier. Before him,
almost empty at this late hour, stretched the Avenue d'Orleans,
the Boulevard Saint Michel, the Boulevard Sevastopol, offering a free course for this headlong race against time. A quick
turn into the Boulevard Magenta, another to swing on to the
Outer Boulevards, then the little Rue de Steinkerque mounted
at racing speed, and he stopped at the bottom of the stairs that
climb the Butte de Montmartre under the very windows of
Juve's house.

"I shall get on quicker afoot, going up there!" he told
himself, leaping from his throbbing car, and starting to mount
the steps. He felt no doubt at all. He had instantly recognized
on the plan found in Bouzille's pocket the house marked with
blue pencil where the prisoner he meant to release was to be
found, and he made straight for it. On arriving, however, in the
near neighborhood of the "Green Rabbit," the tavern adjacent
to the ruined building, he proceeded more cautiously.

"No weapon! I have no weapon!" he reflected, "they took
everything from me at the Depot… Very well! my fists will do
instead… Anyway, I must not lose a second; I must go straight
ahead." Yet it was a mad enterprise surely. He had himself said
the cellar was most likely haunted by Fantômas; Fantômas
might be waiting for him there, revolver or dagger in hand,
ambushed in the gloom, undistinguishable in the dark, thanks
to his traditional and sinister garb of black. Yes! it was sheer
madness to go in. But enter he did. One look had assured him
that no one seemed to be on the watch… And then, how *could*
he be prudent? Was he not come to save Juve's life? Does a man
calculate chances when each passing second threatens the existence of the best and dearest of friends?

The reporter slipped into the building, and caught sight of
the trapdoor. Dragging it open, he plunged into the semidarkness of the basement. At first he could see nothing. Then, his
eyes growing accustomed to the dark, he made out the metallic
mass of the strongbox.

"Juve! Juve!" he cried hoarsely. His voice awoke no echo

in the silence of the place. Then he hurled himself against the great chest and beat on it with his fists.

"Juve?… Juve?…"

A shiver ran through the young man from head to foot. A weak, choking voice had reached his ears:

"Quick! quick!… I am stifling!"

"Juve! Juve, it is I."

"Open! Open! Quick!… Genius! Genius!… Be quick!"

Tears welled in Fandor's eyes, tears of rage and despair… Open the chest? Oh! he would have given his life to be able. But surely it was an impossible task for him to perform? He had no tool; he could not even see clearly. Like a madman, a maniac, he tore at the safe with bleeding hands, but his utmost efforts failed even to shake its equilibrium.

"Juve!… Juve!… Courage!… Yes, I am going to open, Juve!… I will call for help! You shall be saved!"

He was speaking at random; his powers of thought seemed paralyzed. Quick as he was ordinarily to devise the most ingenious, the most daring schemes, he could find no plan to try, no expedient to attempt.

Again he knocked upon the steel walls of the strongbox.

"Juve! Juve, I say! Can you hear me? Courage, courage, man!"

The answer came—in a voice feebler than ever. What was it saying? What did this word signify he just caught indistinctly, this word that seemed simply meaningless?

"Genius! genius!" Fandor said it over to himself. And then, trembling with newborn hope, he thought he understood—he did understand! That word? Why, it was *the* word, the keyword of the letter-lock that secured the safe.

Mastering his agitation, forcing himself to recover his calmness, conquering the tremor of rage that shook him, he seized the milled knobs that worked the letters composing the cipher of the lock. Could he manage it? In the dark he counted the nicks, unable to make out the letters, shuddering to think he might make a mistake.

"I… U… S" he spelled out the last three letters; he pulled the door towards him—and it came open!

"Juve!" he cried frantically. But there was no answer. Was he too late?

Then he stooped down, and crept half inside the iron chest, feeling in the gloom with his outstretched hands.

"Ah!" he exclaimed suddenly, "he has fainted…"

A body lay there, crumpled up together, like a dead man's. The suspense no doubt had been too agonizing for the prisoner to endure.

Mastering his own emotion, Fandor threw the body across his shoulder.

"Saved!" he murmured, "he is alive!"—and at one bound reached the floor above.

But *was* it Juve he was carrying? By the light of a distant streetlight he scrutinized the features of the man he had rescued.

"M. Havard!" he groaned, "the Chief of the Criminal Bureau!"

At first Fandor could make nothing of it. He seemed to be dreaming—a grotesque nightmare. How could M. Havard have fallen into Fantômas' hands? How came he to have been caught in this trap? Then a terrible thought flashed across his mind. Was he the only one in the strongbox? Who had brought him thither? Suppose it was Juve who had taken him to the house? Suppose both of them were at the same time in Fantômas' power?

"But I will find out!" the young man swore, and picking up again in his arms M. Havard, who was groaning painfully, he left the house and reached the street, panting under the burden he carried. Right opposite was a space of waste ground, enclosed by a crumbling paling.

"Nobody will see him here," the journalist considered. "Besides, I shall be back in a second,"—and depositing the Chief against the palings, he ran back into the house. Fearlessly he descended once more into the cellar, went back to the iron chest, and leaned over half inside.

So agitated, so feverishly anxious was the young man at this moment he heard nothing, saw nothing of what was going on behind him…

In the shadow, another Shadow stirred… A shadow? No! a human form, clad in black, a human form dressed in a close-fitting suit of black tights, a form without a face to all appearance, for its face was hidden behind the floating folds of a black hood…

And this shadow advanced, gliding silently across the floor, till it could touch Fandor. A cry rang out, a scream of horror and hate, a name: "Fantômas!"

But the sharp clash of a closing door cut short the cry—the door of the strongbox shutting to and imprisoning Fandor.

A silence. Then a jeering laugh. Then a hard voice, cruel and menacing:

"Fandor is a fool!… I was sure he would come back again!… To have taken him when Havard half filled the chest might well have proved dangerous… And now he is taken, there is nothing to hinder me making an end with Havard…"

A naked dagger flashed in the gloom of the cellar. Soon after, into the deserted alley, a terrifying shape crept out, casting a fantastic shadow in the moonlight… And, dagger in hand, the horrid figure long and carefully searched around.

Was M. Havard to fall under Fantômas' knife? Was Fandor for good and all in the hands of the Lord of Terror? Had Juve lost the game—and his revenge?

*　*　*　*　*

The dawn was breaking. Awake at last, half dead, trembling with apprehension, all his cheerfulness gone, Bouzille was gazing through a crack in his cupboard door at a faint beam of light that slowly grew brighter as the sun rose.

"If it ain't awful!" the old tramp was groaning, "a man can never be left alone… First it's M'sieur Fandor… then it's M'sieur Juve… then it's Fantômas. If it ain't one, it's t'other! It's this, and it's that! Bouzille here, and Bouzille there!… I'm always knocking up against some trouble!"

His gag hurt him. He tried to unfasten it, and partly succeeded. Then speaking louder and almost distinctly, he went on:

"Anyhow, a chap can't satisfy everybody, there ain't no way of doing it!… There's Fantômas, *he* says as how I mustn't tell nothing. Then there's M'sieur Fandor, he will always know everything. If you blab, says Fantômas, I'll *do you in*. Very good! But M'sieur Fandor says back, if you don't speak, I'll run you in! God's truth! I'm fed up with it! I only wish they'd make it up betwixt 'em."

Bouzille started groaning worse than ever. The old fellow indeed was one who liked an easy life, and now found a certain pleasure in giving vent to his self-pity.

"M'sieur Fandor," the unfortunate prisoner went on again, "M'sieur Fandor's not a bad sort. He'd be obliging enough, left to hisself. But there, evil communications corrupt good manners, as they say. A-tying me like this was one of M'sieur Juve's games, I wager."

Whereupon Bouzille incontinently began to tremble. Fear in his case might be compared to an intermittent fever. It showed itself by fits and starts. At one time it disappeared altogether; at another it gripped him with overwhelming force, disabling the trembling wretch from doing a thing or even keeping his wits together.

"If only I knew why he nabbed me," he sighed. "Maybe it was because I wouldn't speak? Maybe too he saw Fantômas and thought I was there expecting him?… My word! but it's no sort of a job to be dumped in a cupboard tied up hand and foot, and not so much as know 'cos why!"

He was speaking the simple truth. He did not, in fact, know what had earned him this awakening out of a long swoon reduced to a condition which everybody must agree with him was singularly lacking in charm. As Fandor had conjectured, the old fellow's fainting fit had been caused by his suddenly seeing in the middle of his talk with the journalist, and behind the latter's back, the tragic figure of Fantômas. At this awful vision the old man had utterly and completely lost his wits. For all his regrettable standard of common honesty, Bouzille was a good fellow at bottom, and it was no selfish fear had so affected him. He had told Fandor nothing so far, and even if Fantômas had been there for some time and overheard the whole of his conversation with the journalist, he had no serious indiscretion to reproach himself with. No! if Bouzille had fainted away, it was simply and solely that, seeing Fantômas no more than a few yards away from Fandor, he had conceived the appalling idea that the fearsome Lord of Terror was about, before his very eyes, to commit the most abominable of crimes, to murder Fandor.

"I risk my head for the lad, and he treats me like this! It ain't fair, it ain't!" grumbled the old fellow, recalling his memory of past events. Then he gave a deeper sigh still.

"But there, no matter for what happened to me! Ancient history ain't never worth troubling about… It's what's a-going to become of me that worries me… This can't go on forever! My legs are swelling… and my hands ditto!… Oh! but he shall pay me for this, shall M'sieur Fandor! I'll appeal to the authorities, so help me!"

He said no more for the moment. He was pondering over a vague, confused recollection of Fandor pinioning him, then throwing cold water in his face. Surely if, in his half-fainting condition at the time, he had not made a mistake, things were not so serious as they seemed. Fandor was clearly not the man to let him die of hunger or thirst in the queer prison he had thrown him into. Sooner or later, but after a delay that could not but be brief, the young man would come back for him.

"Then," the old fellow thought, "of course I shall wheedle the lad round. I'll give him the plan I've got. For sure, in return he'll let me make off… And off I'll make, never fear—straight for Fantômas' place. God's truth! That's only common prudence, I reckon. 'Master,' I'll say to him, 'it's the truth, and I won't try to hide it, a nasty thing's happened. M'sieur Fandor, he's pinched the plan I had of the house I was to take them victuals to.' He can't do nothing else, I think, but thank me for telling him. And there, both of 'em'll be satisfied, anyway."

Bouzille had reached this point in his lucubrations, making

up his mind, in fact, shamelessly to betray first Fantômas for Fandor's benefit, then Fandor for Fantômas', when suddenly he fell silent, his heart stopping dead in his bosom. Outside the flimsy cupboard door he had heard footsteps!

"Saved!" thought the tramp. But next moment he was shivering with terror.

"Saved? But if it was Fantômas?"

He had never thought of that, till then. Yet was it impossible it might be Fantômas had come to find him? Might not the Lord of Terror be coming perhaps to ask him how he had carried out the errand entrusted to him?

"Oh, dear! oh, dear!" thought the old man, "which of the two is it? Trouble is, I've got to pitch a different tale to each of 'em…"

Wisely, at first, he lay low. Silence could not well compromise him. Moreover, if Fandor turned out to be the newcomer whose steps he heard, there was no need to call to him. He knew quite well where Bouzille was. He would open the door of his own accord.

But, three minutes after, the tramp was tormenting himself with another dreadful thought.

"And if M'sieur Fandor went away again without setting me free?" he asked himself. "Times he's a bit spiteful like."

Then he adopted a middle course. Without naming any name, he let out a cry of distress, exaggerating the agony of his voice: "Help! help!"

A voice answered roughly, an unfamiliar, hoarse voice: "Hold your tongue!"

"I am stifling!" replied Bouzille.

"You deserve to!" said the voice.

"That sounds like Fantômas!" thought the old fellow, and he ventured:

"I've got nothing on my conscience, so help me! It was M'sieur Fandor… Hmm… Well… that's to say…"

"Hold your tongue!" the voice repeated the order. "Fantômas isn't far off. Remember…"

At this, the old man smiled to himself. He knew now. As

they informed him Fantômas might not be far off, obviously the statement came from someone who was not the Lord of Terror.

So Bouzille burned his boats.

"M'sieur Fandor," he groaned, "don't be unkind. God's truth! it wasn't my fault I refused to speak… I couldn't no how… Fantômas was just back of you… He'd have killed me, for sure… It's God's truth, M'sieur Fandor, so don't go bearing malice. It's not what a pal should do, it ain't, leaving me to rot in this here cubbyhole!"

As no answer was vouchsafed him, the old man started afresh, more pressingly still:

"Then, come now, must be fair… What I didn't tell you before, I can still tell you, can't I? But if as how you kill me by leaving me to perish o' dryness in this here damp cupboard, why, I shan't never tell you then. That's sure, sure as sure can be, and no mistake about it!"

Still not a word of answer or encouragement.

"M'sieur Fandor," besought the old man pathetically, "if I catch the rheumatics, that'll be your fault… Come now, must be reasonable. You and I are pals. Granted! but that ain't no reason I should quarrel with Fantômas. He's got a long arm, you know, M'sieur Fandor, and I don't like getting into trouble, I don't. You understand that, don't you?"

Bouzille heard a laugh. Was he gaining his point then? Was Fandor calming down under his appeals? He became more insistent than ever.

"And then you know," he whined, "it's on your side I am really… Once let 'em chop off Fantômas' head, and you'll see, I'll never, never go near him no more!"

"Scoundrel! traitor!" thundered the voice—and the door was torn open. For the first time in his life perhaps, Bouzille found not a word to say, his throat so dry he could not utter a sound, his brain whirling so madly he thought he was literally going insane. He had made a mistake. It was not Fandor standing there before him—it was Fantômas!

Stern and menacing, in his black-gloved hands a black revolver, the Lord of Terror stood before the open door of the cupboard, motionless at first, his flashing, cruel eyes gazing through the eyeholes of his hood at the poor cowering wretch.

A second passed—a second Bouzille was never to forget! He suffered a thousand deaths! He felt he was giving up the ghost! He was dying by inches! And then Fantômas' wrath burst upon his devoted head.

"Traitor!" he yelled, "pitiful traitor! Oh, ho! you are Fandor's pal, are you? and Juve's?… At bottom, you prefer them, do you?… You wish to see me guillotined, do you?"

The Lord of Terror put out his arm. He gripped Bouzille, still bound and helpless, by the collar of his coat, dragged him from his cupboard and pitched him rolling at his feet on the kitchen flags.

"You deserve to die," he went on in his cold, cruel tones. "I give you two minutes to say your prayers…"

The safety catch of his revolver clicked. The sound seemed to wake Bouzille from the torpor into which the apparition of the Torturer had thrown him.

"Master! Master!" he cried hoarsely, "hear me first!"

"What have you to say?"

"Why, that I was humbugging! That I knew it was you! That…"

"You dare…"

"No, no! I don't dare, not I!… If I said that, it was because I thought it was M'sieur Fandor…"

"You contradict yourself, idiot!"

"Oh! that makes no matter, Master! Certain sure, I'd say different again, if that might pacify you!…"

"Coward!"

"Oh, no!… or rather, oh yes!… It's truth! and an unlucky devil into the bargain. All *I* want is to live peaceful… and…"

"Dastard!"

"So I be—and as much as ever you please! I'd just like to see *you* facing you, as I am this minute! You're that comforting to a man…"

"Come, a truce to useless words!"—and Fantômas' weapon

was leveled straight at Bouzille.

"Oh!" screamed the tramp, "tell me at least what it is I've done."

"You betrayed me…"

"Never!"

"You sent Fandor…"

"Sent him? Where to?"

"To Montmartre—to the help of Havard…"

"It ain't true! He went there on his own!"

"After guessing the address of the house?"

"After… Ah! yes, that's true, for sure! How the devil else M'sieur Fandor…"

Only Bouzille could have mixed up together like this accents of terror that were only too sincere and excuses so cleverly contrived to mislead. Suddenly Fantômas began to laugh.

"Come, speak out, man!" he encouraged his victim. "Make a clean breast of it! Did you, yes or no, tell Fandor who you were cooking for?"

"But I didn't know!"

"Did you give him the address?"

"Why, no! I saw you, and that cut my whistle!"

"Then how do you account for his knowing all this?"

"Why!… why, I can't account for it… or at least… oh! God's truth! it's all my fault. In fact… I mean to say…"

"Say it then… out with it!"

"Can't no how, Master! Funk's just tied my tongue… But if I was sure you'd let me live…"

"Bouzille, I give you two seconds to make up your mind…"

"Then, here you have it—truth is, he pinched the plan off of me."

Once more Fantômas' revolver described a curve that brought the muzzle within an inch of the old vagrant's forehead.

"Bouzille, I am going to spare your life—for the moment…"

"Only for the moment?"

"Yes! But it depends on you whether it isn't for good and all…"

"Oh! it depends on me, eh?"

"A truce to jesting. Listen to me. I am going to pardon you, but on one condition…"

"Am I at liberty to refuse it?"

"You can choose death instead!"

Fantômas seemed to be bantering his victim now. Perhaps, after all, his anger had been assumed?

"You are to be my companion and follower," he proceeded. "And you will not forget this—at the slightest act of disobedience, not so much as giving you word of warning, I will kill you without a qualm. I mean you to be in my hands like a man without a mind of his own, a tool. You understand?"

"Only too well. What is it I am to do?"

"You will know all in good time…"

Fantômas bent down, and with his dagger cut the bonds that paralyzed the tramp's legs, and ordered him to stand up.

"Right oh! right oh!… But I've got pins and needles all down 'em… And my hands? You're not cutting the cords at my wrists?"

"No! I have no need of your hands…"

"But I…"

"Silence! Remember you have no right to have a mind! Come…"

Bouzille shuddered from head to foot. This clemency Fantômas showed him was not just as comforting as should be. As a fact, Fantômas never forgave those who had been so unfortunate as to do him ill service, even unintentionally. Had he not struck down with his own hand, sometimes for involuntary offenses, the most trusty and the most trusted of his accomplices?

"'All's well that ends well,'" Bouzille said to himself, "but suppose it don't end well, certain sure I shall rue it! Then I'd best get away,"—and he cast a scared look round about him. But to try to escape from Fantômas, to attempt flight he knew only too well was simply to devote himself to death… So was it not the wisest course to follow docilely in the footsteps of the Ever-Illusive?

"We're going far?" he asked in a shaking voice.

"To Paris."

"And if folk see me with you?"

"Well, what then?"

"God's truth! but that would compromise me."

"Bouzille, I beg you to hold your tongue and keep your silly thoughts to yourself."

Fantômas uttered the words in a tone that left the old man no alternative but to obey. In fact, without paying the smallest heed to the poor wretch's tottering limbs, that seemed to double under him, the Master of Terror pushed him out of the house and conducted him to a motorcar standing before the door with all lights out.

"Get in!" ordered Fantômas. "And remember!"—and he laid his revolver beside him on the seat.

"Oh! I shan't forget," declared the tramp. "I have a first-rate memory for some things…"

But the car was already in motion. This time Fantômas was unaccompanied. He had brought no chauffeur with him and was driving himself. He had merely thrown round his shoulders one of those big sportsman's overalls that entirely conceal the clothing worn underneath. Similarly, the leather helmet, like those aviators use, which he had pulled on and which covered head, forehead, and neck, back and front, hid, with the help of great goggles, the black hood he had not removed.

"Not a word!" he said peremptorily—and under the expert hand of the brigand the car proceeded at a good traveling speed not likely to attract attention, that quickly brought them to Paris. More heedful of the octroi regulations than Fandor had been at the same barrier, Fantômas pulled up, and handed to the official his petrol ticket.

"Nothing over the allowance?" the man demanded, and receiving the answer "No!" let the vehicle proceed on its way.

"My last chance gone!" groaned Bouzille. "Certain sure, I wanted to make a bolt of it, give a shout for help… Yes! but my memory's over good… He'd have caught me again!…"

Still as scared as ever, the old man did not speak again, though all the time asking himself with growing curiosity where Fantômas was taking him.

"Not to his own place, anyway," he concluded. "Nor yet to M'sieur Juve's neither, for sure. Yet this is the road."

The car, in fact, on reaching the Place d'Anvers, turned as if to climb the Butte, then stopped alongside a stretch of waste ground.

"Now listen to me," said Fantômas, laying his hand on his companion's arm. "Fandor is there…"

"There? M'sieur Fandor is there?… Where d'you mean?"

"In that cellar…"

"In that cellar? Then you've captured him?"

"I have!"

"But you're not a-going to kill him, surely? He's not a bad lad—a bit quick-tempered… a bit pigheaded…"

"I know. He's your pal!"

"Oh! my pal," the old man protested, realizing the foolish thing he had said. "Why, no! not to say my pal, he ain't—only the sort o' chap as stands a glass now and again… not over often, mind you!… So that's how 'tis."

"Do hold your tongue, chattering fool! Listen here—Fandor is there… alone… a prisoner… waiting for death… in a pitiful plight, do you see?"

"Then, if you pity him, let him go, Master!"

"I told you to hold your tongue!… I have brought you here, Bouzille, because I want you to help me soothe his last moments… Yes! and do you know how?"

"No!… How?"

The reply came in precise, measured tones:

"By bringing Juve to him!… Yes! Juve the police officer Juve!… Juve who is not to escape me any more than Jerome Fandor will escape me now!"

12. A Stern Sense of Duty

Fantômas' tone, as he proclaimed his resolve that Juve should not escape the vengeance he was already free to exact against Fandor, had something so grim and terrible about it that Bouzille was appalled. True, he did not feel any special affection for Juve, who had always rather overawed him, but he was not a man of sanguinary impulses. Far from it. He was one who loved life, one who enjoyed simple pleasures, a glass of wine at a friend's expense, a day's fishing on the banks of a quiet stream. All the tragic happenings inspired by Crime or Duty were beyond his purview.

"Well, well!" he groaned.

"You understand!" Fantômas asked.

"Oh, yes! I understand very well! It's another foul blow preparing! And I'm to take a hand in it… I'd rather get away."

"Hold your tongue, and listen to me! It's your life you're playing for. You forget that perhaps?"

No! Bouzille was by no means forgetful of the fact. Indeed, the revolver Fantômas held, the muzzle pointed straight at the old tramp's head, would have sufficed to refresh the memory of the most giddy-pated!

"Hold your tongue!" reiterated Fantômas, "and try to understand me. One single movement, and it's all over with you… You take me?…"

Then he spoke at length. With clear incisiveness, the peremptory incisiveness of a man accustomed to command and exact from his servants a passive obedience, the dread Arch-Criminal explained to Bouzille what he expected of him. It was a vile comedy he had devised and which he now insisted on Bouzille's carrying through. The old vagabond was to wheedle out of Fandor a letter that should serve to entice Juve into the trap. And to gain this abominable result, Bouzille was again to act the traitor, to play the part of a false friend to Fandor.

"Oh, dear! but it's a sorry business, this here!" grumbled the old fellow as Fantômas finished his explanations. "Certain sure, it'll turn out bad!… If I don't do what you want, Master, you blow out my brains; and if I do do it, it's the guillotine for me!… Yes, it's a damned sorry job! I'm like the nut betwixt the jaws of the nutcracker. No mistake about it, it's poor old Bouzille will pay the piper."

The old rascal was trying to turn it into a jest, still hoping to wriggle out of the vile fix he was in by dint of his wit and effrontery. But a push from Fantômas drove him towards the ruined house.

"Go on!" he commanded. "And tell yourself this—I never miss my mark when I shoot!"

"Oh, dear! oh, dear!" moaned the wretch, "and to think the mark is my mother's son. True, I can try this dodge…" and he began tottering and staggering on his legs. But Fantômas' fierce eye was upon him, and steadied him and drove him forward, inexorably…

He entered the cellar, and saw the strongbox. His face distorted with fear, the sweat starting on his brow, he knocked with his fist on the iron wall of the chest.

"M'sieur Fandor!… M'sieur Fandor!"

At once a stifled voice, that yet shook with rage, answered: "Here! Who is it?"

"M'sieur Fandor, it's along o' saving your life!"

"But who is it? Who is there?"

"Bouzille, M'sieur Fandor…"

"Bouzille!"

"Yes!… I'm not a spiteful chap. I ain't… So I'm come along out o' kindness like, 'cause I wish you well."

Fantômas stood at the speaker's side, his revolver pointed at the other's head, and it was on the brigand's face the tramp read the words he was to say, the words he was forced to use. He was no fool was Bouzille, and he had perfectly understood the instructions of the dastardly Lord of Terror!

"By god! but you're a good sport, old Bouzille," asseverated the prisoner. "So open the door for me… I tell you, I was half mad, I was making my will, and getting all mixed up in my accounts… Open the door, quick! quick!"

"Open the door, M'sieur Fandor!… But how?"

"The word is 'genius.' You've only to spell out the word with the letters on the lock… Make haste! Fantômas may be coming back…"

"But, M'sieur Fandor, *I* don't know, *I* don't, how to spell words. I don't know all my letters!"

"Great God A'mighty!… Why, then…"

"And anyway I've never owned a strongbox, I haven't! I don't understand these devil's contraptions!"

"Well then, shout—cry for help!"

"So as, afterwards, Fantômas may kill me for it. Why, no! M'sieur Fandor, I like you very well, but I like myself better."

"Then don't save me… Be off with you!"

"Very good, M'sieur Fandor! Only don't be hard on me. As I'm here, I'll tell you the notions I've get in my noddle."

"What notions, man?"

"M'sieur Fandor, you saved M. Havard's life. He'll surely come back to your rescue?"

"If he isn't dead… or in a coma. I was expecting him, yes! But he ought to be here by now."

"Then suppose I brought M'sieur Juve?"

"Juve? But where is Juve?"

"Oh! don't you worry your head… I know!"

"Then, run, by God! What are you waiting for? Run, I say!"

"Yes?… But if he don't believe me? If he's suspicious? He ain't o' the trusting sort, ain't M'sieur Juve…"

"I tell you, Bouzille, if you say I'm in danger, he'll not hesitate…"

"To clap me in jail… That's a dead cert."

"Well, they'll let you out again same evening, when I'm safe out of here."

"And won't that be the devil's own to-do! Fantômas will know it all, and come on me, he will!… No, thank you."

All the while poor Bouzille was taking his orders what to say from the brigand's cold, cruel eye, while the latter's revolver all the while was grazing the wretched man's temple. Meantime, in his strongbox prison, Fandor was enduring a very agony of alternate hopes and despair. That Bouzille should have come to his rescue, this did not surprise him so greatly; that the old fellow refused to compromise himself in the eyes of Fantômas surprised him still less. He knew his man—a cautious personage, averse to all perilous adventure. No doubt Bouzille had resolved to set him free to escape the retribution he feared at Juve's hands; but he had no mind to do anything to bring down the dreaded Fantômas' retribution on his head. Evidently it was this twofold apprehension that was prompting his acts.

"Do as you please, Bouzille," the young man admonished him, "but if you let me perish, to a certainty Juve will…"

"Will know of it? I've no sort of doubt he will! M'sieur Fandor, listen here! There *is* a way… For sure Fantômas won't be back yet awhile… I know he won't…"

"Well?"

"Well then, if you wrote a word to Juve? A letter from you—a letter you wouldn't mention my name in, that would make him come, certain sure!"

"But how do you mean?…"

"You've no pencil? No paper?"

"Yes! I have… But how to pass the letter out to you?"

"Oh! that's no difficulty… Look you, by the little trapdoor… Yes! there's a trapdoor through which I was to pass in his meals to M. Havard. You can't see it, but I'll let down a bit of string, and you tie on the document to it… I'm ready to plank down the cash for the postage stamp too, never you fear!"

"Bouzille, it's an express letter, a 'pneumatic' we must send."

"A 'pneu,' eh?… Well, so be it! I trust you to pay me back, next time we meet."

Five minutes afterwards, under escort of Fantômas, Bouzille was quitting the ill-omened cellar. The old fellow was as white as a sheet. This letter he had cozened out of Fandor, and had just handed over to Fantômas, was it not Juve's death warrant?

Back again in the street, Bouzille asked:

"And now I can go?"

"To find the police and tell them what's doing? You're joking!"

"But our bargain…"

"So ho, Bouzille! So you don't know I have no more need of you now, and that those who are useless to me…"

The old man's face turned livid. Oh, yes! he knew very well that Fantômas remorselessly got rid of such as could always betray him, but could no longer serve him to any good purpose…

"Spare me, Master! Spare me!" he stammered. But Fantômas only shrugged his shoulders.

"Come now, no more of that!… Perhaps I shall let you live… Yes! if Fandor and Juve perish, I will give you your life… Come! follow me!"—and he dragged him, his hands still tied, to the motorcar.

…Three hours later, in his quiet rooms in the Rue Tardieu, whither he had secretly returned the evening before on his arrival from Sceaux, Juve was in a state of profound agitation. He was doing nothing, stretched on a sofa smoking cigarette after cigarette. He was pondering the incomprehensible news a telephone from the Prefecture of Police had just brought him— the escape of Jerome Fandor and the prolonged disappearance of M. Havard.

His servant came in and handed him a "pneumatic." No sooner had he looked at the envelope, written in pencil crookedly, with a shaking hand which was different for the name and for the address, than he broke into an oath.

"Curse me! why, it's Fandor!…"

Instantly, indeed, at sight of the queer, untidy envelope, on which Fandor had put his name, while another person had completed the address, than he felt a presentiment of evil.

"From Fandor! From Fandor who is in danger!" he muttered, and tearing open the letter, Juve read the message with haggard eyes.

Cramped and confined as he was in the dreadful prison Fantômas had devised, Fandor had traced only a few lines, in which, as was his way, he had bravely veiled the horror of his situation under a mask of gaiety:

"Blunder upon blunder! Juve, it still goes on!... I am in Fantômas' hands, shut up in a strongbox in the cellar of the ruined building adjoining the tavern of the 'Green Rabbit'... S.O.S., Juve, as the ships in distress say. Without you, I shall be done for. But take precautions; the rescue is bound to be perilous..."

Evidently Fandor had hesitated about his concluding sentence, as the trembling of the writing showed:

"And if you arrive too late, goodbye! Goodbye with all fond affection! Those who fall are not to be wept over, but avenged!"

"Unhappy man!" groaned Juve, striding distractedly up and down his working-room. Oh, yes! he was forgetting his calm self-composure, was the detective, that calmness he habitually preached as an indispensable condition of success in police work! He too, like other people, could lose his head when he heard Fandor was in danger, when once again the struggle was renewing, more tragic than ever, against the redoubtable Lord of Terror.

"In five minutes I will be there," he swore, and he seized his revolver and made hurriedly for the door. Suddenly he stopped dead with a choking cry:

"And... suppose it is a trap?..."

Alas! did he not know that all handwritings can be imitated... And that Fantômas' cunning ruses must now as always be taken into account. Clenching his fists with a cry of impotent fury, Juve picked up again the missive he had just received and examined it afresh:

Why, yes! It seemed these were truly Jerome Fandor's pothooks... If the letter was a forgery, it was an admirable work of art.

"Well and good!" said Juve, "in five minutes any doubt will be out of the question."

He was calm again now. Cases are quoted like this, where, after a serious accident, surgeons have been obliged, there and then, to operate with their own hands on the bodies of their nearest and dearest. Juve could conceive no worse torture. But he was bound to save Fandor's life. So be it then; he would use every means known to him as a police expert. Running quickly to his desk, he picked up a pencil lying there, and with a penknife scraped off a pinch of fine black powder from the leaden point.

"There!" he muttered, "nobody can imitate it!"

What did he mean by "it"? The truth is he had just remembered an easy test, that anyone can make and the result of which is beyond dispute. Of the powdered black lead the detective made two little heaps; one he sprinkled on the envelope, the other he scattered over the letter itself.

"Now is it, or is it not, Fandor's handwriting?" He shook the powder gently, so as to spread it over the whole surface of the two pieces of paper… and next moment odd-looking patterns appeared both on the envelope and the letter—lines and markings showing the imprint of fingertips, reproducing with the utmost fidelity the convolutions of the tiny furrows in the skin that are seen in every single individual, but which are never alike in any two persons and which never change all through life.

"If it was Fandor who wrote, his fingers rested on the paper, and left their imprint there, which the black lead makes visible. It is his other imprints I must now look at," and taking a bone slip from a drawer, he examined it through a magnifying glass. In a minute all doubt was resolved.

"On this slip I have the imprint of Fandor's fingers taken at leisure. Now, the markings on it correspond with those I have just brought out. Therefore it was undoubtedly Fandor who wrote this…"

Then he got up and consulted another similar slip and added:

"And it was Bouzille whose fingers touched this envelope."

…Juve ground his teeth with rage.

"To work!" he cried, "no more hesitating now!" He took a step towards the door, stood still for half a second, then decided:

"And if I do, nevertheless, fall into a trap? If they are ten to one against me? Well! This will do their business for them!"

"This" was a sort of sausage of canvas, tightly corded, of the size of a small breakfast roll.

"A dynamite cartridge, fitted with automatic detonator. Nothing like it for ridding oneself of a group of antagonists… Of course you kill yourself at the same time you finish your opponents, but it's a good piece of work done when Fantômas is one of them,"—and the police officer dashed out of the house and away up the steep hillside of Montmartre, entirely regardless of the breathlessness that increased at every step. As he ran, he was still thinking.

"Have I foreseen everything?" he asked himself. "Yes! I think so… I release Fandor. Then I hide and wait… When Fantômas comes, either he is alone and my revolver is all I want, or he brings his accomplices with him, and I let fly my cartridge and we all go sky high, they and I together!"

He arrived, panting, at the ruined house… All was perfectly peaceful.

"Nobody?" thought Juve. "Seems it's not a trap after all?"—and in two bounds he was inside the building. Next moment he was in the cellar, and by the dim light falling from a grating saw the top of the iron chest.

"The unhappy man!" he said once more, and next moment was pounding the iron with might and main.

"Fandor! Fandor! Do you hear me?"

"Delighted to, Juve!"

"You're not hurt?"

"A trifle knocked about. But we can talk presently… Door, please!"

The laughing tone completed the merry turn of the phrase Fandor used in imitation of the call of a tenant waking his concierge at nighttime to demand admittance.

"Wait a bit!" said Juve, quite calm again now. "It's a letter lock, but I'll force it in two seconds, I swear…"

"Good! But it's not worth the trouble… The word is 'genius.'"

"'Genius'? So you know the word?"

"Yes! I used it to help Havard change his quarters. Don't try to understand now, if you're not in the know. Open the door, do! *Concierge,* wake up, please!"

"What a child it is!" laughed the other, and began turning the milled knobs…

…Alas! behind him, in the darkness, without a sound, came gliding across the floor as a mist glides along the floor of a valley, a vague form that grew more definite every moment. At first, it was only a darker blot in the general gloom. Then the blot took shape, became a human figure.

A man was there. Shod, gloved, clad in black, in a suit of tights clinging closely to his body, he wore a hood, with two eyeholes through which blazed the fire of two flashing eyes.

The man raised his arm. His hand held a sharp dagger, the point of which he laid against the nape of Juve's neck. It was the chill of the cold steel first revealed his presence to his victim.

With a start the police officer turned… and saw… and understood.

"Fantômas!" he screamed with a yell of hate—and in the fraction of a second he realized the hideous truth. Yes! it was Fantômas, mysterious and menacing, who stood before him.

Resistance was impossible. Taking advantage of his enemy's surprise, he seized his opportunity, now planting the sharp point of his weapon right against the detective's breast. Let him make the slightest effort, the smallest movement, and the brigand would surely strike home. He held his adversary at his mercy.

"Fantômas!" Again the cry escaped his victim.

"Save yourself, Juve! Run! run!" Fandor shouted hoarsely from the inside of the chest.

"One second, Juve, and I kill you!" announced the Lord of Terror ferociously. "One second for you fully to taste the pangs of death! Ah! ha!"

But Juve was not listening; he heard, he saw nothing now. His thoughts were whirling in a mad dance, his brain working at a giddy speed. He reflected:

"He is a Monster!… He is Crime personified!… He is the Lord of Terror, the Torturer, the Genius of Evil!… It is my duty to kill him, yes! my duty… But must I kill Fandor? Have I the right to do that?"

Then, in an instant, his resolution was taken; Juve resolved Fandor must share his own courage, join with him in his sublime self-sacrifice.

"He would wish it!" he thought. "What matter if we die, the two of us, provided we purge the world of Fantômas?"

And Juve dropped to the ground, quick as lightning, hurling against the nearest wall his dynamite cartridge…

The explosion that followed seemed to rend the very bowels of the Earth.

13. The Palais de Justice

"Matter of taste, of course—but I don't like the taste!… And as for the other—it lies heavy as lead on the stomach!… I think I'd better be going, eh? As my rescuers don't seem to be coming, must just save myself—no doubt about that!"—and Fandor tried to shift his position.

Night was come again—a cold, dismal night with a fine drizzle that never stopped. Fandor, however, could not reasonably complain of the weather, for the very good reason that he was still ten feet underground, literally buried under the debris of the house, which was completely gutted. His mouth was full of plaster; a ponderous beam lay across his chest.

"Pleasant this!" he exclaimed, as he noted the futility of his efforts. "If this goes on, I shall just have to wait till they rebuild a door for me to clear out by!"

He gave a laugh and shook himself still more vigorously. The young man, indeed, was quite uninjured and in full possession of his usual self-composure. A little before, it is true, when he first recovered his senses, he had begun by asking himself, with that numbed indifference characteristic of men just escaped from alarming catastrophes, what had happened to him. But his memory had presently come back to him.

"Why, yes!" he told himself, "the whole place blew up… my box was turned inside out… and the house came tumbling about my ears!" Then with a shudder: "And what of Juve?" But he was utterly unable to imagine what had been his friend's fate.

What exactly had happened after the terrible moment when he realized how the police officer who had hurried to his rescue was at grips with Fantômas? He had no means of knowing. Who had thrown a dynamite cartridge? The criminal or the officer of the law?

"Mysterious!" Fandor said to himself, "and no less mysterious the results obtained…"

Pinned down as he was among the ruins, Fandor could still make out that he had been pitched almost into the middle of the cellar, but he saw no traces either of Fantômas or of Juve… Had they both of them escaped? Or, on the other hand, had they both perished? Or else, had one of them only succumbed, and the other got off scot free?

"Yes, three suppositions, of which only one can be justified… Ah! well, let's get out of this, and we shall soon know!"

Only, unfortunately, it was a great deal easier to resolve to escape than to carry the project into execution. As for the task of elucidating Juve's fate, this he must of necessity postpone for the present, but meantime there was another thing that struck him immediately—the absolute silence that reigned in the devastated area.

"That proves," he calculated, "that the explosion happened some time ago. Obviously the noise must have brought the police to the spot. Obviously a search must have been made to ascertain if any lives had been lost… Perhaps they rescued Juve, and Fantômas… In any case, it's certain they did not see me…"—and he came back to his first determination to get out at all hazards.

He set to work again at once, redoubling his struggles to get free. The smallest movement caused him excruciating pain, one leg being twisted halfway round and threatening to break at any moment.

"A damnable state of things!" he groaned. "Well! I've just got to choose; either I must die here, or it's a case of 'nothing ventured, nothing gained.' Best take my chance, by god! and have done with it…"

So said, so done. With boundless energy, risking every moment the dislodgment of some stone that would have crushed him to death, he worked desperately to release himself.

"It seems to me impossible!" he grumbled. "But there, one is mistaken sometimes,"—and so it proved in this case. Nothing could resist the young man's strenuous efforts. First one foot was free, then a hand, then his body from the waist upwards.

He had been toiling for perhaps two hours in the inferno of the shattered cellar when at last he emerged into the open air, exhausted, livid, bleeding, but safe…

"At last!" he cried. "And now, no mistake but I must drag myself as far as the funicular. Devil take me if I know what time it is. Midnight perhaps? No! not so late! I can see from here the reflection of the bright lights on the Grand Boulevards."

He thought no more about it. He was staggering and swaying on his feet, all but collapsing on the ground, and it called for all his remaining energies to reach the little funicular that connects the summit level of the Butte with the Place Saint-Pierre and the terminus of which is exactly opposite Juve's house. But there a final disappointment awaited him.

"Hi! there! mason," an employee at the station hailed him, "are you tipsy? Can't go down no more tonight, my man! Last trip's started!"

Fandor did not even answer. Gripping the palings, he had to drag himself painfully down the steps that run alongside the railway track. At last he reached Juve's house. He rang for admittance, climbed the stairs, and sank breathless at the door of his friend's flat.

"It is I!" he stammered to the old servant who hurried to open the door. "Juve? Where is Juve?"

"Why, I thought he was with you, sir."

"He was… he was in the house that… blew up!"

"Like M. Havard, then? Ah! what a calamity!… And Monsieur Havard who hasn't come round yet!"

"So, he is here?"

"Surely! The firemen found him lying in a faint on a piece of ground over ten yards from the house where the explosion was. The sergeant had him brought; they had recognized him…"

Fandor was too exhausted to make any immediate reply. Jean had led him, carried him would be nearer the truth, to a sofa at the far end of the vestibule, and he had sunk down on it. He was thinking:

"Yes! the police were in error. Finding the Chief of the Criminal Bureau lying in some waste ground near the scene of the explosion, they had naturally enough supposed him a victim of the catastrophe… And nobody had hazarded the conjecture that beneath the ruins, Juve, Fandor, and the dread Fantômas might be entombed…"

Only, the longer he listened to old Jean's statements, the more poignant grew his suspenses. Alas! If they were without news of Juve, did not this go to prove the dreadful truth that he had fallen, or at any rate was in Fantômas' hands?

"If he were dead, they would have found his body!" thought the journalist, "but if captured by Fantômas, what can have been his fate?" He felt like weeping and swearing at one and the same time, poor fellow, divided as he was between grief and rage. When two men were in danger, and one of these was Juve and the other Fantômas, was it inevitable that Juve should be the one injured?

Suddenly a step sounded on the floor, and a voice was heard saying: "M'sieur Fandor… It's me… I've been waiting for you, I have… Oh! but I'm bothered to death, I give you my oath on that!"

Fandor stared in amazement at the figure that had appeared at the top of the stairs and slipped through the open door of the flat to the journalist's side. A woman was it? a man? impossible to say! Wrapped in an enormous greatcoat, clumsily holding up a woman's skirt that showed below it a masculine pair of trousers, wearing a cap on top of a feminine chignon, yet at the same time displaying a beard roughly clipped short with scissors, this was the grotesque apparition Fandor beheld.

"Why! what?" the young man stammered. "But I…"

"No, no! You're making no mistake… It's really me!… Me, Bouzille!… Only I've disguised myself… along of the trouble I'm in."

"The trouble you're in?" the journalist repeated the words mechanically.

"God's truth! M'sieur Fandor, it's no sort of life, it ain't, everybody's against me—and I ain't done nothing… Oh! but I found it tedious-like watching out in the Square to see when you'd be coming back."

But Bouzille might have been talking Chinese and Fandor would have understood him quite as well. He had "watched out," it seemed, in the Square Saint-Pierre for his return? So then he knew he was going to return? The reporter put a random question:

"Everybody's against you, eh? Whom d'you mean by 'everybody'?"

"The police, to begin with… then, Fantômas… then you… then M'sieur Juve—particularly M'sieur Juve!"

"Ah! Juve, poor old Juve!"

"Why, yes, yes! M'sieur Fandor… No mistake about it! I wager he twigged the dodge… And yet, if I did take a hand in it, if I did ask you to write the letter to him, it was all because Fantômas forced me to."

"Fantômas! The letter to him!… Ah! you villain!"

Instantaneously recovering his strength under the whip of his anger, Fandor sprang at the old scoundrel's throat, ready to strangle him.

"There!" groaned the tramp. "What's come over you now?… It's cruel, that it is! I come here of my own free will—and then you…"

But Fandor had suddenly begun to stagger, his arms beating the air wildly. Once more a deadly faintness threatened to prostrate him. Bouzille supported the young man, with many expressions of compassion.

"In a way of speaking," he mumbled, "you go doing too much, you do, a-leaping at my throat, and the like… What sort of good does that do you?… A deal better have a quiet talk, eh? Look you, I'll tell you what I know."

Fandor gazed at him, his eyes big with wonder, but the old man, without seeming to notice his astonishment, began his tale—a simple tale enough. After recounting how he had been released at Sceaux by Fantômas, then how the Lord of Terror had come near killing him, he related under what dire constraint he had begged Fandor to write the letter he was to send to Juve to entice him into the villainous ambuscade.

"And then," he concluded, "the letter once dispatched, put in the post, Fantômas did not know what to do with me. I was in his way, you see. So then—my hands were still tied—he lashed me to his car, and his car he hid in the waste ground… Next thing, up comes M'sieur Juve, running—my word! how he did run!—'Ho, ho!' I says to myself, 'there's going to be ructions now!' And I never guessed better in all my life. The whole blessed show blows up! And there's my car flies all to flinders… and now the petrol catches alight! Of course, I don't miss the chance to set the ropes as bound me alight too. Then, just as I was making a bolt of it, up comes the firemen. But there, I ain't curious, and I didn't never stop. I hadn't no mind to stay loitering round, not me!"

Bouzille gave a short chuckle, then keeping an eye on Fandor's face, without much seeming to, he went on:

"But where to go to? I was in no mood for company, for sure. So, I trots off, as you might say, to a friend of mine, a tailor, secondhand slops the fellow deals in. Oh! I made no bones about it, I just dressed up as a woman. And then I comes along this way to have a look round. Well, at that very moment they was bringing Monsieur Havard here. I saw him go by… and Fantômas was taking M'sieur Juve along…"

Fandor was on his feet in an instant, wild with excitement. These last words of the old man's seemed to have turned him into a lunatic.

"Fantômas was taking Juve with him, you say? Speak out, man, for God's sake!"

"That's just what I'm a-doing, M'sieur Fandor… Certain sure, he was taking him along… and quick step too… in a car!…"

"But how…"

"Don't come a-near me! I'm going to tell you! There was a whole gang of fellows there. They were dressed up, I reckon, as detectives, policemen. And Fantômas, he wore a scarf, a three-color scarf, what?"

"A police commissary's? You are sure?"

"I saw it with my own eyes, I tell you."

"But he was taking him, where to? Speak out! Was he hurt?"

"Hurt? No! not much. Scorched a bit here and there; nothing

worse than that… More by token, the master was holding a handkerchief under his nose! Couldn't help but see that…"

"A handkerchief? He was doping him asleep then?"

"Might be so, yes!"

"And that's all you know?"

"Hmm!… Yes, and no…"

"Well, out with it!"

"Oh! not so fast, M'sieur Fandor. Another day, I won't say… But tonight I'm in a hurry. The air of Paris ain't nohow good for me. It's my cough as it makes worse. Must be off to catch the train…"

"Bouzille, you don't leave this room till you've told me…"

"What I knows? Well, look, M'sieur Fandor, as true as true, here's another thing, I'll tell you nothing, I won't, nothing more, if so be you don't hire a plane for me tomorrow to carry me quick away. It's to take or to leave. I don't want to meet Fantômas no more, never no more!…"

And for once under the old fellow's bantering speeches could be guessed a savage determination about which Fandor could make no mistake. Bouzille was now afraid, desperately afraid of Fantômas! The old man was ready to do anything rather than find himself again in the presence of the Lord of Terror. Had he not, in fact, come to find Fandor in order to propose a bargain with him? Was he not offering to tell him what he knew about Juve's fate on condition of his leaving Paris being organized by the reporter?

The journalist made a supreme effort to recover calmness. He questioned:

"How did you know I was going to come back here?"

"Hmm! I knew that… and I didn't know it… I was after hiding in the constructions making in the Square Saint-Pierre; it was just by chance I saw you… I wouldn't tell you a lie, you know that."

"And you'd better not! Well, listen now, you know *I* always keep my promises. Bouzille, if you put me on Juve's track, if you tell me what you know, I give you my word I'll arrange, first thing tomorrow, to get you started on a journey to anywhere you choose…”

"Even a long way off?… Even to… to Lyons?"

"Even to Lyons!"

"Then, M'sieur Fandor, I'm ready to talk, I am. This here's what I know. It's like this, M'sieur Juve, he's at the Palais de Justice, that's where he is…"

"At the Palais!… Are you gone crazy?"

"No, I'm not… Whereabouts exactly, that I don't know, but in the Palais de Justice he is, for sure."

"But what makes you think so?"

"M'sieur Fandor, it's there Fantômas goes every night— Fantômas and his fellows. Of course it weren't he told me. But I know it all right… Before you came, that night at the 'Ami Ralle,' the night we came upon each other in the chimbley, I heard him talking… Yes l it's in the Palais he hides… And it's as chimbley-men they're there; that's the lay they're on."

"Chimney-men?"

"Yes! workmen as repairs the chimbleys. Why, bless you! among the crooks, all the chaps for months past are made up as chimbley-men—in blue smocks, you know, carrying chimbley-flues under their arms… And Fantômas too, of nights, when he's got nothing better to do. And just now, as he was haling Juve off, with the three-color scarf and all, I twigged his blue trousers showing below his togs. Why, I said to myself, I did…"

But Fandor was not listening. There are accents there is no mistaking, tones of voice that *must* carry conviction. Again and again no doubt Bouzille had lied to the journalist. Many a time, to extract a few pennies out of him, he had tried to mislead him. But this time he was sincere—manifestly he was speaking the truth.

Alas! for all that, his revelations were of the vaguest. Juve, it appeared, was at the Palais de Justice. But it is a world in itself, the Palais. Juve, it seemed, was in the hands of a gang of pretended chimney-men. But what was the game? How could chimney repairing have anything to do with the tragedy preparing?

Whatever his perplexity, Fandor never hesitated. Mastering his weakness, he summoned the old manservant, who appeared instantly at his call.

"Jean, I'm going to lock up Bouzille—yes, Bouzille there—in Monsieur Juve's own bedroom. Under no pretext whatever must he leave it, and nobody must be allowed to see him. You, Jean, I shall hold responsible for this."

"Monsieur may rely on me."

"And now, Jean, where is Monsieur Havard?"

"In the master's working room… But he is asleep. The nurse has just told me so."

"Let him sleep, then… Jean, any of those 'Indian pearls' left?"

"Oh, yes! Does Monsieur want one?"

"I want three, Jean."

"But it's frightfully dangerous to take three all at once," Jean warned the young man—and the worthy fellow was perfectly right. These so-called "Indian pearls," pills compounded of mysterious Oriental drugs, and which Juve valued highly, had been given to the police officer by a Fakir in gratitude for some favor received. Made of a poison unknown in Europe, they possessed the property of galvanizing, literally galvanizing to renewed vigor, the most fatigued, the most worn out, the most utterly exhausted man who had recourse to their virtues. A factitious energy, certainly, the energy procured by means of this magic remedy, an unnatural, unhealthy, momentary vigor, followed usually by terrible nervous prostration. But, if ever man did, Fandor at this moment needed some such drug to give him the strength requisite for the work in prospect—the rescue of his friend.

In reply to the old servant's warning he said simply:

"I think, my friend, there's somebody like to be running a greater risk than I'm taking!"—and the gallant fellow swallowed the three pills without a moment's hesitation. Half an hour later the dope was beginning to take effect.

"Now, Jean, not a word about me to Monsieur Havard, you understand… And now to work!… I'm going to dress."

"How, sir?"

"How?" replied the journalist quietly, in a reflective tone. "How?… Why, as a chimney-man, to be sure! Yes, that's how! At Rome one must do as the Romans do, Jean, eh?"

Juve's wardrobe contained costumes of all sorts and kinds, so Jean found no difficulty in providing an outfit calculated to give Fandor entire satisfaction.

But was the young journalist, thanks to this disguise, really going to find and rescue his lifelong friend? Was it not, alas! only too probable that, once fallen into Fantômas' hands, the police officer was irretrievably lost?

*　*　*　*　*

It was seven o'clock in the evening when Fandor reached the Palais de Justice, and the last rays of the setting sun threw a fairylike mantle of molten gold about the vast building.

"Beautiful!" exclaimed the journalist, "but tragic!"

Involuntarily the young man shuddered. He was thinking at that moment of all the grim episodes of the fight against Fantômas which had had for their scene this immense edifice. The memory of the mysterious affair of the living Dead Man, of Jacques Dollert, haunted him…

"Ah, well!" he said to himself gravely, struggling to master his feelings, "the past is past. The future is the thing that counts, the question of Juve's fate!"

As he pronounced the police officer's name, his voice trembled. He was by this time terribly anxious about his dear comrade. At first, in the confusion of mind resulting from the explosion he had so luckily come out of alive, he had hoped for some sort of undefined miracle. He had told himself *it was not possible* Fortune had yet once again turned against his friend. Often we hope against hope. Fandor had begun by supposing that perhaps Juve was presently to reappear triumphant. But hour after hour had gone by, and now Bouzille's statements, vague as they were, left no more room for doubt. Juve was actually in the brigand's power; he was lost, if he could not succeed in rescuing his friend from the hands of the Lord of Terror.

"Now for it!" cried Fandor. Like all energetic men, he felt a contempt for words, complaints, fears. He invariably looked destiny straight in the face—and set to work.

"A reconnaissance first!" he decided. "If Juve is in Fantômas' hands and if Fantômas is hiding in the Palais, perhaps I may find some clue?"—and he made the circuit of the building, gazing up at the facade, scrutinizing the passersby he encountered, examining even the eaves of the roof. But nothing seemed of any particular interest. Below the clock, the police were on guard as usual, entirely unconcerned. At the foot of the grand staircase a sentinel paced tranquilly to and fro—evidently a tour of inspection on its beat. The administrative offices were coming out, one after the other, chatting cheerfully together. On the front overlooking the southern arm of the river and the Mint, not a light to be seen in the chambers of the Examining Magistrates.

"Why, of course, at this time of day the Palais is empty. A round of inspection or two to guard against fire... and then nothing more!"

He shuddered again. The thought of the immensity of the deserted building filled him with despair. Where to search for Fantômas' band? It is a world in itself, the Palais de Justice! And it is by no means very difficult to hide in it. There are some rooms under the roof, for instance, where the records of the prison committals are stored that are never visited. Meantime once more back on the Boulevard du Palais, Fandor came to a definite decision.

"Come what may," he thought, "I'm going to try to get in. Once inside, I must adopt what method of search I best can." He crossed the pavement and went up to the small door that gives access to the stairs leading to the great hall, the Salle des Pas Perdus. An employee was still there, sweeping the steps unconcernedly. Hearing someone coming, he called out to know where the intruder was going. Then turning round and observing Fandor and his getup, he added:

"Oh! you're one of the chimney gang, eh?"

"Yes!" answered the journalist, his heart thumping hard in

his breast, "yes! I'm with the other chimney-men."

"Well, hurry up then! You're a bit late, and the ganger don't look to me an easygoing chap!"

"That's a fact!" declared Fandor, and passed on. A great hope had risen in Fandor's heart. There were chimney repairers in the Palais, it appeared. Who were they? Fantômas' men, no doubt, if Bouzille had told the truth. Mechanically he felt in his pocket for the little electric torch he had been careful to take with him and the good revolver old Jean had handed him, like a man who offers his master a weapon as other valets have an umbrella or a stick ready.

"Well, we shall see!" grunted Fandor, but instantly correcting himself. "No!" he added, "just the contrary, one can't see a thing!"

This was quite true. In the fading light the great hall was very dark, full of menacing shadows. Indeed, the whole Palais was bound to be plunged in darkness at that hour of the evening.

"Forward's the word still!" cried the young explorer. "Perhaps I shall hear noises that will guide me… And, anyway, best get away from the man there. He crossed the spacious vestibule of the Courts and entered the Galerie Marchande. No echo reached him save that of his own footsteps ringing on the flagstones.

"I shall never find him!" he groaned, in a sudden panic.

He passed the bar robing-room and returned by the gallery on which the corridors of the Examining Magistrates open. Everywhere the silence was absolute.

"Suppose I go up on the roofs?" he thought. "Chimney-men, they're chaps who work up there among the chimney pots."

But there was nothing to show that these bogus repairers, no doubt scattered about the building like genuine workers, even took the trouble to pretend they were doing jobs on the roofs.

"No!" declared the young man. "If the officials suppose chimney repairers to be at work here of nights, that's because it's a question of jobs that could not well be done in daytime…"

Then his reflections came to a sudden stop. Far away down a corridor a lantern appeared, swinging to and fro—evidently a tour of inspection on its beat.

"Oh, Lord!" swore Fandor, "if I'm seen wandering about, I shall be caught for sure!"—and he turned to fly. But where to hide? The Palais corridors are long; by the time he reached the turn of this one, the patrol would be upon him. On the other hand, to run was to make a noise…

The young man bit his lips with rage till the blood came… "In two minutes…" he was calculating, when a bright idea struck him. Why not just hide behind one of the big stoves that stand at intervals along the corridors? The patrol would not for an instant suspect any trick. All that would be needed was to creep little by little round the stove as they came on, so as to keep out of sight. Quick as lightning, Fandor glided behind one of the enormous radiators.

But no sooner was he ensconced than a startling surprise all but drew a cry from him. "Full up, mate!" a voice was saying in a tone of banter. Then, next moment: "God A'mighty, why, it's a patrol comin' along… You'll get yourself nabbed, my man! And you ain't even got your gown on."

Fandor had not had time to reply—supposing he could have uttered a syllable in his present state of agitation—before the patrol came up, passed by and peacefully pursued its appointed way. It was a moment the journalist was not likely to forget!

Henceforth, no trace of hesitation was left in the journalist's mind. A man was hiding in the stove. This man was undoubtedly an accomplice of Fantômas, and he had mistaken him, Fandor, for a comrade. In a swift spasm of doubt, he asked himself:

"Am I right in hiding from the patrol? Ought I not rather to give the alarm, and have this intruder arrested?"

But in another minute he was laughing at his own simplicity: "Warn the Palais keepers as they went by? But the men would never believe him, they would take him for a lunatic or a criminal. It would take time to explain matters, and meanwhile the man would escape. In any case would not Fantômas get wind of the arrest, and disappear, dragging poor Juve away with him elsewhere?"

Now the patrol was right in front of the stove; then it moved on and vanished in the distance. By working round the radiator, as he had planned, the journalist succeeded in remaining unseen. Thereupon the voice resumed:

"Eh! but you've got a nerve, old chap!… You *are* one of us, ain't you?"

"Why, o' course!" declared Fandor, putting on the hoarse voice of a regular apache.

"Say, mate!" the voice went on, "if as how the Master was to see you, what d'you suppose he'd do to you? Break your bones, eh? Not there to time! Not wearing no gown!… Upon my word! They'd likely try you along with the other one…"

"For sure!" Fandor answered at a venture.

"Who is the other one, by the by?"

"Don't know… A cop, they do say."

A "cop"? A police officer? Juve?… Fandor's blood was boiling in his veins. But he felt he must be calm at any cost, must not betray his agitation by a single word, a single gesture. Mastering his nerves, and speaking in a drawling, indifferent voice:

"No gown! you said, didn't you? Why must one wear a gown?"

"Oh! you *are* a tenderfoot, you are! The Master's explained the lay often enough!… It's along of the sucking lawyers as come to the Palais evenings, to practice, d'you see, and for lectures. So, by clapping on a gown, a man's less likely to attract notice,"—and, with a hoarse laugh, the fellow concluded:

"'Tis death! but it's a rum game!… There's permits for half a dozen chaps—and blast me! if there ain't a hundred playing round. You'd think everybody in the place was a chimney bloke."

"For sure!" Fandor chimed in. "That's so!"

"So now you're going to put on your togs? Say, mate, the gowns, the best ones, they're in the presses…"

"Righto! I'm off to take one."

"And then it'll be time you join up. The chaps should be ready now… Ho, ho! but it's a rummy go!"

The journalist thought it needless to say more. He was beginning to understand a great many things, and he was getting more and more startled. Without a doubt Fantômas and the members of his gang were in the habit of hiding every night in the Palais de Justice, pretending to be honest chimney workmen. No less surely, in acting thus, they had some definite object in view. But what was it? "They're going to try a cop," the scoundrel hid in the stove had said, the man whose providential mistake had enabled Fandor to gather all this private information. Did it not show that Fantômas, pushing his effrontery to the extremest bounds of possibility, meant to hold a Court of Justice, a monstrous parody of a Court of Justice, in the very building dedicated to the vindication of the Law?

The journalist's thoughts ran at random over the many other abominable farces of the sort already played by Fantômas. Was it not the brigand's custom thus to amaze his accomplices by such fantastic transformations? Used he not, in this fashion, to exploit the credulity of the wretches whose admiration he excited?

But it was no time for further reflection. It was a time for action, swift action, regardless of consequences.

"Heaven help me!" sighed Fandor. "I'm going to join Fantômas' men,"—and he hurried to the bar robing room, where in all haste, exchanging coarse jokes, half a score individuals were dressing in advocates' gowns, telling each other:

"No kid! Must notice the numbers! The Master insists on that. Everything must be put back in its place when we hook it…"

Fandor did not hesitate. Taking advantage of the prevailing darkness, he slipped on the first gown that came to hand. No doubt the last regular tour of inspection for the night must have been the one he had seen go by, for as he left the robing room, he could not help a shudder of fear. From each one of the big heating stoves in the Palais came out men already gowned and quickly set off for one and the same point.

"Best follow the crowd," thought the journalist, clenching his fists with fury as he went. Was it not an appalling thing, a fantastic horror, this fresh proof of the audacity of the Master of Men's Lives and Fortunes, the Arch-Criminal, the Genius of Evil? In mid Paris, in the very Temple of Justice, he had called together this army of lawbreakers who were his accomplices.

"There are at least a hundred of them," Fandor reckoned, "and who can doubt but the whole Palais is haunted by them?"

Then he stood speechless, thought annihilated. The wretches he followed were making for a great door, standing wide open, the very sight of which made the young man tremble.

"The Criminal Court!" he muttered.

Now the throng began elbowing and pushing, all the bogus advocates making a rush, all eager to secure the best places in the Court.

"So much the better," thought Fandor, "the more there are, the more chance I shall have to escape notice,"—and he threw himself into the middle of the crush fighting to get a seat on the already over-full benches. No doubt about it, the ruffians felt quite secure against surprise, quite convinced no spy was there to betray their doings. Nobody, in fact, took the least notice of the intruder, who reached, without any very great difficulty, one of the wooden benches where under ordinary circumstances the genuine barristers sit. Hardly was the young man seated when with startling suddenness a voice yelped out, in marvelously faithful mimicry of the nasal intonation of a crier of the Court:

"Silence! The sitting is begun!"

Almost instantly the electric lights flashed brilliantly, and the lamps on the Judge's bench were lighted. This marked the beginning of a time of seeming nightmare, when Fandor was to ask himself again and again if he were not dreaming, if he were not the victim of delusion, if what he saw *could* be real. The precise formalities of a solemn sitting of the Court of Criminal Assize were scrupulously observed. No doubt, in the ordinary course, the Court only enters on the usher's announcement and is not found already installed on the bench when the light is turned on, on the very rare occasions when cases are concluded after dark. But, in the main, how closely the hideous travesty devised by Fantômas copied the reality!

Dumbfounded, doubting the evidence of his own eyes, Fandor beheld the whole scene of a trial by jury at Assizes complete in every awe-inspiring detail. A clerk of the court was at the table where that functionary usually sits. Facing him the Advocate General was turning over the leaves of a bundle of papers. On the bench the Judges had taken their places, wearing the red robes that confer such a tragic dignity on the exponents of the law.

All this Fandor saw in one comprehensive glance. But he saw yet another thing, a thing that struck a note of monstrous, grotesque horror. The presiding Judge, the President of this Tribunal composed doubtless of murderers, wore, falling over the white ermine of his robe, making a sable blot on the deep red of his costume, a black hood that hid his features. How fail to realize then who it was had the audacity to initiate these infamous proceedings, who it was had the effrontery to preside over and direct them?

"Fantômas! It is Fantômas!" Fandor told himself, his heart beating so fiercely in his breast he thought it must burst. But he gave no sign. In this vast Palais de Justice he was alone, hemmed in by the gang of the Arch-Criminal's accomplices. What could he do in such a plight? At the slightest word, the smallest gesture of protest, was he not certain to be murdered there and then, without even having the satisfaction of selling his life dearly? He kept telling himself, the gallant fellow, while beneath the wide sleeve of his barrister's gown he was digging his nails into his palms:

"I must hold my peace!… I must wait!… I must *not* betray myself."

Then, again, all thought became impossible under the bewildering, maddening effect of the infamous comedy. Rising in his place, the clerk of the court spread a sheaf of papers on his desk, while the calm voice of the Judge announced the opening of the sitting. From where he stood Fandor riveted his gaze on the flaming eyes that darted fire from beneath the black hood.

"It is he! he, Fantômas!" he reiterated inwardly. He recognized the voice of the Genius of Evil.

"Give the order," Fantômas proceeded, "give the order to bring in the prisoner."

At the word, Fandor hardly checked himself from springing up in his seat. His heart, his affection told him who the prisoner was to be whom this bench of brigands was about to try. His eyes followed the functionary who crossed the floor of the Court and made for a door in the wall, which he opened. He strained his ears to hear the final order the sham official was giving in a cheerful time:

"Constables, bring in the prisoner!"

A sound of footsteps followed, and, clad in the blue clothes of chimney workmen, but each carrying a heavy service revolver, two men issued from the private passageway where real prisoners do actually await their summons to enter the dock. These constables, these fellows dressed in the workingman's smock, were they murderers too? There could be little doubt of the fact, but Fandor found no time to consider the question.

Behind them walked a man, handcuffs on his wrists, his right ankle fettered by a chain, the other end of which one of his jailers held. He came on, very calm and self-composed, his head held high, his face not even pale, supremely scornful...

At the sight, Fandor could barely restrain the cry that rose to his lips, a cry that, stifled by sheer force of will, sank to a mere murmur, a sob:

"Juve!... It is Juve!... It is my poor, unhappy friend Juve!"

14. "Remember!"

A deep hush of excitement and anticipated triumph greeted Juve's entrance. A ferocious joy gleamed in the faces of all these abject wretches Fantômas held in thrall under his despotic sway, when they beheld before their eyes, delivered into their hands, abandoned to their hate, the man of all others they dreaded most, the renowned police officer.

Involuntarily Fandor turned his head for a moment. Beside him, on the benches where crowded, in barristers' gowns, the worst ruffians Paris, that great, wicked city, shelters, as the jungle shelters its beasts of prey, he saw faces pale and contorted with fury, eyes lit up with the lightnings of ferocious hate.

Yet such was the Master's authority that not a cry was raised, not a thought found utterance. Fantômas had decided Juve was to be tried, and this trial was about to begin. These enemies of society were ready to play out the infamous farce, which, moreover, gratified their love of cruelty. Did not this so-styled trial, this burlesque assize, did it not afford them the opportunity to gloat over Juve's death agonies?

Fandor turned away his eyes, sick with horror. Could he save his friend? Was it not sheer madness to dream of any such thing? He was alone. The comparative darkness that prevailed in the spacious courtroom just sufficed to guard him from being seen and recognized. Was he not bound to think of the dangers he was himself running? No! not for one second did he remember them. Slightly turning his head, at the risk of drawing his neighbors' notice to himself, he looked round to scrutinize the faces of the jury. Doubtless Fantômas had assigned this post of honor to his chief lieutenants. But the seats usually reserved for gentlemen of the jury were empty.

"Is it the whole assemblage that is to give the verdict?" Fandor asked himself. "Or does Fantômas reserve to himself and his assessors the whole privilege of deciding?" But no time was left him to debate the point. Dry, peremptory, harsh—recognizable among a thousand—Fantômas' voice commanded the prisoner to rise. Juve did not stir.

"You refuse to obey the Court? Constables, force him to his feet!"

At this, Juve stood up.

"Fantômas!" he began.

"Call me: 'My Lord'!"

"No! Fantômas, I will not lend myself to any of the grotesque tomfooleries of your devising that mark this so-called trial… Fantômas, I will yield to force—for you are a hundred to one against me—but that is all! You are a malefactor, you and your companions are malefactors, criminals. Acknowledge you as my judges? Afford you the amusement of this farce? Never! Your place is not on the bench, but here, in the dock, the place of shame. One day, I tell you, you will find yourself there; it is bound to be! At that moment, if, as is now probable, I am no longer alive to repeat my words to you, I think your memory will recall them: Fantômas, Justice is a holy thing. Fantômas, when they come to try you—as they surely will one day—you will realize the boundless contempt I feel for your pretense to hold a legitimate Court of Justice. You, Fantômas, will on that day base your sole and only hope on this and nothing else, the character of the judges who will try you, and who will be honorable men! I have no more to say to you and I will say no more, save that, should I by any chance retain my life, to my last breath I should hold it to be my bounden duty to track down you and to track down your accomplices!… Now do with me as you will!"

Calm as ever, entirely master of himself, Juve resumed his seat. Meantime in the body of the Court, the scoundrels crowded there, as they listened to this detested champion of the law, broke into angry mutterings.

"The blustering villain!" a voice cried.

"Hold your tongue, mate," another voice protested. "After all, he's got the knockout, he's a goner!"

"Silence!" yelped the crier.

"Prisoner," Fantômas now began in a voice of hardly restrained passion, "I have made it my duty to let you speak. The defense has its rights, and I respect them. But I warn you—make no more insulting speeches. Else I shall have you gagged."

Then, without leaving the police officer the time to reply—who indeed showed no wish to do so—he went on:

"Officer, read the charge!"

No! it was certainly not quite according to precedent, the fashion in which this bogus Judge conducted this bogus Assize of Justice. But what of that? Was it not, first and foremost, Fantômas' object to impress his accomplices, to give them a startling proof of his audacity and power?

Fandor, biting his lips not to scream with rage, struggling with all his might against a mad impulse to spring up, dart forward, leap at Fantômas' throat, heard the crier of the court drone out:

"The Police Inspector Juve is hereby charged with having, by all means in his power, as well by force as by fraud, alone or in company of others, striven to arrest the King of Terror, Fantômas.

"Is, in especial, accused of having, in order to attain his monstrous ends, invented the personage of the 'King of the Receivers,' and under that false character attempted to get into communication with the said Fantomas."

The announcement was greeted with loud applause. Just at first, it is true, the machinery of Justice, grossly as it was parodied, had made a deep impression on the occupants of the Court. Many of these—all perhaps—must often have thought of this Court of Assize, asking themselves if an hour would not come when between these walls they would hear the verdict condemning them to the dread penalty of death. But already familiarity was breeding contempt, as they told themselves this was no real trial; it was an officer of the Criminal Bureau, an enemy, a "cop," who was for once taking his turn to stand in the dock, that terrible place a man enters alive, to quit it already doomed to the grave. Truly, there was nobody like Fantômas for staging such comedies, that were at once a defiance to all humankind and a retaliation on society at large.

"Silence!" the usher cried again, and the Judge bade the clerk proceed.

"Is further charged, the said Inspector Juve, with having, still under this fictitious character of the King of the Receivers, a personage nonexistent and invented by him, taken measures which resulted in seven good comrades, seven of the best, falling into the hands of Monsieur Havard's police.

"Lastly, is charged with having, of malice prepense and no less by his example than his counsels, provoked the journalist Jerome Fandor likewise to engage in a strenuous campaign against the aforesaid Fantômas."

Having said his say, and caring little no doubt for oratorical flights—he was hardly likely to have had much practice in that line—this brigand, this fictitious Clerk of the Court, resumed his seat with a sigh of relief, and the case proceeded. Addressing the police officer—he had never taken his eyes off him since his entrance nor so much as made a single movement—Fantômas questioned:

"Prisoner, to your feet! You have heard the charges. What have you to say?"

But Juve simply shrugged his shoulders without a word.

"You admit the facts?" demanded Fantômas.

Another shrug was the only answer Juve deigned to make him.

"Silence is a confession of guilt." Fantômas shot out the words savagely, enraged doubtless to see how the police officer's contempt robbed this masquerade of all its effect. But even now he never moved a muscle. Surely this statuesque immobility of the man, when his voice was shaking with passion, was a supreme proof of the empire he preserved over himself.

"Juve is done for," thought Fandor. "Juve will perish under frightful tortures,"—then once more his thoughts were, arrested. Again he stood spellbound by the development of the tragicomedy. Fantômas was calling upon the Advocate General to open his case. But, if the dread Lord of Terror played his part as

Judge of Assize with some show of dignity, his associates were evidently far from being well versed in theirs. Hampered by his red robes, the wretch who represented the Advocate General lurched clumsily to his feet.

"Upon my soul!" he replied, "I don't nohow think it's worth my while to gab!… What dirty tricks this here damned policeman, this King of the Fences, has played us, I and all the other fellows know, we know only too well, we do!… I say then, let's judge him right away—and talk about it afterwards… To start with, it's getting late, and there's a patrol comes round toward two o'clock. Mustn't forget that!… Juve's life, anyway, ain't worth risking our getting nabbed!"

The self-styled Advocate General had not finished speaking before Fantômas took up the tale again.

"You appeal to Justice," he said, addressing Juve. "Very good! I ask you, prisoner, do you want counsel to speak for you? I am ready to give the word…"

But Juve now appeared to be paying no attention to the Judge's remarks. With an insolence that admirably expressed the scorn he felt, he had closed his eyes and was ostentatiously trying to go off to sleep.

"You hear what I say, prisoner?" repeated Fantômas. Again his voice trembled. This drama from which he had hoped such striking effects was falling to the level of a silly, trumpery burlesque, so little heed did Juve pay to the proceedings. He could not bear to think he was never to see the prisoner trembling with fear, that he could never win one shudder of horror from his victim.

He repeated his question, still preserving the same stiff attitude of immobility.

"You have quite decided, Juve? You refuse all assistance from counsel?"

Verily Fantômas must have been marvelously master of himself, for he did not so much as give a start when a young, fiery, sonorous voice suddenly rang out:

"But *I* claim my right, *I* demand leave to speak for the prisoner!"

In an instant the whole Court was in an uproar. Juve himself had looked round.

"By the Lord!" he muttered hoarsely.

In the gloom, however, very few could distinguish the features of the man who had uttered the demand. Then Fantômas' voice hissed:

"You ask to speak in Juve's defense? Your name, I beg!"

"I do not wish to defend Juve…"

The sentence was still unfinished when a youthful figure was seen climbing over the benches, dashing for the witness stand…

"I do not wish to defend Juve with words, to plead for him… I am here to avenge him, and avenge all Fantômas' victims with him. Now, brigand, hands up! Not one movement, the rest of you, or I kill your chief. Hands up, Fantômas! Surrender, I say!… You want to know my name? I am Jerome Fandor."

Jerome Fandor! The clear-cut syllables of that hated name were no sooner uttered than amazement, consternation seemed to turn to stone the wretches filling the Court of Justice.

Now the light fell full on his face, and all could recognize him. And all could see with terror the revolver the young man held leveled at Fantômas' head in a hand that never trembled. Yes, the wretches, one and all, now stood silent, motionless, like statues. At first they had thought it was a jest, a joke on the part of some comrade. But no! it was verily and indeed the journalist who stood there, alone, in the middle of the court, his revolver pointed at Fantômas, holding their leader at his mercy, ready to fire if they did not do his bidding.

"Life for life," he was vociferating. "You are a hundred to one against me, but you can do nothing. One movement from any one of you, and I fire… Juve, old friend, if anyone stirs, warn me! Once Fantômas is killed, then we are ready to die together, Juve, are we not?"

…Yet surely, had not Fandor lost his wits to be acting as he did? What chivalrous qualm of pity stayed him from firing there and then? Did he really imagine that, merely by threatening their leader, he could keep all these scoundrels in check?

Was it not easy for any one of them, in the semidarkness, to take his revolver too and shoot down the young man before he had himself fired?

He began again with reckless daring:

"Now, listen!… I order you to take off Juve's handcuffs, to knock off his fetters—or I fire."

His hand never shaking, the muzzle of his weapon still pointed straight at Fantômas, the young man's tones were those of a master compelling obedience.

"Release the prisoner!" ordered Fantômas, "he must have his way!"

But why was the villain laughing, so it seemed, as he spoke the words? Why this burst of ironical applause from the audience in the Court?

Still Fantômas had made no movement, not one slightest movement. And now his voice repeated the command:

"Release the prisoner, officers!… That's right… Now set him to stand beside Fandor… Right again… And now I deliver them into your hands, the pair of them!… Knives! knives!"

At last Fandor understood. If no one so far had attempted to make a dash for him, if Juve had been released by Fantômas' orders, and handcuffs and fetters removed, it was because the brigand mocked at the young man's threats, because he laughed at the weapon leveled at his head. He did not even move. But his words were a defiance to Fandor. He had delivered the two men into the hands of his accomplices, and called on them to use their knives—what was this but a scornful challenge to his enemy to do his worst? In a flash of thought swifter than lightning the journalist realized the truth.

Meanwhile Juve had leapt into the body of the Court and was running to his side, afraid at last, shuddering at the thought of the danger run by his friend.

By this time the Court was in an uproar, all in it springing to their feet and dragging from their pockets keen-edged daggers. Then Fandor hesitated no more. He had said: "A life for a life!" Was he to spare Fantômas, risk seeing him escape yet again, for a mere scruple about not being the first to attack—to attack this enemy of the whole human race? It is sheer weakness not to slay—no matter how—the wild beast that knows not, and never has known pity.

Then he fired! The ball must have struck the Judge of the Court full in the chest, but the wretch did not fall, did not even flinch!

"Betwixt us two, Fantômas!" yelled Fandor, and he fired again, emptied the magazine of his browning!...

...But at that moment a cry of rage burst forth.

"Fly, fly, save yourselves!" a frantic voice was screaming, the voice of the Advocate General. "Quick! quick! the officers are upon us!"—and it was true; alarmed by the shots, a patrol of the Palais keepers, making a peaceful round of inspection through the corridors, had rushed up. In an instant the Court was a scene of wild confusion. Brigands and veterans were fighting furiously hand to hand; more keepers were hastening to the rescue.

...But little cared Fandor for the moment. Fantômas had not fallen; he still preserved the same rigid immobility he had shown throughout the trial. It was bewildering, maddening!

"Killed on the spot?" the reporter asked himself. With one bound he was on the bench—from which the two assessors of the Lord of Terror had fled. Fantômas never stirred!

Fandor bent forward—and a hoarse cry, a savage oath escaped him:

"Damnation! It is a dummy!"

The man in red, the Judge of Assize, might well show a never-varying immobility; it was a dummy, a mere lay figure. That was why he had faced Fandor's weapon leveled at his heart with such intrepidity; that was the explanation of the scornful indifference with which the blackguard audience had greeted the young man's threats.

Fandor turned pale with rage.

"Yet I am positive," he thought, "I recognized his voice!"

Then he gave a cry of pain. From underneath the ponderous desk behind which Judge and Assessors sit a man had sprung out—a man clad in a suit of black tights fitting closely about his supple form, a man shod, gloved in black and wearing over his face a hood black like all the rest. His right fist was enclosed in a sort of steelwork cage, and he had raised this mailed fist and struck with all his strength, with never a word, with hideous violence.

The blow felled the journalist, who dropped, his face bathed in blood, his senses all but gone, stunned like a boxer after a knockout.

"Fantômas!" he stammered, "Fantômas! He was there!"— and then he knew nothing more save vaguely in a dream that the uproar of the fight was dying down. It was still in a half dream that he felt them lay him on the floor of the Court, un-buttoning his collar, then of an agitated voice saying softly:

"Fandor!… Fandor, my little lad!… My *dear* lad! You have saved my life. It is thanks to you I am alive!"

The journalist tried to stammer out the one word "Juve!" but his strength failed him, and the voice went on:

"But Fantômas has escaped! And he must be recaptured!… Listen! Do you hear? Do you understand?"

"Yes!" came the answer, faint and feeble.

"He fled along the quays. Then, on the point of being taken, he escaped by plunging into the Seine… You will give out I was drowned in chasing him… You will say that?… You will remember? You will announce his death too…"

But at that moment Fandor lost consciousness altogether. When he opened his eyes again, he was in bed in the Infirmary at the Depot, and doctors were bending over him.

"There," one of them was saying, "he is coming round. You feel better, do you? Well, look here, I have good news to tell you—thirty-seven of the scoundrels have been arrested… Alas! Juve has disappeared… He was there, was he not?"

"Yes! yes! certainly he was," stammered the patient. "You, thank God! They knew you by the papers you had in your pocket… Just now you were holding a letter in your hand. Do you know what it means?"

"Let me see it!"—and Fandor read, traced in a reversed handwriting, disguised beyond possible recognition, a single line, at once a warning and a prayer:

"Remember! Remember!—and never worry your head!"

Thereupon the journalist shook his head, declaring:

"Oh, no! I don't know what it means!"—but as he said so, he could hardly restrain a smile.

15. Politeness to the Fair Sex

"Let us recapitulate the facts! To get things clear, one should always recapitulate. It is an axiom among the wise… Yes! Let us sum up and try to establish with all desirable clarity the data of the situation…"

Fandor was alone in the little room that was his own private office at *La Capitale,* and wrapped in a cloud of smoke sufficiently accounted for by the numberless cigarette ends that strewed the floor round him, sat absorbed in his reflections. His chair was balanced on its two hind legs, and by way of making himself still more comfortable, he was resting his feet on the mantelpiece, his boots supported by the frame of the looking glass that surmounted it.

"Well, the situation is like this—no getting over the fact. If the affair in hand goes wrong, Havard kicks Juve out of doors… and for me, *La Capitale* sends me about my business. Two highly undesirable consummations! Now will the said affair end in smoke? In one word, it is Juve's funeral… or pretty much that!… Ah! but, if he weren't a rascal, my good old Juve, he would surely come, before they buried him, to say two words to me, to give me his instructions,"—and therewith Fandor went off in a great shout of laughter.

Now, if Juve's burial—Juve whom he loved with all a son's affection—occasioned such unrestrained merriment on Fandor's part, this was obviously because the journalist had faithfully carried out the instructions contained in the little note that had been handed him as he left the Criminal Court. "Remember! and never worry your head!" the message read—and he had remembered and was *not* worrying in the slightest degree.

The young man had very quickly recovered from the effects of the attack made on him. Returning to his office at *La Capitale,* after a visit to M. Havard, who could hardly help now receiving him cordially, he had written a series of highly sensational articles, proving with all the conclusiveness in the world that Juve was dead, that he had died a victim of duty, died by jumping into the Seine in hot pursuit of Fantômas, who had himself plunged into the river to escape arrest…

Be sure the journalist had lavished all his practiced skill as a writer for the papers on the carefully guarded wording of these articles. While leaving his readers firmly persuaded that the facts detailed were authentic and definite, he had nevertheless left a door of escape open, had done a certain amount of "hedging," as they say. The last of the series concluded thus:

"In the hurly-burly of the tragic night when we saw, fighting and eventually succumbing, a friend we shall always mourn, did we actually see what our eyes seemed to show us? We ask the question, for indeed there are moments when we are assailed by doubts. There are minutes when we cannot admit that Juve is really dead, when we cannot moreover believe that the Fantômas nightmare is forever ended! Let no one rob us of this forlorn hope! There are heroes who rise superior to death; Juve is of the number. We who knew and loved him, who can boast of having often taken a share in his campaigns, we can never believe he has forever left us. No! we are faithful to our love for him, in our eyes Juve will never be counted for dead!"

"First rate," Fandor told himself after casting a rapid glance over the concluding sentences of his article. When Juve reappears, I trust I shall again find opportunity for some fine sensational writing. I can see my headline at this moment: *I told you so!* The better to enjoy his laugh, the young man swung to his feet. But then, in the act of lighting another cigarette, he suddenly fell serious again.

"But why," he was thinking, "why the devil *does* the beggar want to pass for dead? It's a fact that at this present moment every clue is broken. Fantômas is not fool enough to come running into our arms. And again, will *he* credit Juve's death?" These were questions it was impossible to answer. Quite possibly Fantômas might be taken in by the false news printed in the press. Doubtless he might believe that Juve had jumped into the Seine, mistakenly thinking that he, Fantômas, had himself taken the same desperate plunge. But was it not at least as plausible a conjecture that the astute Arch-Criminal would never let himself be so easily duped?

"Live and learn!" was Fandor's conclusion. "Yes! Juve and I, we're both alive, and I suppose one day we shall learn… Hello! come in!"—the last words in answer to a knock at the door of his working room. A messenger boy appeared. "They've sent me to remind you, M'sieur Fandor. No doubt you're so upset you forget the time? But everybody's going. The boss is downstairs already…"

"Really? Thanks, my lad. Yes! indeed, I am dreadfully upset!"—and Fandor heaved a deep, deep sigh. Then, when the boy was the other side of the door, he began to whistle softly to himself in the most cheerful way.

"Well, let's off to the funeral! My word! What glorious weather! Confound old Juve, he never does anything like other people. I'd a sight rather be going into the country than attending a burial ceremony."

Another peal of hearty laughter, and then, as he put on his coat and brushed his hat, he asked himself:

"By the bye, I wonder if he'll be there—the corpse, I mean."

But Fandor was putting it too strongly. It was not really Juve's burial that was to take place. Well used as he was to push his newspaper stunts to the farthest bounds of reckless audacity, Jerome Fandor would never have chosen to countenance a sacrilegious ceremony. The simple fact was *La Capitale* had opened a subscription among its readers, male and female, the lists of which had been filled up in a week, and that powerful organ was presenting to the City of Paris a bronze plaque to be affixed to the walls of the Prefecture of Police…

"A burlesque funeral, if ever there was one!" reflected the journalist. "The dead man himself will be the last to take it seriously."

So thinking, Fandor left *La Capitale* and was driven to the spot where the commemorative ceremony was to be held. Arrived there, he assumed the most woebegone air and chose a seat in the last row on the platform that had been erected.

"Quite a crowd!" he said to himself. "The Prefect... Somebody representing the Minister of the Interior... M. Havard... and all the quidnuncs in Paris... My word! If Juve is here, he must be the proud man today!"

But he dared not laugh. At this ceremony, the dedication of the plaque commemorating the virtues of the vanished police officer, was not Juve's best friend bound to be in the depths of woe? Yet, in spite of himself, the journalist had much ado to restrain his mirth.

"And Juve himself," he thought, "how he must be holding his sides! Come out, handkerchief!... And to think that perhaps Fantômas is here looking on. Why! he too may even have been one of the subscribers!"

But Fandor soon wearied of these pleasantries. Albeit he knew quite well that his friend was in excellent health, and that this lugubrious ceremony was due solely to Juve's own desire, he found it difficult to escape the contagion of the general sense of affliction. Of course he was well aware that Juve was alive and well, but he was alone in possessing this knowledge. It was in perfect good faith the official bigwigs present exhibited signs of sadness in which the throng of mere onlookers participated. From the platform, M. Havard, still pale from the effects of the terrible dangers he had himself encountered, reviewed in a few heartfelt words the career of the famous police officer.

"He was the embodiment of high courage and high intelligence," he concluded. "It was hard to say which was the more admirable, the scorn he felt for danger or the genius he displayed in the never-ending ruses his futile brain combined. His death is a loss which the whole Police Force feels bitterly. Juve was irreplaceable; his like can never be found again!"

...Just as M. Havard pronounced this peroration with evident emotion—for he had the deepest feelings of respect for Juve, if he was a trifle jealous of his successes—a fat, red-faced woman, in a light summer frock that seemed too small for her ample proportions, who was close to Fandor on the platform, suddenly shrugged her shoulders contemptuously:

"Upon my word! They make too much of it!" she exclaimed.

Fandor looked askance at her, but the good lady went on unabashed:

"Brave perhaps… I don't say no… It may be so… And yet, it don't need much bravery, does it, to belong to the Police?"

Fandor clenched his fists. Whom was she speaking to, this fat dame? Was it to him she presumed to address these offensive remarks? It seemed so, for she turned deliberately towards him, as she concluded:

"And as for being so marvelously intelligent, this Juve they crack up so—why, no! The simple truth is he never succeeded in catching Fantômas!… If only someone else had been given the job!… Don't you agree with me, sir?"

"No! madam," Fandor told her coldly, "I don't!"

"No doubt because you don't know the wheels within wheels of the matter. *I* have my own private information… Juve was a good, worthy man… nothing more than that!"

"Indeed?"

"Yes! I came here myself just to see how far they'd carry out this folly, this farce of making a hero of the man. Why! he was even a bit of a coward… he was actually face to face with Fantômas more than once…"

"You are sure of that?"

"Quite sure!… But he was that fellow Fandor's friend—a journalist, and we all know what that means, don't we?… Yes! yes! Fandor used to boom Juve, advertise him!… 'Scratch my back, and I'll scratch yours,' as they say."

"Better and better!… And I, madam, do you know what I am?"

"Why…"

"I am polite to ladies, madam!" declared Fandor… "extremely polite!"

"Eh?… what's that you say?"

"'Extremely polite,' I said… I respect women—even old and ugly women, even mad women—even you!"

"Sir!"

"And that's why I say no more than to express my most profound and complete contempt…"

"But, really…"

"Now, I mention one thing more, and that is, if I am polite to ladies, I am far from forbearing with men… So, if you have a husband… or a brother… anyone, I don't care who, who can be answerable for what you say…"

"But, sir, you insult me!"

"Precisely!… So, I repeat, if you have a husband, a brother, a cousin, anyone in fact who will give me satisfaction in your stead, you will please inform him of my address… I live in the Rue Tardieu, fifth floor, the door to the left… I shall be happy any time to receive a visit from your friend, and I promise you he shall not go away again without something to remember me by. Your servant, madam!… Ah! yes, my name? It is Jerome Fandor. Yes! and Jerome Fandor will never stand by to hear Juve's memory insulted!"—and Fandor took his departure, leaving the fat lady visibly flustered and indignant. The ceremony was drawing to a close, and groups of officials were crowding round the Prefect and M. Havard.

"Time to be going!" Fandor decided. "I have nothing to say to these folks. I have no right to let them into the secret of Juve's being alive, and it would perhaps be going a bit too far to confirm them in their error by letting them see me here… Yes! let's be off; it is the more discreet and proper course. Besides, I am supposed to be in great grief, and my place is not among mere idle onlookers…"—and the young man turned on his heel and made for the exit.

But he had not taken twenty steps when a hand tapped him on the shoulder.

"Sir!… if you please."

The journalist turned about and saw a perfect stranger.

"Sir?" he said in a note of interrogation.

"You are really the journalist Jerome Fandor?"

"That is so. Whom have I the honor?…"

"I am the Comte de Saint-Pix, sir!"

"Delighted!… You wish to speak to me?"

"I wish to teach you something you do not know."

"Then, pray, speak out…"

"Come, sir, I did not think I required…"

"But you do! You have just used language to the Countess…"

"Ah! I understand now… You are the *cavaliere servente* of that lady?…"

"Her husband, sir! I am her husband."

"Do you insist on my offering you my congratulations? They will not be sincere."

"I insist on your dropping this bantering tone…"

"Impossible. It is firmly attached to my person."

"Let me tell you, sir, jesting is out of place in affairs of honor!"

"Are we engaged in an affair of honor then?"

"I am an officer, sir, on the retired list."

"You were cashiered?… What was the reason?… stupidity?"

"Sir! You are a rude fellow…"

"Sir! I have already had the pleasure of proving as much to your wife; if you make a point of having your face slapped…"

"Oh! You are a lucky man I am leaving Paris tomorrow morning."

"Why lucky, pray?"

"I should have sent my seconds to see you."

"But I am quite ready to box your ears without these formalities…"

"We should have met…"

Fandor took a sharp step to his rear.

"Excuse me!" he said. "I have long made it my practice never to provoke anyone… But if you insist on fighting, you don't suppose I am going to decline your proposal?"

"I told you I was leaving tomorrow…"

"Let us fight today…"

"Why, never! Seconds…"

"Is it absolutely necessary to have seconds?"

"You don't know me…"

"Nor you me, my good sir!… But, that's not the point. Look here! Your wife made some silly speeches; she insulted the memory of Juve. I spoke some sharp words to her. Now, will you allow that Juve was a hero, and I…"

"Oh, ho! You're drawing back?"

"Stepping back, yes; but not drawing back otherwise,"—and this time, having used up all the stock of patience he could command, Fandor, stepping back yet another pace, bestowed on the Count one of those blows that mark an epoch in a man's life. After which, he observed very politely:

"I am now at your orders, sir!"

Then, as the other seemed to have lost all self-control and to be on the point of flying at his throat, he repeated:

"Yes! entirely at your orders… big gun… revolver… machine gun… anything you like!"

"Swords! But you are not used to that weapon?"

"You shall see… Your time?"

"Three o'clock in the afternoon…"

"Very good! The place?"

"Are you agreeable to the Ile de Croissy? I propose we meet there, as it is a lonely spot…"

"Agreed! You will bring the weapons?"

"If you leave it to my discretion…"

"By all means! No seconds?"

"No seconds. I am only passing through Paris, and…"

"Say no more! It is exactly the same to me. I will endeavor not to kill you…"

"A truce to words, Mister Journalist!"

"That's right. Say nothing and be on your guard! Till we meet this evening, Mister Half-pay!"—and Fandor departed for good this time.

At first, to tell truth, he could not help laughing.

"Well," he muttered, "I never thought Juve's sham funeral would earn me the honor of fighting a duel! Good! It will teach me to keep my ears open… Truly that fat woman was a bit too much for my temper. As for her husband, he's a nincompoop… But he can't well be a coward…"

Then suddenly Fandor's face fell. He frowned and seemed lost in thought.

"A nincompoop?" he repeated. "Hmm, that remains to be seen, after all… Mightn't the nincompoop in the business turn out to be myself? Here's a mighty queer sort of a duel, take it how you like—a duel that seems to be a put-up job, an affair provoked of set purpose… No seconds! An out-of-the-way place!… Devilish suspicious!"

The young man walked on a bit farther, his eyes on the ground, thinking deeply.

"Could it be Fantômas? But no! Fantômas would never be so reckless as to challenge me to a duel in which he would be risking his own life… Unless, indeed…"

There he stopped. There are notions that seem at first preposterous, then little by little take definite shape, come to appear reasonable, inevitable… This lady who spoke so ill of Juve at a ceremony actually held in Juve's honor… This husband, who suddenly appeared on the scene and espoused his wife's cause when the latter had undoubtedly shown a conspicuous want of tact…

"Queer! very queer!" muttered the journalist. "And yet I cannot fail to keep tryst. I must, I am bound to be on the ground. I should be dubbed a coward else—and quite right too!… Yes, I shall go… but I'll keep my eyes skinned…"

As he spoke, Fandor came to a full stop on the curb of the sidewalk on seeing a taxi coming towards him, on the step of which an old vagabond crouched precariously.

"A cab, my noble lord?" the old fellow whined.

"Yes!" Fandor agreed. "Here you are, my man!"—and handing a tip to the vagabond, Fandor directed the chauffeur:

"Rue Tardieu, No. 1—and drive hard!" and climbed into the vehicle.

Then a choking cry rose to his lips, a cry of sheer astonishment. On one of the cushions was pinned a paper, on which was written a brief message:

"You might have kept quiet, my lad, and no harm done! Thanks all the same! At present I know nothing, but I am suspicious. Whatever you do, don't touch the point of the swords. Barring that, all goes well. Yours truly…"

The note bore no signature, but was one needed?

"Oh, ho!" chuckled Fandor, as he finished his perusal, "here's a vagabond, dead though he be, strikes your humble servant as thinking pretty much the same as himself!"

Then he added, with a laugh in which gravity and mirth were nicely blended:

"Ye Gods! but it's thrilling! This duel, why, it's the devil of a sporting event!"

16. Where? When? How?

"I'm not inquisitive, not a bit—except when something puzzles me, but I *should* like to know the reason why Juve warns me to beware of the point of the swords."

Fandor was breakfasting at the moment with a first-rate appetite, the appetite of a duelist who feels no qualms at the prospect of meeting his opponent on the ground a couple of hours later. To avoid coming across acquaintances, he had chosen an unpretending wineshop, had taken his seat at a small table and, his eyes fixed on a newspaper he was not reading, was pondering all the mysteries that still encompassed him... That the note he had found in the cab had been left for him there by Juve, this of course he never doubted for one moment. The proceeding was too entirely characteristic of the police officer's methods for his friend to feel any hesitation in attributing the warning to that individual. But what did puzzle him was the motive that could have led Juve to give him advice of the sort. Did he suppose that the Comte de Saint-Pix was simply a new avatar of Fantômas?

"But no!" Fandor assured himself. "If he thought so, he could immediately have attempted an arrest... Did he merely suspect this? Yes! That is likely enough... In any case, if Juve has chosen to pass for dead, this was undoubtedly because he hoped to come upon the Ever-Illusive at his mock funeral... Still all this does not tell me why I am to beware of the point of the swords. Devil take it! To beware of the point of a sword, that goes without saying, don't it? No need to insist on that. It's not with the hilt, as a rule, these weapons of offense prick you!"

With his usual fine optimism the young man quickly abandoned the attempt to elucidate a mystery which he could reasonably expect soon to see cleared up. He finished his dessert, swallowed his coffee boiling hot; then in the calmest and most cheerful mood, entirely undismayed by what lay before him, he left the restaurant and bent his steps in the direction of the Gare Saint-Lazare.

"An hour's bumping in the train," he grumbled, "then we come upon our good friend. Either I'm much mistaken or Juve will not be far off."

After taking his ticket, Fandor walked the length of the train that was to carry him to Rueil, scrutinizing unobtrusively the passengers getting into the carriages. Nothing special drew his attention. The journey was equally uneventful, and when by way of the little stone causeway that connects the Pont de Chatou with the railway bridge, he approached the central portion of the island, he felt bound to admit:

"Perhaps I am wrong? Indeed, Juve did not seem sure of his facts. This Comte de Saint-Pix is maybe just a simpleton?..."

Five minutes later the journalist found himself still more convinced he had been mistaken in imagining tragic developments in connection with the duel he was to fight. The little island lay so peaceful in its mantle of greenery under the afternoon sunlight that it was hardly possible to picture so calm a spot the scene of dramatic happenings.

"The whole business," Fandor told himself, "is going to end up with a scratch I shall make on my man's forearm... and that'll be all!"

He was not, if the truth must be known, a very accomplished swordsman, but he was a born fighter. Incapable of fear, he was always able to keep perfectly cool and collected, and this made him a dangerous opponent.

"No feinting!" he told himself. "Parry and wait, that's the game. There always comes a moment when one sees an opening. The only difficulty, and the one thing needful, is to know how to wait."

Soon the young man came to a halt. The meeting was to be in the large meadow that occupies the middle of the island in front of the villa in a bastard romanesque style well known to all boating and boat racing men. Arrived at the appointed place, the journalist examined his surroundings. The locality was peaceful to the last degree. An old fisherman, loaded with a whole paraphernalia of tackle, was struggling with a hook caught in the long grass fifty yards off. Close inshore a barge was moored, one of those up-to-date lighters, built of sheet iron and of heavy tonnage, that dispense with the help of tugs, being provided with a motor engine and a screw of their own. Aboard this particular vessel a man seemed at that moment to be busy doing some repairs to the machinery. One moment the throbbing of the engine made itself heard, then all fell silent again, presently the noise started afresh.

"It's all just as it should be," Fandor reflected. "The worthy angler won't trouble his head about us. Anglers have eyes only for the fish—which by the by they don't see. As for the lighter, she'll up anchor and away soon as the damage is made good."

Then nonchalantly, tasting for once in a way the peaceful restfulness of the country, the young man stretched himself on the grass.

"My word!" he remarked, "one is fine and comfortable here! I wonder if that idiot don't mean to come."

But at that moment the "idiot" put in an appearance. He had evidently ferried over to the island in one of the Grenouillere boats, and he carried under his arm a long parcel wrapped up in green baize, the contents of which it was not difficult to guess.

"The swords!" muttered Fandor under his breath. "What a fire-eater!"

Then, with a shrug, he added:

"Silly fellow to resent my smacking his face!" But the time was past for joking. Drawing himself up to his full height, throwing out his chest, swaggering delightfully, the Comte de Saint-Pix was drawing near and saluting Fandor.

"I have not kept you waiting, I hope?"

"Not the very least," returned the journalist. "Besides, I can quite understand you were in no great hurry to come..."

"Because?"

"Why! because you are very pale, my dear sir..."

"I pale? You lie, sir!"

"Granted!... Perhaps it is your hat that throws a shadow over your face, after all. You don't remove it?"

"I ask your permission to keep it on… My eyes are weak, and the bright light…"

"Very good!" Fandor accepted the explanation. "At your orders…"

But he stifled an oath as he reflected:

"All the same I should have liked to look him in the eyes, this hectoring bully. Either I'm crazy or his mustache has sprouted surprisingly since this morning. But nonsense! I am full of silly fancies!"

No doubt if his opponent *had* been Fantômas, he might very well be wearing a false mustache, one that was not identically the same as it had been that same morning… But why insist on inventing complications so unlikely?

"I am a fool!" Fandor assured himself once more. "If the good man was Fantômas, Juve would know it… Well, Juve is not here… It follows…"

"Shall we leave the choice of swords to luck?" the Count now asked.

"If you like."

"In that case, choose one without looking. I'll do the same."

"Agreed!… or rather no! I don't agree. It's not the usual thing. Let's settle it this way, toss a coin in the air and choose heads or tails which shall have the one to the right."

He had suddenly remembered Juve's warning: "Don't touch the point of the swords!"

Choosing with eyes shut, might not his hand easily graze this or that part of the weapons?

"As you please!" the Count consented. "See, the sun is not in our eyes, whichever way we stand. Will you choose your end?"

"It's really all the same to me."

"Then let us stay as we are… By the by, who is to time the rounds for us?"

"Don't let's have any!" Fandor calmly proposed. "The best way will be to fight to a finish…"

"Be it so!… You are ready?"

"At your disposal!"

"On guard, then?…"

"By all means!"

No! it was not Fantômas who faced Fandor, and the journalist grew more and more convinced of the fact… True, from the moment of his opponent's arrival, he had taken pains never, even for one second, to let him out of his sight, and this might account for the fact that he had ventured—supposing he was the Evil-Illusive—on no criminal attempt… But all the same Fantômas—so thought Fandor at any rate—would surely have betrayed himself in some other way. This Comte de Saint-Pix, after all, was a brave man. His behavior could hardly be more honorable. A swaggerer? Yes! There was swagger in the way he fell on guard, swagger again in the impertinence of the last words he took it upon him to say.

"Sir!" he announced, "I beg you not to spare me in any way! Strike without scruple! For myself, I have never cared for duels in play. I warn you I am going to fight without pity or favor!"

The Count gave a queer laugh as he uttered the words.

"Ah! that raucous laugh, I know it surely?"—and again his thoughts turned to Fantômas… But no, no! he was not going to let so vague an impression influence him.

The journalist asked nervously:

"Ready?"

"Yes!"—and with a silvery tinkle the two blades met.

"We must…" began Fandor, but he never ended. He stopped dead, in alarm and amazement, while his enemy simultaneously gave a cry of rage, of fury. The utter unexpectedness of the thing was astounding. Something whistled through the air, like a projectile… and lo! a hook, weighted with a lead, and thrown with all the dexterity of an expert salmon fisher, fixed itself in Saint-Pix's hat!

An oath, a yell, and, thirty yards away, with a twitch of the wrist, the angler landed his catch, tearing off the duelist's hat.

Fandor stood astounded. He thought he was going crazy. So great was his stupefaction he could do nothing for a moment. It was not only the man's hat the hook carried with it. It was a wig. It was a sort of mask as well—a thin skin of silk artistically painted, a membrane so delicately fashioned it seemed to be actually and literally human skin! Before his startled eyes, the young man beheld no more the face, already grown familiar, of the Comte de Saint-Pix, but the haggard features, beardless, vigorous and stern of a stranger...

"Fantômas!" screamed the journalist, while, shaking his fist at the old fisherman who came running up, revolver in hand, Fantômas—it was none other—thundered in mad rage:

"Juve! Juve!"

The denouement was utterly unexpected, bewildering, like a nightmare. Chased by Fandor, his retreat cut off by Juve, Fantômas was tearing at headlong speed for the riverbank.

Did he mean to plunge into the stream? No! With one bound he reached a tree and scrambled up among the branches.

"Hurrah! hurrah!" shouted Fandor. "We've got him!"

He had drawn his revolver himself, and Juve was hurrying up to his support.

"No quarter!" roared the police officer. "Fire, if you get a sight of him!"

"Trust me!" was the young man's uncompromising answer.

Both had instinctively taken cover behind the trunk of a big elm. Fantômas could not see them, that was certain. Would he not inevitably be forced to come down? Would he not be at their mercy then? It was no lay figure this time Fandor would have for target.

"So you knew all the time, Juve?" he asked hoarsely.

"Yes! It was a sure thing! And you were going to be murdered! The point of the swords was poisoned... But hold your tongue... pay attention!"

"Oh! We've got him this time, Juve!"—and the young man was on the point of recklessly stepping a pace or two nearer, when a cry of fury escaped him, a cry re-echoed by his companion.

The lighter had rapidly got underway; with all the power of its engine, it was forging ahead, tautening the mooring rope first, then in another minute tearing up by the roots the willow to which the rope was tied. With a mighty splash the tree pitched into the Seine, and away, towed in the lighter's wake. Clinging to its branches, appeared Fantômas, grinning like a demon.

"Fire, fire, Fandor!" yelled Juve.

But the volley was all in vain. How, with a revolver, hit a flying and already distant mark?

Fandor could only growl: "So the man in the lighter is an accomplice?"

"Looks like it, eh?" answered the detective. "There, he's climbing on board."

"Well, then, at the lock, eh? Let's run, Juve, run! We'll catch them there…"

But the police officer refused. "No!" he said, "they won't go through the lock. Look again—they are only two on board, he and an accomplice… and… ah! I thought as much!…"

From the massive flanks of the barge suddenly a balloon had bellied out—one of those balloons, inflated with hydrogen, that, quite moderate in their dimensions, yet possess a power to rise rapidly that is amazing. The gas-filled globe shot up to a great height and was borne away by the wind. Clinging to the rail of the car, Fantômas and his accomplice stood bowing with mock politeness to their baffled pursuers.

"Oh!" groaned Fandor despairingly, "if only we could know where the wind will carry them!"

"Oh!" Juve echoed, clenching his fists, "if only we could guess when we shall get a chance to fight him again!"

And both together, they sighed in chorus: "Only to discover how to beat the scoundrel!"

Already the balloon was no more than an almost invisible speck on the horizon, but still Juve and Fandor stood there motionless and pensive, forgetting past dangers, cursing the truce this escape must mean and calling on the Future to afford fresh fields of battle—if only these battles were destined at long last to end in victory.

THE END

www.ingramcontent.com/pod-product-compliance
Lightning Source LLC
Chambersburg PA
CBHW072257130726

47910CB00012B/2057